the
evolution
of strangers

+

Jonathon S Kendall

2013 Curious Apes Publishing — First Paperback Edition
www.curiousapespublishing.com

Copyright © 2013 by Jonathon Kendall

All rights reserved.

No part of this book may be reproduced, stored in a retrieval system, or transmitted in any form, by any means, including mechanical, electronic, photocopying, recording, or otherwise, without prior written permission of the author.

Cover Art by Nicole B. Schmidt
www.nicolebcreative.com

This is a work of fiction. Names, characters, places, and incidents are the products of the author's imagination or are used fictitiously. Any resemblance to actual persons, living or dead, is entirely coincidental.

Published in The United States of America
ISBN 978-0-9910088-0-3

For Auren…

"I was born lost and take no pleasure in being found."

— *John Steinbeck*

Chapter 1

"KISS ME," SHE SAID.

So I did.

It wasn't romantic. It wasn't soft or hot or cold. It wasn't eternal or fleeting. And it certainly wasn't as exciting as I had expected. It tasted like a kiss, just a simple kiss. But that is exactly what I had been waiting for — the brown eyed, pale-skinned, normal type of kiss, with an old love in passing — like breathing — kissing Andrea is like breathing.

Technically she was cheating on her boyfriend. Technically this was wrong. Technically this was a mistake — all a big mistake. But no matter — she came back to me, on her tip-toes, for one more kiss.

And her boyfriend saw us kissing but no worry — my friends rushed him out of the party before he could make a scene or kill me or both. So she cheated, and I hate that, but she cheated on him, and with me (such a beautiful sin).

I would start my road trip in only a few days so the timing couldn't have been worse but that's the way it goes, I guess. So we stood there calmly with the time we had left together, staring at each other intently — looking for a change, studying our cracks and all our old spots — but it was all the same. We already knew each other's every crevice. We knew every inch. So we looked at each other without awkwardness — with solid eyes and natural blinking.

I told her I was happy that she had come to the party to see me before I left and she smiled and I kissed her again. I told her I was glad she was near me after so long and she said she felt bad about her boyfriend but wanted to stay with me for the night anyways so I kissed her again. I kissed her all night, in fact. We drank spirits and danced there together, fully expecting the lights to blur and the memories to jumble — too many drinks until the morning.

We locked ourselves into my bathroom — one of only two bathrooms for a party of 300 people, all of them knocking on the door asking us "how much longer?"

"It's my house. Go dance!" I would yell at them banging on the door, and slowly they understood — we weren't coming out.

"I've missed you," I said.

She told me the same and we talked. We talked about a lot of serious things and a lot of not so serious things. The world outside the bathroom was bouncing with hired DJ's and jungle juice, spilled beer and wasted wine — all of the expected college debauchery. There were people swinging from the ceilings and breaking into the neighbors' — so many black lights the smoke glowed. The cops even stopped by a few times but Aden calmed the situation quickly. Everyone ran away but came right back for more dancing. Though we ignored all of this and stayed inside together.

Even when the morning came, falling in through the cracks under the door — we stayed inside still. We hadn't been together in months and it felt relieving — like a sip after rehab.

So we kept talking and talking like this, trying to make up for lost time — but sadly, that's exactly what we didn't have — time.

So I said goodbye politely — and left her there alone.

+

THE ROAD WAS VIBRATING furiously beneath our feet before we entered the car — the air smelled of burning expectations — and each passing moment bent to our memories like flowers to the sun; so we ran to The West expecting the soul of the world to shrink into us. Its daunting diversity often frightens us into stagnation — but this time we were fighting back, armed with books and journals and packed trunks and maps and light, bright shining lights to penetrate the night. We had everywhere to go and everything to see, but knew that our country was waiting for us—that it always had been waiting.

With one last deep breath Aden calmly asked, "Are you ready?"

I didn't answer directly but with a nod, he exhaled slowly and turned the key. Ann Arbor passed through our mirror as she had a thousand times before, but this time it was goodbye for good. Neither Aden nor I really had any specific reason for going. Surely we had our explanations out loud, often differing to the point of humor—"to sleep with America"—"to spread love"—"to know our country better"—"the adventure of a lifetime"—"to find ourselves"—whatever that means? But no matter the cause, we were only there to let our America flow through us.

I only remember one specific conversation for that first gap, Ann Arbor to Chicago, and that is not to say that it was the only one—rather that our memories are pathetic and don't do our lives justice. The vivid detail of each moment would be better if left pristine and not left for dead in the underbelly of our minds. Those wise, heartfelt moments are abundant if we were only given the hindsight to play them back to ourselves with perfect lucidity. If only we could watch the movie of our relationships with those whom we have separated, I imagine we'd find love pouring out from the beginning. Couples would feel their hearts pounding right before the first kiss. Parents would see their children as newborns forever. Houses would always seem fresh and full of possibility.

Yeah, that would be nice.

"Do you realize that we are going to keep driving until we can't drive any longer?" Aden speaks with a peaceful authority most of the time but this question was coming from a place of wonder.

We both knew the answer but it was so outlandish, preposterous even, that it hadn't dawned on either of us to treat it rhetorically. I spontaneously twisted to look back as our home faded farther away, stared for a few moments in silence, plopped back into my seat and fervently responded, "Fuck yeah!" like a teenager using the word for the very first time.

"Fuck yeah!" I shouted out the window and pumped my fists. I hit the dashboard furiously, bounced up and down, and smiled—I really smiled this time.

All the while Aden's hands were vibrating on the steering wheel and in neither of us really knowing what to say due to excitement and adrenaline—we kept repeating the same statement in different ways. One of them would click, or make this all make sense?

"To the ocean!"

"To California!"

"We're heading west!"

We laughed all the way to Chicago anxious for the first small talk we could find. We knew our story was something worth telling even though we didn't know what it was. We talked about our dreams and all the adventures we'd face and all the people we would meet and how our lives would be changed forever and how we would publish our story in Rolling Stone and save the world from itself and lift people out of poverty—all by driving.

See—this was the start of a two month long therapy session, though instead of a couch, we'd talk out our dreams a foot from each other, with seatbelts on (just in case).

We drove and drove like this for the better part of the night and in those moments I saw Michigan for the very first time. I called her home because my extended family lived there, my parents were raised there, and because of my university of course. The cities breathe and pound out steal, plumes of smoke, and "trucks built Ford tough." If something is really "American Made" it should come from Detroit or Flint, I thought. The rest of the country is just faking it.

See—Michigan is full of hard working people—honest people, the union crowd and their daughters. The girls wear what the teenagers in California did a few years ago and the guys mostly watch football and work with their hands, but they are polite and decent all the same. And in the Upper Peninsula they hunt and they fish and have beards and flannel shirts. They wear hats and hiking boots and work in coalmines like my Dad and Grandpa did. And they are named Uncle John—all of them. The women love their husbands and teach their children to say please and thank you. It's nice. I love Michigan. I do. But it speaks a little too softly for my taste and settles down too quickly the same.

So although I appreciated Michigan's nuances, it just wasn't for me. I needed something bigger, or smaller, something with more wide open spaces, with more people, or with less people; I needed something different—something new. And when you have nowhere to go except somewhere else—every direction is forward, loud, and beautiful. So staring out into the fields, passing by chain restaurants and small town stadiums, I whispered to myself, *"Let's see something new."*

And the road trip begins…

+

INDIANA PASSED AS IT always has and probably always will. We had vague ambitions to see Indianapolis on our way back up from Miami before heading home but those decisions were all too far off and except for a recognizable name, Indianapolis didn't seem to offer us anything noteworthy.

So we drove.

The smoke stacks of outdated factories peered over Lake Michigan with a hesitant apathy, matching our own. We simply mumbled non sequiturs to ourselves about how sad Indiana is—about how sad we are. It's a graveyard for a forgotten industry, I thought. Moms brag about Indiana the same way they do their children—"Did you hear that Bobby got 4th place in the local wrestling tournament?" See—Indiana isn't empty enough to be interesting or busy enough to visit, so it settles in as the eternal fourth place finisher, knowing it doesn't even deserve a medal. But it's OK with that. It understands in a way—and so it's passed through.

+

IN COLLEGE ADEN AND I wanted to change the world in Elkhart, Indiana by registering lethargic voters in the projects. It was my first time in a ghetto and outside of a few essays and books crammed into sociology curriculums I hadn't close to sniffed the real thing. The houses all looked the same, like giant cardboard boxes stacked on top of one another.

And everyone was black. *Everyone* was black.

I asked a woman to register to vote and she paused for a moment while a youngster came up to the door and stood next to me. I wasn't scared as much as confused. She gestured for me to "wait here" and shuffled inside to grab something from the kitchen. She came back calmly with a small bag of white powder and handed it to the boy.

It wasn't sugar.

And life continues like this of course — women still sell bags of mystery white powders to teenagers, uneducated, hopeless, and stuck in UPS packages. And we left knowing this — knowing that we didn't do much. And maybe we never will? But at least we tried.

Now though, I want to go back. I desperately want to smell and feel Indiana with every ounce of my being — as I do with all places. I'm hooked on everywhere.

Traveling is the most powerful of addictions. It latches onto our subconscious and physically changes the way we look forward. The world transforms from space to possibility and people mutate from everyone to someone. But I didn't know that yet, so Indiana whizzed by, meaning nothing to either of us — a hiccup until reaching Chicago.

So we marched on in warp speed through the turnpike, passing lonely semi-truck drivers. And I thought of their stories, each of their stories — each unique and full of experience and loss and wisdom for the road. I wanted to stop and pick their brains or call them on am intercom and have long heart-to-hearts with them as we all trudged through the darkness together.

One would tell how he was once a college graduate who fell on hard times and blinked once too often, and one day he woke up old, in the middle of Oklahoma, driving Coca-Cola to a Great Plains 7-eleven. Another would sing of romance and cheating wives and country songs in real time. Many would speak of drugs and prostitution and others would be secret Obama supporters and others would have dark histories kept in the vaulted book shelves of their minds. They would laugh for companionship and enjoy all you can eat breakfasts on their way to nowhere.

"It's all about survival—and it's all about the road," they would say.

I looked to Aden in these moments of silence but most often his reaction was inward. He'd nod to himself, ignoring my gaze completely—too busy telling his own stories to himself— figuring it all out. And I know he will—"figure it out." Someday he will.

See—though I knew Aden, I didn't. Because how can we know anyone really, when we can hardly trust ourselves from one day to the next? We are all crazy, talking to ourselves with furious anticipation for the next thought—for the next step. And so too Aden would fall silent to his mind, and if like an equation, I was determined to figure him out even before *he* did. All we have are pipe dreams and possibilities, I thought, but for now, we're in this crazy world together, partners in wanderlust, passing the world back and forth to each other like a hot potato, waiting for everything to cool down.

But I doubt that was what was really on his mind. He was probably analyzing some social interaction he had had the day before, figuring something out. See—Aden has to figure it out. And he doesn't know what *it* is, but he's obsessed with it nonetheless. He stares at books late into the night and reads articles and bleeds deeply for knowledge. And I mean knowledge-knowledge. He hates Jeopardy—or so I assume. I mean knowledge for the ages. He digs epiphanies and life philosophies. Sure— he ascribes to them like I ascribe to changing the channel but in those moments of clarity he is completely obsessed. He believes deeply in the power of people and the world and looks out with possibility.

The horizon isn't an idea to him—it's a place to go. Like the ancient travelers of past chasing the impossible, the horizon is always evaporating away from us. But Aden believes that he can literally be there, at the end of the ocean—stand on top of it even, meditate, and know it. This probably comes from his upbringing, as is the leading explanation for all things "personality," but I give him credit for coming out of his childhood all excited no less.

If I know anything, I know that we all have reasons and excuses to be fucked up, but society can't survive if everyone has justifications for their actions—eventually we grow up and say, "This is who I choose to be." Eventually we make our decisions and contemplate our lives from an intellectual hindsight that requires maturity, even if it *is* faked.

And so is true with Aden's family. He grew up Jewish, hippie, and urban all the same, which makes for nothing less than a complicated self-identity. His best friends get stopped by the police for no legitimate reason except that they have cornrows and wear their clothes baggier than the suburbs would like—they laugh without hesitation and live for rap music and smoke marijuana to feel rather than to think. And yes, they are black. And yes, the narrative changes when you are black.

All the while his mother teaches drama to aspiring Beverly Hillers and apathetic teenagers who need an arts credit to graduate. She wears flowing costume-like clothes and lives so unpredictably and in the clouds that Aden can't help but spiritualize each step. And on top of this his father runs around the world learning languages, going on middle-aged dates, building edifices to his madness. So between the grounded reality of urban youth, the airiness of new-aged spiritualism, and the straight lines of architecture—Aden has a lot to think about.

So I play devil's advocate to his fleeting beliefs and laugh at the absurdity of it all, at the obscurity of it all. I drive forward with him into the center of America, ready for the ever-changing weather.

Chapter 2

CHICAGO CAME SOONER THAN I would have liked, as every place does.

Chicago is a city in its purest sense. The suburbs and the McDonalds-ridden off-ramps buffer the skyline to begin, because there are so many damn lights and the stars hide behind the thick black clouds, and the sounds of the streets and the cars burst your eardrums into chaos — but don't doubt that the skyline comes — oh how it comes! The earth curves over Chicago violently, like after first reaching the summit of a mountain, looking down on each valley with perfect clarity — Chicago the same, bursts into your sight aggressively. The whole highway is full of parents in SUVs pointing and smiling and saying to their children, "Oh look look!"

I turned to Aden grabbing his shoulder, "Look! No seriously," pausing for emphasis, "seriously look!"

And so we looked and stopped our bustling minds for a second as the skyline appeared in the distance. I thought of slaves finding The North and freedom. I thought of the great trade ships leaving the ports for Latin America. I thought of the trains from New York heading to the next real place of opportunity. I thought of the Italians and the Mexicans and the Poles and the Gypsies and the Greeks and the hope. I thought of the restaurants and the American Dreams and the towers and the communities and the bridges, metaphorical and literal — I thought of the whole Midwest pointing at all the bright lights of Chicago saying, "Look-look! This is who we are."

Aden turned up the music louder than necessary and we pounded our fists to the dashboard and danced with our arms. I bounced up and down and swayed my hips to the boom-boom of European electronic DJ's. We didn't know what it was called, the genre, but we knew we liked our music hard and rough and energetic—like an energy drink in note. It didn't need words or a message, our music, but it *did* need to demand a reaction. So we screamed in verse to each passerby as we zoomed into the heart of Chi-town together.

This would begin a theme of ours, lowering our windows with the music—all the windows—so that each person we passed would know that we were coming—and bringing with us a party, our little party. We would come rushing into each city or farm with bullhorn intensity, obnoxious, loud, and dancing.

Because, of course, it's always important to dance.

+

WE WERE HEADING TO Gavin's house somewhere near somewhere else, somewhere in Chicago. Although our minds had been fully wrapped around the road trip for months, deciding to find places to stay hadn't been discussed. I blame myself fully for this. I had promised, as I always do, that everything would work out because, "I think I have family there or something." And per normal, I did. I made a few quick phone calls to the family-network and was tipped off to my second cousin who was doing tech work in Chicago, somewhere in Chicago. I didn't call till the morning we left.

I figured Karma would lead the way.

Gavin and I's relationship up until that point had consisted of mutual attendance at random family gatherings. I knew his personality and core, not at all, his face, kind of, and his name, only slightly more than kind of—but someone in his family was somehow related to someone in my family, somehow, somewhere, and in our family that's enough to guarantee shelter and a warm meal. It has something to do with being Mexican I think?

"Hey man it's Kristopher. You're my cousin I think. You know my mom right?"

"Oh yeah man what's up?"

"Well I'm coming to Chicago tonight and..."

"Oh perfect! Give me a call when you arrive. You can crash at my place."

— and that was that.

We found Gavin's apartment in the Ukranian District. I know nothing about Ukrainians except for what Andrea told me but whatever I knew would have probably been beaten out of their individualities after having been in the U.S. for a few generations. The monster of conformity and assimilation does wonders to cultivate districts of immigrants who all want a better life, but still yearn for the familiarities of their old country.

...And so goes the Ukrainian district.

It looked like bare old America to me, but what do I know?

And so we are clear — Andrea is my ex and the love of my life and the sunset over the Pacific and the stars in the desert and the post cards from everywhere all in one. She is a walking symphony of adjectives in perpetual crescendo. I spent most of the trip trying to forget about her and deal with her pounding into my mind so that's what I'll do now. I'll write about her later — yes. Maybe later? It's always "maybe later" with her.

+

GAVIN IS FRANTIC WITH life so had to leave a club just to meet us at his house. Though I know he didn't mind leaving because we were just another adventure he could get mixed up in. He greeted with hugs and familiarity, a goatee, freshly pressed pants, a black dress shirt, and anticipation.

He now lived somewhere in Chicago, sure, sounds good, but he grew up in Iowa. And Iowa was a bunch of corn and highways to me then, so I was surprised at his worldliness and liberalism.

We stayed outside for a while, soaking in the night and each other, talking about our family and catching up on each other's lives for the past twenty years. We didn't know each other—really—our aunts would argue otherwise, but the reality is that we were strangers meeting for the tenth time. But that's not a bad thing I guess—we're all strangers to each other in a way. All of us. We only "know" about three people plus our parents and even *they* surprise us to the heavens sometimes.

The living room, as promised, was already equipped with a set aside corner for us to sleep. We had our spot to throw our bags and souvenirs and pillows. We had our spot, even if for only a few days, and that was comforting. After the introductions, we talked about our elevator pitch histories and futures, drank all the beer and laughed—and then we fell asleep in our spot.

Nothing more happened.

I woke up still drunk in the morning to watch a tennis match. I don't know why, but I like sports. They energize our madness for moments of insanity and then return us to perspective just as quickly. But we all need a little madness I think.

Then we walked into downtown, stopping at a gas station to get ice cream and labored our way across square blocks and sordid street lamps, allowing the melted sugar to settle around our hands and arms. After all—it's not Fourth of July without messy ice cream hands.

We could see the buildings, touch them with our cameras, but didn't heed Gavin's warnings that, "it's farther than you think. You should really drive in." Fuck that. We had planned our future only as far as the end of the road trip so everything before us was set within the confines of a car, so we were already anxious to get out and walk around. We continued sauntering along, ready for anything—right up until the point when we realized we should have driven. It *was* farther than we thought.

Whatever. It's always whatever with problems.

Downtown Chicago should be called small-sky country since you can only peak into the window right above you. The rest is metal and glass as far as the eye can see, upwards and onwards. Aden explained a little about the architecture but I didn't really listen. He knows a lot about a lot of things, but especially architecture from the snippets he heard from his father growing up. That is nice and all but I have no patience for numbers or geometry. Squares are too predictable. Right angles bore me. But I don't appreciate art either, not really, so take it or leave it.

The magnificent mile is magnificently clean. We eventually arrived there and took a few pictures and looked at all the tourists thinking we weren't a part of them. We *were* though, and would continue to be throughout most of our lives. There are only a few places where we aren't tourists but I guess that's OK — so I thought of being home, but soon realized that I didn't have one.

I had no "home."

I had filled every hour of my adolescence with predictable time slots and meetings and practices and tournaments and moments with friends for that very reason. I wasn't just a suburban soldier — I was the general, leading the pack of my generation into carefully defined societal roles, marching us onwards in unison towards colleges and acronyms to stick onto the fronts and backs of our names. Those letters mean nothing outside of business cards but they were my Holy Grail for about six years.

I didn't drink or smoke. I dated a then-virgin Christian and went with her to Bible camp. I hated it but I went. I was the president of that and the best at this and the leader of some other thing. It was all planned and organized. I was going to move and build my own home almost to spite the hand I was dealt, because even then I knew I didn't have one. My family switched houses every few years so I fell in and out of favor with my parents every few months. I stood firmly in the same area code for all of high school but was never in the same place for more than a moment. But even then I wanted to get out. I think we all do, in a way.

I barely remember college I worked so much and lived in five different apartments in five years. I was somewhere different every summer because I couldn't bare living wherever my parents did. So the world spun around me and I stood still, being so sidetracked by every day that I forgot about the everyday. I was good at it for a while, sure, sounds good, but then it all became too overwhelming—so I ended up bad at it and broke up with Andrea.

Whatever.

But maybe the Magnificent Mile would one day be my home, I thought? Maybe I'd meet the love of my life while walking through corporate art and phallic fountains? Then I'd move towards white-picket-fences and nine-to-fives. Maybe? Though probably not. I didn't even want that—not that I knew what I wanted—but certainly not mantle pieces and fire places. No sir, I'll pass and have a heavy dose of "what's next?"

So we eventually found ourselves at the Taste of Chicago—a festival for food—a giant panorama of smells and people all pushing their way through lines for giant fatty turkey legs and dripping corn on the cob.

USA! USA!

…I called Andrea because I was bored but she didn't answer. That put me in a bad mood but Aden didn't notice as he frantically searched for a bathroom and a cell phone signal all at the same time. He's a pinball with consciousness, I thought. I suggested he call from the port-a-potty but he ignored me.

So we decided to head into the masses anyway, though it was immediately apparent that we didn't fit in. We were part of the whole, sure—we wanted some food and the place was a poster stereotype for "diversity" so neither our color nor our creed had anything to do with it. It was our gate that didn't fit in. We needed more space to walk widely and slowly—like giant elephants unafraid of everything below us. Even so—everyone swarmed us ass-to-crotch, shoulder-to-arm, chest-to-back, like a thousand sardines caught in a fisherman's net.

There were so many people I didn't see any of them.

We needed more space.

I need more space.

+

THE LINE AT PIZZANO'S Pizzeria wasn't a line as much as a swarm. Aden was impatient after about thirty seconds, or hungry, so decided to have a little chat with the hostess. He informed me that she was stunning, as most hostesses are, and was told we'd somehow be given first priority or something or another. We were seated within 15 minutes inside and ready to eat.

"So how did we get in so quickly? There are a million people outside waiting for a table," I asked him honestly.

See—I have always been one to wait in lines. I think it polite. Civilization can't function without organization—otherwise we'd all be cutting each other down for the next spot in line. But Aden sees himself as an exception, or exceptional, and therefore looks at societal norms as puzzle pieces that are constantly realigning themselves. The picture is always the same but each piece doesn't necessarily have to fit perfectly. He says that we all live on a giant chessboard—our words and body languages our knights and bishops. So he believes that he can talk his way into and out of all situations, most often to his detriment—but this time it worked.

"I flirted with her and she told me she'd move us up the list," he said frankly.

"That doesn't make sense."

"Yes it does. Of course it does. Listen—she comes into work and puts on her makeup because she *has to*—but if she wants to make an exception or bend the rules it won't hurt anyone except for her boss, and then his boss—and she's probably never met him. Sure there are procedures but she didn't make them, she doesn't *believe* in them. She's a cog in the wheel man. She *wants* to buck the system, even if subtly. We all do. So I just complimented her hair a little—empathized with her—and looked at her even—so she did us a favor. It's simple—people do nice things for nice people."

He sounds like a hippie half the time and an investment banker the other half, so although I understood what he was saying, I wanted further clarification — "Sure, but don't you think it's unfair that we are sitting before we should?"

"What do you mean by 'should?'"

"Yeah yeah yeah — there aren't any 'shoulds' that we don't create together as a society. I get it. We ascribe to themes and rules and systems, like "standing in line" and "waiting your turn" and "money is a real thing" and your point is that it doesn't have to be like that. Sure I agree philosophically. But eventually we have to get real and understand the brass tax. We *all* can't get exactly what we want whenever we want it. That's too American. Without lines and rules there is chaos to the nth degree. What if everyone complimented the hostess to get ahead in line?"

I knew his answer before I finished the sentence — "That would be great…then we'd all be real. We'd all be seriously living in each moment rather than racing to the next thing-to-do. We'd all be complimenting each other. But for now, if being nice and genuine gets me karmic perks because the rest of the world is too busy looking through each other to notice anyone then who am I to say, 'no thank you. I will not accept your gesture of affection?' Who am I to say that?"

All of this, to me, was beautiful and spiritual — but also a little disingenuous since I knew where he got these ideas: books about relationships, sexual and metaphysical, and new-age Zen Buddhism. But that's a little too critical, I think. Where do we learn anything anyways, except from books? So I digressed — "OK you are right — but that's a fairy tale man. It's not going to happen in real life."

"Sure it can — and it does. It's just that we *choose* not to make it so. Do you know that the U.S. makes enough food to feed the whole world a few times over but we waste so much of it and don't think about anyone else but ourselves, that half the world lives in poverty? This is utterly and ridiculously fucked up. We have the technology, and are creating more technology each day, that when put together it would allow all of us — and I mean all of us — to live and do exactly what we were meant to do — whatever we decide we want to do?"

He looked at me with a seriousness you wouldn't expect from someone who was espousing a society run by machines whereby we'd all live in utopian ecstasy. But he was dead serious. See—Aden is always dead serious, even when he sounds crazy.

Though thankfully the waitress saved us from an infinite regress of circular logic. Aden looked at her and ordered the way he always orders—"Well I think everything looks splendid on the menu, so I have a question…"

The waitress nodded fleetingly as he continued without needing a cue— "If you were to get any pizza, yourself, regardless of price, without worrying about health concerns, or any other stupid reason, if you had the freedom to choose whatever you wanted—what is it that you would order?"

She told him and he said pleasantly, "I'll have that."

See—he always orders the waitress's favorite meal. He has his own tastes, but often likes stepping deeply into the shoes of those around him—to feel their emotions, their likes, their dislikes, their desires, wants, and needs. He likes to feel people without actually knowing them—even if for a moment. I smiled and ordered whatever I ordered.

"Do you remember when we first met?" he asked me.

"Of course."

"We had dinner at a place just like this. It was a Chicago style pizza joint…do you remember?"

"Of course."

"Do you remember what we talked about?"

"Of course not."

"Really?"

"Politics?"

"No man—well…kind of? Whatever. We talked about our futures. We both wanted the same position in student government, so instead of running against each other we met for dinner to see if our ideas were compatible. Remember?"

"Something like that—yeah."

"Do you remember what we wanted to do specifically?"

"No."

"Of course you don't! Because that's never the point. Actually I had very different ideas than you for how student government should function and had very-very different ideas than you for what we should do that year…but it didn't matter. We clicked because we just clicked. We both went to dinner and realized that we had some commonality—our hearts were in the same place. We both wanted to change things for the better."

"Yeah but that doesn't necessarily mean that two people will always…"

"See man, that's where you're wrong. Two people with very differing opinions don't have to necessarily disagree with each other. They can find some commonality, some humanism, and come to that ever-important common ground. Which is exactly what we did—and now we are best friends."

"I think there was more to it than that…"

"No," he insisted, "we come from very different perspectives and we don't necessarily agree on everything. Correct? You know this to be true. But we went to dinner and ate that damn food together and came to the conclusion that despite our differences, it was better for us to work together than to be enemies."

"OK?"

"…and now we are best friends!"

"So?"

"So the point is that if we give one another a chance…give one another the opportunity to show the most benevolent versions of ourselves—we'll like each other. All of us—we'll all like each other."

"Are you talking about the hostess?"

"Yes!"

"You're full of shit."

He laughed and said, "Yeah—maybe? But we got our table now didn't we?"

I laughed and said, "True."

So we held our bellies and walked home in splendor. The Taste of Chicago was just letting out as we entered twilight together. The streets were blocked with families and balloons and couples hand-in-hand, with the gangs of youth sprinting around the city around us—with two friends stuffed from the flavors of America taking it all in, with just enough room for more.

Because, of course, there is always room for more.

+

BOOM! JOLTED FROM MY core I ran outside to see what the commotion was all about. Fireworks—of course—of course there were fireworks.

I insisted that Aden be proud to be an American with me if only for a few moments so rushed him out onto the balcony. A stone's throw away from us, directly across the street, we could see the bustle of middle aged men running to and from large canisters, setting off bombs of sparkles into the sky just above our heads. Our eyes followed each explosion from intention to lighting to take-off to flight to release. It was the most intimate fireworks display I had ever seen. I felt the ash settle on my arms and legs, so my first thought of course, was to quickly cover my beer bottle so as not to taste the residue of violence.

But soon the streets were full with shouts and patriotic music pumping from bar speakers. People lined the sidewalks with lawn-chairs and empty beer bottles. Everyone was drunk on life and pride (and beer). Aden needed to feel a response so he bellowed out hellos and god blesses to all the strangers. I joined in and we sang every word of, "I'm proud to be an American" at the top of our lungs and swung our energy across the expanses of pavement, across and over and under the metal. Boom, bang, and pow — it was great to be alive and we knew it. And for a moment, all the bright colors and lights of America fell into us like a crying kaleidoscope.

Right then Gavin called us from a club and needed a ride home — or didn't — but we wanted to drive anyways, we needed to move. The pent up energy of organized explosions feet away from our hearts cracked open the city. We rolled down the windows and turned up the music as loud as the speakers would take. We zoomed through the city walls with furious anticipation for whatever was around the next corner — with explosions of fireworks leading us all the way there. And people addressed us — in a way they had to. We were attention whores even on the road. I danced belligerently while sitting down, as if that were possible, and Aden smiled feverishly. We were in a jet shooting down the illuminations in front of us, crashing through intersections without reason. It was a sacred and drunken journey through the causeways and alleyways of downtown.

When we arrived at the club Gavin and three others piled into our self-proclaimed taxi. And there were girls whom they had just met, and guys standing on the sidelines disheveled and broken. Gavin had won his girl for the night. It was the game we all played — boys and girls dancing to the music of our hearts in giant nightclubs, jumping up and down, ready to escape whomever we came with if only for a taste of that new life force.

We all fall into each other, it seems.

I thought about Andrea for a moment but then compelled myself to forget her just as quickly. See — we had a city to fly around and through and out of. We had life in front of our faces. We had things to do and places to see.

Andrea could wait.

Aden took the corners too quickly so we all banged from one side of our seat belts to the other. Finally arriving back home, we reminisced about those loves lost and the fireworks and the future — our mutual future together. It was all only a matter of time until the next great exploration of space.

+

ANDREA AND I MET under difficult circumstances, a few years prior, on the cusp of her first mature relationship. Her then boyfriend was charming, handsome, incredibly polite, and undeserving of what transpired but I honestly couldn't help myself. And to make myself feel better I blame Andrea entirely for our beginnings without remorse. But I thank her equally. I had been some version of intimate with a few of her best friends. So they all warned her — "You have a boyfriend. Be careful. Please don't like him." She therefore went into our first meeting with preconceived notions and labels, some true — others exaggerated for effect.

Aden was there when we first met at my apartment for drinks. Andrea slid through the doorway as if floating, with a blue sundress, subtle makeup, and flawless skin — angelic without trying. Aden and I secretly met outside the bathroom to debrief soon after she arrived — "She is perfect," I told him without asking for reassurance.

He agreed, maybe, but I wasn't in the mood to intellectually analyze anything. In fact I didn't really care what he thought. I couldn't stop swallowing and my chest pulsated to the point of embarrassment; I actually thought she might notice, so I gathered myself and walked into the living room full of past flings and an angel, acting as if I hadn't noticed her at all. I was intimidated, sure, but in knowing that I had a square enough jaw to match, I would hardly seem affected.

Though after some witty banter she offhandedly mentioned her boyfriend.

"Oh you have a boyfriend?" I asked her. "You are much too pretty to *just* be my friend — so you had better leave." I was half serious but glared at her stone-faced as she chuckled. I didn't crack a smile and pointed to the door.

One of her friends added, "Yeah he's serious — he doesn't believe in platonic friendships."

I don't.

She ignored me, uncomfortable, and changed the subject. But I would bring it up later in the night multiple times to make her feel uncomfortable and flirt — asking her, "Why are you still here?"

It was self-defense and a tactic all the same. A girl *that* beautiful knows it, even if a little insecure, and therefore can't be drooled over. Girls like that are used to guys falling over themselves so I acted indifferent — and of course it worked.

After a few more chance encounters we began to meet each other on purpose. The more this happened the less interested she became in her boyfriend — and two-plus-two our story began. A few more things happened after that and eventually I found myself at Sears Tower in Chicago without her.

Whatever.

+

WE DISCOVERED THE ONLY free parking spot in the city, behind a dumpster and in front of a Mercedes, and this made sense in a way. Our parking spot was a great metaphor. See — in a lot of ways, this is a story about the middle pushing out towards the edges. Aden and I weren't dumpsters nor were we flashy cars. We were $30,000 a year. I had read Bret Easton Ellis and Henry David Thoreau all the same — but something was missing. I grew up healthily ambitious, with disdain for neither wealth nor poverty, but I seriously couldn't relate to five dollars in my pocket and hitchhiking though I wanted to, nor could I understand the excessive abundance of Hollywood and penthouses though I wished I could. So we parked ourselves in between the two worlds most fantasized about in our culture, between the extremes, and walked and walked and walked into the towers of Chicago's past and present, pathetically normal.

"So I was thinking that after this trip is over we should fly to Ethiopia," I suggested to Aden after seeing a pretty Ethiopian girl near the bathroom.

"Done and done — but when?"

Aden agrees to all adventures spontaneously as I do — which is why we were in Chicago in the first place. We probably should have been studying for some graduate school exam or putting in resumes for Washington D.C. organizations but we weren't, didn't want to, and had no plans to in the future. We were there — right there — and we were going to Ethiopia someday.

"Does it matter when? We're going."

+

WE WENT TO EAT at a famous Mexican restaurant. Some man had brought his local flavors into the Latino District of Chicago and it flourished. American Dream manifesting — "win one for the gipper."

We walked in to practice our Spanish.

And we ate the food of the Earth, my food — rice, beans, pork fat, tortillas, hot sauce, and fried meat. We ordered whatever we thought looked good which ended up being two meals for each of us — disgusting and heavenly all at the same time. It tasted like grade school.

"I love beans. No — I *love* beans, " I said. "If I'm ever on death row I'm having my grandma cook me beans and tortillas for my last meal."

"What do you mean?"

"Beans make me feel alive. It's such simple food — but I love them."

"Really? You don't seem to identify with being Mexican very often?"

"You know—that's sort of true. I had a conversation with Andrea about that very thing about a year ago, before we broke up. She once said we were a 'mixed couple' and I balked at the thought."

"Well," he said cautiously, "you technically are, or were, ya know, a 'mixed couple.'"

"Because I'm brown and she's white?"

"Yeah."

"Right. But I don't know—I don't feel like I have much of the culture except for what's on the surface."

"Yeah?"

"Yeah. I mean—I like the food right? And I can't help but dance when music is on. And I desperately want to speak Spanish fluently. But to be honest—my town was so white, and my dad was so white, that I never really understood the whole 'Mexican thing' too well."

"You never felt like the 'other?'"

"Occasionally—but not really."

"How does that make you feel?"

"Like a poser."

"Dude—you're not a poser."

"I am, in a way."

"No you aren't."

"I am—see, I never had the difficulties of my grandparents for example. They are Mexican-Mexican—with all the struggles and the effort and what not. It was different for them…"

"Yeah but that's just because society is getting better."

"I don't know, to be honest. For example, my grandpa moved to Michigan on the back of a truck with all his family in search of work. They had to sneak into theaters to watch movies. My grandma had to take advanced math tests to convince her teachers that she wasn't mentally retarded...."

"Why?"

"Because she didn't speak English."

"So that makes her more Mexican?"

"Yeah — it does — I feel like the struggle gives her more credibility."

"I mean — sure — that sucks, but that doesn't mean she is any more Mexican than you are..."

"...And here I am, after all their struggles, gallivanting around the country for my own amusement. It's pathetic."

"Bullshit."

"It's not bullshit. My grandparents had *real* struggle to deal with — *real* oppression. And I've benefited from all the perks of their hard work and what am I doing to honor them? Saying 'I love beans' doesn't do them much justice."

"Bullshit"

"It's not bullshit. For example, my grandparents were migrant workers...migrant workers. Like, they picked stuff from the fields when they were real young and had more than a dozen brothers and sisters. They were children of the Earth and loved the Virgin Mary and all piled together on a truck each winter traveling back and forth from Michigan to Texas and back again. That's their story man — they followed the work and headed to The North, and I mean the *real* North, the North of our dreams — with stories of patriots and legends and the Underground Railroad and the Civil War and all that. I bet they were so alive back then — not like today where we're all distracted from each other with all this damn technology. We spend too much time with too many people and too many sounds so we never really get to know anyone not really. My mom tells me that she always had homemade meals — always, and they were rolled out from my grandma's sweat — each tortilla tasted of love and sacrifice and all that drama. And my grandpa didn't get a legitimate job until Affirmative Action. So Kennedy and General Motors changed everything them right? — and my grandpa got a huge pay increase, like three times what he was making earlier — can you imagine that? — and then their children — the great generation — they went to school at universities. Well my mom didn't because she was the first in her family and therefore still a little traditional, or a lot traditional I mean, but whatever, the point is that eventually the younger ones got themselves educated and married and moved into the suburbs. I even lived there for a second. Seriously — my family is the definition of the American Dream. My grandparents picked vegetables and here I am selfishly perusing the country to 'find myself' because I know everything will work out regardless. Talk about change of priorities eh? It's not like I'm worried if I'm going to eat tomorrow. But that's the reality for a lot of people ya know? But that was their reality. And we just ordered four huge meals for the two of us and God knows we aren't going to finish half of it. And all the while, today, right now even, right now as we sit here talking about all this bullshit — people are starving somewhere. Fuck man — what are we doing? What are we supposed to do?"

"We're supposed to eat this food in front of us," he said not wanting to get too serious, "all we can do is eat it — it's already in front of us, and if we don't, it will just get thrown away."

"Yeah man, but that's not the point. Of course you're right, 'we have to eat it,' but it's still a little disgusting no? And you and I don't settle for disgusting right? Or do we?"

"Apparently we do," he said pointing to the food in front of us.

So the silence bellowed out from under the ruffles of passing cars and backroom Spanish conversations. I imagined the two men behind us discussing last Sunday's sermon and their daughters' softball game — maybe a little politics but nothing too heavy.

"You really don't think you're doing anything?" Aden asked, "You think we aren't doing *anything*? You speak like you're disgracing your family or something—like you owe them something?"

We interrupted each other, "Of course I do! If they hadn't…"

"If they hadn't what? If they hadn't survived, or worked? What? Let me tell you something about you and I being here man. Your family is great and you love them and I love them but the odds of anything happening—anything—I mean anything!—the odds of anything in this world happening is zero over infinity. Period. Like me for example—blah blah blah long story short—my Jewish grandparents met because of WWII. As in, without Hitler and all that sadistic mess I wouldn't be here, and probably you wouldn't be here either, at least not how you are presently, with me. Isn't that twisted? Sure it is—"

I wanted to get in on the conversation, "For sure, but what does this have to do with…?"

But he didn't let me—"Your family is your family man and you are you and you can't change that. For example, the Vanderbilt's aren't happier or luckier than us—they are people with wants and needs and desires and bad days all the same. And that is the point—if you think your family had it all figured out you are wrong. They still don't have it figured it out. So kiss them goodnight and appreciate every second you have with them and cry when you think of their history and where they came from and where you came from—that's a damn good story—but don't tease yourself with fairytales. They made mistakes too. They were selfish at times. They are really real, and no matter how you spin it, they'll always be real."

"Whatever."

Neither of us had anything more to say so we took our time sifting around the last morsels of fat puddling on our plates. I looked out the window and laughed inwardly at all the chaos and questions we were faced with, and suggested that we leave. So I paid our bill, kissed the waitress goodbye like a good Mexican, peace-signed the still eating clients, took a deep breath—and pushed the door to my future wide open.

This conversation would continue though—into the ether. It would resurface later disguised in costume or as some other issue. But no matter the context, specific wording, or setting—we were only ever talking about one thing, asking ourselves the same question over and over again—"What should we do next?"

It was decided that we would leave Chicago and chase the setting sun across the howling plains before us. So we did that.

Nothing more happened. We had to go.

Chapter 3

THE OLD WAY OF going about meaningless road trips without destinations or timelines was to hitchhike and meet strangers at bars and sleep with them and talk to new characters on accident. Stories of the road were different way back then — before computers in our pockets.

See — this trip was transpiring right at the cusp of a great technological revolution and we could all feel it. We all had only recently crossed over into this world of immediate hedonistic satisfaction. Everything seemed new and different — faster. Everything had changed since our childhood. Now the world is all a giant mess of 24-hour haircuts, I thought, and delivery beer and drive through marriage licenses and computers and screens and television shows and advertisements and a whole host of other crap, which was all collectively and slowly sucking the soul out of our humanity. See — the train stations are all empty nowadays. The teenagers cry for cell phones and text their friends sitting next to them. Everything is predictable and planned and the stars just don't shine as bright with all the damn television screens penetrating the stillness of the night. Technology is racing past us and we don't understand it nor want to — we're just riding its coattails into the upended future without any forethought. It feels good and easy, like an addiction, like a drug — so we keep plugging ourselves in. But what of the side effects?

Whatever. We don't care. It all feels too good.

See — 40 years earlier we would have found a stingy motel for the night and walked to the local saloon and would have hollered at the moon drunkenly, feverishly, without a plan to worry about, and then houses would open closed doors for us and have us over for supper. Yeah that would be nice.

People were more trusting back then and the road was safer and people would look each other in the eye and ask for help, and if not they would steal it I guess, but even that was a little more polite because at least it was genuine and random — authentic people meeting haphazardly, with the universe throwing all the animals together and smashing them into one another and then running away, back and forth, back and forth, but they didn't know what was going to happen next and that was the beauty of it.

No one knew anything really except for their own thumbs and the loneliness of backs of pickup trucks and real hunger. But no matter the difference, I guess, because our hearts haven't changed. They can't. We all still want to help strangers and are still fascinated by real pilgrims. We still need journeymen to shake our shoulders and still need stories to tell — we all need loud personalities and slaps in the faces to wake us up sometimes. Our souls yearn to help and give and hug one another but we're all so damn afraid nowadays, and our doors are locked so tight that we can't get out, let alone allow anyone in.

It's sad.

But Couchsurfing is my generation's answer to that fear. It's a website that combines social networking with traveling, whereby wanderers stay with hosts stationed all around the world. So Aden and I used it, technology, all the same — cleverly lambasting all those things that we know and love just to make ourselves feel better — like environmentalists with Hummers or anti-gay activists with callboys.

Everyone is a hypocrite to their ideals sometimes.

So in Iowa City we had plans to stay with such a couchsurfer named Faith. We chose to stay with her because her name was Faith and thought it wildly karmic and beautiful.

+

SHORTLY WEST OF CHICAGO and into Iowa geography recovers its original constitutions — open and wild, with only small single story houses speckling the horizon. The cars feel foreign to the whole, where the road is out of place and penetrates the land—carefully, lovingly, but without its permission. The asphalt juxtaposes haphazardly with the yellow corn, the pink air, and the green sunsets—all with inlets of blues and hazy browns speckling the horizon. The black sticky road ought to be peeled back in over itself though, and rolled up like a has-been red carpet. It's too dark, the road in Iowa. It doesn't fit. But neither did we.

There weren't any passport checks or significant lines to cross—just the Mississippi daunting—but that was enough. We were leaving the safety zone of Illinois—no more of the loud noises and muffled yells which lulled us to sleep in the city. And that's what I noticed most, there were always sounds and commotion and walking-distances in the city but west of the Mississippi there are only flat lines. The East yells towards all the room in The West, over the dividing rivers and the truck stops waiting to hear an echo—echo, echo, and yet The West falls silent. It only listens, and whispers stories of the cities and points and laughs at all their funny noises.

And I noticed the telephone lines looking like a child's example for drawing perspective. The two sides of the road repeated the same story over and over—pole, wire, pole, wire, pole, wire, pole, and then another wire as far as the eye could see until the two sides met in the distance. We were driving towards the point of a metaphysical triangle and all I could think about is what this would be like on a hallucinogenic—which wasn't completely out of the question. See—it often takes substances to do anything fanatical but temperance to keenly feel. And that was going to be a problem, this balance. So we joked about our future two hours in front of our faces because that's as far as we could see and sang a few songs and pointed at red barns because they were *really* real and were *really* red like in children's books. And we talked about California because oh California!—but somewhere in the causeway between that conversation and the next I couldn't help but think of the echo still—pole, wire, pole, wire, pole, wire, wire, wire, and all those wires crisscrossing through every house. We're all connected, I thought. We all forcibly connect through giant cables and posts that we stick along expressways in Iowa. And one day our children's children will laugh and say, "Can you believe grandpa had to plug in his computer? Can you believe they had to deal with all those wires? They were so primitive back then."

But we'll sit them on our laps and explain why — "You see junior — we all just wanted to feel one another, we wanted to speak and connect — so we built a giant spider web of electricity and light all across the country from Iowa to New York, house to house."

And I wondered what they were all saying to each other, all those families phoning back and forth, not knowing that there in Iowa I was listening in. I listened as we drove and heard the same story over and over…

There was a father who told his wife he had to work a little late and there was a father who wasn't really working a little late and two single women were meeting for drinks because they both really needed one and a teenager told his girlfriend that he loved her and they would always be together and a daughter cried to her grandmother after being told of the divorce and then a travel agent confirmed a man's one way plane ticket to Paris and there was this Mexican who just got citizenship and there was the old woman who refused to buy a cell phone because she didn't trust them and a wrong number turned into a blind date for the night and some girl just found out that she had cancer and she cried and her mother cried too and an adopted child spoke to his real parents for the first time and all those conversations, all at once, they all flooded into my mind, coming and going like a hyperactive mosquito.

Oh, and there was the conversation between Andrea and I that never happened because she didn't pick up the phone when I called her.

Maybe later?

+

IN IOWA CITY, WHERE Faith lived, the roads winded in and around off the highway — feeling off balance. The equilibrium of expressways causes curves and stops to seem too roundabout and out of place, inefficient even. But the shortest distance between two points is usually boring, so we turned the wheel, over bridges, past court houses, seeing quaint roads, old timers, and tight spaces, until finding our own generation there near the college. We had to go deep into the city, you see, if it can even be called such a thing, in order to find its pulse. We pressed down hard with our whole bodies into ourselves until the thump, thump, thump was clear—the heartbeat. We turned the music up to match—thump, thump, thump, until the beat unified and transposed itself—until we entered a simple college town—one not unlike our own.

Anxious to meet our first stranger of the trip, we passed through the town too-quickly and got lost and called our host for directions and flirted on the phone with her to ensure an awkward first encounter.

"I just got off work," she said, "so let me know when you are here. I'm just getting home."

Faith sounds innocent over the wires and satellites of the phone. She sends out signals of Midwestern hospitality and high pitches. I imagine if a lady bug could speak she would sound just like Faith—her tone smiles through speakers.

"Well we are just outside your house I do believe!" I had to shout because the music was so loud and Aden needed to release energy so he too shouted into the phone and my ear the same.

"Yeah love, we're here!" he said.

Like cartoon characters unreal, we slapped the sides of the car, drumming on trunks and head lights, dancing under the blazing July sun, midday rocking. Faith walked out of her apartment complex slowly, as if on safari—objectively too close to the lions and tigers, but if by God's will she couldn't stop moving onward. She stared unsure if to make eye contact. We barely acknowledged her presence with an off-handed nod almost unrecognizably—though she didn't interpret us rude. She was simply intrigued by such a showy first impression—two dancing idiots not present for any particular reason except to suck all the full-body experience possible out of each parking lot.

"Are you Kristopher?"

She turned her head slightly as if to say under her breath, *"you can't be serious?"*

But we were, and are very much serious—so we very much seriously ran over to her, big hugging-arms open, kissing her on the forehead unapologetically, demanding that she understand only one sentiment—"It is wonderful to have finally met you."

And it was. We finally had our Faith. We rushed to gather whatever garments and toys we'd need for the night—pillow, hookah, trucker-hat, funny t-shirt, potato chips, ready-set-go. Aden led the pack as if knowing where she lived though he didn't.

+

A FEW YEARS PRIOR, Aden and I went to Costa Rica for a week of excess: hiking, drinking, bungee-jumping, drinking, zip-lining, drinking, I forget, drinking, something else, and drinking. It was spring break and it was college and that's what you do so I don't regret not remembering much, but one moment in particular still feels uncertain. While entering a hostel in Monteverde on the southern Pacific coast, overlooking the ocean gulf, a lone Israeli swung effortlessly nestled in a hammock. After common introductions through her broken English I offered, "I'm American," but she quickly replied that she already knew this fact.

Maybe she had recognized my accent but in her English being so elementary and so painfully pronounced, I had to enquire if only for curiosity's sake—"Well how ever did you know that?"

"You walk like an American," she said.

I still haven't a bone of an idea what that means but if I could venture a guess I'd say Aden fits the description quite perfectly. He leads with his chest like a gorilla protecting its territory—arms back, fingers curled upwards, not clenched, relaxed—but ready. He walks straight and purposefully, always knowing where he is headed to, and advertises his destination plainly by way of crystal blue eyes. His head rarely wavers to the side while his hips nearly swing out of their pockets to take up more space. He's shy of 6 feet but stomps around like an insecure giant with a chip on its shoulder. His walk doesn't fit, or I guess it does at times, but it reminds me of someone who *learned* that particular brand of movement. It's unnatural to the rest.

And don't get me wrong — Aden is a good-looking guy: brown hair short, usually tapered by a five o'clock shadow models would envy. My five o'clock takes a week and looks out of place and blotchy and really objectively and terribly ugly — but Aden's, the opposite. I imagined he looked thirty at twelve and I will look twelve at thirty — and I'm not sure which is worse but for now I'm envious of his stubble. So the walk matches the face, sure, or should, but for a moment looking at him speed walking towards an apartment he'd never before set foot in, broad shoulders awkwardly pulled back and chest out, I couldn't help but ask him inwardly, *"What are you trying to prove?"*

Though that conversation would filter itself out naturally later in the trip after I'd built up the courage to finally ask him out loud.

+

FAITH'S APARTMENT HAD just endured a string of rabble-rousers for the last few years, so it looked and smelled the part: half spilt alcohol, half girly hair products, and half late night food remnants. It reminded me of my apartment, to be honest, so I quickly threw my bag down next to my spot and felt strangely comfortable. There was a fellow Couchsurfer already there — he'd parked himself quite humorously on the couch, laptop open, already writing of his journeys. His most obvious feature stuck out magnetically though. I gave Aden a look only best friends could translate and he agreed with a lift of an eyebrow — *"holy shit look at this guy!"*

Jake was skinny and quite small. He wore run-of-the-mill eyeglasses sporting a pretty intense red goatee, forgettable enough if it weren't for his arms and legs being completely saturated in colorful tattoos. It wasn't a number of tattoos neatly lined in a row — it was as if he was wearing a long-sleeve ocean on his arm. The other arm was less memorable but still fully filled in. Now of course the proper way of dealing with such an encounter is to not deal with it at all, but rather to calm the firing nerves of your mind and treat the person appropriately, normally, with a blank slate. "Don't judge a book by its cover." Etc. But fuck — Jake looks like Alfalfa meets Hell's Angels so I couldn't help but worry.

He introduced himself shyly and amiably all the same but I could still see more ink than skin — and in knowing he was fully sick of answering questions about his physical appearance, and with me not wanting to rock his proverbial boat, I began the conversation softly with, "so what's up with the tattoos?"

Alas — curiosity often exceeds propriety. I just couldn't help it. He knew though — he understood — so smiling calmly, letting go of my firm handshake, he offered openly, "What do you want to know?"

Much to my surprise he answered all my questions with passion and genuine interest. Though, after the inappropriate quiz while introducing ourselves blandly I asked Jake what he did for a living. Fully expecting some version of ex-convict (or full time comic book enthusiast, tattoo artist, aspiring truck driver, drug dealer, or some combination therein), he explained, "Well I've been traveling around the United States for a bit now and my goal is to see a baseball game in every American stadium. I love baseball. It's nice having the summers off because every year I can enjoy some new crazy adventure."

I saw it coming before he finished but didn't realize the severity of my stupidity until he said — "As I said I'm from Maine, but after the summer I'll go back to teaching. I have a kindergarten class."

Jaw. On. Floor.

So it was settled just then — I was getting a tattoo. Period. I decided right then and there to get one and considering my view on life changes with the wind — this may have been a risky endeavor, but in such moments of full expression it would behoove me to capture those feelings for an eternal reminder to myself. My life would never fall into perfect symmetry. There surely would be moments of absolute depression. But in those instances of desperation I want to remind myself how to live correctly and spontaneously. And since I was in a wonderful headspace just then, fully digging the world's lessons and serendipity, I would use that energy to print my life's slogan firmly and deeply upon myself—knowing that what is written never dies.

Aden wasn't as excited at the prospect outwardly but I could tell he was mulling over the same rational. Later in the trip he would in fact get a tattoo, an exquisitely scribed single word on his wrist, on his own accord, on his own terms, and visible for all future girlfriends and employers to see. It would be simple—the word "Love" deservingly capitalized.

As Kara walked into the apartment she had no idea how much she would transform me, nor her I. None of us had any clue for that matter—all of us together in the same room for the first time, all sizing one another up with first impressions and snap judgments, unsure if any of us would mean anything significant to each other—like everyday strangers. And I saw Kara uncharacteristically uncertain in those few moments. The door had opened quietly in the middle of a conversation. She offered a reserved hello saying she was one of Faith's roommates before running off to the bathroom to clean up. She was smaller than average but carried strong features that altered my perceptions immediately.

Her hands were soft and chin strong—eyes average brown with matching straight hair, average weight—like a tomboy who had only recently come into her own. She carried youthful, full breasts that she rarely showed off to their full potential. She is attractive but there's nothing obvious to explain why. She has to stand still to be noticed.

I immediately contrasted that with Faith as she sat on the couch chatting with Aden, or flirting, which is ultimately the same thing for adults. Jake said something and I spoke back at him about our mutual road trips and how I envied his purpose—how I yearned for a purpose, any purpose. He said he equally envied my freedom and that got us talking about his plans and my lack of plans but the whole time I couldn't help but stare across the room deeply into Faith's eyes. It was suitable that she and Aden hit it off immediately since both their sets of eyes belonged on an album cover or deserved to be sung about in song lyrics by their heartbroken exes. They both deserve exes—though neither of them had any.

I'm used to Aden though and am also predictably attracted to the opposite sex so I continued staring at Faith. Her eyes — they are like pieces of art in need of appraisal. They danced circles up my spine and twirled me through rings of, "Wow your eyes are fucking ridiculous! No seriously…"

I said this out loud interrupting Jake — "I'm sorry if that makes you feel uncomfortable but…I just couldn't help it."

She curled around herself and retreated into saying, "Oh — thanks."

We'd both soon get lost in each other's personalities more than anything physical so I'd forget her eyes soon enough, and she'd never hold me to the comment, but sometimes there is only room for "wow."

See — I was attracted to both Faith and Kara for different reasons but wasn't ravenous by any stretch of the imagination, and it showed. But just when I started to feel really-really comfortable with my surroundings, with Faith and Kara, with Jake and the idea of staying with strangers, another variable came bursting through the door. Vanessa, a third roommate, was followed by a very large University of Iowa football player. They only nodded before hiding away into her bedroom. The football player left only a few minutes later so either he had stamina issues or he had simply walked her home. I chuckled and decided that the answer didn't matter. Shortly after, the girls rushed off to the bathroom, Faith, Kara, and Vanessa, to paint their faces and change their clothes. I took the opportunity to soak it all in, nod gently at Aden as if to say, "*This is going to be great*," and quickly called Andrea.

She didn't answer though.

Maybe later?

+

ANDREA GREW UP WILDLY conservative. She was home schooled, frequented her church more than the grocery store, worshipped Jesus and George W. Bush equally, didn't watch rated R movies well into her twenties, and generally prescribed to all things Biblical until only a few months before meeting me.

So when her father came to visit, and subsequently to meet her new hippie-boyfriend, it was not smart of me to wake up in her bed the morning he arrived.

Knock-knock the door sounded. Knock-knock her heart pounded.

"Holy shit my dad's here!" she yelled at me still underneath the covers. "Fuck-fuck-fuck-fuck-fuck! You have to go…"

"Where?"

"uhhhh…."

"I apologize for being rational here, but you live on the tenth floor so unless you expect me to jump out the window…"

"Shhhhhh …Fuck! What are we going to do?"

"Tell him you are an adult and you sleep with your boyfriend?"

"That is not an option. Fuck-fuck-fuck!" She was frantic, and my lazy acceptance of the situation as "not a big deal" was hardly comforting to her.

Knock-knock.

"Andrea?" her dad shouted from outside the door, "Are you there?"

"Maybe just pretend like you are out?"

"No — he'll know. I'm sure my sister already told him I was here. She's an idiot you know…"

"Well I wouldn't necessarily say…"

"Oh shut up and get dressed. Fuck-fuck…fuck!"

"Does your dad know you use that word?"

"Get dressed!"

I quickly put on my clothes—a disheveled t-shirt, dirty shorts, stinking tennis shoes, and uncombed hair. I looked like the poster child for "get away from my daughter" but I didn't much care. For so long I had argued with her about her sinisterly oppressive upbringing—that she ought to simply stand up to her parents and tell them that she had moved on, past the suffocating rules of the church and its inhibiting and hypocritical morals—but somehow that didn't do much to convince her. She would usually say, "They are my parents—I have to respect them," which was true—but that stance didn't do much good for her that morning.

"I'll tell him I was already here. I'll tell him I came over this morning to use your computer because mine is being fixed?"

"OK—good idea. Let's do that."

"Andrea! Answer this door Andrea!" her father shouted still waiting outside her apartment. He knew something was up.

"You look like hell," she told me.

"No I don't! Well—maybe I do? …I look like morning sex."

"Shhhhh!" she smiled and gave me a kiss. "Just don't say anything. Please?"

"Of course."

Her dad works for the CIA so was probably watching me from some CIA watching device as I frantically wet down my hair and put on her deodorant, all on his video phone spying machine—but we wanted to at least pretend like he was an idiot. It made us feel better. So I gave him a firm handshake and lied appropriately, nicely, and calmly. I offered the requisite gestures and talked about how, "I had to work late last night, so I had to scramble this morning to use her computer, and oh it's so nice to finally meet you, and no I didn't just have sex with your daughter, because she's still a virgin, and still goes to church every Sunday, cross my heart, hope to die, hand on the Bible, I swear," and all of that.

He nodded and grinned through his teeth all the while thinking, *"This asshole deflowered my baby girl."* So all in all it was a very typical first encounter between a father and his daughter's boyfriend.

And after a surprisingly successful day spent with her family, we walked back into her apartment without saying much. After eating she motioned me into her bedroom and said, "You did very well. I think they like you."

"Even though I looked like sex?"

"Yes," she said while taking off her shirt, "…even though you look like sex."

+

AS I REENTERED THE house in Iowa, visibly angry that Andrea was ignoring my calls, Aden gave me a look that I interpreted perfectly — "*be here,*" it said.

I stood still and took a deep breath to recalibrate.

I am in Iowa, I thought.

Andrea is not here, I thought.

"Let's rock out some alcohol to get things started eh?"

We hadn't eaten dinner but forgot unknowingly on account of the new setting. The girls yelled to us directions to the liquor store through muffled doors and hair dryers that we didn't understand.

"Did you get any of that?" I asked Aden hoping he had.

Aden said he knew exactly where it was — "Something about going down a street to the left and then there is another street and we should turn or something?"

"Yeah I got the same. Fuck it — we'll find it," I said.

And so we went.

And that was the point of the trip, I think — the little adventures and conversations and decisions without justification. We were all sick of logic and foresight and worry and hassle so we ventured into the darkness of Middle America reaching out to feel something, anything. We blinded ourselves to objectivity and objects equally. We wanted to bump into everything unexpectedly and feel around a little — trying to guess at what was in front of us. We let America touch us however it desired, like a massage of accidents.

The local liquor joint was the new world and every street was a changing tide and our compass was happenstance but we made it just fine.

And there it was, gleaming out from carved shelves and blank white walls — Everclear, the holy grail of teenage legends. It was illegal all over the civilized world except for states like Iowa I suppose, or rather, it was legal in Michigan too but could only be purchased at pharmacies in disguise as rubbing alcohol. It wasn't discussed whether or not to purchase said fire-water, only how much of it. We rushed home to explain our enthusiasm.

"We — have — Everclear!"

We nearly busted down the door banging and screaming before Kara came to let us in, "Calm down children. What's the problem?"

"We have the opposite of a problem my love — do you realize that Everclear is not legal in Michigan, or Ohio, or Indiana, or Illinois, or New York, or…fuck! This is incredible. What proof is this? It's like a horse tranquilizer in liquid form. Do you have shot glasses? Let's go. Let's go! Come on now let's rock out!"

Jake laughed and Kara made a few statements to infer the extent of our ignorance — "If you read the bottle you will see clearly printed a warning about taking shots."

"Oh whatever," Aden said continuing his rant, "this is a very important point in our adult lives — we're taking shots regardless — the label is irrelevant."

Kara began to again explain why this was a bad idea but I quickly stopped listening. We all took shots except for Jake because he doesn't drink or smoke and only reads the Bible for fun—well I don't know about the Bible part, probably he doesn't read the Bible, maybe he reads the Koran or nothing or fiction, or something? As wrong as I was about him about his tattoos it wouldn't have surprised me. The point is he was our walking DD for the night and we loved him for it. The shots tasted like acid and bleach combined and we all gagged and exaggeratedly flailed our arms in the air and barked out expletives to the road.

I jokingly snapped at Kara, "Why didn't you warn us about this shit earlier? I'm dying over here."

From there—everything sped up. The carpet began to shake beneath our feet so we couldn't help but jump around and move. I attempted to start a conversation with Faith about her interest in writing but I couldn't keep my balance—the ground was still shaking furiously. "Do you write a lot? What do you write? Aden—give me that hula-hoop. Vanessa—have another drink!" Smack—I hit the wall and another drink spilled into my open mouth. Fast. I braced against the floor on all fours and Aden tripped over me trying to comment on Jake's shoes. Fast. "Do you ever try to match your tattoo colors to the clothes you wear?" Vanessa came sprinting into the living room and Kara accidentally poured her a double shot of vodka. Fast. "This is a toast to all the moments that deserve a toast!" I stumbled into a deep conversation with Vanessa about our Latino connection and I looked caringly all around her and them and at Aden. Fast. She said she believed in love and Aden shouted out in agreement from across the room. Fast. "Where are the sombreros?" The Earth continued to shake furiously and we all spun hula-hoops around ourselves to catch up. Kara was the best due to her womanly hips and general coordination. Fast. "That's kinda sexy you must know." I was the worst due to my being the worst. "Why thank you!" Fast. So we blurred the lines of vision and reality until everything turned into light. The whole world turned into light. Faster. Bright shining light. "Do you believe in god or God?" Faster. Everything was colliding. We were all colliding. Much faster. We cranked up the music juxtaposing deep house with country and explicit hip-hop and laughed our hands to our stomachs. Fast. "Are we supposed to feel like strangers?" Someone yelled and someone else yelled over the other person and we all screamed about going out to party with the cows. "I think we are all gods in a way." Fast. "Do you have any weed?" Aden banged into doors and we took frequent bathroom breaks to collect our thoughts or meditate and forgot to wash our hands and kissed and hugged and continued to meet and dart forward together. "No we don't." Faster. "I think this place is haunted." The Earth shook and split into two and we had more drinks until we leaned on each other singing and decided what crazy outfits to wear and what characters we would be for the night. Much faster. "We all can decide to be whoever we want whenever we want," and we discussed this point and without explanation or disagreement and so we all toasted to "risk." "I don't know what will happen tonight but do you mind if we stay another day?" Faster. The ground shook some more and the wind swirled in and blew us outside sprinting towards more foolish ideas.

"Please stay another day," Faith begged us.

And everything sped up from there. Aden tripped and got back up. Fast. "Let's rock out." We adjusted our giant sombreros. Fast. "Nice dress!" It wasn't Halloween. "We are already rocking out." Faster. Saw a pizza joint. Faster. Decided to go there after the bar. "Can you write me a poem?" We ran across the street. "I feel like feeling." Came back to the same side we'd just left. Wanted to feel the other side. "Jake, are you sober?" Fast. "Why are you guys really here? Really?" Gazed at the stars and saluted the homeless man. All the homeless men. "Iowa smells funny." All the homeless women. "The streets are alive!" All the homeless children. Where's the bar? "Look at the stars in Iowa man!" Why are people homeless? Faster. Headlights and passing cars and peace signs. Much faster. "I can hold my liquor." "You're going to love this vibe." Do they not have opportunity? "Kristopher, stop walking in the middle of the street!" We should give equal opportunity. Faster. Aden said shut up. "Come to the sidewalk!" Fast. Shut up. "Get out of the street!" Noticed I had brought a giant American flag and was wearing it as a shirt. Fucking faster! The bar looked like a bar. Aden went in. "Sometimes they have drinks for a quarter." Aden made friends. We toasted to each other. "Country music?" Aden rapped. "We drink in here." Faith stole Aden's hat. Pictures. We sat down. "Who is that?" There was a table. Remember. Something. Loud. "Look at me for a second." Kara stole Faith's hat. Orange. "Dude we have to stay." Video. Feelings. "I love you guys. Jake do you love me?" Ridiculous stars. Wanted to see the stars. "We are all the same thing." Fucking ceilings. I hate ceilings. "What if we could read each other's minds?" Faster. Vanessa in Spanish. "How about a jazz club?" She speaks Spanish? "I'm getting another drink." Kara looked beautiful. "I like your name Faith." Jake changed my life. "Speak Spanish!" Best Friend. "I rap like a boss from the streets." Faster. Staring into tables. Folded arms. Faster. "Oh my god you are so white!" Swirling. "Do you have a home?" Bathroom. Faster. Drink. Drink. Feel. It. Faster! "I wish I had money." Picture flashes. Last call. Faster. Dance. "Are we foreign?" Much faster. Twirl. Dance. "I'm not from here." Hope. Live. Look. "Get down from there." Jump. Orange hats. "Please forgive them." Giant sombreros. Bouncers. "Go blue!" Bouncers again. "I hope you have a beautiful life." Where are we? "Meet a pretty girl and marry her." Where am I? Friends. Run away. "Get down from there." Faster! "Where to next?" Everclear! "Kara!" Oh shit…we took a shot of Everclear? "What's up Aden?" Why did we do that? Slow down. Everclear. Slow way down and think for a second. "Look around man we're west of the great Mississippi." Kara was staring at me wearing Aden's orange hunting hat. Slow down. Aden saw Kara and me ignoring the rest of the crew and blurted out, "you two are in love!" I stared at Kara and calmly replied, "yes we are," and the whole table erupted in belly laughter. Slower. Kara told everyone to shut up because, "We are momenting." Slower. I started to laugh and hugged Jake next to me and pounded Aden fist to fist. Slow down. And then we decided to leave.

From there everything started to slow down.

"So man, what's up?" Some guy from outside the bar was asking me.

I needed a second to compose myself and stop the street lights from spinning so addressed him confused, "Nothing really. What do you mean?"

"You know, *this*," he looked me up and down smugly, pointed at my wardrobe and repeated, "What's all *this* about?"

I took a moment to comprehend what was actually happening. I looked back at the pack and they were all mingling around unsure where to head to next and it was only then that I noticed Aden, Jake, Vanessa, and Faith were all wearing miniature Mexican sombreros. I forgot. My eyes rolled up and in noticing a giant shadow above, I reached upwards and felt the remains of what was in fact a very large papa sombrero. Also while lifting my arm I felt extra cloth placed near my forearm — the American Flag resting on my shoulders. Of course — this was surely a strange outfit for a random Tuesday in the middle of July, especially compounded by my t-shirt which read, "*Voting Turns Me On.*" In finally realizing why the fine gentlemen before me had brought to my attention such a strange assortment of flags and awkward hats and cheeky mantras, I responded in time.

Very slowly I stroked the flag and tipped my hat to him saying, "I still don't understand the problem?" — fully understanding the problem.

"Not a problem man, just wondering why you are wearing this?" He was trying to humor his friends at my expense but certainly wasn't looking to pick a fight.

I only briefly glanced at him before walking away — "because I want to man," I said, "…simply because I want to."

Aden roared with delight so he too sobered up momentarily to soak it all in. He mimicked me, "Did you hear that guys? Kristopher said to this dude 'simply because I want to' all calm like. And that's what it's all about isn't it? Huh guys? We're all just doing what we want. I love you guys."

He put his arm around Kara, "I seriously love you." He was all juiced up on Everclear and high on the evolution of strangers. We all were.

The pizza joint was right next to a black dumpster, hanging around back alleyways, getting mixed up with the wrong crowd.

"Hey!" Faith shouted from across the way to an average looking delivery guy just pulling in. I hoped he had been tipped well — cheap college kids.

"Hey you!" she repeated.

Faith is shy at first, actually just insecure, but it manifests itself more obviously than she would like. Her hands are in her pockets even when she's not wearing any. "Hey man — you got any pizza back there that you were planning on throwing away?"

Maybe she flirted or flashed him? Actually probably not — she probably didn't flash him — but it makes for a better image. Either way she and Aden returned with a free large pizza.

"See guys — ," I wasn't paying any attention as Aden stuffed his diction with the first slice. He sounded like he was whispering through a closed door.

"See…listen," he mumbled drunkenly. I still couldn't understand a thing until he swallowed fully — "Jake — you know man, right? Why did we get this pizza? Why do you think?"

He wanted to answer but Aden finished first — "…I'll tell you why Jake. Well first because Faith over here — come over here Faith! …Look at her Jake. First, because…Faith — come over here! Faith! OK she's not coming but that is irrelevant. First — because Faith is charming and beautiful. She has the knack, ya know? — just sweeping in like a superhero when all other sources of food are lost, saving us from hunger. Are you hungry Jake? I guess we really aren't "hungry-hungry" like kids in Africa ya know? — but her deed was noble all the same but — well — what was I saying? You know I think we should get some snacks or something. Vanessa! Where can we get snacks?"

I fell into his trap and lost all semblance of articulation. Drunk.

"Aden, dude — hey, Jake — Jake, listen here real quick. Aden? So I was thinking; I was thinking we should give the pizza to a homeless guy or something right? It's sad being homeless and we aren't homeless. No? Yeah you are probably right. Regardless — snacks right? Vanessa!"

"Oh — no no no no no no no no no NO! I remember now," Aden said remembering his earlier point, and took Jake and I under his outstretched arms like an entourage, "The first reason we got this free pizza is still Faith and because she rocks out but second — or most importantly — first? — or the point is the real reason for this wonderful gift bestowed upon us by the great food gods of the street and such, the real reason my friends is — love. In order to get free late night food you just have to send out good vibes and love and live fully and the world shall reward you. That's the truth man. You just got to live it and you'll get pizza. It's beautiful like everything else."

Grabbing a piece and forgetting about the homeless I added, "true words my brother."

Jake must have thought we sounded like hippies, or nudists, or nudist hippies from cult documentaries — we belonged at Burning Man or Woodstock, not the middle of Iowa. But he surprisingly agreed.

"I can dig that. I like that," he said.

He doesn't say much but he says a lot.

Though, somewhere in America a couple was breaking up. Somewhere there was a funeral and somewhere there were guns and somewhere there was regret, so we thought it fitting to go to bed just then. I went to sleep wanting to slow way down, if only to feel the adrenaline of acceleration all over again.

Chapter 4

I HAVE A GRANDMOTHER who doesn't believe in sleep. She says she doesn't have enough time left to spend any in bed. And that is mostly true, right? We never tell stories of that one time we took a nap. But surely there is surely something fantastical about dreaming — about losing ourselves in our imaginations, like children at recess. When we dream we lay back into our subconscious and let the darkness wash under us — a magical world without sensory perception where thoughts roll onto a frictionless plain of endless possibility before us. It's an alternate dimension of models and loves lost and comic book powers. And sometimes the story changes midway through or we go back in time; often we see ourselves true, or while falling down, with the ground rising up towards us — faster, faster, and faster, just before everything crashes.

So I blinked cautiously, still groggy from the drunken night before, but decided to sleep a few moments longer. So there in my dreams I danced between the inside and out, hesitating to fully rise because I knew that the moment I decided to wake, all the ego of my world would come back towards me with full force. I'd be forced to acknowledge things like yesterday — I'd be forced to articulate memories into stories. They would be discussed and filtered. Meanings would be assigned and details would be lost or amplified. There would be "a point." And that frightened me.

See — I often prefer my dreams to real life. They seemed more real.

And my dreams felt like this...

I stood unaccompanied in the middle of the Sahara. I wore only sticky brown shorts made of some earthly fabric tied with a thin tan string — no pockets or hems. I was ancient. Beads of crystal sweat made the long journey down from my hair follicles to the tip of my nose, leaping out towards the sand. I couldn't see anyone or anywhere to go so I picked a direction and ran away towards the sun.

I followed the sun across miles of desert heat until there upon the horizon a mother-tree revealed herself to me. She had thick brown arms and one thick black trunk reaching far into the sky. But even in her grandiosity, she looked near death, pathetic, skinny, and hung low. Once she offered chilling green hugs but now only slumped like a retired athlete.

I walked up to her, unsure what to do or how to react. We were both dying inside so I touched her softly, empathetically, walking around her entire diameter in solidarity. I brushed my index finger over her bruises and her creases, careful not to pull off any bark.

I closed my eyes holding her trunk and walked, and walked, until suddenly my thumb fell into a deep carving. And in stepping back I read four distinct words etched into her wood – "You are not alone."

…Just then I woke up.

Jake was already awake and looked relatively pleased to see me alive, "How do you feel?" He asked this only marginally concerned.

"We'll see. I need some water," I said.

Aden was still sprawled out like a stretching daddy long leg on the adjacent sofa. His hairy chest and legs were fully exposed, unabashed and unworried. He must have taken Faith's advice quite literally so "made himself at home" rather openly, sleeping only in a thin pair of crumpled boxer shorts. All the blankets had piled themselves next to him on the floor during what must have been a restless night of bathroom breaks and darkened half-dreams.

"Aden," I grabbed his shoulder and shook him gently. "Aden man – it's time to get up – or at least put a blanket over you or something."

I looked at Jake chuckling and rolled my eyes at all the resting limbs – "Aden! Buddy…come on man let's be humans for a second. Wake up."

"What? Yeah, what's up?" He looked around dazed but didn't see anything due to his terrible eyesight. "I need my contacts," he said.

I let the luster of the day speak for itself so shuffled to relieve myself while he gathered himself. Upon reentry into the living room, Aden had already slipped on pants and glasses. Faith had woken in the meantime and was sitting next to Jake with an oversized men's t-shirt stretched over her knees and chest. None of us said anything in particular but knew we were all thinking the same thing — feeling the same thing. Kara sauntered out of her room while I stood in the kitchen. She was still wearing Aden's orange trucker hat — a good sign for positive first impressions if I'd ever seen one.

With my hands planted firmly upon my hips and after a fully expressive deep breath, I scanned the room and said rather prophetically, "so what now?"

Jake half serious mentioned that his plans were to leave for Chicago that afternoon to meet some old friends and continue his festivities with them. Faith chimed in annoyed because she had to work most of the afternoon at the local hotel. She said she "served cold buffets to lonely businessmen too tired to complain. "

Aden responded appropriately — "Those are both terrible ideas, you should both stick around here with us."

I added for emphasis — "OK, Jake, here is the thing, Aden and I had every intention of speeding through all this middle section of America in order to get to LA as quickly as possible. Just yesterday this was our plan. But in one day, or better, I will say night — in one night Iowa became a destination rather than a pit stop on to bigger and better places. But come on Jake — there are no 'biggers' or 'betters'…"

I looked at Aden knowing he was in agreement.

"…I know you feel it as much as I do," I said, "I know we all feel it. So stop looking at your itineraries and big red dots on the map. Here we are right smack dab in the middle of the breadbasket of America, where people sweat and drink and smile with the lightning — and it's wonderful right? So stop kidding yourself. You are not leaving. You are not leaving! Let's go get some food."

Kara looked at Jake shrugging his shoulders as if to say, "*OK*." So it was settled—we all needed one more day together.

Though just then I received an email a few hours later from a friend still in Ann Arbor. It was simple and clear—Andrea had kissed someone since I left and he thought I deserved to know. I swallowed fully to stay calm and closed the laptop quickly. There wasn't a settled molecule in all of my body—my core expanded inside out.

Aden suspected something was up so asked me in his typically optimistic way—"What's good man?"

"Oh no...nothing...I was just checking my bank account. All is well," I said.

See—sometimes I lie through my teeth and smile carefully when confronted with emotion of any kind. I'm not proud of it but it's true nonetheless. For the entirety of my life everything has been "*all good*" and that could be classified as emotionally stunted by some but I choose to think of it as a useful defense mechanism.

I wanted to leave everywhere and go nowhere but settled for—"Can we get a tour of the campus?"

We passed a used bookstore that Aden insisted we visit on our way back. He had already packed about 35 books in the trunk because he couldn't decide which he would want to read.

"Who knows what my mood will be?" he had said.

And that was telling—I thought of books as escapes or examples of beauty but hardly wanted to use them for therapy. And who's to say that that is what Aden did exactly, but all his books had a "how-to" spin to them and claimed to fill very specific holes in one's life. I was reading Hunter S. Thompson while he read something about male archetypes? He needed books depending upon his momentary disposition while I reveled in the anticipation of one day calling myself a writer. I idolized prose and studied its composition like a scientist but hardly *felt* anything.

Aden though, is made of emotion, and one day he'll realize that that's why nothing seems to fit. Everyone else is thinking and predicting, but Aden is made differently in his core, and therefore desires to "understand" *how* to think. If he only knew that it was everyone else that needed to "understand" *how* to feel—like him. Oh then what splendor. Oh then what he would impart upon the world. Oh then what he could teach us all…

We then rushed off into the heart of campus. After passing the pedestrian causeway and hearing stories of smoky tailgates and drunken parties, Kara introduced us to the old capitol building of Iowa, transporting me back in time.

So I dreamed once more of the past…

Suddenly all the red brick and asphalt vanished. I turned around and saw the hopeful Iowa merchandise muted, and the store fronts changing. All the colors smelled old but secure. There weren't very many women but rich boys threw balls in the square — they wore strange shoes and dress clothes with big brown buttons. They were nineteen-year-old gentlemen, shipped off to university to continue the aristocracy. A horse and carriage pulled a farmer's princess in white lace with her red elbows — and all the gentlemen prodded the way young boys do still today, and the grass was vibrant and raw — it grew wild like the west. Humble Negroes pushed sharpened wheels to landscape order into the folly. I wanted to go back there with all the empty dirt roads and the wood fires. Forget all these modern expectations — let's read Shakespeare in the summer sun, I thought, and invent sports at midnight. Let's un-hallow this space and make it pure again with rain and pie.

…Then a stranger took a picture of the six of us with a camera phone from his pocket. And we looked comfortable there, arm-in-arm together, because we were. So the stranger took a picture of strangers, and then walked out of our lives forever.

Faith took us to the largest lecture hall on campus. I leaned over the railing from the second floor of the room and told everyone I was going to jump.

"Do you think I would hurt myself if I fell from here?" I asked jokingly.

They all yelled in serious tones they'd soon use with their children—"That is not funny. We're going down the stairs." I thought them good mothers so obliged them all the while missing the rush.

And there stood a solo piano in the middle of the empty stage. Jake put it quite nicely—"This looks more like a concert hall than a place of academic achievement."

"I don't think there is much academic achievement either—but I get your point," Kara said before sitting next to Aden on the piano.

He played something that we all recognized but fiddled around with the keys to make it a little snappier. Of all the gifts I've received from genetics, nurture, or by some higher force, without question I have been given the anti-talent for music. It's not that I don't hear music, I do—I hear it, but my fingers can't translate it—like a boy raised by wolves unsure how to arrange all the sounds of organized humans. For me, a piano is about as useful for making music as a leaking bottle of ketchup—like it or not—there is going to be a mess.

On the contrary Aden hears all the melodies behind the melodies and will often notice some random backbeat in a song. "Do you hear that?" he often asks me. "Right there…ting ting ting—bang! You don't hear that? Alright listen right now…right there…it's sort of faint but without it the song wouldn't be the same. Do you hear it?"

"Oh yeah I hear it, right there, yeah—OK—yeah I get what you are saying," I say, completely ignorant to what he is saying.

See—sometimes it's better to feign comprehension than to hear all the frustrations and complaints. I just don't get it and surely never will. I've accepted it. Just let me dance, I think. Because, of course, it's always important to dance. So that's exactly what we did but without music to confuse me—right next to the biology building, shadowed by the old courthouse, was a beautiful flat yard of grass—like a football field without lines or stands. And oh how we danced!

The only ones watching were couples on leisurely strolls and professors hurrying to office hours. A few students intermittently jogged by and saw Kara spinning helplessly in circles, head-back, arms-out.

"Try it Kristopher. Try it!" Kara yelled like a schoolgirl at play in her backyard, "if you put your arms out like this and then spin around…and you keep spinning and spinning and spinning and then you pull your arms in…!"

She screamed with delight and fell down to the ground smiling profusely. Faith was next and Jake settled in for pictures. But in me being too anxious to watch her finish I began just the same. After a few of my own tries Aden too decided that it was socially safe and therefore too joined in.

"Afterwards it's like a natural high. Sure you are dizzy but there must be some chemical released in my brain or something because — I feel forcibly happy after I spin," Aden said. "No wonder kids do this — it's their version of a drug. Spinning and sugar."

Aden predictably was trying to "figure it out," but Kara retorted quickly yelling at him, "Aden! Stop talking! Just spin!"

I agreed with her so decided to outdo myself and spin with athletic intensity for as long as I could. I took a long deep gasp because I knew I'd have to hold my breath through the spin, and so began slowly to warm up. One spin, two spins, a little faster, and then the third spin — and then I widened my strides and turned my arms rubber and they whipped around like spokes on a tire. Four spins, and five spins, and all the bright colors and the green grass and the white blocked buildings and the black road and the flag pole reaching into the pictured blue sky and the yellow lines and the road, six spins, seven spins, and eight spins, it all blurred away into rainbows and impressionist paintings and nine spins, and ten spins, and then my head flailed back towards the past and there was Aden but he looked different now, eleven spins, and someone yelled out nothing, and twelve spins, drilling towards the center, and the blissful white clouds and where was everyone, and thirteen, fourteen, fifteen, and the spinning released me from all the damage of life, and I was high on my own accord this time. The road was all gone.

I fell down hard on the dirt and the field kept spinning but I didn't feel out of place. I was used to all this commotion. And as it slowed down, I saw Faith and Kara and Aden too spinning their lives away with a fevered intensity. People were watching jealously, wanting to be that free, so I waved to them to join but they couldn't, they couldn't because they were too afraid to let go. No matter — we spun around in circles waiting for the sun to change — feeling alive, maybe for the very first time.

Amidst the ecstasy though, I felt a tinge of guilt while lying openly on the floor, so worked to push it away. In lifting my head slightly I saw only Jake standing still trying to stay above the insanity. He thought it contagious so lingered close enough to catch us if we had faltered, but held back enough to give himself an alibi just in case. It makes sense — he had a kindergarten class to go back to and the real world to face. His ride had an expiration date. Ours didn't.

"I have to relieve myself so I'll be back shortly," I said while slowly picking up the pieces that had been scattered all around. I needed to be alone.

So I walked stubbornly back into the biology building and found the bathroom quickly. In washing my hands I felt the cool filtered water all around and splashed some on my face. I looked into the mirror, alone in the middle of a bathroom, somewhere near somewhere else, somewhere in America. It was just then that the ceiling caved in and the walls collapsed. I was trapped — looking out into myself, caught between the past and all the tomorrows to come. I splashed more water on my face and covered my neck as well. There I was, looking as I always do, but everything had changed and I knew it. Andrea was sprinting towards the exit sign and it was all my fault.

There it was — violent heartbreak. I'd never felt it prior, in that I was always on the giving end. It felt like death. I envisioned Andrea with someone new and dry-heaved into the sink, gripping the sides of the porcelain. I ran the cold water into a cupped hand and drank in a forceful gulp, running the other over my face to mix in with the tears. *"I just needed to cool off,"* I'd say. *"Man I can't believe my allergies,"* I'd answer. But truthfully—I was air in water—rushing towards the surface to escape this foreign universe. And I cried too. I cried without hesitation or abandon. I cried and cried and needed more water so covered my head again, again, again, again and again—to wash it all away. Though while staring into myself for the better part of fifteen minutes I realized there was no going back—so I quickly stiffened under my tears. I said out loud to myself, "you are not alone," and walked outside to once again quietly hide with Aden in public.

+

"I FEEL LIKE I'M seeing Iowa City for the very first time," Faith said while peering over a bridge down towards the river.

"This is such a beautiful campus with beautiful people and such a great vibe. It's a college town but has a peculiar hue of something—it smells different and…oh look over there at that building! There are probably thousands of students that go into that building everyday like it's a rundown carnival ride but hell—it's beautiful too. Look, look at the marble columns and the red bricks and oh look at that carving! What is that?" Aden was giddy with the setting and so spoke honestly.

Kara agreed with Faith—"I guess you are right. I mean I guess it's just that—I was always known that I was going to go to school here and I've known the campus since I was young and even when I arrived I was more interested in the parties than the landscape. Give me a moment to look around…"

"Yeah definitely take a moment to look around. We'll all look around," I said. And I meant it.

We walked along the river like molasses falling into the light and held hands and shoulders. Time was moving too fast and the cars were too big and we needn't be distracted by anything except one another—looking around together, seeing the same old places virgin.

But just as the moment was creeping towards perfection Kara blurted out in her usual way — "Oh look...I've peed there!"

"What? Where?" This was unexpected.

"In the parking lot over there behind that Buick, except I'm not sure if it was a Buick then. I've left myself all around this town marking my territory. Well that's what I tell myself — mostly it was just that I needed to go really badly. Good thing I like skirts," she explained without hesitation.

See — she owns herself fully and is therefore proud of her every statement. So I admired that about her awkward honesty, thinking it cute rather than gross.

"Maybe you'll find somewhere new for tonight?" I said while walking into the aforementioned book shop. I ordered a milkshake and spoke with the owner about why he sold milkshakes in a bookstore.

"...mostly because people like milkshakes," was a logical answer so I turned to Jake for more agreeable conversation.

I sat next to him on a shaky bench made for children. It all fit quite nicely so I watched his own version of madness — him stuffing children's books under his tattooed arms. I had forgotten about the kindergarten class. But more madness still — Aden looked at books about sex and personality. Kara was gushing over a book titled "Cunt" and read the back cover loudly without pause and screamed about feminism and its real definition. I thought to myself it all sounded interesting, or maybe it was just that Kara was interesting? And Faith was skimming through titles with her finger, head cocked sideways, searching for a book to catch her eye but wouldn't have mentioned it if she had found one.

Their story was much the same as mine and Aden's but certainly more feminine — and curiously less extreme. Kara was the popular loud one who had no pause button and Faith kept up enough but was rarely in charge. They influenced each other and loved each other and ping-ponged back and forth and cried when they needed to — but Faith was softer. She smiled less often but bigger when she did. And that's a lot like

Aden and I but those nuances will play themselves out later, and in context. And I'm not sure who is who anyway?

Aden naturally has more natural hesitancy towards the world — I'll call it fear for now. But in him being acutely aware of the extremes, often he is the one pushing our boundaries on purpose. We live on the same giant plain in life, the only difference being that I'm colorblind to the edges. So I often lose sight of my direction and end up walking in circles — and if I *do* reach the edge, I don't acknowledge it — I can't — so I step off and fall as if on accident. Aden will look at me with awe and think, "*how did he walk off the edge so easily?*" while following me into the abyss, because he must.

Oppositely, Aden sees all the fine lines and edges illuminating in the distance way before we get there. He looks off to the horizon with apprehension and curiosity equally. He makes moves on purpose, turns right and turns left and drags me tenaciously towards the edges of his dreams. He looks down first, slowly extends one foot over the edge, balances for a moment, takes a deep breath, and jumps purposefully. And I follow him ignorantly off the rim not sure why it's such a big deal, until I take that last step, and then I feel the rush. Only then do I say to him, "*Wow! Thank you for taking me here. Thank you for taking me to this new place.*"

And so it goes in this way — us leading each other equally to feed the flame, to keep the candles of our lives burning well into the early morning.

+

"WHY DON'T WE CHILL out and just *be* for a while? How does that sound?" Aden suggested with everyone in agreement. "I'll go grab the hookah."

I had never smoked nor planned to during my adolescence but soon after Aden had introduced me to the sweetness of flavored tobacco I was hooked. He had been present for all such introductions. The first time I drank was on my twenty first birthday. Aden made sure all my drinks tasted nothing like liquor — and so personally used strong mixers to mask the flavor. The party raged and the cops came and everyone hid in closets in my room. The police gave me a noise violation but we all laughed it off, as you should on twenty-first birthdays.

From there the drinks grew stronger and eventually we forgot to use mixers. Aden, too, taught me the technique of taking a shot. It was only he and I in my kitchen so I wouldn't have to bear the public embarrassment of spilling and coughing all over myself. And in the same way, without judgment or pretense, he offered me my first smoke. I'd been curious for months so when I asked him to help me through the process he obliged and gave me guidance. Again—just the two of us in my kitchen, coughing, and laughing about the coughing, until the smoke reached its proper location and connected unapologetically with my mind. I felt off, but calm, because he talked me through it as he always does—him leading me to my limits and offering reassurance while I take the plunge.

So there in Iowa we placed the hookah in the middle of the floor and all sat Indian-style watching Aden load the sticky tobacco into the smoking chamber.

"You are going to love this flavor. It's called Irish Cream and tastes like caramel," he said peacefully.

Faith took the first hit and smiled dreamlike in approval. We insisted that Kara go next because they were our hosts—it was only proper. The room already smelled of s'mores and relaxation as I grabbed the long tube reaching from the middle out, touching my lips gently. After blowing all the air I had inside outward, the only option left was to breathe in deeply to suck in all the flavor possible. As the smoke saturated my lungs its chemical components melted into my bloodstream. After only a few heartbeats I felt my legs grow weak and my hands still. I looked upwards and watched the air thicken above me as if looking slightly above the fire. It tickled past Jake's face but he didn't flinch although he'd never take a hit. No tension. And there it rocked me solid, a few heartbeats past my neck and on to the top of my head—there it sat. It's certainly a mild buzz if it can even be classified as such, but by combination of heat and company I felt wholly present.

Aden sensed how pleased I was so asked just to hear my reaction — "Feeling good man?"

I was in the middle of my second pull so didn't want to exhale just yet. I closed my eyes and pushed my head down slowly as if to stare at the floor, then looked up, relaxed my eyes, and nodded yes.

"Yeah man — for sure. I'm glad you feel good. He feels really good," he said reassuring the girls.

Then Faith took the tube and asked, "So that's what you two are all about eh — feeling good? Like you don't have any specific motivations that I can tell for being here, or anywhere, but I can speak for Kara in saying that you guys live deeply. I mean today I feel like I saw my campus all over again. You guys live very intensely."

She closed her eyes the same as I had and passed the hookah to Kara without looking. She held the stem in her left hand loosely, swaying. Kara took a hit and said mid breath, "I think we are all feeling very good right now."

Jake added, "I agree," in his way — so that we all knew he felt it too, though soberly. Or maybe it was second hand?

This is where I would have normally taken over the conversation and asserted my beliefs plainly upon the room but I fell silent as Aden set in motion what was to be an emotional hatching of unprecedented power — one that would lead us to forever change our perceptions of the word "stranger."

He began gently — "I understand what you are saying Faith but let's not forget that you are all equally a part of this equation. If we walk into a room 'guns blazing' while everyone stands still, with their hands above their heads, there is no gunfight right? You have to shoot back and duck behind the tables and dive through windows for there to be any drama. Otherwise the director is mad and everyone is bored — otherwise we are just sadistically pressuring the unwilling. So I must politely disagree with your premise that we live deeply as if you have no part in the outcome. You are not bystanders."

Jake added, "Well what caused this? Where does this come from? You don't seem to care about anything in particular, except for everything? It's weird."

"I don't know," Aden said for us both, "it's as if the road whispers to us not to miss out. There are a million things happening right now, good and bad, and we're all only this small little piece of this implausible mystery we call life. We're all sitting here in this room staring at one another as if what we do matters—as if anything really matters? None of us know anything about anything except for what feels good. But even that can't be cause for our motivations—life not about living deeply I don't believe, because what does that even mean? What have we done? It's not even about choosing or happiness or sex or travel or any of those clichés. For me—it's about action. Movement."

"…living like it's your last day and all that jazz?" Kara suggested while inhaling profoundly. The smoke dripped from her cheeks like pellets of black water. She steamed out the next few lines noticeably hushed—"I think that's a problem with people," she said.

Then she paused to inhale one more hit. The sweet nectar palpated through the room and outwards through the windows. A slight breeze washed in and out with a liberated consistency. "We print slogans on billboards," she said, "and list them in our favorite quotes and cheers to 'tonight' but as soon as someone does something remarkably unusual—they are chastised. 'She drinks too much.' 'Why does he wear that?' 'Why don't you just go there and do that like the rest of us?' All the simple beauties of life are beaten out of us by nuns and soldiers all wearing the same thing—the fucking conformity is stifling."

"Well it's easy not to conform when you don't have to answer to anyone. We have an unusually freeing situation—traveling around the country without expectations. Our parents and the television already told us what we *should* do but we're past the confrontation. We've already made our choice," I added. I tried to explain even though I hadn't a clue what I was talking about. I just knew the trip was bigger than outright rebellion.

Kara asked us all to hold that thought and ran past our peripheral vision. She came back smelling of butter and skin.

"This is from Africa," she said and I thought just then to myself how Africa is always lumped in together with itself. Surely there are thousands of languages and dialects and fires of different hues there but Africa is often singular in description — at least for Americans. They all need the internet or medicine or something right? That's all we know. But so too is America consolidated under one accent or president to the rest of the world. Half the world gets their cultural understanding of America from episodes of Friends and how can they not, I thought. How can we not assume unless we go there and eat it up ourselves?

She confirmed — "I'm not sure where from in Africa. Maybe it's all over? But my point is that there is a tree that seeps this shit and some company sells it and who cares because it's soothing. Try some."

It came in one of those girly cylindrical shapes that are usually reserved for wrinkle creams. It was yellow with careful black writing. I placed one index finger placidly near the top and felt the solid melt into my body heat. My mom had drilled a thousand traditional rules into my head since the age of awareness — one of which was "not to take more than is offered." I always had to take the least amount and be the last in line and ask before you take seconds and don't chew with your mouth open and put your shirt on and take off your hat and look that person in the eye and pinches under the table and private bathroom breaks for scolding. So with my mom's voice a constant force on my shoulder, I heard her whisper to me, *"Don't take too much. It could have cost a lot of money. Be polite."* So I only took a pea sized portion and blended it around my forearm.

"Don't be shy — take more," Faith said speaking for Kara as they often do for each other.

I wasn't used to that suggestion so snapped, "I'm not being shy," more harshly than intended.

Kara fought back, "Then stop being a pussy and lather yourself up."

I half chuckled at the evident lack of sexuality present for such a command. And I needed Aden in such awkward situations to lead me, so he scooped out an adult portion and covered his knees and ankles rather energetically. Jake then went to town and we all scampered for more wet heat and covered our necks and faces and looked at one another through glistening eyelids. This worked to heighten the already peaceful living room — transforming ourselves into sexual heathens on the cusp of collapse. Everything was elastic and smooth and so we touched one another and sucked each other's smoke in through the firm air, unaffected by anything happening outside.

If such a moment had repeated itself in a porno some inspiring orgy would have unquestionably ensued. We all would have loved it and one another equally and so would have fallen off the edges of our inhibitions together into one of those moments you replay in your mind and wonder how it ever came to be. But often there isn't a defining moment when you want one. Defining moments are more unpredictable than that. So instead of taking our clothes off bare in between the couches, we emotionally made love to the experience with a concentrated intensity. I reached to the hookah and took another hit, and another, and another, and held in the high deeply, feeling it rush past the ceiling. Aden closed his eyes and so we all did too, and so we fell silent — because there are no words in spontaneous meditation.

But Jake broke the silence with — "Do you think it is 'chance' that we are all here right now?"

"That's a heavy question Jake," I said. I spoke for the first time in a while.

"That's a very interesting question, or maybe *the* question — 'choice' and 'chance' and 'fate' and all that, because it all has to do with why we are here. It's a spiritual question, in a way, is it not? It's a question that if answered, would map out a blueprint for our lives. If it's 'choice' that rules everything, then we have the freedom to devise our lives, but then the entire burden rests heavy upon our shoulders. On the other hand, if everything is being predicted for us, then we should stop worrying and just let it flow, but then we might end up sitting on our grandma's couch into our forties on account of the free pizza and football games. So who knows? I don't think either answer makes anything easier. You still have to react to life."

Everyone else had their reasons and opinions so we mostly just spit into the wind, around in circles, until the conclusion was anything but a conclusion. Kara and Faith agreed that life was a mix of both fate and choice and Aden then offered something about love being more important than either. I simply took a deep breath of smoke instead of responding. Often times the most philosophically engaging conversations are the least fulfilling, it seems. Because who likes a story without an ending?

Then...

"I died once," Jake said.

The expectations of such a preface are hardly worth noting except to say, "it'd better be good." All the weight of life and death are intertwined so tightly in such a sentence that we all decided that anything we had to say in response would prove inconsequential. All the senses and smells engulfing the area were sucked out. We all held our breath in the vacuum of Jake's story, like prisoners wanting to stick around for just a little longer.

His introversion screamed at the top of its lungs but no one heard a sound. "I remember the day vividly," he said. "I was on a drive and I was hit and I can't really describe the damage. Like, I thought to myself just before it happened that I was going to die and you won't believe how that moment felt. Crazy. I can't even describe it except to say that I was very worried and um...calm, ya know, all in one. You can't do anything except accept your fate in a moment like that. I don't know. But I should have died. Well I guess I did for a moment or two. The car was beyond destroyed and honestly I don't know how I survived. But...well...it's all a mess in my head but I have the scars still."

He lifted select parts of clothing to show us but I kept holding my breath. He continued — "So after that day I told myself I had a second lease on life ya know and that I had to make something of it. So, I guess, well...that's a large reason why I'm here this summer by myself ya know. Does this make sense? I've always wanted to see all the baseball stadiums so I figured I might as well do it right? Who knows when the next car accident will happen? Right?"

The room was branded in pin drop silence for quite a time. I gazed at Faith's eyes for grounding but they looked different than before. She splattered them around in all directions, but somehow was calm inside, contemplating as we all were. Trying to compartmentalize a near death experience next to recollections of one night stands and memorized rap lyrics and resentment for ex-girlfriends and the details of final exams — it just doesn't make sense — it just doesn't fit anywhere neatly in our brains. Rather, such stories of death infiltrate each separate memory individually, demanding clean perspective, challenging our very reason for existing. And so it seems that stories are cleaner without death — as is life.

Someone said something to change the subject but none of those words made any sense in comparison. So we did the only thing we knew to do — we drank.

From there everything sped up. The pub found us singing karaoke without microphones and dancing on the bar. We were asked to leave but instead laid down flat and pulled up our shirts and stuck limes into our mouths and shared public kisses tasting like tequila and breath mints. I kissed her and she kissed him and we drank from belly buttons and licked salt off necks until we were all satisfied with the flavor of the night.

Kara sprinted back to the apartment and Aden lost himself and Jake gaffed soberly at all the insanity thinking, "*They've done it again.*" And we did — even bigger than yesterday — all hyped up on hookah and rock n' roll.

Though eventually we all collapsed into our respective spots, except Vanessa was there this time and casually invited me to spend the night with her. And so I woke up the next morning fully satisfied in her warmth. But this story is of course not about sex so I'll leave the details for imaginations, because often that is all we ever have anyway.

+

IN COLLEGE I GREW to love running like beer and bad sex. It's "good enough" and everyone else likes it so why not? Therefore I experienced many frenzied nights of running through precipitation listening to Beethoven or Bach at the tip of midnight. I would laugh with Ann Arbor, getting to know her intimately after all the students and their commotions ran into their houses for shelter. I'd be alone with my city, zipping past libraries and pizza joints, hailing the taxis in solidarity.

See—as you watch your lover sleeping, enjoying her peace equally with yours—you become familiar with her breath. You see her life force expand and retract—inhale and exhale. So the night is intimate. It rejuvenates life. It connects us.

So insomnia too familiarized me with Ann Arbor. We were connected because I saw her at her most vulnerable moments—those without the heavy distractions of city congestion, when the lights are dim and the moon is bright, with the rain pouring down filling her drains. I ran the streets and found the familiar places devoid of calamity. They were empty and dark and stagnant and blank. And in those spaces, peering in through mirrored windows, I'd see that they are tanks without fuel. They need us, the streets. They want us. America beckons. Etc. But if you really want to see her and become acquainted with her nature— you must see her at night. You must watch her sleep.

And so I did there in Iowa City—running, watching the sun rise over the east, enough to sprinkle droplets of heavy heat onto the muffled farmers and the shadowed grounds of The Midwest. They all thought me crazy for venturing out so early after such a late night, but no one knew exactly when we got back or how or why for that matter—so I shrugged it off and ran into Iowa City, my feet clenched to dirty shoes.

It hadn't rained since Ann Arbor and wouldn't all summer as we hopscotched through the north and south, avoiding the storms as if on accident. But I missed the idiosyncrasies of thunder and hot chocolate, so mused myself with expectations of tornadoes in Nebraska. See—no one looks up to the rain after grade school anymore, but I still enjoyed the impulsive sting of a drizzle during a run, so I wished just then that Iowa would grant me relief from the rising sun and send her rain to drown me in all the most beautiful ways.

The ground felt cold against the clapping sounds, against the cracked sidewalks, against the new trees and the forgotten stop signs. Clap-clap my joints bolted, stretching tendons, clap-clap through the dust and someday peace will come to me, I thought. I lost myself in crosswalks and numbered street markers. I saw the old trucks and there was a Walmart too and changing reds to greens on the stoplights, with little white men on the crosswalk signaling my safety even though I ignored them. Clap-clap as a train obstructed my run. It inched onward to Des Moines and then Sioux City—Denver, Vegas, San Fran and back again carrying hobos, singing carols with packs of all sizes. They'd rest their weary heads between the coals of West Virginia, I thought, and sink back into their dreams for the next great place. I saluted them, the hobos, and they I, as the rolling wheels picked up steam, now a few inches at a time. Clap-clap and blowing whistles oh how they blew, but I didn't have time to wait so I grabbed onto one of the ladders of the train and jumped all aboard.

And for just more than a second I flirted with the old ways—wanting to stay on just long enough to hop off at the next city. I'd call Aden to pick me up. I'd tell him all about train jumping and real wandering. I'd tell the story for ages until it flattened and spread out and I'd tell everyone that I slept until Mexico by the time I was a grandpa. Stories always expand in this way. They seem to exaggerate themselves with time. But I hadn't brought my phone so jumped off the other side of the train and continued my run back to the parked car rather normally. But if for a moment though, I entertained the thought, and that was enough for me to smile all the way home.

After a shower or three we bid farewell to Jake and exchanged contact information but this time both parties had every intention of keeping in touch. We had to. And we did! We'd see him later in Los Angeles as planned, after zigzagging our own paths across America separately. And Vanessa and I hugged goodbye pleasantly and maturely all things considered, and exchanged contact information the normal polite way—with neither of us actually expecting to keep in touch.

And without real time limits or any of that mess, Faith, Kara, Aden, and I packed the car tight and decided to grab a quick bite to eat before letting go for good. We chose a Middle Eastern buffet, which Aden loved, in him being the fun kind of Jewish, where he mixes melted cheese with meats and chomps down bacon and milk with beef and leavened bread — sometimes all at once even. I think he lights a menorah and knows a few Hebrew words — like a "Christmas Day Catholic." So we ate the stuffed grape leaves and lamb, gyro meat and feta — olive oil, leafy salads and hummus of all varieties — all the flavors of far off lands in Iowa, like the kings of past demanding foreign spices.

What a feast! And we laughed so hard for so long that the restaurant had no room for staring. The shy Arabic whispers all rose up into juicy grins and belly laughs. Aden started crying and fell off the booth and held his stomach and what were we laughing about again?

"What are we laughing about?" Aden stuttered from the tile and no one knew but that's the game. Though near the end, half still giggling, Aden threw out one of those sentences that are usually ignored like bad pickup lines. What he said should have withered away, blending in with the low tones and the hums of the backroom dishwashers, but with all the expectations I can muster — it didn't.

"Why…hehe…you know what?" he looked at me and paused to build his composure, "ha…you know what? You girls should — haha oh god I can't stop laughing this is great…you should — haha, you should come on the road trip with us I bet you'd have a blast!"

I joined right in and said sarcastically, "Yes! Yes you should quit your jobs today and come with us."

And then…

Absolute. Silence.

Glassy eyes and strange expressions sure, sounds good — but absolute silence. The moment was thick and dynamic with possibility. Now granted this story had been written a thousand times before for romantic comedies and comeback-kid westerns — the story of the farmer's daughter swept away to Hollywood by a fast talking city slicker promising late nights and big tent revelry. The protagonist always got the girl and she was the hometown cheerleader who was bigger than the tractors, at least in spirit. It's all so cliché. But this was real life fantasy because they actually said yes. They dumped their previous plans and bought one way plane tickets to the City of Angels where we'd pick them up. And who knew for how long they'd be with us or where we'd venture to? — but who cares because all the wholly fucks in the world couldn't match this.

Sometimes, it seems, there is only room for "wow."

I played the story back to myself — two boys stay at two girls' house whom they've never met and a few dinners later they decide to quit their jobs and buy one-way plane tickets for a road trip to nowhere.

What is a stranger again? What are you supposed to do with a college degree?

And so it was settled. They said yes.

Kara, Faith, Vanessa, and Jake each moved me into submission. I would have predicted laughter, some banal conversation, a bed to sleep, and Aden and I having our own adventures. But that didn't happen. Our connections felt deep and fell immediately upon our hearts. I heard them, enjoyed them, met them, and they too I. And maybe no one can really ever know anyone else — sure, sounds good — but it can't hurt to try.

Chapter 5

We met Glenda. She hadn't washed her hair in a while—I noticed a ring and strong hands. She stood upright but very much on purpose, as if gravity kept her off balance and out of sorts. I was reminded of waitresses in famous movies with a line or two and their ways of fading out of the scene.

"Do you need a room?" she asked annoyed after a few minutes of waiting.

"No we're just headed to the bridges of Madison County. We saw a sign a few miles back on the highway but I'm not sure if we're heading in the right direction. Could you help us with directions?" I asked her.

She was a legendary photograph waiting for an artist. Behind her hung empty frames and brown walls burnt. I looked around the tiny room packed of NASCAR memorabilia, a shrine to Jimmy Johnson and dusty earth tones. The local trophies were mute too, placed carefully on the dilapidated bookshelves. She fit back in time, it seemed, like the rest of western Iowa, there in her salmon NASCAR shirt, with her elbows resting on rotting wood long past its prime.

"Oh ya'll aren't too far away. There are twenty or thirty bridges or so just down the road there a ways. Are you hoping to see any one in particular?" She spoke mostly without adjectives.

"Well I didn't know there were so many, actually. Is there a bridge that you recommend in particular? We are due in Nebraska tonight so we'll probably only be able to visit one."

She suggested—"If y'all go down this road out here for a few miles there is a sign for one of them. Y'all will see."

That day I was wearing a black t-shirt with printed white block letters. It said YOU ARE HERE. I bought it after reading some Echart Tolle and Alan Watts in one of my spiritual phases — when I was obsessed with Buddhism or some shit. When I wear it I always get people walking up to me laughing or pointing, some of them even say they like it. It's a very true statement for the reader — YOU ARE HERE. But even more true for Glenda still. For her it was a declaration for acceptance — she didn't have much of a "way out" even if she wanted one. Wide open spaces are sometimes a prison. Her life, I assume, will always be spent behind motel counters until the wrinkles eventually cut in so deep that one day a newspaper will write her obituary — *"Local motel owner dies of boredom."*

Aden kept talking to her and so she began to cheer up on account of his big smile and pleasantries. He liked her I could tell and therefore wanted to show her everything he could see.

Walking out of the office and back into the car Aden said regretfully, "I should have invited her on the road trip with us — even if only for a little while."

"I know man but we don't have room in the car and I think she belongs here. She fits here," I said.

"I don't think anyone belongs anywhere."

He didn't really believe this of course. A part of him wanted to with all the grandeur of travel, but in reality he was actually searching for a spot that fit him. I was as well. We wore different highways and temperatures, loosened up through cities and unnamed towns together, and we loved travel, we really did — sure, sounds good — but we figured that after trying on all the people of our country — eventually we'd look in the mirror and finally buy the damn thing.

We wanted to find a home. And not just a place to *call* home. A home-home. A real one. But we were too frantic to settle anywhere just yet and we knew it.

We saw a sign that read "Bridge of Madison County" with a hand painted arrow pointing to the right. So we turned right. The gravel stone road kicked up plumes of smoke but we wouldn't disrupt the traffic. We couldn't. There was nothing to disrupt—no traffic to speak of. The road winded up and down and right to left with eight-foot corn stalks lining either side. For a while we questioned the sign and thought ourselves on private property. It all seemed so "in the middle of the nowhere" to us city boys.

In fact, I very much expected to stumble upon a dilapidated red barn filled to the brim with the dead bodies of lost travelers. An old man with rotten teeth and whisky stained overalls would run out screaming "Private property! Can't you hippies read?"

He'd shoot a shotgun into the air barefoot and Aden would say something about love and try to give the old bugger a hug. But he'd just yell at us—"what are ya' homos?"—and kill us dead just for fun.

But eventually I snapped out of my mind and all the dirty stereotypes after finally seeing The Bridge, next to an enormous cornfield (of course).

"Why don't we go into the corn first eh? I've never been in a cornfield," I suggested for no apparent reason.

And of course it wasn't "necessary" to go explore a cornfield, this would be dull, even, for most—but so it goes like this when you travel—always sticking your arm down much deeper than necessary into the black hole of life. But we need it that way. We are life junkies—Aden and I—taking sweet hits of breath and smiles daily. We're addicted and therefore are sometimes tough to handle. We roll into cities like tornadoes, sucking up our surroundings into memory banks and camera flashes. We meet a few people as we do—greeting them inappropriately with hugs and taboo talks and immediate comfort. But then we go, as the tornadoes do, and leave people stranded without words. But I enjoy that feeling—leaving a memory—it's my fuel—leaving an impression, challenging the status quo, living more fully than, and running helplessly into the mazes.

We stopped the SAAB in the middle of the road, completely confident that no car would pass while we were gone. No need to lock the doors. And so we stepped gigantically over the ditch and shook hands with the first stalk before crawling all the way in. The corn smelled sweet and clean like a garden center. And everything in front of my face looked the same, like a green-blindness, so I looked towards the westward sun.

Aden shouted through the corn — "Think about it man, Glenda voted for Obama! Think of our Glenda my man. Iowa is the California of the middle with their caucuses and gay marriage — these fuckers voted for Obama! Like imagine that — the dude who owns the corn we are presently running through walked into the voting booth and on one hand he had a white war hero Republican and on the other he's got a black newbie liberal, fully equipped with Hussein as a middle name, and he checked off the Obama box man. These farmers are rad out here."

I agreed, though didn't say so out loud.

"We should leave," I said. "I've had enough of the corn."

So we finally came to the bridge. And it was polluted, of course, by carved graffiti but somehow it added to the flair — in half of it being two names with a heart in the middle. Without knowing how many restorations had taken place I observed the bridge incredibly sturdy, but altogether useless. I'm sure the bridge once had some use but at present it simply led from a hobbled parking lot towards the edge of some private property. It reached over the water sure, sounds good — but the river was all but two feet deep at its high end and led only to a big pile of nothing.

"Why is this here?" I'd have asked the tour guide if she existed.

Iowa has the most thoughtful tourism industry known to man, I thought. It doesn't charge anything for anything. If I were the governor of Iowa I'd ship buses of Bostonians out to corn fields and let them play for five bucks a pop — two bucks extra for a tour of the bridges to nowhere. English teachers would eat it up with poetry assignments and reading lists for Steinbeck and Twain. But that's all capitalistic and city-like so doesn't quite fit out there with all the silence of rural Iowa.

Just then Aden calmly walked up to me and said, "So I'm pretty sure I just accidentally kicked a giant swarm of bees into a frenzy. It was an accident. Don't panic. Be chill."

"Well on that note," I said. "We should probably leave."

And so we took one last long walk through the bridge's passageway of I-love-you calligraphy and spotlight oranges, all the while surrounded by buzzing bees.

"If we just maintain our chill energy they will be chill," Aden advised. So instead of sprinting back to the stereo system and air conditioning in fear, we simply and calmly walked back to the car like Buddhists to satiate the bugs. And neither Aden nor I were stung even once. So we thanked our lucky karma for its mercy and looked towards the sun.

"I think we got lucky. These bees aren't city bees," I added while closing the door, "they aren't used to the antagonism."

+

MISSY, A COUCHSURFER, HAD expected us two days prior, so we mercilessly pressed down hard towards the blue-green-yellow-orange-red-to-black nightfall to collect our thoughts and reach her house before midnight, watching time's daily rainbow set over Nebraska. Neither of us said a word until reaching Lincoln.

"Is that it?" Aden asked and pulled off to the side of the road, rubbing his eyes for the blur. We turned down the music from unlawfully-loud to way-too-loud and lurched towards the front porch, leaving the car running just in case.

The door was wide open as it should be in Nebraska. I saw Missy skipping towards the door, wearing a white smile and a blue dress. She quickly showed us our spot in the living room with a premade futon while introducing us to her boyfriend. Israel, his name, was tall enough, with a tan, big nose, and wore a beard like a hippie would for show.

"I really appreciate you having us over on such short notice and sorry for not arriving on time but we got caught up in Iowa of all places," Aden said to begin the small talk.

I noticed a four-foot tall hookah on the shelf next to our couch.

"You smoke hookah?" I asked. "For some reason I didn't expect that in Nebraska. We actually brought one with us for the road trip."

Up to this point Israel had said only "hello" and "welcome" so I was surprised to hear his second sentence — "Oh yeah I was raised in Mississippi," he said with a twang, "but I'm Iranian by blood so I grew up with shisha. Do you two smoke anything else?"

Aden lives so sporadically, so violently, so sumptuously, that marijuana takes him to dark places behind his mind. The last six months were full of Aden's revelations about energy and his childhood and he just couldn't take it anymore. He needs to see everything in front of him as is — otherwise the light is too bright.

"No man," he said to Israel, "I'm sure Kristopher will partake but I don't smoke anymore." This was a good decision because when Aden goes off on a tangent he never returns.

Missy carried herself softly and feminine in the ways feminine girls do who aren't sure of their own beauty. Never was she a looker in high school so probably grew up confused about her worth. She had apple cheeks and a thin layer of baby fat all over, but with her strawberry hair and model-pale skin I'd safely call her attractive. She looked and spoke like Nebraska, always smiling, pointing at premade beds, mostly quiet until spoken to.

Israel on the other hand believed strongly in his opinions. "We have some homemade beer if you guys would like to try," he said while packing a bowl on his lap, "we're pretty amateur but it's not so bad."

We gladly accepted a glass and passed around a few hits until we all felt adequately comfortable with the new setting. I hadn't changed out of the YOU ARE HERE shirt and Israel said he liked it, and so asked me what it meant.

"For me it's more philosophical than sassy — there are a lot of times when we are in our heads, ya know, or I should say — there are a lot of times when I am in my head, so it's just a reminder of what we have — this moment — this time," I explained.

"So like existentialism or something?" he asked.

"No, I mean, yes, I guess…but that word has a lot of implications that I don't particularly align myself with. At the core, sure — but we all know that word is misused a lot. I'm not trying to be some Camus-style selfish prick that hedonistically lives for whatever desires I happen to have at any particular moment." I paused and then continued, "It's more of a healthy awareness of what's in front of me. And I'm not trying to be obtuse I promise, it's just that, I guess, it's more about people who text while at dinner with someone for example. It's about being polite and enjoying company at present. YOU ARE HERE — so *be here* ya know?"

Missy passed me a homemade beer, and Israel finished a home grown hit, in a hometown city, wrapped up in smoke and all the thickness of conversation. So I felt at home while high just then, and in a way I never expected to nor spoke of honestly. See — I didn't own my freedom like I did my decisions. There has always been a vale between the high and real life — as if they were mutually exclusive. So I'd often fall into those moments of marijuana-induced clarity throughout college in an attempt to make sense of all the possibility before me — but I would do it assuming I was doing something wrong. See — when you are young the world is all too big and intimidating with the future. But weed focuses everything into manageable chunks for a bit. So I liked it — though I rarely spoke of it out loud.

What it does — if nothing else, is allow us to focus on the particulars of life which are otherwise overlooked due to our hyperactive perceptions. When you are stoned — you feel, you really-really feel. You taste and only taste. You listen like Beethoven's ear pressed to the floor and you see vividly like a blind person coming into sight for the very first time. You pick out smells from wines and cheese tastes so damn good and the sex makes you believe in God with a capital G. It's spiritual, in fact.

Andrea and I would often fall into each other in this way — through nights of laughter and cross belly touch, with moonlight hugs and background music for enhanced eye contact. Our sober versions cared little for the outside world of people and problems — but when we were high, our distain for everyone other than each other was even more pronounced. We'd have sex like bees worshipping each other as The Queen. After a hit or half a bottle, everything outside would vanish, leaving only our kisses to soften the blow, to distract us from the difficulties of life. So we'd lock ourselves inside and listen to the rain pounding outside, matching its rhythm with our bodies, in some magical attempt to find proper nouns amongst the constellations.

I believed in her so audaciously that the roof collapsed a few times onto us, or so it seemed, but we hardly noticed above the music. We already were music. But the song ended, as they all do, and so left us treading water, yelling about happiness from across the ocean.

I'm not happy though. Not now. But maybe I will be? Maybe later?

Israel blew smoke near his cat named something or whatever, hoping for a good time, and began to talk about the Mississippi of his heart.

"It's about the land—really—when you get right down to it," he said, reminding me of a drifter in his use of grandiose pronouns. "It is" and "they all say" and "there once was" and "one day" and "what it's all about is..." and yap yap yap.

We're all guilty of the same thing—sounding bigger than we are, but surely travelers take the cake and exaggerate to the moon.

"The land looks different now after the factories opened up just down the way close to the wetlands," he continued. "The brush used to spread all the way up the great river—until the pollution set in."

Aden was still sober—"That is a shame but I do believe truly that we as a society have the technology to feed everyone if we all just agreed to it."

That was a little out of context, and a little strange sounding, but Israel knew it was all part of the game—travel and youth and big dreams alike. It's our scary version of small talk. Cut the crap and tell me why you get up in the morning? What makes you cry and when's the last time you felt really lonely? How often do you bleed? We go way down into the souls of people purposefully.

But Israel was one of us. And that's why he and Missy would never work; he's too fast for her—a stampede passing by. She'd hold her beer like a cliff and Israel's hand like a balloon about to burst. She could reach out and feel him but would never squeeze too tight for fear of bursting her own bubble.

"So you mentioned Mississippi," I managed, "but what's your story?" This is my go to question for a number of good reasons—trust me.

Missy rested her hand on his knee, bracing herself for the truth.

"Well I'm actually just passing by much the same as you," Israel answered. "I've done odd and end jobs all through Nebraska and Oklahoma—I just came from Mississippi, living with my pops for some time, but I'm headed out to Denver sometime soon once I can gather the money together."

Denver, the North Star for voyagers of land—always blinking of expectations and mountains. We would go there soon but for now listened to Israel's story of back-and-forth regression.

"Are you going for good or just visiting a friend?" Aden asked.

"Well I really don't know," he said while looking longingly over his shoulder at Missy.

He hurt her and she wanted him to stay and he knew all of this but that wasn't the way his blood flowed and we all knew it. And it wasn't that he didn't love her. He did. He loved the way she looked at him and held onto him like a small child, but he was too caught up in the already rushing currents of his life to stay with her much longer. All he could do was wave goodbye, lovingly, beyond the horizons of Colorado.

See—Nebraska isn't somewhere you move *to*, even for love.

He continued about naturalness and the Earth and about being connected to it—"I take jobs in different towns and I have a friend in Denver who promised me some work and shelter but I'll come back to Nebraska one day. Nothing is permanent right?"

In Iowa Aden had mentioned that he wanted to feel more one with the dirt and the grass so I wasn't surprised when he perkily told Israel he half admired the farmers and field hands getting all mucky in the humidity.

"Oh yeah man — that's super cool of you to think that, especially since you're from the north," Israel said in response. "You should definitely try it but be careful. Some of these kids, not too much younger than we are, go for summers working under a farmer and get pretty messed up from it. They aren't paid anything near minimum wage because of some legislative loophole. The farmers have all the power out here."

I chuckled a little at the thought and he continued, "They don't have much for way of fun and go a little crazy." He took another hit and gestured for me to finish it off. But I already felt just about perfect so turned down the offer and suggested he continue talking about growing plants.

He swallowed his first couple words slowly, "But working with the Earth…is…" he took another hit, "is exactly — what — we are supposed to do…ya know?" and blew a plume of smoke towards the ceiling. "If you get right down to it and go deep down within yourself, physically, we're all made of the same thing. We all come from the Earth: the plants, trees, rocks, water, grass, mountains, dogs, and cows, and shit — it's all from the Earth. This is just flat out undeniable fact — nothing spiritual about it. At one point we weren't here and now we're here talking and that's pretty damn cool right? — but it's still true that we had to come from something and that *something*, before the nothing, that *something* was the Earth. So to me, it's pretty obvious that we all *are* the Earth."

That was all grand and beautiful and wonderful and all of that. I agreed, mostly, but I couldn't take all the metaphors even if I understood them so I quickly left to take a shower to wash everything off and clear my head.

When I woke up the next morning, Missy was sprite — a homemaker "tidying up" like she'd actually use the phrase on purpose.

"Well how do you feel?" she asked. "Was the bed alright for you?"

"Oh Missy," I said using her name out loud. See — people like to hear their names out loud. It makes them feel important. "The bed was seriously wonderful. The last place we stayed was a couch — wonderful people — but this bed you made here was all made up and done up just the way I like. So honestly, seriously Missy — thank you very much."

"Are you going to stay another night? I don't think I ever got your plans?"

"Funny thing is we don't really have any. We have to be in LA in a few weeks to meet up with some friends but the in-between is pretty up in the air for now," I said honestly. "We can find another place for tonight if you need the place for yourself. Maybe you and Israel want a nice night to yourselves before he leaves?"

And I saw in her face just then a sheltered sadness, and so immediately regretted bringing up the issue. I said — "I mean — I guess what I am trying to say is that we'd probably like to stay one more night, at least so that we can really get a good feel for Lincoln. But we actually had a few other couchsurfing hosts offer their space so it wouldn't be a problem to move locations if that would be easier for you? You know how couchsurfing is — some people stay a few hours and others a week and who knows how you predict any of it right?"

"Oh no you two are welcome to stay," she said. "Actually — Israel and I are pretty busy today so I won't be able to take you around but maybe you want to have breakfast?"

It was already past noon. I like breakfast past noon. And I especially like people who eat breakfast past noon. So the day was hot and started with omelets at the self-proclaimed oldest stand-alone truck stop in America, right on old Route 66. I didn't know what that meant really but the eggs were nice and Aden won a tiger in the claw machine that we'd forevermore use as our mascot. We called him Mariachi in honor of sombreros and Iowa.

After that we saw as much of Lincoln as we could in one day. It reminded me of Madison, Wisconsin which is a huge compliment. Aden and I drove there one weekend on a whim to see The Wolverines lose a football game, to be heckled mercilessly for all of four hours, to eat dumplings and cheese curds, and to look at Lake Michigan from the wrong side. Lincoln felt similar in it being a capital and a college town all in one.

Aden refused to don a shirt most of the day though I covered up long sleeve style, wearing his orange hat and thick rimmed glasses which were missing their lenses — all for fun and attention. There was the Love Library and The Quad, a statue of an old man and a Woolly Mammoth, the intimidating football stadium that we snuck into, and nostalgic street names like Sesame. We took pictures and videos of random students and stopped strangers to flirt with them and invited everyone on the road trip with us. Very typical. Then we ate Thai food and heard about a concert for the night and bought some funny clothes from the second hand store which we'd regret purchasing later in Wyoming — but that will come later.

We drank only mildly, unsure if we needed to leave the next morning but still burst into an unnamed club later that night, ready to dance. Because, of course, it's always important to dance. There was half a person tapping his foot on the dance floor looking up at the DJ but everyone else was way too cool for school so stayed back towards the bar and cupped their beers near their chests like social shields. Aden and I were not cool enough to have an opinion about school and wouldn't see any of these people outside of the next however long we decided to stay, so naturally left our inhibitions at the door — and danced our asses off.

The empty dance floor, wooden and dull, for us — turned into an Ibiza whiteout of thousands, tens of thousands all pounding and jumping in unison. I closed my eyes and let the music pour up into me like upside down gravity. Bam, pow, boom — chick-chick and wham, over and over — the beat pounding through my unabashed punches and shuffles. Pow and zoom, up and down — dance and dance and dance and dance until the floor moves for you. Etc.

So eventually a few people trickled onto the dance floor knowing they couldn't look as ridiculous as we did. We gave everyone a social crutch and so they too began to dance. One, two more, and then a few more started to sway back and forth. The DJ was good, too good for Nebraska even, and should therefore one day run away towards more appreciative crowds. Today I imagine he's probably somewhere in a basement with headphones on, with thick base beats blasting his ears, listening for someplace new.

My eyes opened for a moment long enough to see Aden dancing closer and closer to the blonde. The Blonde. The way male youths of America dance purposefully into a mounting position—the way they dance is like an ugly foreplay—like a meandering pedophile. I hate how my generation dances. I fucking hate it. -Aden had heard this lecture a thousand times but still didn't care so twirled his blonde around closer and closer to him. But she was rhythmically terrible. This was sadly and obviously apparent right off the bat, so I immediately forgot about the speed of courtship and ran towards Aden.

"Try and get her to dance Salsa!" I screamed above the music.

So he twirled her around and laughed and shrugged about tempo. I gave her friends some brief attention so they wouldn't steal her away from Aden, taking pictures and dancing wildly in front of them for their amusement. I thought I'd have to stay with them all night calling them "hey you" after forgetting their names for the twelfth time. I'd ask them to buy me a drink because it was only the chivalrous thing to do and they'd giggle the way most girls do. But none of that really happened because Aden grew tired of leading and having his feet stepped on after only a few minutes. He is a good dancer so hadn't the patience for lessons.

So we left, and sprinted in and out of a few more hotspots, playing freeze tag with the barstools, until finally spilling out onto the streets with everyone else. There were Nebraskans everywhere, getting in fights and holding hands equally, some made out with exes and others walked home alone—but no matter, we had more colors to see.

"Where are you all from?" a big black man asked us forcefully as we walked back towards the car. He asked like he was used to people trembling at his voice but Aden and I are familiar with Detroit so began a conversation with him calmly.

"We're from near Detroit—on a road trip across the country," Aden said. This man was big, with chains and sweat, and stood next to his sidekick who was just as big. He hollered across the crosswalk at a "big booty'd girl" not actually expecting her to turn around. It must be hard to be black in Nebraska, I thought. Though this is a guess.

"Oh well you better get the hell out of Nebraska," he said. "There ain't much here except for some cows and they be boring and shit."

I sneered at the stereotypes but treated him in a way he'd hardly been used to—with respect. We weren't intimidated because he was a student, probably younger than us, just trying to get by. So we talked with him like this for maybe ten minutes on the side of the street, there under the yellow lights and the black reflections. We learned about each other but forgot the details just as quickly, bid farewell and moved on—farther and farther west.

+

"GET UP MAN—KRISTOPHER—Kristopher! Sorry to wake you my man. Well actually I'm not…Kristopher…I know how you like your sleep but check it out!" Aden yelled at me. He pointed backwards as the light hovered below the back window.

See—I had asked him to wake me at sunrise because I like sunrises like everyone else.

Aden was speeding away from daybreak. We had decided to leave Lincoln shortly after the night out and time for writing, 2:30 in the morning.

"Where are we?" I wondered while stretching out the window. "…And is it me or are we going incredibly fast?"

Aden cocked his head to the side and smirked—"I mean not *that* fast haha. And where you ask? We're on a great highway in Nebraska. Does it matter which? What's in a name?"

I felt ill at ease while looking around hoping to see another car. Where are we, I thought. No really — where are we? There isn't anything for hundreds of miles, I thought. Nothing.

...I munched on some crackers dropping crumbs over the already filthy car to calm my nerves.

See — it's not that I *like* people — it's that I *need* people. I need their touches, their voices, and their chaos. I grasped this more with every passing mile.

I hadn't seen so much space in all my life, only then realizing that being a city boy has less to do with where one lives and more to do with how ones feels comfortable. People make me feel at home. The country is great for some but it pulls at me too softly. There is a predictability with the country — when you wake up, what happens, who you see, what you do. But I need confusion, if nothing more than to feel something- anything.

It's nice being a city boy. It is. But we were sailing the car on an ocean of land without care for speed limits or crash landings, something impossible during rush hour. I felt like a tourist for space — with all the busybody skyscraper types lining the prairie for a glimpse of emptiness. Soon the trucks would coat the center of our country, I thought, selling t-shirts reading *"I was nowhere"* — selling postcards too — and people would settle for the new economy, buying houses and building suburbs into all the empty space.

See — every somewhere used to be a nowhere. Nebraska is just taking its time.

When we're young we're taught that the world is round like why the sky is blue, things fall because of gravity, and electricity comes from a kite — sure, sounds good — but we all know these things. They aren't up for discussion or analyses. All until you find yourself in the middle of Nebraska, alone on a highway, chasing the human experience.

The Earth, I contend, is in fact flat in Nebraska and I will not accept any argument to the contrary. Flat — fall of the edge into a never ending abyss with killer octopuses and sea monsters — flat. The disorienting — "far as the eye can see" type of flat — the flat of our nightmares.

We turned right onto state road 183 heading north for South Dakota and read a peculiar sign next to the gas station over yonder—"Stop for Gas. Next Station 300 Miles."

A few miles passed without seeing another sign or any sign of life. More miles the same, then ten more, twenty more, a hundred miles of nothing—and after an hour of careening northward, still there wasn't a single car. No cross street. No house. No barn or animal. No faith or river. Nothing.

I rested my temple on the window, too lazy to carry my own weight. Aden pressed firm upon the pedal, worried only of hitting too much air.

He sped up asking, "Let's see how fast this can go eh?" without really asking.

I gave him a droopy thumbs-up without looking, still focused on the window pressing against my skull. The SAAB was born from jets so flew across the tar as if floating—faster and faster—all the while my head against the window still. I cracked the back pane slightly and rested my extended arm only faintly outside to feel the wind rush past. More than a hundred and thirty miles an hour, up and up and racing towards Canada and I put my head against the window still. I blanketed my face, neither smiling nor unhappy, pressing my lonely cheek against the window, leaning full force into the door, ready to fall out.

Everything was so beautiful—we learned how to disappear completely.

+

THE MORNING OF OUR one year anniversary together, Andrea and I woke up and kissed each other softly.

"We made it," I said.

"Of course," she said while snuggling into my chest. It had never occurred to her that we wouldn't "make it." I was the one who had doubts, but not her. For her—this was only the beginning.

We walked around campus, skipping all our classes because they didn't matter. We ate ice cream because we always ate ice cream. We walked around downtown because we always walked around downtown. We ran a little through the local park because we always ran through the local park. If you hadn't been privy to our most intimate thoughts, you'd have never known it was a special day. Because in many ways—it wasn't.

"I have to go to office hours," I said to her just before dinner. "…But at 7:00 pm meet me at that Indian place on Main Street. And wear something nice."

She smiled.

I bought flowers. I wrote her a long love letter. I made reservations at her favorite restaurant and set up the table a few hours in advance. The "exorbitant tip" that I had promised the waiter would ensure the night's perfection. It was all planned. It was all prepared.

I was finally ready for something special.

So as she walked into the doorway, everything else fell away. Only *she* glowed, there, before me. I don't remember what she wore because I never remember what she ever wore—a blue dress I assume. Something like that. Nothing mattered except for her energy. I was so excited, so outlandishly anxious, that I hardly had the nerves to kiss her—like it was our first date. She kissed me though, politely for the public, and sat down at our extravagantly decorated table.

"You look nice," she said.

I smiled.

See—she rarely complimented me normally. "I don't compliment you because you are too cocky already," she would often quip. So the fact that she complimented me was a big deal. Trust me.

"You know what?" I asked her.

"What?"

"I never see anyone else when you are around."

"What?"

"Still—after a year—when I go out with you dancing, or to dinner, or while walking through the streets with you—I don't see anyone else. You are such an intense distraction to my own senses that it's as if nothing else exists when I am with you. You give me tunnel vision. So thank you for saying that I look nice—but let me insist that today, and for all days— you *always* look nice. It's actually quite pathetic how I feel about you. It's almost embarrassing."

She smiled. But again—for her this was all already understood. The fact that I even had to say it out loud more worried her than comforted her. She was so enamored by us, so constantly sure of our never-ending future, that it hadn't donned on her that words were even necessary. So she just smiled. She smiled as if to say— *"same to you."*

After dinner and after more unnecessary articulations of my love for her, without ever using the word because I was too scared, I finally motioned to the flowers and to the still unopened letter.

"Why hasn't she noticed the set-up," I lamented. "Doesn't she realize this is not just some random dinner? I put a lot of thought into this goddamnit!"

"What?" she asked.

"The letter?"

"Oh—this is for me? I thought it was just part of the table decorations."

"Do you see flowers or letters on any other table? I set this all up a long time ago."

"You did?"

"Yes." God she frustrated me sometimes.

"Oh," she said apathetically and read the letter.

For the past month I had spent countless nights sleeplessly worrying about that letter. I thought about what to say while walking to class, while lifting at the gym, and while staring deeply into her eyes. *"What will really wow her?"* I had thought.

After finishing the letter — the simple yet profoundly articulate letter — the letter which would catapult us into a whole new level of intimacy — after finishing that infamous letter, she placed it in front of her doggy-bag and simply said, "thank you," with the same intonation she would use only moments later with our waiter.

"Thank you? That's it?" I wanted to scream — "And how about the fucking flowers? How about the necklace I gave you earlier today? Thank you? Fuck."

We walked home holding hands which was a big deal considering I rarely, if ever, held her hand. "I don't think it is necessary," I would argue with her. "We are past PDA," I often said — "We don't need it."

So she held on tightly to my hand all the way until reaching my apartment. And we made love softly with music in the background, no more intimately than any other night. And while lying with her there, I finally asked out loud — "Did I do good today? I really tried you know."

"You do good every day Kristopher," she said calmly.

"That's nice," I said, "but I *really* tried today. The flowers and the letter and the ice cream and the gift and yeah — I really did try. Did you enjoy yourself?"

"I enjoy myself every day Kristopher," she said.

"Yeah?"

"I don't think it's necessary," she argued with me. "We are past flowers and dinners," she said — "We don't need it."

"Yeah?"

"It was all beautiful and terrific and I'm lucky to have you. I am. I truly am. But I already knew that before tonight. You know what I enjoy more than fancy dinners and necklaces and getting all dressed up and all of that? You know what I most enjoy?"

I smiled.

"I enjoy you. I enjoy us. I enjoy the nothing. I enjoy lying in bed with you and holding your hand. I enjoy *this*, Kristopher," she said softly while kissing my neck. "I enjoy *this*."

And she was right. What was so pleasant about us, what fit so perfectly, was not that we enjoyed the same things or even that we had the same values—what most mattered was the nothing—because nothing ever really did happen with us. We were in a constant state of euphoria without any of the details. Because the details didn't matter—or they did—but only her details—her smile, her warm hand against mine, her leaning on my chest there in that moment. So we meditated on each other's nothingness just then—and were happy.

Everything was so beautiful; we learned how to disappear completely.

+

STILL IN NEBRASKA, I kept my head against the window, with my fingers tickling the outside for attention, thinking of "settling down" as a dirty word.

And so I daydreamed...

Aden and I had wives sitting in the back yelling at the horses to keep going, sipping on moonshine and pointing towards the storm coming ahead. Aden asked if I thought this ground was fertile for potatoes and babies, and I laughed and joked about my Giselle in the heat — how she loves it when I tickle her with the glass of my teeth. He slapped my knee and pointed towards a clearing just beyond some rolling tumbleweed. "Let's go there," he said. "There's good land over there."

In the middle of nowhere, I thought, we are all tumbleweed.

"Can you believe people actually live out here?" Aden bemoaned, this time out loud.

"It's honestly a little creepy," I said. "They must have been around here for hundreds of years or something because no one *moves* out here that is for damn sure," I added with my head still against the window, too lazy to acknowledge eye contact or speed limits.

The road was so hopelessly empty that we kept at the 130 mph pace without decision or care. Aden continued — "So at some point someone just decided to come out here, probably heading for California or gold or dreams and decided, after looking around for a few moments, 'yep this is where I'll stay,' and then just straight up stayed. Can you believe that shit?"

"I think I would be conservative if I lived out here," I said. "There is no sense of perspective — what's the good of the government and taxes if there is only one road for 300 miles and the nearest hospital or police station takes two hours to get to? I wouldn't give a shit about anyone but myself and my family out here — Republicans make a lot more sense now."

Then in the middle of the expressway, or some version thereof, we stopped. Stopped. Stop. We needed lunch. And it didn't make any sense to pull over to the shoulder even if one had existed because we hadn't seen another form of life or machine for over an hour. So while munching on peanut butter and jelly, we settled on top of the car in the middle of the highway — turned on some Willy Nelson and swayed back and forth with our America, listening for shouts of freedom coming from every direction.

+

I FELT LIKE I was stuck a cobweb without a spider there to eat me — waiting for the long haul of starvation. Everywhere as far as everywhere reaches was blank — beyond boring, insanity inducing, and eerie. We had tasted chocolate and spoke English out loud at a gas station a few miles back so felt socially rejuvenated enough, but as soon as the people fell out of sight across South Dakota, everything creaked back towards solidarity — the lonely kind.

See—South Dakota mirrors itself on both sides, spreading upside down all the way along Mexico and back up again. So we kept driving, trusting the signs, envious of the planes overhead, wanting to feel anything but abandoned. We had only each other and the dust, dreams, and half read books about dreams.

Aden now slept next to me on the open road, *the* open road—stretching from Sioux City towards Mt. Rushmore and up into Yellowstone. The North, the real north, is known for its stars and trees more than anything else—so there were merely RV's and vans of arguing families, with teenagers rolling their eyes at the bad reception, all only half looking behind cameras with one eye shut. The far off horizon point steams and smudges the frame like a child coloring outside the lines.

The atlas showed three red cross lines until the Badlands so I planned to stop at all three—each for gas and stories. The first reminded me of death and the White Man. I stopped at the local grocery store to buy snacks and energy drinks but ended up sitting in the car for about twenty minutes, Aden still lying next to me sleeping.

It was a movie in real time—every car was old and beat up, past its prime, held together by necessity and duct tape. Every person was American in the old way, the real way—before computers, before fast food, before microwaves, before electricity, before cars, before trains, before guns, before horses, before disease, before countries, before flags, before made-up identities, before pollution, before ships and synthetic cloth, before power as a verb. These people weren't Native Americans—they were Before Americans—rushing in and out of the grocery store with plastic bags and dimpled faces, dimpled faces and cases of beer. I sat in silence, watching the comings and goings of my most ancient brothers—off to party in the new ways, drinking in desperation rather than for celebration.

The second stop was advertised for a hundred miles with dozens of handmade billboards leaning against two-by-fours. "1880 Town" they read, in big bold letters written with a shaky hand as the paint dripped down towards the grass. There weren't graphic designs or taglines—hell there weren't even computers or much forethought, just sides of barns standing straight up with simple South Dakota words like *Great*, *Old*, and *Fun* over and over again.

I was sold.

Aden woke up from the sudden stop and I smiled saying, "We're here," as if that meant anything. We had no "here."

We played football in the parking lot because we felt like it and bought some food from the shop before actually entering. "What's this place anyways?" Aden asked, not angry or even curious, just matter of fact.

"I don't really know," I answered. "For the last 100 miles there wasn't anything except signs for '1880 Town Up Ahead' so I figured it made sense to stop. It looks like a ghost town or something eh? It'll be good enough."

Aden nodded and bought another trucker hat that said "1880 Town South Dakota" with an ugly picture spray painted on it. He still didn't really know what the place was or whether it was fun, or even whether we were going to go in. He didn't know the price or the significance, the history or the rationale, but for some reason I'd have been surprised if he hadn't bought a souvenir. It's his way — decide you're going to jump first, then look over the edge, and *then* check if the harness fits (while already falling). I don't understand it really. But I bought one too to fit in.

It was a ghost town. Except for the highway next door there wasn't pavement for hours. So we walked around the dirt road surrounded by the sheriff's office, the jail, and the post office, the train station, the washhouse, and the baker's house — inside the mayor's quarters, the church, a butcher's place, the blacksmith's quarters, and an all-purpose shop. We settled on the saloon to waste the majority of our time in, similar to the men in 1880, except that we had plans to leave.

We bought beverages and watched two old cowboys play funny songs with children as backup singers, their proud parents egging them on with video cameras. I imagined their lives would continue on without Aden and I filling up the peripheral through Christmases and graduations — the way all lives do, each of us individually riding the trains of fate, constantly switching tracks and directions. It's a crazy life, this life, and especially when we're in it together, listening to country music in 1880 Town.

"Look at her," Aden said while pointing to a burlesque dressed girl shyly making her way to the stage.

She tapped to the music for all the tourists and smiled because she had to. Her job demanded that she smile. Her outfit was a silky ocean-green dress, lined with black lace and a pushup bra, with white stockings and dark noisy shoes. She danced shoulders-back confident, but in a way that made me question the posture. See — she was only in the dawn of her beauty — not quite ready to cast a shadow — too reticent for the stage. She had big blue eyes and skin to die for.

…I had to talk to her.

We finished the show and our drinks equally and then watched two musical cowboys duel each other outside the saloon. Some of the children were chosen to play along and we all laughed and cheered with an empty noose hanging in the background. But it all fit somehow. The whole town was a stage.

Though we soon found the girl and flirted with her amicably, inviting her on the road trip, telling her stories of adventure and mountains.

"So how did you end up here?" I asked her looking around, emphasizing the fact that we couldn't see any houses for the horizon.

"Oh I just live up the street actually," she said, and we laughed. At first trying to laugh *with* her but soon realizing it felt more like *at* her, so shut up promptly.

"It's just that," Aden tried to explain, "It's just that there aren't any houses as far as the eye can see so I guess I just don't understand what you mean by 'up the street?'"

I noticed just then that she was more beautiful than I had originally thought. She was younger than I thought too. She had a line of freckles on her left cheek and a cute little figure, womanly but soft and innocent.

She'd probably been with only one person her whole life, and probably quivered throughout. So I fantasized about her in the hay, with the moon shining, just her and I, naked in a barn together.

"You should seriously come with us," I suggested. "We'll drive you to Mt. Rushmore tonight and then we can take you back in a week. Have you ever been to Denver?" I asked her, and I meant it. We would do it if only to show her new cowboys.

"No," she said. "I would go but my grandma owns this place and she would be mad if I left."

"Do you have a boyfriend or something?" Aden just outright asked.

She blushed red soul all over her cheeks and turned away cutely. "No," she said politely. "But," she said, "it's just that...well...I don't know..."

We nagged her for a while still, up until she finally convinced us that she actually, in fact, did, *have to* stay. So we gave her hugs just then, leaving her lost and smiling through her hair. But that, sadly, is the eternal story of goodbye — fading away into the distance, thrilled for retellings and blue skies and little white lies.

...Goodbye is heavy water.

The third stop was advertised even more frantically with bigger versions of "Great," "Fun," and "Old" lining the road for miles. Aden was driving by this point and so stopped at the Petrified Rock Garden, the third red line on the atlas. And for clarity's sake, I must share that when we stopped here and the ghost town equally — there wasn't anything else. There is a two lane highway running perpendicular sure, sounds good — but the big signs weren't lying. Compared to the infinite echo of distance before us, anything with a voice box was worth seeing.

But, sadly, the Petrified Rock Garden was neither great nor old — only fun due to the shock. It cost five dollars to enter; we bought our tickets from a pimply teenager who handed us two perforated papers almost ashamed — like he was sticking it to us. But it's a job and we knew it so didn't blame him. The garden was in fact a large field, go figure, littered with turned over tree trunks and old stumps. We laughed and laughed at the ridiculousness — or more at the business model.

"This is hilarious dude," I said. "Some farmer had a bunch of old tree trunks and…now granted they are really old, but…actually, look, here this one says it is a million years old. That *is* really old. I actually have never touched anything a million years old before except for the ocean, but you know, well, so — yeah I guess this is legit? Kind of? You get what I mean man? Right? — Look — some guy had a bunch of tree trunks that were old, granted, but still tree trunks no less, and figured that there is so much boringness around that he could make a profit by comparison. He sat around his table and convinced his wife that building a fence around rocks and charging five dollars a pop would actually work. And fuck if I'm wrong because it worked didn't it? Here we are staring at a garden of rocks…"

But this was all true, I thought. Exciting is relative. South Dakota is naturally empty so you have to fill in the gaps with your mind and play amongst the fallen trees to feel alive. It is a state for the dreamers, whose imaginations paint the horizon vivid with madness — it's a state for the artists and the travelers. It knows itself calmly like a near death experience, because in a lot of ways, that is exactly what it is.

Later west near Wyoming, we exited for the Badlands. This is adventure, I thought — the kind with rock climbing and safety equipment, red chalk and heavy breathing. So in order to properly ready myself I stopped at a gas station and ate a buffalo hotdog — the way they did in the olden days — the days of real men and buffalo hotdogs and slushies. Yeah that's the stuff.

The Badlands are, generally speaking — nothing. But that wasn't really all that surprising considering everything else in South Dakota was similarly boring. I don't know how exactly, but the Earth, somehow, throughout the millennia, managed to carve into itself giant crevasses, some of which reached into the air hundreds of feet. They cut into the ground like a horizontal ant farm weaving for miles. And when you are in one of these tan fractures, you can't just climb up; the earth breaks off at every hold so you have to find the natural inclines which usually takes some searching for. So while playing in the rock maze, with towering sheets on all sides blocking the sun, I ran around like a child out of practice. But amongst the heat and terror, there comes a point when you realize you are, in fact, lost — and alone. But then you realize it's sort of nice — because, of course, we all want to be lost — at least sometimes.

Because really — losing yourself and finding yourself are synonyms in hindsight.

Most of life comes in unexpected flashes — we fall in love when we don't want to and make money only when we don't need it. It's a come as you are world that rewards coincidence and idiosyncrasy equally — we make conscious decisions and then pray for chance. So there in the dirt — I believed in nothing except for magic and disorder.

+

ADEN WEARS WHATEVER HE wants and I'm envious to the hills. He just owns it, whatever it is, and walks around shoulders-back like he couldn't care less. His style is unpredictable and full of owned folly but he pulls it off effortlessly. One night in college, for example, he came out of his room wearing a Japanese kimono as if nothing was unusual and shuffled into the cab. Another time we went to the nicest club in Detroit, him wearing a neon orange winter coat and ultra-white glow in the dark sunglasses — neither of which he checked at the door. And I remember our last night in Ann Arbor together, the night of Andrea and I's last kiss, just before leaving for the road — I remember how that night Aden wore a silver NASA-looking puff vest like everything was just fine.

See — Aden is a riot in Technicolor.

One of those jealous days, before a concert, I ran to the local hippie store and bought a manifest rainbow, a tie-dye cotton t-shirt, emblazoned with giant red hearts both front and back. But this was out of place for me. See — my style was more collar and belt. There is a word for it I think? — dull. But Aden changed all that with bursts of color and zigzags.

He influenced my style and freedom the same — always challenging me and asking "why not" over and over again under his breath. But the shirt—now I had it—and wore it with pride and so it became part of me. Slowly though. I'd first wear it to festivals or Democratic workshops—places of patience and sensibility. Then I'd dress as a hippie for Halloween, then as a hippie for class, then as a hippie while out at dinner. I wasn't one, a hippie, but I held the t-shirt sacred for its symbolism. It changed me.

It's the way that we present ourselves that really defines us, I think. Because what we think, what we care about, and what we know of ourselves—all that is only the tiniest littlest fraction of our whole. It's what we do and how we smile that really counts. It's the We and the They that really makes the world turn—labels and quick definitions, slogans and snap judgments, and we all better just get on board. We are what we impart, sure, sounds good—but we are defined by how people react to us. So the shirt changed me—into someone who actually wears those types of things and therefore goes about my business with some individuality, without care for brand names or fads. And it feels good and everyone knows it.

So I wore my shirt to Mount Rushmore happily—with an American Flag as a cape and bright green flip flops and an 1880 Town trucker hat. I wore it because I wanted to, sure, but mostly because Aden taught me how to.

Though I soon found myself in a verbal tussle with a veteran who told me I was desecrating the flag by wearing it as an article of clothing. My first thought was to say that, *"it isn't the flag, it is my flag, and that is the point isn't it?*—But he was a veteran so I told him I hoped he enjoyed his evening instead. It's always important to be polite to veterans, I thought. But he kept at it so I told him I hoped he enjoyed his evening once more. And then he said something else for the third time, and then a fourth sentence, until everyone became a little uncomfortable, especially with all the children. So I ended up telling him to enjoy his evening a dozen times before fleeing the scene with *my* flag still on my back.

Aden and I then ran up as close as we could to the monument, head-back, neck stretched long-ways, like we'd feel Lincoln's sweat if he had had the chills. And honestly, while looking at giant faces carved into the rock, it's hard not to feel loyal. Someone plays the national anthem and everyone is merrily on vacation camping in the real America as it's called, and the bright spotlights shoot up, illuminating our four commanders, and the weather is perfect, and the stars are twinkling, and hell if you aren't a little proud after all?

Freedom rings. Etc.

But then the mind starts pumping and I realized that the monument was quite similar to the propaganda machines we read about in text books, the ones with giant gold statues of Stalin or Hussein, Mow or Kim Jung Ill. Mount Rushmore is probably worse even—"Fuck the gold statues," my country said, "let's dwarf the hell out of a mountain and carve something so massive we'll need dynamite to pull it off. Yeah, that's the stuff."

But we have *something* of a democracy so our leaders don't build their *own* statues, I thought—they *earn* them if they do a good job. Right? Or if the history books decide to say they did a good job? Either way I felt much better about our situation so stared up in awe, glad for my passport. And I guess that's the point of a monument. They are supposed to demand patriotism.

All the while lightning shown off in the distance and the sky crashed with sound.

"We better get out of here, eh?" Aden said.

So we both said farewell to the friends we had made at the top of the path, bemoaning the rain to come. And in leaving the parking structure we turned on a song called *Chicago,* already missing the Midwest—trying to feel a little normal with familiar melodies. And that's the funny thing about travel—we leave and search in airplanes with backpacks stuffed with escapades and scribbles—all the while we compare for home. But, I think, life would be smoother if we all missed today rather than yesterday.

Yeah, that would be nice.

The rain never actually came, though, but the sky *did* explode. Turning in and out of a dreary highway dead of light and scuffling for traction, we there met the night's son—lightning splitting open the sky like cracking glass. It was a new era of storm, a new category above classification—the titans before gods, turtles all the way down, and all that. The magic of the sky was exploding tentacle lasers all across the horizon before us, showing daytime instantaneously amongst the night's stars.

"This is exactly how I would picture an alien invasion," Aden exclaimed slowing down to look through the windshield. "I mean—come on man. No way this is real! This is…I mean fuck dude just look at this shit."

I tried to take a picture or a video or something—anything—but my fingers were too frantic and therefore I couldn't finagle the damn buttons but—"Wow," I said. "Holy shit. Man. I mean oh my god man. I don't—I mean. I think that… Man oh man let me tell you what. Right?" And I continued like that, not making much sense, but what else are you supposed say when the sky is falling?—All you have are your mumbles and your eyes.

Then the hail began, rushing down like white demons pelting the car from all angles. It was a blizzard of brutality—with streaming waterfalls of rocks pelting the car, and holy god we better get out of here…

Shelter.

We need shelter, I thought.

"You know how we talk about hail as if it is a real thing but we rarely ever see it in real life? You know how we've all said things like 'did you see that hail yesterday?' but we don't really mean it. Really we mostly just see rain, maybe a few solid pebbles, sure, sounds good—but then we talk about the storm for the sake of conversation as if it meant something. You know how we do that? I mean, I know *I* do that. But this is not that sort of storm ya know? I mean—this storm feels like it is from God or something. I feel like Zeus is throwing down baseballs at us. There are ice-baseballs hitting our car like a pitching machine. Holy shit Aden look at that one! Fuck. Fuck. Fuck!" I shouted.

"We need to stop somewhere," Aden agreed frantically. "I'm pulling into the next motel we see. Ahhhhhhh!"

He screamed at the gloom, caught somewhere between his survival instincts and his curiosity. So we ended up at a Holiday Inn parking lot running in and out of the lobby checking if we really wanted to stay. A hotel? It didn't feel right, like we were selling out.

Do you believe in miracles, I asked myself, or do you believe in clean towels?

I sprinted from the automatic doors into the car, panting and a little battered still from the stinging hail.

"Can you believe this shit?" I stumbled. "Well here is the drill — they have rooms and they aren't that expensive but it's a Holiday Inn man? How do you feel about waiting it out? I feel too corporate staying here — plus the sounds of outside are more forceful from the car. Right?"

"Yeah man. Sounds good," Aden said exhausted.

He fell asleep almost immediately the way he often does. I stay awake alone in the night and he wakes up alone with the morning. I'm not sure which is worse. But when the silence comes, even amongst a storm — I feel her. It's the mind silence that gets us — when we don't have anything to look forward to or remember except the front of our brains pounding out the same name on repeat. Andrea. Andrea. Andrea. Andrea. Andrea. I hate her. Andrea. Andrea. Andrea. Scratching on repeat. Andrea. God I miss her.

Earlier I had bought a postcard from the Badlands tourist store. I had no real intention of sending postcards because they feel braggadocios to me. Postcards say, "My life is better," no matter what you actually write. But I bought one anyways — convincing myself it was for my mom or dad, sister or the grandparents, someone else...anyone else.

But just then I pulled it out of my bag and stared at it, Aden already asleep. The picture was a brown glow of sun behind a tan moon rock — "The Badlands" it said — with room only for an address, a name, and a message. So I started writing softly, unsure who to write it for, but whatever it was—it meant something. I could tell—it *would* mean something. And my heart skipped, faster, and faster—it pounded with rapturous fury into the night. I wanted my pen to move fiercely under the canvassed stars, but in the stillness I could only think to write, "I love you."

Though maybe that would be enough?

Maybe later?

Chapter 6

CRAZY HORSE MONUMENT IS being built in honor of the Lakota people—the namesake of The Dakotas. The Battle of Little Big Horn and names from the earth—it's a place of meaning imbedded in the ground, with gods and spirits, humans and stories, all harmonizing like the most perfect quartet. You could almost touch the history in the air, if you felt strong enough.

I could go on, you must understand, but I forget. See—the Native American story isn't sexy enough. It's a monument that punches you in the neck, sure, sounds good—but by the time you are doubled over the pain is gone. It's a hit and run story that you tell and awe over, you insist things like—"that is so bad" and "I know, it's such a disgrace"—but then you do nothing about it. Obviously it's nice to feel like an activist two feet away from the problem. But only when you cross the ocean of South Dakota do you find out what you really care about.

So I cried for my native brothers, I did, but I forgot why a few hours later—and moved on towards Wyoming.

+++

"You know The Midwest ends right here don't you?" Aden said.

"Actually, I think it ended just west of Chicago but I get what you are saying," I said.

See—Aden and I had had a series of arguments with locals in Iowa and Nebraska about the definition of "The Midwest"—arguments about which states were to be included in the definition of "The Midwest" and which were not. Etc. Stupid conversation, I know, but a conversation we had no less.

See — people from The South naturally include Iowa as being a part of The Midwest no doubt, as they should, but those from Ohio, the true middle, those from Pittsburgh or Minneapolis, for them there is a whole different expectation for people of The Midwest. So the argument continues. And I even heard vague arguments in favor of South Dakota — but I took those arguments only casually, even less than Nebraska, but I could at least hear the rationale out loud without vomiting. Wyoming, on the other hand, is unquestionably *not* the Midwest, and I will not hear any argument to the contrary.

Though Wyoming is also not the Great Plains in it being too far north, but it's also not Big Sky Country because it has too many trees — but it's also not rocky like Colorado, nor does it have the bustling culture of the Pacific Northwest. There is a quiet isolation in Wyoming that reaches further than geography. It doesn't fit, Wyoming. Partly because the people aren't close enough to each other to collectively decide on a culture, but mostly because no one really cares. Even Idaho, being boring and closeted, at least has a well-known crop and a skyline. Wyoming, though, fills empty acres with only cows and farm animals, like a children's books manifest — so we can't help but chuckle. I hope politely, though.

Wyoming and Hawaii are America's islands, it seems — and Puerto Rico when it's convenient.

"Look how cool that ground is," Aden exclaimed, pointing at the ground. "The soil is turning red and crystal. It is vibrant."

We had already passed the imaginary borderline and therefore couldn't quite understand the landscape. There is life in Wyoming, different than South Dakota, but still a sense of flatness, even with hills in the distance. It contradicts itself.

"Yeah it's super beautiful," I agreed with my hands still on the steering wheel. We were headed to Devil's Tower. I had been there before when I was younger and remembered it as a giant cylindrical rock shooting up into the air straight and ostentatious.

"You think it's beautiful? Dude it is *not* "beautiful." Honestly I can't believe you think it is just beautiful? It is the most beautiful thing ever. God you are so negative." — Aden said this mischievously. He plays this game often — challenging me to describe something more positively than him — but more for the challenge than the positivity.

"Yeah I know man. Super beautiful," I said almost identically as I had before.

"'Super beautiful?' he questioned me. "That's all you got? Come on man that is the worst description I've ever heard. I can't believe you. I mean seriously — can you believe this guy?" he said turning to the imaginary neighbor sitting outside the window. "This guy over here thinks that life is 'super beautiful.' I mean here we are rocking out in the most beautiful, mind blowing, stunning, loving, and fantastical backdrop ever and all you have to say is 'super beautiful?' That is beyond lame man. Let me out of the car."

"Right," I said annoyed.

"No I'm serious man. Do you see that red cross line over to the left?"

"Yeah this place is incredible. I remember the last time I saw Devil's Tower I didn't really appreciate it. I remember climbing through all these giant boulders but I was too small, too small and too fearful to…"

"You were scared?" Aden interrupted. "I can't believe you were scared of rocks? That is super lame man. I bet these rocks are going to be the best rocks in the world."

I tried to play along — "…Yes the best rocks in the world," I said.

"…'in the world?' Haha this guy thinks these rocks are the best in the world? I mean these rocks are the best rocks in all the worlds combined, the universe even! — fuck, bigger than the universe! — these rocks *are* the universe.! I mean comeon man you can't just describe these rocks simply as 'the best in the world' — haha can you believe this guy?" he said again to the imaginary third person.

He was playing. I know he plays. In a lot of ways, what a cool game right? — trying to describe the world more positively, bigger, and greater than each other. Who can open up their mind to the possibility of the ultimate positivity? ...He has a knack for bringing out the best in people, challenging their perceptions of good and bad until there is only good. I get it.

But it's annoying.

There is an inherent negativity underlying the whole exercise — because someone has to lose. Someone has to be put down. It's the innate "you are stupid for believing this or that" element that bugs me to the stars. So rather than deal with it, I closed my mouth until reaching Devil's Tower.

Though he kept up knowing that he was getting to me, like a bully on the playground. Granted he didn't carry bad intentions — Aden never had bad intentions — he just wanted to play the game. He wanted to challenge me. And he wanted to win. But I had no desire to cooperate in a game of "who's cleverer" and it showed. I didn't respond to any of his quips for the better part of an hour and it got to both of us.

So we parked silently with him still at it. While talking on the phone to his mother he mentioned how I would for sure get us lost because "that's what he does." He didn't actually believe this but he was on a roll, fully under my skin.

As we walked up to Devil's Tower, he asked me what was wrong and I said nothing. He called me out on it knowing there was in fact something wrong, so I told him I didn't understand his need to make fun of me for no reason. I felt like a kid being picked on by a bully, a bully and a best friend all in one. So he apologized and we got over it quickly, ready to attack the trail together. This would prove to be our only "fight" for the full trip. It was needed like a cold shower. Sure it is shocking and feels shitty at first glance, but the effects are undeniable. We'd talk about it in more depth later, with the black-black night, driving towards Denver.

"Shhh," Aden whispered to me, crouching down into the tall grass. "Look at that deer," he said.

There are three paths labeled for color and severity at Devil's Tower. We picked the most daring of the paths predictably, and so circled the whole tower.

"What do you say we get off this path?" Aden suggested.

"What path?"

"Yeah I know but you see that opening up top? ...I bet we could climb through it and come out the other side, on top of that big boulder? — let's do it for the picture if nothing else." Aden wasn't really asking. He said this while running up the slope towards a steep crevice in the rock. It was only wide enough if we turned to the side and balanced back to palm, squirming all the way up towards the sun like expert rock climbers — except that we didn't have equipment or knowhow.

"What's it look like?" I yelled to him still far behind.

"Come on up and see for yourself"

So I did. But the view wasn't enough. It's never enough. One more hit — one more shot — one more fling, and one more night out — one more cut and one more bruise until we learn. But we hadn't learned of death or real pain just yet, so chased our own ambitions farther and farther up.

"This is beautiful. Take a second to look around." — and then — "Let's go higher."

The original crevice, which once loomed so daunting above, was now only a speck hundreds of feet below us, well off the path. See — it called to us, the end, like a tangible place — but all we ever found were new beginnings. We paused only a few times to check our footing and glance at each other as if to say, "*This probably isn't safe.*"

And it wasn't.

The boulders grew bigger and simultaneously nervier. They grew farther and farther apart so eventually we had to jump and climb, or swing, using a loosened root from a hobbled tree or whatever. We hopped from one boulder to another mimicking our journey — with no real path or sense of direction, the end found us more than we found it. And then we reached a section of the hike "dangerous" by any definition—so without anything to save us except raw purpose, on all fours, carefully—we traversed the aslant rock well into dusk. We grabbed each other's forearms to pull each other higher and wedged our trainers into wet corners—eventually reaching a point of only return. Devil's Tower was standing right next to us, and not like the pictures from carefully positioned lookouts or doctored videos—we saw it naked and touched its belly. We couldn't go any farther without superpowers or a helicopter so turned with our backs to the outstretched earth and looked upon our home in luxury.

"Ahhhhhhhhhhhhhhhh!" A deep breath.

"Ahhhhhhhhhhhhhhhhhhhhhh!" One more deep breath.

"Ahhhhhhhhhhhhhhhhhhhhhhhhhhhhhhhhhhh!" and I couldn't breathe.

I cried out for my country waiting for the echo, echo, echo—for someone to tell me how it all works, but all I heard were the birds chirping in time, singing a beautiful song opposite the rainbow.

Ahhhhhhhhhhhh...

We were even more careful going back down because on our way back down we saw multiple signs warning us about "rules" and "the path—"you must stay on the path" —"you must stay in line and wear the uniform" —or something or another.

Sure we could have died, but where's the fun in safety?

The plan had been to run around the tower, see some nature, and speed down to Denver for a night out—it was Friday no less. But after all the climbing and slipping it was well past closing time so the moon was settled dazzling overhead. We turned on the car lights for posture and pulled out a map (old school style), and searched together for a town worth driving to.

This is harder than you'd expect in Wyoming. So we picked the biggest red dot that rested next to the biggest name with the biggest font. We figured that would be sufficient for drinks and dancing.

Our fingers pointed towards Gillette, Wyoming.

Gillette, Wyoming — get ready.

+

A WAITRESS DIRECTED US to "Mingle's" a few blocks down the street, so we went in full of purpose and amusement. A Wyoming bar in a little nothing town late into the night, without a place to stay or expectations for shelter — we'd try to meet some locals and have a gay old time.

But that — sadly — is exactly what we had, a gay old time. Earlier in Nebraska I mentioned buying clothing from a secondhand store that we would regret later — this is later. I bought a black t-shirt with a picture on the front of a 70's running man in multicolor, wearing a head band and short shorts. At Crazy Horse I had bought a handmade bracelet so was wearing that too, along with the 1880 town trucker hat and square rimmed glasses. I thought it was funny. Aden wore a v-neck white t-shirt and a sheer charcoal sweater, unzipped. He was also wearing flip flops and a whicker top hat. He thought it was funny.

For Detroit or Ann Arbor this is mild and would therefore go unnoticed amongst the bedlam. We could carry on hitting on girls calmly and no one would blink twice. In Detroit, we could also go along being Mexican and Jewish without a problem — forgetting about our skin tones and nose sizes arbitrarily. But we were reminded very quickly upon entry that Wyoming is in fact *not* Detroit.

There were two types of people at first glance: Iraq War veterans and Latino gang members. And to our best efforts, we didn't fit in with either. It was noticeably segregated but more than half the men were wearing cowboy hats. It was a fashion show for Bald Eagle and American Flag styles — colored headbands, and pistols settled into holsters attached to blue jeans.

Fuck.

This town had about 200 people and 100 of them were working in the Walmart, though the other 100 must have been in this bar drinking and staring at us. We were outsiders in the creepy-scary-movie sort-of-way — so instantly we thought about turning around and walking straight out of the bar. The local patrons would cheers and make a night of making fun of the faggots.

But we would have none of that madness. We simply swallowed our pride and lumbered towards the bar. Luckily the bar was small so felt packed and therefore we could more slide by people rather than flutter like peacocks all showy.

We ordered Bud Lights to fit in. For some reason a gin and tonic didn't seem appropriate?

…Aden rushed towards the dance floor after about five seconds. Though I tried to stop him, grabbing his arm.

"Fuck man, none of the guys are dancing," Aden said to me, trying to pull me off of him. "There are a bunch of girls out there alone. I'm going in."

"Aden, none of the guys are out there because they all are too busy making fun of us," I said, "or cleaning their deadly weapons. I would advise against it."

"No man — we belong here just as anyone. We're American too. Right? I want to dance. I'm going to dance."

"Right," I agreed, but only because I knew there wasn't any arguing with him. "Well — at least understand that all the guys sitting around the dance floor are all probably dating the girls who are dancing. So listen, you can dance — but the girls are off limits. Their boyfriends *will* shoot you. It's not worth the risk. We'll be in Denver soon."

"Well you are coming too," he insisted, trying to pull me towards the dance floor.

"I promise you. I promise you…" — I said this staring directly into his eyes — "I promise you that I am not."

And so that was his cue to run off onto the dance floor, square dancing like he knew what he was doing, looking like he didn't know what he was doing. All the while I stood on the sidelines while he flirted with all the girls not heeding my warning. And for a moment I envied his freedom. There was still something holding me back — call it nerves or superstition but I didn't trust rural Wyoming. It was the scariest place I'd ever set foot in, more than in downtown Chicago or 8 Mile, Queens or skid row in Seattle. I have walked straight into the ghetto without missing a step, but not here. Looking around at all the shaved heads and cowboy boots I felt like a foreigner lost at sea. My heart was beating and my eyes were wandering and my beer was shaking from the chills.

I needed to leave.

Though Aden in that very same moment was twirling a girl around in circles ignoring the choreography of line dancing. He was smiling ear to ear as if to invite the other guys on the floor. *"Come on it's not so bad,"* he was saying to the crowd. But they were all too cool for school so sat still in circles facing the dance floor.

It's not that he was ignorant to the danger — he just didn't care, and somewhere deep within his heart, he knew that everything would be fine.

God I wanted to be that free. I wanted to be that stupid.

But just then I saw a man in a flannel shirt point to Aden and punch his fist nodding to his friends.

Time. To. Leave.

I signaled over to Aden and smiled tightly at the guy next to me. He stared deadly right back without a smirk as if to say, *"Get out."* So I took his advice earnestly and yelled at Aden.

I told him what had happened with the flannel shirt and he said matter-of-factly — "Well it sounds like we should head out."

And we did.

The whole situation lasted all of 15 minutes; our beers were still cold and half drunk. It was the least American I had ever felt — and what a pity too. But in a lot of ways it makes sense because it was Wyoming after all. Wyoming arms itself with Jesus and guns, and its men are trained to use both.

+

THE MOON CALLED SOUTH for Denver, so we drove well into the morning through long stretches of black highway, passing only a few truckers — reminding us of Indiana. We sped up, keeping with the light, tunneling through the darkness. We were piercing the space, running away from Wyoming as fast as possible, unaware of sidewalks or exits.

"We are cool right?" Aden said offhandedly. He didn't mind that I was already sleeping because the conversation wouldn't be easy regardless.

"Of course we are cool. What do you mean?"

"Well it seemed like you were pretty upset back there at Devil's Tower. I was just fucking with you man…"

"No I know. Listen, I know what it's all about. It's just messing around but you know me man. I don't enjoy that type of messing around. How many times have you ever heard me insult someone out loud?"

"Well not to be a dick, but plenty of times actually."

"Really?"

"Yeah man. I mean you get away with it though. People always laugh it off or you say it in a way that is just blatantly honest like everyone in the room was already thinking it. It's the *way* you call people out on things that is different — so it doesn't seem to bother them."

"Right — I mean for sure I'm blunt but I don't ever say something to put someone down on purpose. If anything I give compliments like free samples. I guess — I mean, listen man, this isn't the point. I shouldn't have opened that way. For sure I have hurt people's feelings, Andrea for example—but I just don't like the malice is all."

"Man there was no malice involved—it's just…"

"I know man. I know. It's like 'who can describe something better?' or 'who can be more positive?'…Something like that right?"

"Yeah it's a game I used to play with Al-O-G and Gary all the time back in high school. We would say some girl is cute and then the other would say 'nah she is fine' and then I'd say 'no she's like a super model' and up and up and up until it became ridiculous. We would be talking about some, objectively, just "cute" girl but somehow that would transform into sentences like 'If I had the pick of any women, computer generated or real—I would only pick her lips because even those are sexier than everyone else combined.' …It's just to be stupid. It's just a game."

"Of course—but it's the inherent 'I'm better than you' that gets to me."

"Well yeah but that's just part of the game."

"Well I don't like that sort of game then. I don't understand that game. I have no interest in being better than you at something—or proving I can do this or that better than you…it just doesn't…"

"But that's not the point!" he said. "The point is to have fun…"

"Yeah but what I am telling you is that I do not find that fun. You have to put the other person down, inherently, to win. It's negative."

"No it's not negative, it's trying to be super positive."

"Yeah it *would be* if you didn't start every sentence with, 'you think X…well that is stupid…because actually…' and then you continue. There is no need for the "stupid" label. Maybe I'm 'sensitive' but it doesn't make any sense to me. Making fun of your friend for fun?"

"I get what you are saying—we just see it differently. I didn't mean anything by it."

"It's bigger though…it's about how we walk, for example."

"How we walk?"

"Yeah…well don't take this the wrong way but you get in fights a lot more often than I do—which isn't saying a lot since I've never been in a fight but you get what I'm saying. Like when we are out at a bar often someone will brush by you and you won't move."

"Not if they don't say 'excuse me.' No."

"Right. But then you are standing all spread out taking up space and the place is packed and some drunk guy sees a girl and brushes up against you…you know what I do? —I just give the dude space to pass. You though—you'll make it very apparent that this guy brushed up against you. You probably won't say anything, but you'll stand solidly not really letting the guy pass."

"…Because he needs to say 'excuse me.'"

"I mean you are right, the guy needs to chill, but what happens when he doesn't? There is a confrontation. There is often a confrontation. And then you have to calm the situation down or step outside or whatever—the point is I've never been in a fight but also I've never even come close to one. It seems like you like the confrontation?"

"No—I like justice."

"That's not it. I like justice too. But a lot of people would say that justice is having to pay for a hotel when you are traveling around yeah? And I'm not saying you are wrong and I am right, all I'm saying is that you don't have to always prove yourself."

"Nope," he said. "I grew up differently than you did. You were pretty popular right? I was one of only a few white kids in an all-black school…*and* I was in the band. I wasn't a nerd exactly but I had to stick up for myself and couldn't get pushed around right? So we play games and develop thick skin and that's the way life is where I come from."

"Agreed. But it doesn't *have* to be. Some guy who is passing by is doing just that, he's "passing by." People don't want to fight. We're all at the bar to meet pretty girls and drink with our buddies and that is the point right? But if you make an effort to cause a confrontation there *will be* a confrontation. I just feel like it's not fun—it can't be amusing."

"I get what you are saying for sure but it's basically about being who I am. I am not going to stand down for anyone and I am not going to be stepped on."

"For sure, don't be stepped on—but maybe move out of the way when someone passes by or lay off when I don't want to play a game of who's better than who? I don't like it. I mean, do you think I let people walk all over me?"

"No but that is because most of the time you are walking all over them."

"Really?"

"You know what I mean."

"Yeah. I guess I do," I said, thinking of Andrea.

+

DENVER FELT LIKE HOME with all the lights and the people even though I was a thousand miles away from Ohio. We woke up at the Holiday Inn and the car wouldn't start. We paid seventy dollars for a local Mexican to tell us we were out of gas. Aden took a shower in the hotel. Aden took a shower in the hotel we didn't sleep in. Aden took a shower in the hotel we didn't pay for. He flirted with the maids. We ate at a real cool Market called "The Market," recommended to us by some hipster girls who gave us free tickets to a comedy show. We went. It was comedic. Then we went to the parking lot and jammed out to some techno and threw up after taking too many Everclear shots.

We needed to recover from the drinking though, so we had a few beers and went to the main street for the nightlife, and dressed up for the first time on the trip. I wore a blazer of all things. We danced the night away, meeting the beautiful women of Denver and kissing a few of them on the mouth and other places. A great little lounge turned into a dance club for the night. We didn't have any place to stay though, so after the bars closed we made it our goal to meet someone and convince them to let us stay at their place within a half hour of meeting us. It worked, strangely, so I woke up warmly in a beautiful stranger's bed and took a bus back to the city. Aden lost his wallet so retrieved four hundred dollars in cash from the bank and met a Farah Focett look-a-like and her friendly blonde teller at the bank. Then we found Aden's wallet in the parking lot. We laughed at the irony.

Everything is perfect, we thought.

Nothing can go wrong on this trip.

We bought a statue of Buddha just in case.

+

YELLOWSTONE FEELS CLEAN. It has been untouched, period, forever — not touched. Trees fall as they do and cliffs drop as they wish. The roads, insignificantly narrow to the whole, are aliens to the ground. They are too organized. They were created rather than have always been. Alas, they allow tennis shoes and synthetic shirts to experience Mother Nature like infants on her chest — gazing out, present, baffled by every sense perception. Yellow Stone is a rebirth, turning us innocent again, so we may rediscover how to actually use our senses.

But even more, Yellowstone is all around us, we just have to open our minds to each moment, discovering our own lives with wondrously sparkling eyes. We saw a ton of bison and elk and saw Old Faithful shoot up into the sky at least a hundred feet. It was spectacular — almost as spectacular as the families holding hands. The vast immensity of Yellow Stone is incomprehensible to me, seeing as though I have never lived outside of walking distance from at least three gas stations and four convenience stores.

There are only two highways running perpendicular to each other in Yellowstone so often we'd find ourselves stopped behind orange signs held by teenagers telling us to slow down. Slow down? For construction? No time — so we got out of the car and threw a football with the music blaring — with a thousand cars all piled backwards waiting on the teenagers.

"What do you want to listen to?" we yelled to the teenager.

"What?"

"What kind of music do you want to listen to? Do you like rock, pop, country...what?"

"I like everything," he said.

"We do too." — the moment was perfect.

To amuse ourselves, we picked the campsite right by the lake. The rangers said it was full of bears fishing at night and was therefore the most dangerous place to stay. Perfect. The day had been lasting of sun and companionship and lonely hearts and so much green it hurt. We had driven around only to stop every few miles to gaze. We had all day for gazing.

But after picking up a few boxes of wood, Aden motioned at me through the window towards a license plate and two young-looking girls. The license plate was significant because it read Michigan and the girls were significant because they were pretty. I knocked on their window and introduced myself as a guy from Michigan and charmed them with promises of bears. They actually were students from our university so the conversation was pretty easy to fall into. We stayed up with them yelling and drinking around the tent until the morning. Apparently The Rangers received four complaints about us around midnight and therefore told us we had to leave the park at dawn — but we were drunk, and already had plans to leave in the morning anyway, so we didn't much care about annoying our neighbors. They were boring and old anyway.

We danced together around the fire, all four of us, clapping and chanting tribally, weary for the sun. We walked down to the lake searching for bears, drunk, happily taking off our shirts and making plans with the nameless pretty girls from Michigan.

"We should all go to Montana," I shouted.

"We can't," they said together. "We have to go back to Michigan tomorrow."

"Have to?"

"Yes—we *have to*," they said.

I hate "have to."

Just then Aden kissed one of the girls and she not-so-surprisingly kissed him back, even though he had only met her only a few hours earlier, and probably still didn't know her name.

"We should probably leave them be?" I said to the other girl.

And I knew what was going to happen! I knew it happily.

I was young. She was young. We were alone in the forested solitude of Yellowstone together. We would walk too close to each other. We would talk about intimacy. We would talk about love. We would talk about travel and become all excited for our futures. We would make claims about tomorrow, the likes of which would never come to fruition. We'd have *that* moment—*that* cosmic moment—hands brushing, fingers tingling, heart pounding, unsure but sure all at the same time. We'd have that infamous walk far away from Aden and her friend. I could have predict it hours before it happened—but somewhere deep inside of me, there all along, there was Andrea—fighting my libido.

Sure there was Denver and sure there was Vanessa and sure this girl would be easy and simple—she'd accept the frivolousness of that night without demanding anything more than a steady orgasm—but in many ways, I was sick of the triviality of sex. I wanted to make love. I wanted to know her perfume. I wanted to know her nuances, her subtleties, and her idiosyncrasies. The truth is—I wanted Andrea.

But somewhere in Michigan she was lying in bed with a new boyfriend, and that angered me. And it didn't anger me that she was actually with someone new—it made sense in a way. Instead, it angered me that I so stupidly left her at her most vulnerable moment, at our most vulnerable moment—where if I hadn't left, we probably would still be together. And I'd have remembered how to actually make love. I'd have still smelled her perfume through the smoke.

But of course I left. Of course I needed this journey, for some reason, any reason—and therefore knew that for all my hesitations I would soon find myself panting with this new girl in Yellowstone—because I was weak. So fucking weak.

I woke up in her tent, still drunk from all the Everclear, unsure how I got there. Aden was in our tent with the other girl.

It turns out they both had boyfriends, mine was engaged actually—and who knows if the world cares but what's love if not a lesson in determination? I learned then that there are only a few girls who actually keep their legs crossed and guys all cheat without remorse. Half the time it's not on purpose, at least the getting caught part—but do we really have that one soul mate waiting for us behind the glass at a train station?

I mean, I believe in fairy tales until they become unrealistic.

Sure I have Andrea and she nags at me every night just before I fall asleep to dream about her—but she's off gallivanting while I am off gallivanting and neither of us had the decency to say the magic words out loud until the very last minute when they don't mean anything at all. You can't say I love you and then goodbye. It's just bad manners. Which is precisely what I did—and then I slept in some stranger's tent because I felt like it, and wanted the freedom of new skin.

Fuck love, I thought.

…And in being in the perfect headspace I thought it was just the right time to call Andrea?

"Hey," I said muted, surprised she answered.

"Hey how are you?"

"Oh I'm good. I'm sorry I didn't call earlier but I lost my phone in Nebraska. I tried many times before that though. I'm sure you are *very* surprised," I joked sarcastically. I'm terrible for holding on to anything past a few days—even love.

"No I'm not—but it's OK, where are you now? Are you calling from Aden's phone? Having fun?"

"Yeah I'm doing fine. It's pretty crazy right now. I'm in Yellow Stone and it's—I don't know? There are so many things to tell you about. It's really pretty I guess, with all the giant trees and we took pictures next to this old stream that has probably been running for the past, well, I don't know but a long time. Everything is just old out here. And I saw a bison! I stood right next to it only a few feet away and Aden thought I was dumb and…actually…how are you?"

"I'm good…"

"No I know. You said that already. How *are you* though?"

"Kristopher…I'm doing really well. I'm really just living in the moment and enjoying myself as much as I can. I have a great group of friends here and just the other day we went to my friend's lake house and smoked. I smoked so much and we ate BBQ and it was really nice."

"That sounds nice."

I was jealous. Whenever she talks about a "friend" she means some guy who she is either sleeping with her or some guy who wants to sleep with her.

"Where are you going to next?" she asked.

"I think we are heading up to Montana but then we are going back down to Los Angeles to meet up with some of Aden's friends. Who knows what we'll do there but it is LA right? It should be fun."

"Right."

"Well…how is your writing coming along? Are you excited for Belarus? Have you been using your new camera? You know how I love your photographs. You are a brilliant photographer."

It's better to give her a whole host of options to reply to or else she'll give you one word answers all night. She doesn't fake interest very well—that is for sure.

"I actually love my new camera, but I'm just not very good I don't think…"

"Of course you are good!"

"Well I don't know. But I am practicing," she said perking up just a bit. "When do you think you'll be back in Michigan?"

This, I didn't know at the time, was a crucial question. Her lake house friend who she had kissed, I would later learn, was courting her just enough after the initial kiss that she was just on the verge of committing to him. So while I thought that they were "official" by this, in fact, they weren't. This had little to do with him and much more to do with her. She can't stand to be alone—and since most girls interpret her diffidence as arrogance, she rarely has girlfriends and thus clings to males, any male "good enough." If I was going to be back in Michigan in time to see her for a while before Belarus she would probably back off and enjoy herself from a distance, waiting for me, but if I was going to carouse around the country while sleeping with random girls until after she was already an ocean away—who could blame her for moving on? But like I said—I didn't know this at the time. I was stupid—as all males are.

"I'll be back who knows when? I think sometime in September. You'll have already left by then right?" I said.

Wrong answer.

"Yeah, I'll be in Belarus. Can you believe it?" She said this sentence like a wave, starting off slowly and calmly, but she crested just soon enough so as to also sound unafraid.

"I think you are going to have a wonderful time. Remember I'll try and come see you and if not I'll come to New Hampshire for Christmas. I'm doing it whether your dad likes it or not!"

I laughed.

She didn't laugh.

Though I could tell she smiled a bit through the phone—"Yeah we'll see."

"Hey listen," she said. "I should get going but it was really nice to hear from you. Enjoy your summer," she said. She said this like she'd never speak to me again.

"You too Andrea. I love you and I miss you."

"Goodbye Kristopher."

Aden hopped in the car ready to recap the night. He was bursting with energy and therefore only briefly asked about the conversation with Andrea. I told him it went well and we pulled away from the camp site to all our neighbors' relief. The girls from the tents had already left back for home. We were heading west, them east, but we met in the middle for fire and regrets—and that's often good enough on the road.

Nothing mattered after that except California.

There was only California.

We were done waiting and as superlative as the journey had been—it was time for a real live destination, in the flesh with horns and sins and expectations, big flashy signs and yellow hair and surfer shorts, the Californian as an adjective version of California. So we stopped in Montana to eat a buffalo burger and ice cream, broke down in Idaho and played more football in a parking lot, drove through Salt Lake City only stopping for the Mormons, slept through Nevada until the lights of Vegas blindsided me to the right, played a slot machine on the border, won a million dollars, or dreamed about winning a million dollars, turned right for California, and stopped.

Stop.

"Where are we?" I asked tousled.

"We're in California my brother!"

"Lovely, so why are we stopped? It's late."

"We're in California my brother!"

"Right. I guess that makes sense."

We stopped because the traffic at 4am was like rush hour in Delhi. I was convinced there was a convention for average cars and headlights but apparently that was the previous week. Who knew?

But with some patience and warmth we found ourselves at the end of the road where the concrete meets the sand, on a beach, where the sand meets the toes of children, and those children play in the ocean with me, heart wide open, staring at the morning shine!

…Though, my feet still felt a little dirty from Wyoming.

Whatever.

So I stood there in my spot, somewhere in California, somewhere on the Pacific shore, somewhere in America, finally understanding the fairy tale: the blue skies and the white lights, the blessed churches tucked away next to blonde liquor stores, the haughty professors, infidelity, the cliffs and insects, with brown military basis, best friends posing for monuments, empty beds and midnight carousing, thumbs outstretched and credit cards and glowing road signs in the night, crystalline stars and giant gaps in between voices, the rusting trucks next to roadside diners, the dust and the gold, and captivating strangers all standing around fully equipped for fierce conversations — and all the directions all colliding — the ocean speaking to us all the same way, and what a beautiful life and how hard it is — all the contradictions all in one, and The Lesson yelling at me through the waves —

Everyone is a stranger, sure, sounds good — but only until you say hello.

Chapter 7

I WOKE UP ON the couch unsure of what had just happened. Kara was head-to-feet entangled on my side and Faith was somewhere on the ground. Aden was just waking up slumped over in a chair, stained and loved up. I saw half a blanket on the floor, a torn pair of pants, fast food wrappers, underwear, and papers of all assortments. Our collective dignity was leaking but no matter, we had the beach and Hollywood for blending into and people to meet from all walks and talks.

The first person we met was the owner of the couch I had slept on. He was a blonde fellow, maybe a few inches shorter than me, average weight, average build, and he didn't seem too smart, but knew pretty much what he was about. He was Oklahoma with an apartment in Los Angeles. At least that's the way he came to me, like someone that was just "good enough," but who had only recently found out.

He was a part of a community of guys who newly became famous for teaching other guys how to get girls. Whatever "get girls" means is up to the individual but it rings of desperation at first, sounds like a science when spelled out, and then depending upon your sex is either interesting or disgusting. Regardless, it exists amongst college students and engineers and computer programmers all around the world, those with just enough money but not enough affection to be content. I thought it was needed at first—some place where nice guys could learn how to not finish last. But of course with power comes great devolution and it spread to reality television and Rolling Stone authors and Vanity Fair and fraternities until it became a game of one night stands and a contest for how many people we've all slept with. It has made notching your belt a competitive sport.

Though this guy in particular had taken the stage a little more comically and written a book for girls about how to properly talk dirty to guys. And his friends have written books and created online manuals about how to best present oneself attractively and therefore find love — even if only for a night. So let's just say politely that you could smell his insecurity on his breath.

"So you guys had a good night?" he said obviously perturbed. I would have been too if random crazy strangers had trashed my house. Except the house had already been trashed well before our arrival, so we thought we were simply adding to the décor.

"Yeah we went to Hollywood I think — or some major street — it was a bar I think?" And that's honestly about as much as I could handle for explanation.

"Where are you from?" he asked while sitting down at a computer desk next to Aden only now waking. He said this almost accusatorially, waiting for the response so he could shoot back with a comment about how *"People from there are..."* or some other bullshit.

I didn't know how to answer a question like that. I still don't. Abroad I say I'm from Detroit, and in the Midwest I say Ann Arbor. See — If I say Ann Arbor and people have never heard of it, I feel like someone just a little too proud of their hometown — like those who gasp, *"You don't know where Springfield is?"*

"No I'm sorry dear but I don't — because there are fifty of them in every state and they all smell the same."

But I digress. It's a difficult question to answer in California because California is "America" in its language and for its flag but different enough to lose out on familiarity.

So I told him, "We are from the east," to sound smart and cryptic.

He ignored me though and quickly moved on to the girls. They would certainly be more engaging, he thought.

And in lieu of not skipping too much I should tell of how we actually came to find ourselves in that beautiful, yet altogether insecure house of Los Angeles — all folded over the couches together.

See — after the bumper-to-bumper traffic and headlights we called one of Aden's friend's from college who had moved there sometime ago. He was therefore generally expecting us, but not our side-effects — like a cleverly marketed diet pill. Though ironically that is exactly what he sold — online diet pills. I sold diet pills and get-rich-quick schemes and he'd make a commission on everything sold. Apparently he is doing just fine in this line of work. His name is Barry.

Leo, another friend who was connected to Aden either from school or somewhere else, was creating a website for the legalization of marijuana — or an online forum for people who wanted to learn how to grow it? — or something or another, online, to do with weed? I think.

These two, combined with the dirty-talk salesmen, were a potent group of hard nights out, hangovers, and occasional bouts of work — which usually consisted of them checking the internet for an hour a day to make sure they were still making money. Now granted I'm giving them too much credit, of course, but I'm also not giving them enough credit. Compared to us, they had their shit fully together.

That morning though, we had avoided the comparison, rushing out into the sinful traffic of Los Angeles before the sun could show its face. We had to pick up Kara and Faith from their red-eye flight. And as we waited there in the lonely corridors of that forsaken airport, I thought of the sun still hiding behind The East. What if we trusted the first light from New York ,I thought, but waited all morning for nothing? What if the nighttime one-day chose to lengthen itself for fear of retribution — and the sun hid away past her cue? What if the sun never came? Would we be scared — worried as if it were a sign for the end?

No — actually we'd have celebrations with Kara themed and all dressed up! Because that's how that girl bounces — sideways and diagonally until finding her way almost slumped over, half behind a living room cushion, feet sweating on my stomach yet oh how I love them so. Faith would cheers to the lasting moon and curse the foolhardy sun for her narcissism while playing the banjo faster than she knew how. See — these girls, Faith and Kara, they look around and nod vertically at everything speaking to them — always in agreement with the stars or even a lazy sun. They are beautiful, you see. Sure, they were still virgin to the road but they were experienced in enthusiasm — so we needed them much like a cigarette after good sex.

They are like good poetry.

We had picked them up at their friend's house — a friend from Iowa. This friend from Iowa was beautiful in being racially mixed, but I forgot her name five seconds after she said it — telling of how much I actually cared. See — I am concerned about pretty girls up until they say their names and then it usually goes downhill from there. I'm tough to impress for a commitment — unless I'm a few drinks in and then it's hard not to impress me — then "everything is beautiful" and "I love you" and all that silly jazz.

So I'm that. But they are Beethoven played with a recorder.

So after all of us had reunited, after all of the pleasantries of friends and all of that, we came back together — collectively noticing that it was "fucking hot" — "no seriously, it is fucking hot" — and so decided to jump around in the ocean together that day. We parked illegally in a shopping mall to "stick it to The Man" and the adolescent bag boys.

They are both equally at fault, we thought.

Then Aden and I played baseball on the sand while Barry flirted with some tattooed girl with funny earrings. Aden, actually, had initiated our group's conversation with her but Aden wasn't forceful enough for her — and hadn't done enough drugs to fit in with her conversations. So he played baseball instead, while Barry made plans to have sex with Aden's girl — the one *he had* noticed.

I'm sure it irked him the way situations with girls always irk him. He always does the right thing — he's confident and good looking — he's open and happy — smart and successful — he's an equation answer for a women's list of desirable qualities. He's the definition of "what I'm looking for in a man." But that never matters — it's not about that, and worse, he *knows* it's not enough. He acknowledges it. He learns it. And then he tweaks his personality to fit whatever he thinks it *should* be. So the truth is that he's not trying to "find himself" out here on the road — he's looking for how to find love.

I wish I was more help but I'm numb to everyone that's not Andrea, sadly, even if I sleep with them.

After relaxing it was time for a burger at a chain famous to Los Angeles. I had never heard of it and was therefore razzed about the Midwest as boring. I would argue sarcastically, "...*boring because a lack of fast food?*" but I hadn't the energy for conversations with people trying to prove themselves to me.

Insecurity annoys me.

Aden and I had a long, serious conversation on the way to the burger joint about whether or not we would actually eat there. It had a drive-through. This was a problem. Anything with a drive-through must have other versions of itself scattered around the area, strategically placed for pleasure and exploitation. This wouldn't be a big deal except that we had promised ourselves not to eat at a national chain restaurant or buy anything from any national retailer while on the trip. We wanted the "mom and pop" America the whole way through and were not interested in making exceptions. This is why we never actually stayed at that Holliday Inn and why we had searched for any place in Idaho that could change a tire other than Walmart. We hadn't gone to any chain restaurants because we thought we were above them, when actually we were beneath them, or at least we wanted to be underneath them — deeper and deeper.

Though we eventually decided that it was a "regional chain" and not a "national chain" so we therefore weren't breaking any rules. Problem solved. Burger eaten in glory.

And so while sitting there talking about nothing particularly important — I think love — I noticed the apparent diversity of our group and the surrounding tables.

"Leo is black, I'm Mexican, Aden is Jewish, Barry is Irish, Kara is Italian, and Faith is something else," I said. "And yet here we all are just chilling here calmly together. Sure that sounds normal enough except that our native ancestries have been killing each other and separating themselves around the world for thousands of years. Humanity has spent millennia putting up walls and carving out borders in the land to distinguish ourselves from each other — with languages and customs. Then bam the invention of the airplane and giant ships full of human cargo and all of a sudden we are all sitting in the sun of LA bludgeoning these burgers together without a care in the world. So, I ask you, how did we all find each other here, all of us, speaking English together, all of us with the same culture?"

Everyone exclaimed something about "yeah that's cool," or, "wow I never noticed that," or "it's cool that we never noticed that," and, "it seems so normal," and shit like that, but honestly I wasn't really paying attention. They all continued this line of conversation until the meal was over. I mean I was glad they contributed to each other but that happens often with me — I open up a topic of conversation because I have to vocalize my own internal ramblings, but hardly do I actually care what everyone else has to say afterwards.

I think we all do this, in a way.

So I thought, not caring, nodding at the dialogue before me, still thinking about the diversity of my country and how it came to be. How do we define ourselves amongst the collage? How do we stand out?

Etc.

I thought this over while enjoying the moist warmth of a perfectly grilled cheeseburger, donned with lettuce and tomato, special sweet sauce and a toasted bun — melted butter and crisp french-fries garnishing the plate. Oh how I love the succulent juices of a greasy cheeseburger dripping all over my hands and mouth. I thought about "connection" and "difference" distracted by wet ketchup and a refreshing sip of ice-cold water. I contemplated the beauty of all our perspectives and stories — of how our grandparents came to see us here all decked out in variation — and then I took another bite mouth still half full. Everyone has sacrificed and gone without and strived for a place void of judgment, a place where we can all eat around the same table—a bright red plastic table with fatty wrappers and oil stains and money enough for super sizes, I thought. There were thoughts and senses and the weather, the blue-yellow weather, and the glistening sun matching the glistening french-fries. We're all connected by the french-fries, I thought. That's why we get along.

Then after some carousing around lost in the traffic blasting hip-hop we finally made it back to Barry and Leo's place. It was still trashed except all the glut was pushed over into one dirty corner rather than put away neatly into cupboards and spaces. And that's where we packed up into more obvious outfits and showered quickly without soap to get all the sand from our ears. Kara and Faith both changed into skimpy little dresses, with their breasts overflowing into plain sight. Everyone noticed except them, it seemed. They wanted to be noticed but they wouldn't notice even if someone was staring right at them.

"I'm so glad I am here," Faith said to me while pouring a round of shots for everyone.

"I'm glad you are here too my love. It's quite crazy that just a few weeks ago I didn't know you existed and now we are here—together, allies if you will."

"Yes you are definitely my ally."

We plopped a shot back but hardly felt it, like alcoholics. Maybe because we actually were alcoholics? Probably not—just young, which is mostly the same thing.

"What's the plan for tonight?" I asked honestly. This was our first night in Hollywood after all, so therefore had to fully rock it out, but we weren't exactly sure what that would entail. Not yet.

"Let's drink first and ask questions later," Kara shouted.

So the first night soon became one of those "memorable" nights that no one remembers. Stupid alcohol and stupid us for needing it. Though here is what I do remember—the bars didn't have a cover, we drank Everclear shots before leaving in honor of reunions, and Aden dared me to kiss a girl without saying hello to her. This surprisingly didn't bother the girl though, quite the opposite actually, so the scene flipped like a movie about debauchery. We ate some late night food at 4am and I nearly got arrested for trying to sneak out of a parking garage without paying.

It was all just drunken youthful stupid madness.

I felt like a well-read hooligan desiring jail for inspiration. And what if I got caught? — No matter — I'd sit in the cell, I thought, observing all the lonely characters for essays and future conversations. I live for the story, you see. All writers do. We are all just trying to put lipstick upon our lives after the fact. We're philosophers with creativity. We believe in "what could be" and "what should be" and it all sounds beautiful but only because we don't like the story as is. Writers want to see things differently than they actually are.

So that's exactly how the morning came to be — starting with a day at the beach and good food, friends and sunshine, shots and drinks and beers and a great night out. And so the next day I woke up as previously described — still wet from the pool, ready to change the world one tourist bar at a time.

+

SUPERMAN WAS STANDING RIGHT in front of me so I felt powerful there with him. See — he was a man just like me — with abilities and faults just like me. He had his bad days and good days. He loved and lost and sometimes he just wanted to be alone. He wore a costume after all, or was that just his way of showing off? But he fits here, I thought — amongst the stars and boulevards and fancy clothes, in Hollywood, next to the guy in an alien suit and the girl dressed as Marilyn Monroe, Spider Man, and the giant guerrilla.

"Only a dollar for a picture with an icon," they shout at The Chinese Theater.

Though we all ignored superman like we had seen him a thousand times before — me, Leo, Barry, Aden, Faith, and Kara all walking along Rodeo

Drive together, looking at all the breezy trimmings. I went inside one of the fancy clothing stores for only a moment to fully wrap my head around all the excess—to breathe it in, to smell the cleaning supplies and taste the cocaine flavored counters, the white marble floors speckled with black granite stone and the remnants of individuality placidly draped all around. It felt like a hospital room scrubbed clean of all personality.

I looked closely at a blank-staring blonde folding clothes and I told her story to myself. But I didn't get much past the makeup. Her high heels distracted my creativity. All I could construct was a miserable life half smiling about thousand dollar handbags. I felt disgusting. I felt like she was disgusting, and worse, she knew it—like a porn star faking it just right.

I imagined how she got up in the morning, that morning, and popped a Vicodin to kill the pain. She downed it with Grey Goose and sunk into the shower—her naked body perfect in all the wrong ways. She washed her bulging breasts, perky but fake, and drooped down sadly. She braced herself against the bathroom wall leaning over, staring at the ground, the water rushing quickly onto the back of her neck. Gliding out of the mist she would stare in the mirror after wiping away a spot from the steam. She would stare in the mirror for quite some time—naked in a bathrobe without makeup, without her hair perfectly parted and shined. She stared at her insides but couldn't penetrate the plastic, one tear gradually falling on her cheek, mixing in with the mascara—so much mascara.

And that's how LA feels to me. It is like a witch-hunt for beauty, mass hysteria for flesh. And so it frustrated me. Who really gives a shit about the brand of shirt you are wearing? It's all made in the same factory in China anyways. I'd like to meet them and feel if they have a soul. Maybe they need it massaged to get all the kinks out?

And there were billboards everywhere for movies and giant faces selling bottled water, smog, and blasphemous cars lining the streets, little showoffs all grown up, and hobos on the ground after just the right hit. But then I thought for a second about the hobos, about how maybe the hobos had it all figured out, those hobos on the street corners losing themselves in some apparent clarity. They saw the world around them clearly and packaged it into sweet liquids and let it pour through them, so that they could not only see the outside, but feel it within them—like a spiritual quest on the tip of a dirty syringe.

What if I sat down right here with my hundred-dollar bill, I asked myself, and let go of everything? What if I made friends with the drug addicts and the pimps? What if instead of listening to funny men talk about funny things all my life, I simply sat down—right here on the side of the street in LA-90210 and felt my deep brown eyes roll back into the ether?

God I want to feel that connection even for its faults.

…

"Let's go get some lunch," Aden said and we all listened.

It was a place "where all the stars go," we were told. All the stars and us. I asked the manager to take my picture and put it next to the Al Pacino autograph. He ignored me though so I asked him again insinuating— *"What, am I not important enough?"*

But he just insinuated right back with his eyes. *"No you are not,"* he said while putting a piece of fish in the fryer.

Then we left and bought a few funny t-shirts, or should I say, Aden bought a few funny t-shirts—and walked around the streets gazing up at the Hollywood sign vacant in the distance. Its letters are hollow to match the theme of LA. I wore a shirt that read "choose a life" in big bold letters as a declaration. I was a walking advertisement for youth and freedom, strolling down the streets critiquing everything in sight while simultaneously announcing my undying love for love. What a joke.

But either way I felt uncomfortable and out of place—I felt judged—and so realized that I would be the worst celebrity in history. The tabloids and the public would hate me equally…

"So I heard you might be dating…?" the interviewer would ask me.

"Fuck off," I would say.

This is ironic, I realize this, while writing my innermost thoughts along the way — but the gaze of someone else is always much stronger than our own. We can often handle ourselves, at least most of the time. But I wouldn't want my personal goings-ons all splashed about in public, but half these stars, on the contrary, seem to revel in it — because it's good for their careers. They wear those tiny little mesh skirts and lose a bunch of weight for effect, or grow out ugly beards to prove they don't give a shit — all the while wearing the most designer flib-flab to ever walk the face of the Earth, and pose for cameras. They fucking pose for cameras!

I mean I do this too but it's different. It's different when I do it — I think.

So we went out again, but this time the classy way — with button ups and dress shoes, taking shots from the bottle on the roof of a cement parking garage, with half-naked truth or dare pictures deleted for precaution. You know — the "classy" sort of classy. But this night instead of going deep into Los Angeles with all the buildings and square jaws, we went to Hermosa Beach for the boardwalk and dive bars instead.

…I drank on the side of the street and stumbled into a something named saloon.

And the next thing I knew I was half a mile into the water on a pier overlooking the pulsating ocean. It all came in chunks, drunken chunks, like memories, memories of staggering over chains and Do Not Enter signs, and Faith next to me all the while, and there were lights too, memories, and then a flashlight pressed against a locked fence — memories and a police officer tall, staring at me like I was a blonde on Rodeo Drive.

Chapter 8

I OFTEN DIE IN my dreams. There is one particularly haunting version where I am forced to play an impossible-to-win version of Russian roulette. There is a giant stage, an even bigger wheel — rainbow colored and shimmering through the sky. My aim is to spin the wheel to the correct slot amongst millions of glowing slices, like an inverted game of wheel of fortune — except the prize is my life. Needless to say I spin and I always lose, and so die, and then I play again and lose again, and so die — again and again and again until I wake up panting in my mother's arms rocking back and forth like a madman in a strait jacket.

In other dreams I've died by falling face down into the ground after jumping from a plane without a parachute. I've died by way of a bullet wound from a confused police officer. I've died in self-induced car crashes, because my dream-self wanted to see what would happen if I veered into a ditch. I've died in a WWII trench. I've died fantastically at the hand of a headless horseman chasing me through my apartment, finally finishing me off with an arrow to the head.

So I've been to the darkness and back again — realizing that I'm not altogether afraid of death itself, just the five seconds before it. It's the forced acknowledgement that gets to us — a desperation underneath the eyelids, hidden somewhere between the dark recesses of our least acknowledged worries and an eerie sense of acceptance — and all the while that frantic heartbeat races to pump just one more drop. Death is a whole body agony — each cell self-identifying past the wholeness that once was, individually sad for the end.

Death is a worrisome final vibration.

But there is a silver lining as always — when you don't believe in a magical afterlife with white clouds and healthy ancestors, cloths and

Greek architecture, you often find yourself sucking the life out of every moment with such a ferocity that you can't help but climb over locked gates, two locked gates, shouting to the incoming surf. See — a tentative fear of death is surprisingly also a freeing recipe for bad decisions.

+

"AHHHHHHHHHHH," I SCREAMED WONDROUSLY with Faith beside me.

But I couldn't explain the beauty of freedom or use drunken yawps as an explanation for societal misconduct so instead of confronting the police officer's flashlight, I ran away farther down near the water, almost off the edge of the pier and into the westward ocean.

"Where are we now? Where is Aden and the rest? What should we do? Is that really a cop? Fuck."

Faith's suggested plan of action was laughter, and the real sort of laughter no less, the contagious version — so I laughed with her forgetting about the possible jail time and stared at her shining. She had too much makeup on and her dress was a little too showy — but no matter — I still wanted all of her. I cared about her like a great memory in the making much more than an object of my affection, but couldn't help but want to kiss her anyways. Not for her sake specifically, but for the pronoun "her" — the feminine. And of course I also wanted to kiss her because the best stories are illegal and done with a girl. This is objective fact.

I would share how we got out of that mess if I knew. It was some combination of stumbling and vomiting that cut us loose. See — after some time we found ourselves climbing back over the fence into the waiting arms of the gang. The police must have found a group of hooligans causing more of a stir than Faith and I, so moved on. Laughing isn't against the law anyway, I thought.

Aden carried me back to some party somewhere in LA, me shouting to the empty street — leaning on his mind and shoulder equally.

There was some scuttle at the party because one of the girls was being sexually harassed by one of the guys at the party because there is always a girl being sexually harassed by one of the guys at all parties. There was almost a fight I think — about honor, respect for females, and an ass-grab. I spent the rest of the night falling on Kara sitting on the floor in front of a beer pong table. She fell on me the same and so I sat there back to the wall, head to the foolishness of twenty-somethings, like looking into a bruised Monet.

"I could totally beat you if I wasn't drunk man," someone said across the table.

"Well you wouldn't be trashed if you hadn't lost so much," another one said faltering.

"Dude did you see that girl earlier? I mean fuck man — I think she wanted me!"

"You always say that…"

"It's your turn. Go…throw the damn ball dude!"

"Yeah! Fuck yeah! I told you we'd come back," the one erupted after sinking the winning shot.

"Three to two now, I was just warming up earlier. I told you I'm going to beat your ass," the other one said and on and on and on and on until my eardrums bled of ego.

I felt myself dreary from all the posturing. I sat there, drooling on the ground, drunk past the point of retention, too tired to stand — convincing myself that I was thoroughly better than these idiots. I knew what was up. I was choosing the fast lane. Yes — this ground is a choice for me — while they were merely naked emperors gallivanting for everyone else's amusement. Yes — yes! I was choosing the dirty ground. I was choosing to drool. Yes. I choose drool.

Then someone packed me in a car and hurried me off to some empty house. Barry was dog-sitting for his aunt on some backstreet somewhere in LA so we took that as an excuse to sleep all over her couches and pillows, sprawling out even on her kitchen floor. I was so drunk I could have slept on a bed of grimy glass and wouldn't have noticed the difference. I only woke a few times to the sounds of Leo and Kara mumbling their bodies together under a shared blanket near the dining room table.

"I don't understand why guys have the freedom to sleep with whomever they want to whenever they desire but I get cross-eyed stares after I do the same?" she had said in Iowa, and proven herself there on a stranger's floor in California.

Kara was free in that way — and not with a slutty sexuality like Aden or me — but with a real ownership of her wants and needs. Or at least she was certainly better at articulating it. I envied that in her — I envied her exacting confidence. She had those butting insecurities like looking at the mirror three times too many before walking out the door, but it was certainly more genuine than a Hollywood girl. She was all puffed out like a peacock, sure, but she was also able to fly so left the rest of us helpless — on the ground, watching her sore well above us into the night.

+

SOMEONE HAD THE IDEA to pack ourselves all tightly into the folds of our backseat and run down towards San Diego and Mexico.

"So there are 5 suitcases, a full trunk, and 6 people," Kara said now sober. "But I think we can fit in one car."

So Aden drove with Faith next to him — while I, Barry, and Kara sat in the back — with all of lanky Leo scrunched at our feet, somehow intertwining into all our legs. It was uncomfortable, of course, but we all sang together with the music blasting out the opened windows and arrived necks creaked and knotted.

And just as we were going to pay for our first blasphemous hotel a friend of Kara's brother called saying that he had extra beds in the Hyatt downtown. So we dropped everything to meet him and check out our new spot.

Jarod his name—was short and typical in all the Midwestern ways: brown well-kept hair, hazy eyes, and a pleasant smile. He shook hands firmly but without trying to prove anything. I liked him right off.

"Make yourselves at home," he said. "My job put me up in this big room so it's better to have company than be here all by myself anyways." He said this like he hated his job albeit the perks and the fancy hotels.

"Life is not about stuff," the universe said to me once again.

We tried our best to enjoy the room but the setting was so bitterly frozen I couldn't warm the mood. With the backdrop of a perfectly folded bedcover and one of a thousand identical TVs latched at its base to a corporate shelf, swung down dryly, adjacent to another ho-hum forgettable footstool—I hadn't the energy to find the bright spot. Hotels are prisons without bars. So I sat there befuddled in San Diego, unsure where the future of the day would take me next. I sat there and contemplated my own existence—and my meaning—and *the* meaning—all those meanings of words and stories thrown together the way we throw them together sometimes. I did this because this is what I always do—I think too much.

I ran downstairs for some privacy in the parking lot, shuttering in the heat, and came across a dreary old man and his son unpacking their stuffed trunk.

"Is this your car?" he said pointing to me.

"Well it's my friend's but mine as much as anything else for now."

"All the way from Michigan eh? I noticed the plates—that's quite a long ride down here to San Diego. I'm just coming from a little ways north of Los Angeles but wow what a ride all the way down here eh?"

"Yeah we're on a road trip and decided that San Diego sounded about right for now."

"You planning on going into Mexico?"

"Yes I think we'll…"

Just then he shouted at me quickly like the whole sentence was just a shoved together sound — "Well let me tell you something. That place is a madhouse I tell ya — just last week ten people were murdered. Can you believe that? I was about to go there myself but no-sir not now. That's more than one murder a day and the next victim sure as hell ain't gonna to be me no sir!"

"Well we'll see. Thanks for the tip," I said shooing him away.

And that was the saddest man I'd met up until that point — all stubbed into his own fear without a sense of adventure left in him on account of his aged self-preservation. That's what it's all about, I thought, that stifling edge where only a few are willing to stand. Sure as hell there was a story for Mexico to be told and retold if only it were given the opportunity to present itself. I wasn't about to let a few ruffians running drugs up and down the coast stop me from anywhere or anyone for that matter. Who was he to tell me I shouldn't go? — of all the terrible things to say to someone, of all the horrendous sins and defunct theories, of all the unsolicited pieces of advice — telling me not to go?

If I go down and love-up Mexico real nice-like I'm sure she'll kiss me softly, I thought. I wasn't scared of Mexico. No not me.

But this guy was different. He was a rough quickie sort of man, drunk to his own ways, set in his own sorcerer's stone. I'm new to this life but not new to my ideals and they'll get me further, I thought, farther down south, or further into the vast and endless space of the future, into that deep ocean of experience to come. Either way, I was ready to go to Mexico despite his warnings.

+

ANDREA HAD PARTIED IN Mexico only a few months earlier, only a few months before the infamous break-up. She went to spite me, because the previous week I had gone to Columbia "without her." She wanted to prove to me that she too could have fun without me — that she too could travel without care for love or our future.

Though, that didn't prove to be true — for either of us.

Her friend from Mexico was rich, so all of her friends were predictably rich as well. Andrea was therefore entertained by free massages and hard dance music, handsome suitors of all sorts spouting love at first sight, and by alcohol flowing into and through her. It must have been a glorious vacation — away from her tyrannical parents — away from her distant boyfriend. But through all the bedlam of youth, during a crazy night while dancing in an exaggeratedly excessive club, the likes of which could only exist in a country where the rich were not simply rich, but excessively wealthy compared to the "commoners" of its mostly-poor citizenry, she found herself being mercilessly hit on by the countless, unnamed aristocracy of Mexico with every passing step. She deserved this in a way. It was expected considering her untamable and untranslatable beauty was uninhabited and therefore obvious — but in her also being a girl, somehow she didn't expect it to all be so noticeable. She didn't expect to have to defend herself so vehemently.

She called me drunkenly, naively even, in the dead of night.

"Kristopher?" she said from Mexico.

"Yes?" I answered perplexed. It was 4am.

"Kristopher! Oh perfect," she said into the phone. "Kristopher you wouldn't believe the night I just had."

"Are you OK?"

"I'm fine...*now*," she said.

I smiled.

"We went to this club that was in some cave or something — I don't know actually. It was crazy. The music was great and we flirted with a bunch of guys — sorry — but we flirted with a bunch of guys so they would buy us free drinks and oh my God I'm so drunk and I couldn't stop thinking about you."

"Are you OK?" I repeated. At this point I was actually worried.

"I'm OK now," she emphasized again. "I'm too drunk though. I had to pay this guy ten dollars—which is a lot of money in Mexico you know?—and he let me use his cell phone so I'm standing on this busy highway and I'm calling you."

"So you *are* OK? Nothing is wrong?"

"Yeah I'm fine but I just...well I just had all these rich guys buying me drinks all night," she said. After she said that, it was obvious to me that she was in fact very drunk. See—she usually hid from me the fact that she continuously, every day even, was mercilessly hit on by every male who saw her. Though I knew this already—it was funny to hear her finally admit to it out loud. She continued—"These guys were all trying to take me home and whatever...and God...I am so drunk...but I kept insisting to my friend that I wanted to call you and she thought I was stupid but what the hell right? —I wanted to call you. I wish you were here with me."

"I wish you were here with me too," I said.

"Why did you go to Columbia without me?"

"I don't know. I just wanted to have some alone time with Aden I guess. I'm sorry if that made you uncomfortable."

"I miss you."

"I miss you too."

"Mexico is great and all," she said, "but it would be better if you were here."

"True," I said. And it still was.

+

ADEN INTERRUPTED MY DAYDREAMING about Mexico and Andrea, meeting me downstairs demanding—"Let's get some fish tacos from a local."

"Perfect."

They were too expensive and a little American greasy but the juices rolled off my tongue onto the saturated napkins in just the right way, and the Pacific blue draft fluttered over my ears with the sounds of rolling waves in the soaking morning—a perfect morsel of a San Diego flavor. We drank lemonade peering off a wooden-rolling balcony somewhere in California, gazing, just gazing.

But a quick splash of gray to the left caught my eye like a falling tree branch in the peripheral. It was a gaudy machine of terror, an enormous vessel of The Navy to keep me safe and warm at night, to keep me eating spicy melted cheese too fast without fear. This freedom of ours in the America of our bedrooms—that simple calm—that slow heart beat—beat, beat, beat-beat, that *real* dreaming that we feel, none of it could possibly exist anywhere except for under an army's shadow, I thought.

"What is that there for?" I asked but this time out loud.

"It's just chilling in case someone wants to invade us."

"Who? Who's going to invade us?" I asked confrontationally. "We've built so many ridiculous bombs and jets here in America—I mean do you know that we have jets that can go thousands of miles an hour—so fast—that they are out of the country before our enemies have any chance to react? What a rush eh?"

"What a rush? Yeah—but aircraft carriers are sickening. They are like the armies of half the world packed onto one ship with nuclear weapons. They're like submarine starships from the science fiction novels and I bet the army has shit that we've never even heard of in those big desserts in New Mexico too."

"Yeah we should go there and see if they shoot us for getting too close," I suggested foolishly.

"No. No-no-no—because, and I'm serious here—they *will* shoot us," Aden said.

"Yeah I'm not a fan of being shot," I finished.

But that was true, our military, it's all gaudy in the same we Americans are, imposing on the skyline of the would-be horizon with its steal constructions and pollution. See — I was conflicted over US politics and international affairs equal to which drink I'd slosh down later that evening. It didn't really matter what I thought about anything and I knew it. Should we invest so much money into weapons and boundaries? What does it mean to be American and why does my passport count for so much? Where is the beach? I wonder if that pretty girl will like me if I say hello over there? Has Obama done a good job? What flavor of ice-cream should I get — maybe gelato? There have been nearly a million civilian casualties in the Iraq War and no one seems to care — why? No seriously — I'm serious — where is the beach?

I sat there thinking about this for quite some time. Then Jarod tapped me on the shoulder.

"Hey buddy — everyone's already left," he said. "We're walking down towards the ferry to Coronado Island. Don't worry about the cost it's on me. We'll be there relaxing in no time."

He patted me on the back.

"Thanks. Just give me a second though. I can see you all down the way. I'll catch up."

I needed just a second longer with the apple pie sun tasting so good on my skin. This is my life I thought — right here, this moment, and none to come and none that already came. This is it. Right here on this pier in San Diego, alone with the birds squawking their white songs, and the fish don't have a care in the world — there is that nice fat family chomping away at slopping French fries with their red striped shirts to match the navy backdrop and they are like a picture of God all connected together — connected with me and this tickling sensation of the wind, and what is the wind? — and I don't care about any "what" or "why" right now except this oily smell and this moment. This is it. I'm made for San Diego and this balcony.

Then I caught up with them and took the ferry across the bay onto Coronado with everyone half-naked spilling over the side, all of us staring at the ocean below, feeling wholly satisfied with the setting.

"This is ranked as one of the top ten beaches in the world," Jarod said.

I am obsessed with devaluing rankings but I also use them when it's advantageous. Whatever.

"Oh that's great," I exclaimed.

"What's that even mean though?" Aden asked as if speaking for me.

"It means a lot of people love this beach. You know that's something interesting about Americans — we always think the rest of the world has better beaches than us but we have Florida and California and Hawaii giving their fair share of beauty to the world. We don't necessarily have to go to Fiji to feel alive ya know?" Faith explained.

"Well of course," Aden continued, "but that's not the point. I'm not saying America doesn't have anything to offer — almost exactly the opposite or else I wouldn't be here exploring it. The point though — is what are the criterion we use for 'best beach' anyways? The people who visit it? The view? What the sand looks like? Cleanliness? Size of the waves? Restaurants and nightlife? How long the boardwalk is? How pretty the girls are? World class surfers, newlyweds, and a family will all have very different definitions eh? And who is voting? — that — more than anything, is the real question."

"This beach, today, for us, will be the best beach in the world," I said to everyone's silence.

And that was it — that moment — that silence, walking hip to hip and sometimes even hand in hand with our friends towards something, a beach today, but towards something no less — and that's all that mattered. Kara and Faith smiled at each other and skipped merrily when they felt like it and their hair waved back and forth brown and straight and healthy and full of youth. Leo and his giant flip flops clomped along the long-long sidewalk across the peninsula and his lanky arms fell towards the Earth like a graceful weeping willow. He was a tranquil giant meandering around and I thought just then that it was fine to have known him so well composed.

Barry, though, was a frantic sort of fellow and so he rather glided in his gate, but with a shaking and uneven, almost-dancing sort of walk. He wore his shirt baggy because he couldn't wear it any other way — his chest and waist were so narrow and concaved that any shirt of any size melted away from him, but in a refreshingly casual sort of way. He just looked around like a lost puppy, not worried about finding his way back home and I loved it.

And Aden just then was Aden in one of those Zen moments he has often. He would hardly have noticed if I had tugged on his ear or scraped the back of his ankle on accident — step and then step — he was on purpose with each movement but without being directly conscious of any of it. He was thinking about the moment at hand, or trying not to think of it and just experience it, only the senses and then let those senses fall away as well, until he didn't exist and no one else did either and he was one with the ether and the void, floating.

+

ONCE, HE AND I had gone to a music festival in Detroit high on energy drinks — so we blended throughout the crowd of shameless dancers and wore our funniest outfits and bounced up and down with our fists pounding out the rhythm towards space and smashed down towards the ground with our calves bustling and breaking backwards — up and down, left and right, arms like noodles wet and whipped. We saw the world's best DJs with the ancient lights beating down a new brightness and what a satisfying and ecstatic scene — tens of thousands of people raving their individual steps with dances of all varieties under the moon, and oh the moon shining so bright illuminating Canada in the distance like a second star across the river. They heard us bawl and jump from the melting city of Detroit — but all the while I couldn't find Aden anywhere.

See — he had wanted to see a different DJ on a different stage. There were four which is customary for festivals, so we separated but the night was so vivid and stark with sound that I couldn't push my way across a few dancers let alone find him amongst the bedlam. I couldn't find him but who cares, I thought — so I bobbed my head up and down like a snake slithering upright and the enormous crowd became one furtive organism with me and around me, and I to them equally, and up and down in unison, and up and down in unison, with my head looking upwards because there is really only upwards in ecstasy, and the boom-shake, and the sweat in my veins and the up and down in unison, and the up and down in unison, though still, I couldn't find Aden anywhere.

So I broke myself off from the whole like a useless Jenga piece and called Aden a few times before he picked up.

"I — am — at — the — back — stage!" I screamed as loud as I could, emphasizing each syllable to the best of my ability with the towering speakers and singing attendees eating my every word.

"I aaa…no…the…back? …I'm…amazing…!" he said.

"Whaaaaaat? Aden — where are you?" I repeated.

"Duuuu…there is this…stage…I'm…" or something or another until I got so fed up I texted him hoping it would connect.

It did. So he texted me — "Main Stage. I'm in the middle. Find me."

So I bustled through the crowd enough to find a clearing to the next stage. I was leaving one song for another, one vibe for another, the outer back stage for the main stage — *the* main stage where at least 10,000 people were all swaying with the DJ's beat. And I was to find Aden "in the middle" of all that?

I passed a girl without a shirt on and another teenager in all black, wearing a gas mask, with spiky pink hair. I nodded towards a couple waving glow sticks in front of their faces but they too didn't notice me. I saw a half lit cigarette on the ground and a middle aged biker with a highlighted face glowing under backlights and neon bulbs — crunch went the empty beer cans — stifling the heat with the moisture of smelling bodies all thrashing against one another. Though I went deeper and deeper still, pushing past a group all hand in hand, their arms raised like a prayer circle bouncing up and down.

"Excuse me," I said but they didn't hear anything above the music.

I am just a part of this entire mess I thought, with the crazy lunatics of my generation blinking at one another in passing, but looking at each other just enough to feel a connection. And on and on, towards the middle — and it became increasingly violent, me shoving people aside who didn't care and just gave me the thumbs up as I strained myself deeper and deeper towards the middle of this shimmering noise — closer to the DJ like a god controlling the crowd with every flick of his finger and each change of pace. Though all the while I just pushed deeper and shoved harder and crawled through a few legs and stepped over fallen couples kissing and farther, deeper and deeper towards the center.

There is no way I'm going to find Aden. There are too many people and I can't see past the person next to me and everyone is so close we are touching and I feel bad shoving people aside even though they feel my excitement and where the fuck is Aden? All the weed smoke and vibrations of the arms and the drenched stickiness on my cheeks from strangers and fuck this — I'm not high enough and I want to find some girls and how am I going to get home if I can't find Aden?

Though I pushed through still — farther and farther. I found a few gay college students in leather tights dancing next to old fat women in Budweiser t-shirts like they were family all along. So I calmed and became angry the same as the beat, back and forth, like the crowd swaying, back and forth, annoyed and joyous, like my life, back and forth — until there, downwards — sitting Indian style in a yoga meditation pose, palms up and eyes closed with the weight of thousands of people dancing and screaming around him, with two-story tall speakers blasting his eardrums, with spit and spilled beer and the fallouts of all the day's frenzy pouring down around him all at once — there he sat, my friend Aden — meditating.

And that's Aden in all his eccentric glory. The meditating madman, I call him. The madcap sage. The dancing Buddha. The oxymoron of man of all in one. So I stood there silent before disturbing him and looked up towards the DJ slowly — then to the group next to me on my right, then at the stunning woman on my left, then at the jumping adolescents in front of me, and then I calmly turned around to smile at the older couple to my back. I even peered over the crowd on my tip toes to see how far I had come from, to see how far I had traveled to be there in the middle of everything with Aden.

Then I gazed back at Aden, still sitting, still meditating, the only one sitting, the only one meditating, there alone in his thoughts — and I smiled a great big smile.

I gently tapped him on the shoulder and said, "Hey. I found you. You ready to rock out?"

I looked up at me with a great smile of his own. "Always," he said while standing up — and then — and only then, did he begin to dance.

+

WHEN WE ARRIVED AT Redondo Beach with the gang intact, all of us fluttering from the sun, I stepped onto the yellow sand and stopped for a moment to gather myself. This was the first time I had encountered wealth, the cookie cutter predictable kind, since I had left. There were enormous cocky houses lining the boardwalk with piercing gates for separation — blue herons and old novels and red bricks stacked tall, fortresses for their wealth. Now understand that I don't blame these people, whoever they are, for buying property right next to the sun and battering the tapestry because I'd do the same in retirement, but it always feels good to point at someone else for ruining everything. So I did.

"Why are there so many people here?" Kara said noticing the hundreds of coolers and beach umbrellas. It was still early yet we'd be hard pressed to find a clean spot except next to yelling children.

"...probably for the same reason we are," said Leo.

"Top ten beach eh?" I said sarcastically to Jarod while padding his shoulder. He snickered and shrugged politely.

We slipped between the polka dotted families and sand pails while the grains all shimmied in between my toes and made the ground fall away, splashing with every step. Aden found our spot nestled just in front of the creamy first-aid stand and the glistening life guards, with a giant fat man to my left stroking his belly while his toddler jumped all over him like a human jungle gym. It took a while to get acquainted with the heat and the peaceful setting of the white sun haunting us over head, but eventually I calmed and fell to my back. Everyone scurried to put on sunscreen before their skin turned leathery like rough parchment — so we touched each other's backs and legs in order to protect ourselves from a sun we should be used to by now.

And slowly our clothes came off — one flip flop and then a skirt, then someone's t-shirt was thrown to the ground, and then Aden flipped off another shoe, and I wiped sweat from my brow and ran my hands through my thick brown hair, and Barry forgot his swimming trunks so just stripped down to his undies which looked about the same as swimming trunks except slightly more risqué in name — and so everyone chuckled as he walked by but he didn't care because he doesn't care about anything like that. Leo had also forgotten his swim trunks, which made me think they had almost done it on purpose, for the sheer joy of being different.

I played catch with Aden again and then jumped into the ocean, it bellowing out until forever, or maybe just until Hawaii but I couldn't see that far. For now, though, it was infinity and splashes and delights in the slippery blueness all around — so we threw giant inflatable balls into the ocean just to watch them come back. The ocean was playing catch with us like a prehistoric puppy that would never get tired.

"It's a mirror for the sky, that ocean," I yelled at Aden.

But he didn't care about that — just the waves pushing him backwards. He yelped and punched at the on-rushing water like a training prizefighter.

"I will take on the ocean!" he touted, "and it will succumb to my will. I am the master of my own destiny!"

"I don't really believe you are going to have any real effect on the mighty ocean my friend," I laughed at him.

"Ah-ha my brother—you are in fact wrong once again! I am and I will—the ocean is mine to control," he laughed too while diving into one of the higher swells and came out fingers flopping all around, blinking the water from his red-blue eyes.

"See," he said looking at me proudly, "I have conquered the ghastly water as Poseidon once did on the eastern banks of the Aegean. Will you come with me brother-god to fight off the wandering evils of this day?"

At this point he was just having too much fun for me with the fairytales and the swagger even if it was all in exuberant rapture. So I checked myself out of the water and back to the girls. They were tanning themselves orange on top of orange towels on the orange sand. They wanted to completely blend in.

Leo and Barry joined Aden in their old-speak just as I was sitting down. They would spend the next hour or so punching at the ocean and kicking it too, as the tide rolled in slowly closer to all the people crowded around the shoreline. They were six foot tall children conquering the mightiness of the mighty sea and talking like old folk heroes, yelling things like, "oh brilliant ship of the American empire come bring us our women to have merry times with and we'll all drink jugs of port wine and pirate whisky celebrating our victory," or "yes I tell you young gentleman, I am the Sir you have heard of through the prairies and the retched plains of the forested north—I come to save this hallowed ground from the beautiful yet ferocious maiden you call La Pacifica off the burly shores of The Angel City—and come forth now young lad, I am here for you, and I'll show you how to punch the Earth till it bleeds."

And Barry even tried to involve himself in the thoughtlessness yelling out, "yahoo yes sir I am the king and the conqueror here to marry your daughter and punch the ocean too yahoo!"

I enjoyed listening to them romp around and Faith and Kara did too I suppose. But I just sat there still, observing the way I observe sometimes, and looked up at the sun as well as I could, because sadly we can't actually look at the sun the way we wish we could. The sun is very much like God in this way — the way God is written about in those old books, about how we'd go blind or die if we looked at him directly. All of that comes from the old astronomy religions, I thought, while pouring fistfuls of sand over my dry white thighs. It's all the same thing this religion talk. I know what is what. What is what is this beach and these friends and this sun and I can't very well look at it I know, but I sure as hell can feel it like a warm coat just dangling there in the magnificent sky. The sun is a smoldering boulder of history and energy, and so it *is* true that it revolves around the Earth and not the other way around, like those big headed scientists would have us think. It *is* our own star. And it is my favorite star too because it has its own dance for half the day and I love dancing. The other stars run away behind the penciled sky during the day — just so that our own star can have its very own special parade, I thought. Every day we come to the beach and we watch the parade of the sun marching across the sky. This is the truest of all the truths. Yes it is circling me today I thought while massaging my frying shoulder with two extended fingers — the sun must only be circling this beach today, and for just me.

Happy, I settled back on my towel and closed my eyes to fall asleep the way you would want to right before death — just serene and peaceful in the friendly sun.

"Let's go get some ice cream," suggested Aden and we all ran to do so.

We walked along the stretched sidewalks from the beach leading clear to the other side of the peninsula. The houses were all quaint and bright with paint and spackled flags, upright grass, and even the dogs chirped with the birds fluttering overhead. It was an iconic scene, all of us skipping on the sidewalk in the California air. We heard a great bellowing horn playing old Michael Jackson and other Motown classics off in the distance. And eventually the street opened up to a park. It was bustling with hundreds of fold-out chairs and plumes of food smoke billowing from heated coals, and juicy chicken bones sizzling and the fatty sauces all baked around casseroles covered in good'ol American tinfoil yes ma'am, and it smelled wonderfully wafting towards my tongue. Yes ma'am it did.

It was a carnival for old people. I observed a sparkly white man in an even sparklier red suit, with cheesy singer hair twirling around a raised stage in the middle of all the retirees. He sang out sing-alongs that we all recognized from the big-name bands of old. The women and their saggy breasts were all grey haired, sitting, with some of their husbands standing, white haired with Coca Cola in their hands. It was like a tailgate without the beer or t-shirts. They all wore sailing shoes and pastel polos. They had "made it" — the American dream on their peninsula with the beach and their Cokes in hand and their grandchildren off with trust funds somewhere so they didn't need anything except this oldies cover band in their park. Though out of the masses all sitting down in lawns eating and listening, there were a few wild ones — the young fifty-somethings all dancing like a gracious mosh pit. They twisted their hips and smiled big like they were at a great music festival for the elderly.

"Let's go dance," I said assuming there wouldn't be any discussion to the contrary.

Aden looked at me strangely and sneered ever so slightly in saying — "I mean — they are super old."

"And...?"

"Well I mean we have the 5:20 ferry to catch back into the city."

"Really?" I said accusatorily. How dare he suggest we that we had a ferry to catch? "A ferry to catch? To do what? To go where? Do you have somewhere *to be*? ...have to wake up for the job in the morning?"

He understood right quick and so admitted, "Yeah you are right — let's dance."

Barry and Leo I could tell, really and terribly did not want to dance. They weren't dancers. They were livers and dreamers and talkers and they did batshit crazy things like walk around the beach in their underwear, but dancing — dancing brought back memories of high school prom for them that they'd rather soon forget. I on the other hand loved dancing, and loved senior prom, so would have none of their hesitations.

"I understand you are not interested in dancing," I shouted back to them while stepping over picnics and old people, "but we are dancing so either you can go back by yourself, sit on the grass and watch us have fun, or you can stop being too cool for school and enjoy yourself."

Neither of them looked at the other but in knowing I was right, they slowly walked towards the center of the park together, albeit doubtful and a little hurt. I kept whizzing past all the food, giving the ladies thumbs up and rubbing my belly saying "yum" and "that looks so good" to make them feel complimented. I was faster than them — faster than their friends — faster than my friends even — jumping from one open grassy spot to the next, having to "say excuse" me after each leap.

"I'm sorry," I said to one lady in particular after having to brace myself on her puffy mop head. "I really am sorry I just want to get over there and I can't find a good angle to get there without being just a little rude."

"Oh no honey," she shrugged, "you go get'em."

So I laughed and kept hopfrogging until the dance area chopped my knees together and pushed my fist into the air pumping. I turned around to Aden just behind me, then Faith swinging her arms in the air, and Kara right there bouncing.

Immediately the crowd noticed us young'ens and therefore made a circle around us. They clapped their hands to us and we to them, and a few of them taught me old dance moves I only recognized from my mother in the kitchen. I learned them and then they said, "Teach me something?" and I said I had no moves I just had a feeling and they all threw their heads back with joy and what a scene. We had 25 years on the next youngest and so they loved that we joined them. We brought, even if for a moment, just a slightly more engulfed flame than they were used to.

"I hope my retirement has dancing in it," I yelled to Aden above the music and he agreed through facial expression.

One lady in particular took an almost awkward liking to me. She wore her hair long almost to the small of her back. She was fit — maybe one of those older marathon runners that ESPN does stories about, and didn't hesitate to show it off. Her skirt was long and flowery, but not only in print—it rustled the same way a daffodil would in the wind. She had a spaghetti strap white blouse, fairly see through, and not long enough to cover her stomach with her hands extended towards the sky. So she reached towards the trees and snaked like a gypsy dancer at Woodstock. Maybe she used to do this at Woodstock, I wondered? Maybe she still does? She grabbed my hand and had me twirl her around and mimicked my steps like I was teaching her something without trying. She asked me where I was from like you would at a college bar. She touched my shoulder and said, "That is so interesting," a few too many times. I loved the attention no lie and she was attractive for her age, but the whole situation was more comical than exciting.

"Cougar?" Aden mouthed to me.

I didn't know. All I knew was that she was probably worth millions with a house on this island and the way she flirted led me to believe that she was either a divorcee or a widow or an adulterer—or maybe the town slut sick of wrinkles? Either way I did my best to hold back. She even went so far as to invite me back to her picnic for some food though I kindly denied her request. But that didn't matter—the day was clear and almost perfect.

We eventually pulled ourselves away though, mostly by request of Leo and Barry's body language screaming, *"I don't want to be here."* We sampled all the nearby casseroles as we walked out, this time a little more carefully.

"That old lady was pretty after you?" Faith teased me.

"Maybe."

I actually regretted not seeing where a little flirting could have taken me. I told everyone I should have let her be my sugar momma.

"I would live on the beach all day and have her order me massages and I'd eat like a king and she'd fly me around the world I tell ya."

"Yeah but then you'd have to sleep with an old woman," Leo noticed.

"Yeah true—but then he'd get to sleep with an older woman," Aden retorted and we all smiled.

We ate quickly before taking the ferry and leaving. It was a Greek restaurant right on the river. It had a beautiful bumper sticker on the cash register that read, *"I'd rather be in Ann Arbor."* The owner was a Michigan Alumni so Aden finagled something free or extra for our meals. He always does this—but it's easier when he has something in common with the victim.

"Let's make this the best night of our lives," he said to me slurping cucumber sauce into his mouth.

"Always," I said.

And I wish that would have been true. God I wish that would have been true.

Chapter 9

SHE WORE A WHITE DRESS. I touched the raw of her knee with my left forefinger softly at first while smiling and listening to her story. Her hair fell gently over the passion lines of her cheekbones; they were stuck in place but kind in their curvature — welcoming her chin like a perfectly shaded blend of highlighted elegance — her skin, bone colored and sharp; she carried healthy shockingly red lips. And that was the only makeup she seemed to flaunt, a luscious rosy mouth echoing the lights of the bar. She placed her hand on mine and pressed my whole hand down tighter against her thigh, just high enough to arouse me if I hadn't already been so deep under the spell of her words.

"I can't imagine being able to do what I want," she said slowly rotating her wrist and glass, swirling the ice and vodka leisurely. I was mesmerized so noticed the evident tan line of a ring on *that* left finger as she carefully watched the ice circle round and round — sliding tight against the glass over and over.

"I just got a text from my sister and she doesn't want to watch my son anymore so I'll have to take a cab all the way back to Silverside soon and then backtrack again past the bus stations. She doesn't care though — it's not like I only get one night out every month?"

She continued — "I'm looking good though — I think? Ever since my son was born I had to fight to get off this weight and now I can only go out once a month and his father won't have anything to do with him but mostly because I won't let him. He's such a horrible man — or boy — he's a horrible child that wouldn't know responsibility if it punched him in the face. I don't want him near Joey even though he offered to take him this week."

She flicked my belt with the palm of her right pinky finger saying all of this not for pity or attention—but deliberately, like she needed someone to listen—just to listen and nothing else. She had heard my story already so knew I wouldn't be a threat for sex nor would I go blabbing to someone she might know. I was a barstool stranger just interested enough for her to let loose. She wet her lips and mimicked me holding her left hand while reaching for my right. On her attempt I leaned in close with my upper body and kissed her cheek faintly with my jaw resting parallel to hers, holding the position just long enough, like a hug without arms. Then she bent back into me and we kissed softly, my thumb holding up her neck, my middle finger near the bottom of her ear. It was calm and emotional for just a moment. But the music kept loud in the background and the laser lights were blinding my depth perception—so the only clear sense was touch—just my lips and hers and this beautiful tainted mother with her heart collapsing down into my hands for just tonight.

"I hope one day that I'll be able to travel," she said looking at me, "the way you do. I'll take Joey around the world and show him everything."

She smiled just that once.

She was hopeful in her frostless beauty, in her blank dress and her fluorescently corporal skin, and she kissed me again. I was happy to see her out though I thought of Andrea all the while. I actually hadn't known her name nor cared for it, not really, I only knew that she had been sitting at the bar alone when we arrived—one of those too-pretty girls much lonelier than everyone expects, a too-soon mother "looking good" for the night. I had sat next to her and asked her if she would order me a drink very coyly and she smirked and asked what I was having. She was a magazine sort of pretty with green pulsating eyes and supple everything—on that barstool alone. I spoke with her then for only an hour, but already knew she deserved more than a messy mix of dried puke and television shows and arguments with baby sitters and even the warmth of a San Diego sun couldn't break her chill. So I'd like to think that she needed that kiss on that barstool with me—at least I hoped she needed me—I hoped that someone did.

I watched her eyes flicker back and forth from mine to the glass, to the bartender, and then back to me again. And for a moment I thought of running away back to her place but instead I just kissed her sympathetically, and sadly, for the very last time.

"And what are you going to do about it, huh bitch?" Smack — Aden went heavy into the bar protecting himself from a tornado of wildly flailing hands.

"I'm sorry," I whispered to the girl in the white dress, squeezing her hand tightly like I meant it. "I think my friend needs me. I hope you have a wonderful life. I truly hope you have a wonderful life and all your dreams come true," I said.

She turned down methodically, crossing her legs, knowing that that was the end — swirl went the vodka, melting ice, and a simple white dress once again lonely at the bar.

"What's going on?" I asked Aden. The bouncer was peeling an angry girl off of him.

Aden laughed a big hearty laugh and smiled while saying, "Oh she wanted to sit on the stool I was sitting on and I wouldn't move so she freaked out and started hitting me."

I assumed there was more to the story but didn't care to ask. No matter the circumstance I was always on Aden's side.

"Oh yeah? — you OK? She clock you one?"

"Nah man — pretty fucked up though huh? Some people are just so violent."

"Let's get out of here. Where is Barry?"

"Oh I think he's outside — he found some tall black girl to make out with or something or another."

"Right."

Barry was indeed making out with a girl who rather looked like a transvestite but maybe Barry was into that sort of thing? We found Faith outside of the bar and Leo not long after. Kara and Jarod had already shuffled back to the hotel room a few hours earlier to have some privacy before all our drunken noise came storming back in with bad breath and half eaten late-night burritos spilling on the floor. Leo looked a little unhappy about Kara sleeping with Jarod—he had assumed he had earned a weekend full of sheet rumbling with Kara because of the night before. But Kara is a big girl and made her own decisions. He shrugged his whole body for the rest of the night.

"Let's get some pizza or something," said Faith. She was drunker than Aden or I at this point.

"Sounds good."

"I agree."

So we walked down the gas lamp district of San Diego, with bars enveloping the loud air—surrounded by hair gel and dashing good looks without tan lines, with the Mexicans and their ocean smells—all of us walking towards the pizza. We stopped, noticing the absence of Leo and Barry and saw them standing at another corner chatting with two girls. We gave them a few moments in their attempts at flirting but wouldn't wait much longer than that.

Just then a short man with gold chains around his neck and an obviously hairy chest yelled at the bouncer of the adjacent bar. We laughed at him inwardly—he was angry that he had been kicked out of the bar, or that he couldn't get in—he was so random in his speech I wouldn't have known the difference either way.

"Fuck you man!" he shouted. "Fuck you and your stupid ass mother fucking haircut and you think you are something special out there in your tight black shirt like a faggot huh? Yeah you! Yeah I'm talking to you ya' faggot!"

I looked at Aden chuckling under my breath so as not to anger him further. He continued—"Yeah it's alright though you twat—I got the biggest swinging dick out here man. Yeah chief—I got a big old Cuban dick that I can use and you just have that small little white pecker. Soy Cubano mother fucker! Big dick yeah!"

"Can I see it?" Faith asked.

This was a terrible decision on her part. The proper action for dealing with angry Cubans with large penises is to walk away. *"Just walk away,"* I hear my mom telling me. Faith was a little too drunk though and therefore felt overly confident. And in knowing that she wouldn't *really* have to deal with any of this if things got dirty, I immediately resented her stupidity.

"Que bonita? What do you want? You want to see my dick…my big dick?" he said having fun with her.

"Yeah," she continued with a challenging tone, "I mean if you got the biggest dick ever then I'd like to see it. If it really is *that* big like you say?"

"Are you listening to her cabron?" he asked me and Aden. "You better keep your woman in check," he said while slowly turning his head to the side.

"I'm nobody's woman," she said egging him on. I stood back passively but screamed in my head *"shut the fuck up!"* I didn't know what she was trying to prove and I had no desire to defend her lack-of honor with a stranger when all I wanted was some pizza.

"Everything is fine man," Aden offered.

"Obviously it is not fucking fine you mother fucker. I said keep your bitch in check," he shouted red, getting right in Aden's face.

Aden tried the Zen approach—"I'm not interested in trouble my friend but I would appreciate it if you didn't call my friend a bitch."

"Ahhh puta! Que me dices? Soy Cubano! Soy Cubano! Voy a matarte puta!" This roughly translates to "blah blah I'm going to kill you" but he didn't know that Aden and I spoke enough Spanish to understand.

Aden responded in Spanish — "You have no reason to kill me. No reason at all."

This was quite sensible I thought. Though the Cuban did not agree.

He jumped at Aden with his hand fiercely clutched around Aden's neck and drove him back a few paces. Aden did some jujitsu move to free himself from the hold almost immediately but the quickness of the violence startled all of us — Aden especially. The Cuban's friends ran towards him and pulled him away. They dragged him away, him still screaming in Spanish about his big dick and killing people and what a mess of a human being, I thought.

We didn't say much after that. What is there to say? We walked back to our spot without pizza almost in shock. Faith felt bad as she should have and so apologized profusely in the elevator. Aden forgave her immediately before the door even opened. And upon arrival we realized there were only soft spots for six people so someone would have to sleep on the floor. We played a rock-paper-scissors tournament to decide who would be relegated to just a pillow and the floor. Aden lost the game so curled up next to a few cushions and the hard floor.

That night Jarod had found Kara more intimately than just his friend's little sister and Leo something similar with her the night before. And I had my white dress. And Barry had won his multiple kisses throughout the night — and all of us had our own beds.

Aden though, had been hit twice by two angry locals and had only the cold lonely ground for comfort. At this point he had no more than his pride and a forced grin — if that. Before I went to bed I saw him clutching his pillow more tightly than normal as he sunk down into his dreams. I wished I knew his thoughts for that night. What ran through his head under the phantom wind of San Diego?

What happens after life smacks you right in the heart?

+

THE ROAD BACK NORTH towards Santa Barbara felt comfortable for me. I drove this time, always slower than Aden would have, but I got us there safely anyways. I obeyed the speed limit religiously because I hardly cared about any other law — so I figured I owed the police at least some respect (but just some).

When we arrived in LA once more we dropped off the boys, saying farewell to Barry and Leo clumsily, incidentally, as if we *had to*. It wasn't that we weren't interested in them — it was just that we were more interested in the new roads ahead of us. So we said goodbye too harshly, too quickly — it felt too definite. See — the best goodbyes are on their way out the door before we even say hello, because at least those ones don't hurt. Often goodbyes are brainwashed and repetitive and feel insincere between families. But worst of all — is when goodbye is the only thing left to say.

No matter, we curved around the winding 1 into Santa Barbara and at the very last minute found a couchsurfer who would take us in. We stopped to shake his hand and introduce ourselves properly, but only for a few moments before asking for a suggestion for food.

"Well that's an easy choice," Steve said, "You have to go to Free Bird's burrito joint."

He was a musician which fit for Santa Barbara. He reminded me of a singer-songwriter look-alike with a scruffily beard, unshaven, but well kept enough. He was about my height, blue-eyed and incredibly casual about opening up his house. If you had told me he locked his doors, ever, I would have needed video evidence to believe you. I don't remember there even *being* doors at his house.

There was a bum of sorts living in his garage, and two English chaps from Liverpool who looked and sounded like a punk version of The Beatles stayed there as well — and three tremendously polite Scandinavian, who described themselves as "wilderness dudes," they were sleeping on the floor. That was a well thought out nine people including our four staying in Steve's house that night — all of us strangers with the doors wide open. Aden would sleep in the hammock for fun.

Later I would use this exact scenario to prove in conversations that in fact people *can* be trusted if you aren't frightened by the idea of using a dirty shower every once in a while.

But that's neither here nor there.

Free Bird's lived up to the hype. It was a glorious pageantry of college students and fresh vegetables, fried onions, beans, and slippery rice all rolled into a perfectly wrapped chicken stuffed piece of heaven. I ordered two of them, a few pounds each, and scared them down my throat against my whiskers like a hollowing sea lion. And I did indeed have whiskers — whiskers and a blanket wrapped around me in the restaurant. My shoes had countless holes on the bottoms of them and the sides and all around the tops of them too, shredded from hiking without proper boots. And my face was unshaven since going out in San Diego a few days earlier and who knew wearing the same shorts for a week was something to be ashamed of? I had been sleeping in the car from LA to Santa Barbara after Aden switched to drive, fetal style in an oversized blanket. We had walked to the restaurant a few blocks from Steve's house and it hadn't occurred to me that I should probably leave the blanket behind. So there I was draped, blanket over my head, looking like a ragtag nun ordering my food.

"Do you need some help with something? Do you have a place to stay?" a student asked me as I walked out of the restaurant with my two towering burritos in hand.

"No. Yeah. We're staying just up the street. Thanks though," I said quickly.

"You just cold or something? What's up with the blanket?"

"I have no legitimate answer for you. I just brought it."

We walked back to Steve's house to sleep without any reason for being there either. We had heard that Santa Barbara was nice but there were a lot of nice places. We chose our lives based upon the happenstance of the strangers we met and the taste of the next town; neither money nor expectation led us — just the road always passing. So we walked in the middle of the street that blessed night, double fisting food bags because there were no cars and if there had been, we'd just have scampered out of the way — the glowing street light and my foot stepping, stepping, another foot stepping, and on to Steve's house just because we could.

+

ANDREA AND I BOTH enjoyed the vibrations of electronic music. It was something that connected us. So one day we went to a house party in Ann Arbor that had promised a DJ and "good times." Aden, a few other friends, Andrea, and I all walked there together not chiefly soberly, but sober *enough* by college standards.

Andrea lifted her hands into the air as she always did, enjoying the music as she always does, not knowing that the whole time I was planning my escape. This was a "college relationship" after all — "it won't last" I had told myself. So as she sat there, away from me, gliding with the music, me dancing halfheartedly — knowing all the while that this was the end — that this quite possibly would be the last time that we'd dance together.

On the walk back to her apartment she stumbled drunkenly, annoyingly even, unsure of how to get home. I talked to Aden a few hundred feet in front her, checking only every so-often to make sure she was still behind us, but without much real care. I left her there, a few hundred feet behind me, her clinging to one of our mutual friends — purposefully not holding her hand.

"You are an ass!" she shouted to me upon finally arriving at her apartment.

"I know."

"You avoided me all night! You didn't even walk me back. Good thing my other friends were there otherwise I would have never been able to walk home!" she said again for emphasis.

"I know."

"Why don't you want to hold my hand? Are you embarrassed by me?" She wasn't really asking for an answer. We had had that conversation many times before. It wasn't about me holding her hand — it was about me *caring*.

"I don't know," I said solemnly.

"It's like you don't even care about me! You know there are plenty of guys who would love to…"

"I know," I interrupted her. "You are perfect. You *are*. You are absolutely perfect but…well…I don't know. I'm sorry. I am drunk too."

I couldn't bear to tell her the truth. I couldn't. As we walked down that lonely road together in the dead of night, her painfully stumbling behind me, I couldn't bear to hold her hand. I couldn't bear to hold her up. Because I knew that soon enough — she would have to hold herself up. I knew that she would soon be all alone.

+

WE HAD A QUICK breakfast and met a few of Steve's neighbors who had never seen snow. This was unfathomable to me — that someone had never seen snow. Maybe in the third world where you can't get away but in the suburban beach that is Santa Barbara it wreaked of laziness more than anything. Sure the beach is difficult to leave, but at some point you'd want to know what it feels like to shiver right?

We spent all day at the beach, this one rocky — reading, playing catch, writing in journals and splashing in the water. But we soon decided to leave the beach and all agreed never to return. We had packed a week of sand into every crevice of our pours; our souls seeped of dry shells, and so too we needed to feel something bigger, like a mountain.

We ended up at a Cajun restaurant and ordered fancy dishes like stuffed crab and unpronounceable cheese appetizers and local brews. It was an expensive ordeal but we had been eating only fried taco-stand type meals for the better part of a week now, so thought our tastes deserved a slight tinge of refinement. Aden chatted up the waitress enough that the owner came out and gave us all free dessert in honor of our road trip and we promised him, "cross my heart," that we'd visit his favorite spots in New

Orleans when we got there—if we ever got there. In fact Aden's panache was the reason we were able to eat in the first place.

"This place was recommended to us by the locals and at this hour the only things left are the Subways and McDonalds. You can't have us come all the way to California, home of the best Cajun food this side of the Mississippi, without tasting greatness?" he insisted to the hostess just as she was locking the door.

"I promise we have no intention of staying here well past anyone else—we'll eat fast and above all, we're incredible tippers," I added.

So we ate in glory and clanked the bottom edges of our beer bottles in celebration. We toasted to our journey thus far and to all the journeys to come. We toasted to the restaurant and to our waitress and to the owner and the free dessert—the comfortable seats we sat in and the clothes on our backs. We toasted to California and Iowa, maybe even Michigan if I remember correctly—and our incredible tans. We toasted to the new people we'd meet and the ones we already had met and to all the strangers that let us into their homes. We toasted to road trips and real freedom and Los Angeles even. We toasted to America in the big sense and toasted to the sheer awesomeness of being alive and how Americans always use that word "awesome" too. We toasted to our shared love of music and wine. We toasted to our families, hopefully they weren't lonely, and to the people who stick around in places for real long times and to the travelers that get to meet them. We toasted above all to each other. We did this all before taking our first bite.

"To life," I had said modestly. And we all agreed on at least that.

After that we entered a nameless bar full of people and ordered our drinks and thankfully split up. It wasn't that I was sick of Kara and Faith—their enthusiasm was gladly appreciated every step of the way. In fact I was more eager to see Barry and Leo gone than them, to have the four of us back together, just the four of us. We of course had spent less than 10 days total with the girls but us four together, it felt natural. So splitting up, even for a night, simply gave Aden and me a chance to have a heart to heart talk, an honest one that would have otherwise been tainted by the presence of any female, with egos and impressions and our insecurities getting in the way (of course). But it was just us now, so none of that debris mattered. It couldn't have even if it wanted to.

"I think I have it figured out," he said as we sat down adjacent to the stools at an empty table. The band was blasting away so we had to speak loudly but not to the point of shouting. I faced the sound and gently nodded my head more in agreement with the beat than anything Aden was going to say.

He started — "Girls in general want a man to be strong — sexually strong — they want to be led in the right direction and told that it is OK for them to want sex."

"What?" I asked.

"Well just hear me out." — He immediately felt defensive although I didn't intend for him to feel such. "It's a simple biological switch. Girls always want to have a male in their life right?"

"Outside of lesbians, etcetera, yes I agree — I guess, as do males want to have a female," I concurred.

"For the history of time the girl has been in environments for the most part where she has had to choose which male she wants. It's all over nature man — when does the girl do a fancy dance for the guy's attention? Never. And here's the thing, we all are still doing a bunch of fancy dances with pick-up lines and showing off our cars and being generally the alpha male — or trying to be. Right? But the thing is that none of that matters if females don't exist. We'd probably be all just scratching our balls and playing football or something," he chuckled, "but what has happened lately is that girls have a million options that they didn't once have. A male bird needs to do a fancy dance for the females because he has to compete with the four other birds doing the same thing right?"

"Right."

"This makes sense. Fanciest dance wins. But nowadays girls are fairly sick of fancy dances. They want honesty."

"As opposed to...?"

"If you are at a bar and you are dressed halfway decent you probably have enough income to be sufficient and girls are forgiving on physical appearance in general because we're all pretty unattractive as a sex outside of a few exceptions and a lot of the times those sorts of handsome guys are gay anyways — well that's not the point — the point is that girls are sick of everyone playing around and showing off. They are turned off by it. Now we are just one of a million dancing birds so if we want to be noticed we have to stand still. If there were still four of us out there like thousands of years ago in a tribe and we didn't do the little dance then the girl would think 'why aren't you dancing?' — and then we'd be doomed, but now it's different. To stand out we have to be honest about what we want and just come out and say it — we have to stand still, and demand their attention — almost stoic."

I looked at him for a while without saying anything but cocked my eyes upwards to show that I was in fact thinking of a response. I listened to the band play, the crowd growing larger with every passing minute. We'd soon have to speak louder and I knew it. But that was OK — I wanted to anyways.

"I'm right," he said sure of his assessment, generally logical as always.

I kept thinking and took a sip of my Rum and Coke. I thought about biology and the sexes, and the history of birds dancing — trying to come up with counter examples and even contemplated agreeing with him for the sake of leaving it at that. I knew he would think of some nearly contrary opinion the next week anyway. So I knew it didn't matter. I knew it deep down.

Though instead of reacting to all this with counter logic or an argumentative tone I very politely and genuinely asked him, "What are you missing?"

"What do you mean?"

I didn't want this to hurt more than it had to so I asked it in a different way—"What would you change about yourself so that more girls would react favorably to you?"

"Oh I don't know. But that's the point man—it doesn't matter—so long as you rock out honesty and love and just tell girls how you feel in an honest way they'll react favorably. They want sex just as much as we do."

"Sure. That is true they do. But what is the point Aden? I'm being vague here on purpose and I don't want to give you the run around but very plainly—what is all this analyses going to bring do you think? What are you really after?"

"I want to be able to walk in a room and know that I could have every girl in there. I want to be the life of the party and I want to spread love and leave everyone better off for having met me. I want to show girls that they don't have to be worried about their sexuality and we should all just let loose."

"OK. I want that too. 'Free love!' I'm all about it. I get it man. I really do. I even get what you are saying about being honest because god knows I don't believe in guys and girls being friends and I vocalize it to nearly everyone I meet. You know this and I know it too and I think being honest rather than jumping head first into the 'friend zone' with a girl you are secretly crazy for is not only stupid but also counterproductive for the end goal—which is to *be* with her. I get it. I agree with you—mostly. We may argue about how to approach said honesty but that's a longer discussion but that's not what any of this is about really. Is it? This is about you and what you have to offer and I promise you brother—I promise you more than anything in this world that you have more to offer than your honesty."

"Of course I agree man—which is why I need to be more honest so that I can be more accessible and then I'll be more successful and therefore I'll be able to show them all that I have to offer. We're on the same page here."

"No we're not," I said sternly. "You are not on the same page as me. My page reads that Aden is a hell of a human being that I am proud to call my best friend. My page reads that you have so much beauty seeping from within you that any girl would be psycho-ward loony not to jump in bed with you if even for the *chance* that you might want to be with her exclusively. You would rain down so much happiness and selflessness and love upon her — god man I know it — and I feel it deep down and I want that for you so desperately."

I yelled at him like a seasoned orator — "...But you aren't going to find anything unless you stop this bullshit crusade to figure it all out. There is nothing to figure out. There is boy and there is girl. There is you and there is her and if you think that all you have to offer her is free love and honesty and a bunch of other meaningless trite than you had better get used to being lonely because that's all you'll give them. It's like your rushing around in a beautiful mansion with your eyes closed trying to feel your way out, thinking you are lost in a cave, when all you have to do is open your fucking eyes and you'll realize you are already above ground."

He knew I was serious by my tone and I complimented him too feverously for him not to react anything but humbly. So I wasn't surprised when he nervously tapped his finger and said, "Yeah but I'm not like you."

"Fuck that," I interrupted him.

"No seriously man," he interrupted me right back, "we are seriously different. I don't know any of *this*. I don't know how any of *this* works." He gestured towards the room in a very general sense, pointing at random people and even making a circle with his index finger between the two of us.

"I don't get this social stuff. I am learning on the job here. I mean fuck — I've never had a girlfriend. I've never even had a girl really like me. You know man, listen, I know you grew up and your mom made you order meals for the whole family so you could get practice talking to strangers. I know that your mom would never speak on your behalf even when you were a toddler and tell people to speak directly to you instead. You were bred to be a social butterfly, comfortable and unafraid in the face of enormous social obstacles — but I didn't have that. I had a situation in which I couldn't get a word in edgewise without my mother freaking out. She's a drama queen and my dad wasn't all that social either and I was the only white kid in the whole town so fuck man — I'm just not like you. It's not all so easy to me. So I have to try and figure this out. You are basically saying, 'just be yourself,' but I don't know what that is. I don't know how to portray what that is. I don't know."

This was heavy so I sat back in my chair rather openly and responded, "Doesn't matter."

"It does matter!"

"Does. Not. Matter." I repeated emphatically above him. "For all your double talk you seem to be doing pretty damn well for yourself. You think Faith and Kara are here because of me? Do you think everyone we meet reacts favorably because my mom demanded I make a fool of myself in public just so I got used to it? Do you think that has anything to do with anything? It doesn't. I'm social — I agree — but no more than you. I couldn't be or else I'd be annoyed with your silence — and you'd be annoyed with me talking so much. Do you think I'm the alpha between you and me? False. False and false again. You decide where we are going to go and what we are going to do much more often than I do. I'm sick of this 'I don't have social skills' crap because that's what it is — it's crap. People *like* you. Get over it. Girls *like* you. Get over it. I almost think you are too scared to just put yourself out there as Aden, because you are afraid of getting rejected in the real way. See — if you hide behind these books and theories and systems and logical conclusions about what girls will like and how they will react, it's easier. Because if something doesn't work you can say 'oh I guess that method didn't work' rather than thinking 'that sucks that she doesn't like me.' Well listen — she won't like you. Another one will and another one will and another one will and then the next one won't and you're just going to have to get used to it. I am. The only girl I've ever loved is off painting the town red with a new boyfriend and I'm dead inside to every female I encounter. Fucking dead in the ground, numb, dead — to everyone. And it sucks. It sucks badly and it hurts but I don't regret any of it because she knows who I am and I her and not like something you 'know' from a book or something you read online. What you need to realize is that you have it. You already have it. Own it. Know it. And stop thinking so much—stop moving chess pieces around—stop over-thinking every step you make and just acknowledge that you have your shit together in a way that is more than attractive to females. I promise you—I promise you promise you—that if you 'try' anything, anything at all with a girl, she'll sniff it out like a bloodhound. The more you try the more you'll fail. The best quarterbacks for example—you think they are thinking about every detailed step of the proper throwing motion or do you think they are just chucking the ball the way they know how? They are chucking the damn ball and it always ends up being a perfect spiral because that's just how they throw. They couldn't throw any other way and if they tried to, they'd probably just fuck it up. Well, you are fucking it up by thinking. So stop. You already know how to talk to girls. You are already attractive and the fact that we are having this conversation is annoying."

Obviously my reaction warranted a response but Aden seemed perplexed. He didn't know whether to be angry or silent or what—and I had no idea which he'd choose.

"Thank you," he said almost under his breath more quickly than I expected.

And then after some time without much talk, after we had closed our eyes to let the music and the moment trickle in real deep, to think about the power of our conversation, I held up my glass as did Aden for one last toast.

"To life," Aden said modestly. I smiled knowing that we both could agree on at least that.

We rounded up the girls and—farther and farther north.

+

I DROVE ALONE, STRAIGHT through the vacant night, up a carving sultry rode twisting inside and outside of itself. I blasted the music noisy with the windows down, with the fiery storm swooping around and turned back and forth in my seat swaying and tapping the steering wheel tight. I felt the physical forces of momentum through every hard turn, but Aden and Kara and Faith just bobbled back and forth sleeping as I cranked the car around the next bend and onto the next, only narrowly missing the semi-truck barking towards me, and hush, listen to the thunder, and the stabbing headlamps and the night—towering shrubs and breakneck tree trunks and the bursting wet objects to come, all tempting me past the yellow lines, towards the grass, if only to see what would happen.

What happens when we leave the well-laden path, I wondered? What would happen if everything ended just now? What of LA and California? Would they miss me?

So I became tired and worried for California just then. I wasn't sure where I was on that putrid highway, hurrying towards Yosemite, just that I was somewhere north of where I was just moments before. And so I thought about God and Aden and life, all alone. And I became spiritual in that moment, as if I had been spontaneously born again there in the front seat of the Saab. The road was my church—so I prayed to the next exit, that it would love me like a savior on Sunday.

Chapter 10

"THERE IS WATER," ADEN pointed, exhausted, and anxious.

"Oh god finally," I coughed.

We had been hiking for the better part of the morning and ran out of water much sooner than we had expected. We were possibly off the trail. We actually didn't know considering how casual the park rangers had distinguished our "trail" from other random clearings. Everything in Yosemite looked like a new trail, each direction called to our curiosities, leaving us saying things like, "I mean—that looks kinda like a path right?" And then we'd all somehow collectively agree that yes, that thing could possibly be a path and that was just fine. The foliage wasn't thick enough to discriminate a cliff from a bear, an enormous elk from its vast grassland, even a stream from the raging rapids.

Yosemite causes disorientation and a peaceful upside down feeling—like everything is in its proper place except for you.

"Do you think it's safe to drink?" I asked Aden stupidly as if he would know.

The water was just a trickling brook and so fell softly, plump, from a bending leaf. Aden pointed out something fairly obvious while gesturing grandly towards the valley below—"I think this has got to be about as clean of mountain water as you can get. Come on now—all the bottled water companies print pictures on their bottles that look just like this to advertise how fresh and pure their water is. Granted they probably get their water from the same water tanks that we wash our dishes with but for marketing purposes ya know?— *this* type of scene—right here without electricity for hundreds of miles—this type of scene is exactly where we can supposedly get clean water, no? If this water gets me sick I've lost all faith in humanity."

"OK I'm convinced," I agreed patiently while holding my empty plastic bottle under the leaking leaf.

The water was see-through and therefore twinkled in the sunlight. I drank an exasperated, gulping portion into my innards and it felt cool beneath my neck. I felt refreshed—and not just physically. Everything came up and into my head and out the top—the crunching motion of the sticks snapping beneath my heavy feet—and the vaulting trees protecting me from monotony. It was a nice moment, drinking from the Earth and not a store.

Aden drank too and we refilled for the girls and yelled for them still a few hundred paces behind us.

"I saw a sign back there for bears," Faith told us in her short shorts and blue tank top. She trudged along with Kara a little scared of the wild animals and the unexpected sounds, but she was still confident in stride, holding a stick out in front of her like an old mountain climber ready to conquer the world.

"I think I saw the same sign," Aden said sternly. "And it's pretty safe to say we are off the path at this point—I think we should head back to where we started from and see if we can't get to Half Dome before sunset."

And off we went because that's what we do when Aden suggests something—we listen and we go.

The trail weaved throughout the burly trunks quite quickly. All the greens blended in beside the pink berries. We scuffled beneath overhanging vines that swung down almost at us, like a Tarzan movie set. We trudged and followed our way up the dirt and banged sticks together next to enormous, impossibly cut boulders. We even ran sometimes too, or what I mean is that *I* ran sometimes with Aden yelling at me to slow down and enjoy the scenery, and I'd yell back at him that I was, and then I'd soar and squawk on top of overturned monster-trees, gnarled from time.

I love to climb. So I played in nature's playground, scuffing the insides of my palms all the way down deep past my skin, chalk white stickiness, and the blood flowing up my wrist with the smashed bug juice—and then mountaineering to the bottom of the crater only to see if I could scramble back up towards safety. Aden simply walked the path with a walking stick—but I, instead, saw the world outstretched in front of me like a recreational area without boundaries—like a heavy rush.

We were on our way to Half Dome unsure why except that a sign had pointed us there, when we saw an overhanging cliff jutting out almost like an island in the air.

"Does that just shoot up like that?" Aden asked perplexed, "Or is it attached to the rest of the mountain?"

"I don't know," I said honestly. We had been walking on the northern, high edge of Yosemite with a thousand foot cliff to our left—the likes of which base jumpers would drool over. It was a sheer flat face, like a vertical runway pointing straight down, except that the small peninsula, near to our eyesight, appeared to float away from the rest of the stretching overhang. We wanted to go there and could see it, but hadn't the expertise for a proper touch. None of us were seasoned rock climbers, after all.

After some close encounters with the escalating crag, leaning outwards in attempts to find a passageway farther south or lying down flat with only our heads leaning beyond the point of solid ground, we grew weary of what was about to be attempted: the sheer vastness of the fall, the shielded heart beat for those of us who dream of the great leap of faith, who want to jump, but then don't, and then think "what if," and then don't, and that's why we are afraid of heights, I thought—not because we are afraid we'll fall, but because we are afraid we'll jump.

But there was a way. There is always a way, I thought.

"Come here," Kara yelled from behind a towering tree rooted only in half the ground, the other half was floating in the air, just the air and a clean drop. She hung onto one of the branches quite literally for her life and said, "If we balance ourselves out to that flat space right over there, we could use the roots of that bush to climb up to that rock right there. Granted we'd have to be careful not to pull ourselves up too strongly or we'll go careening off the other side, but it looks just wide enough once we get on top — think of it like a balance beam — then we'll all be able to fit on that peninsula looking thing, over there near the edge. Wanna go?"

Near the edge. Near the edge. It was unwisely dangerous and "off the path" without argument. It was a death that the park rangers wouldn't lose a wink of sleep over...

"*Serves'em right,*" *the old mountain man would whisper to the other. "If you are trying an uneven balancing act with a thousand feet down on both sides and you fall — guess what'll happen? You'll die. Stupid kids.*"

And sure we *were* stupid kids but the edge called to us still, like a poem in the wind, like the cusp of history, like it meant something — as if it were actually important. So we did it despite the danger — one by one traversing the edge, holding on tightly to whatever we had left of ourselves, and we leaned on one another, and got a little dirty along the way, and almost fell down a few times, we slipped, and we gritted our teeth down hard — and it wasn't easy and I was deathly afraid the whole time but to the delight of the gods and the stars we made it. So we sat there on the edge of that cliff, with the world empty beneath our feet in all directions, with all the angles of the universe sprawling out in front of us and we hugged one another because that's what you do when the world ends — you hug one another.

We had found it — that blurry line between the bitter cold of our fear and the shining glare of a dream come true — that eternal line between the hopes of our parents and the youth of our peers — we finally found that line, sitting the on the edge of California, the edge of America.

But even that wasn't enough. It never is. Nothing is ever "enough." See — we had to kiss the top of the sky! We were told that Half Dome was the flagship attraction of Yosemite — "a view to end all views" — or something or another. So we hiked farther — a seemingly endless hike of grunts and jumps and the trickling condensation of our will dripped from our foreheads bit by bit, drop by drop, until we were left almost empty —

asking ourselves if it was all worth it, asking ourselves if we had the capability to fight through. Miles and miles, up and up, and it never seemed to come.

"We must have wandered to the other side of the national park because I feel like we've been hiking for hours by now and I still haven't seen a sign saying we're going in the right direction," Kara lamented while sitting on an overturned log, dirtying her backside with maggots and bird poop.

More important than her shame was her rest. See — she heaved heavier than the rest of us and so stopped every half-mile complaining of dehydration. It was a warranted concern, but I didn't care in my athleticism. I was impatient with her needs — the slow methodical way to which she labored up every step like it hurt. She bothered me probably for the first time just then — and so I smiled inwardly thinking that I had finally found her flaw. It made her more human and therefore more likeable.

Stop for Kara, and then go farther, then stop for Kara, then go farther — though eventually we did find that sign and she was right. We had originally gone in the wrong direction which is why it took so long, but after an entire day's worth of climbing we finally came to the final step, the final hike — the part where you can see the top with your eyes and so yearn deeply to feel it with your touch. The peak was still a good half-mile more and as is the case with all challenges, the end of the hike arced more steeply than anything we had previously encountered. So we stood there staring up towards the path in front of us. I started jogging up it if only to reach the end quicker. Aden yelled at me again to slow down and enjoy the view.

"The view is from the top Aden — the view is from the top!" I yelled back at him still running up the now rocky path.

"I thought it was about the journey?" I heard Aden ask rhetorically, faintly in my peripheral.

It was in fact about the journey, I knew that, but I had already been journeying for the entire day, with views of animals and erect trees and humbling valleys and I felt it, I got it, though now I wanted to get to our destination. I wanted to be done with all my journeying.

And it's always the same right before a destination during travel, when we attach ourselves solidly to the more obvious reasons for going somewhere. Sure the café in Paris with the funny little dog and that crimson red beauty in the corner is something we may remember on a day of leisure—but on our way to the Eiffel Tower we don't notice anything a block away. We can't. It's obvious why we are there. We're not there for the scenery—we're there for the goddamned Eiffel Tower.

So too I continued running, leaving them all behind and so got to the top quicker than I had expected. I looked around and it was in fact a sight worth seeing—it was in fact the highest point, the top of the mountain—so I understood why there was an older couple there with me, even if they *had* driven most of the way up. They at least made the final hike under their own feet and that was admirable for old people. I looked and looked but more observed than felt anything. I then peered back down and saw Aden a quarter mile away still walking towards me in the sky and even farther down was Faith and Kara sitting, resting. I saw Faith's arm around Kara's, their heads together resting on each other—Aden all alone. So I took one last glance at the blue and at the old couple, and ran back down towards my friends.

I realized just then that the view was in fact just a view, and consequently more representative than anything else, representative of something, call it the journey, sure, sounds good—but certainly this moment was more about being with my friends than candy for my eyes.

I only quickly acknowledged Aden with, "let's go help Kara," because I knew he'd understand me—all of me.

When we arrived at her still half sitting, she looked up at me gaunt and obviously perturbed with the entire situation. "We should have brought water," she said. "This is dangerous and my legs are burning."

She spoke sternly, as if we were her children and didn't want to wear our coats in the winter. I didn't say anything though. I just cusped her shoulder gently so she would understand my sentiments through my touch, without words. I knew I had been selfish in running ahead, in pushing everyone faster and faster. I thought I was doing them a service at the time—allowing them to feel the world as I do, all swift and hectic, without pause for self-critique. It was a difficult, very difficult moment of calm for me just then. I could feel the outsides of my molecules bursting at their seams, like a crowded anxiousness, and a part of me still wanted to run back up to the top and leave them all behind—but my hand stayed with Kara. I looked at Faith and hugged her with my free arm and they knew what I said. They knew I was sorry. And in a lot of ways their forgiveness was bigger than they knew.

"You know guys," I said this time out loud, "I'm really glad we are all here together."

They all nodded inwardly with their heads still down towards the ground, all of them exhausted but in complete alignment. So we walked slowly this time, together. And it took quite a while and we stopped at least three more times until we reached the top, but we reached it together no less—so the view sparkled much brighter than before.

+

THAT NIGHT I RESPECTFULLY asked our neighbors at the campsite for fire wood. We had forgotten to buy some, and in our pitch black searches we came back to the pit with only thick sticks—nothing that could be considered real solid wood. They were senior citizens, probably grandparents though I didn't ask, but looked at me like I was there equal. Worse even, I felt as if their lingering eyes looked down upon me—and not in a manner of superiority, but rather like a mountain climber who after reaching the top looks down upon those below with envy—wanting to do it all over again. The old man saw my youth in each blundering step I took, and heard the politeness of my tone, and so spoke to me gently and straight, like a man who knew he was near the end of his life—like a sage giving advice to a youngster. His wife sat back in her seat holding his hand as I stood over them and smiled a great big smile with real trust and solitude—she was happy there in the woods with her husband, by the fire, taking it all in. I could tell.

I hauled a few logs at a time back to my site only a short walk east, taking their fuel and their fire, less for them and more for me, over and over, and they smiled again and again, each time feeling the metaphor deep within themselves. Their hands clutched stronger each time as they watched me in my strength and my enthusiasm take their fuel. I felt conflicted as I always do, in that moment, but in the end I relegated myself to the belief that they had already lived their full lives. I told myself that they had in fact already traversed their dreams and traveled their world, whatever it looked like back then, and came to their end together in the woods and therefore didn't mind passing their time in quiet observation.

Later that night after eating healthily over the fire and talking about feminism with Kara and Faith, which mostly means Kara and Aden arguing but hugging shortly thereafter, I took a swig of wine and thought of our old neighbors across the way.

"I think it is very nice that the old couple gave us their wood for the night. I'm going to go offer them a bottle of wine to show our appreciation. And maybe if they want to join us they will — I bet they'll have a lot of interesting stories," I told everyone not really asking.

When I arrived at them, bottle in hand, they were still touching, as if they were Siamese twins who knew that the surgery was possible but rather preferred the feeling of constant connection. I offered them our bottle and our company equally. They whole-body-grinned in delight without moving much — I could see it in their subtleties, in their quiet facial tics underneath all the wrinkles.

"Oh no," the gentlemen said stroking his white-white hair, "We don't drink anymore at this age. We've had our times."

He looked at his wife and she glowed understanding the inside joke and then continued — "But I do have something that I could offer *you*."

"Well you don't have to…I mean, I really appreciate the wood from before and…" I said but he didn't really hear me, already rummaging through his bags in the tent. I could see his silhouette like a shadow puppet dancing beyond the fire.

He came out palms up together, like he was taking communion and I was the priest. Resting gently upon his chapped fingers, from the tip all the way down towards his wrist, was a crystalline bud beautifully cared for, almost orange around the edges.

"You smoke right?" he asked me assuming the answer was yes. Before I could nod in agreement he giddily asked me another question — "They call this 100 Kush on the streets. Do you know why they call it 100 Kush young man?"

"I'm sorry sir but I don't."

"It's because on the street this is $100 an eighth!" he gleamed.

"Oh…right," I said almost confused. I didn't know if he was trying to sell it to me or just show it off or what?

"So yeah — I guess I can get some money from the car or…" I said. I was obviously perplexed and didn't really want to buy it but he was an old man and so I had to tread carefully so as not to offend him. Old people are treated like they don't know better, like children, except they do in fact know better. They just don't care. Old people can get away with anything.

"Oh no no no," he comforted me, "this is my gift to you. I'm old and retired and I get this stuff from my doctor and I have the money so don't you worry about it. Go take it to your friends and enjoy the night. But don't inhale too much right away — it'll hit you hard if you aren't careful with it. Take a puff and see how you feel, wait a few minutes, and then if you want to go higher up then take another puff. Remember this. I don't want you scaring yourself if you aren't used to California bud."

So there in Yosemite of all places, I had the best weed of my life, and for free no less. The gang was all pleasantly surprised as I retold the story full with voices and character development and wild gestures. I would get up from my seat to play myself and then I'd exaggerate the old man and his wife slumping around next to their camper and they all laughed watching me. I spoke loudly too, hoping the couple would hear, listening to themselves through my voice, seeing themselves through my eyes —

how wonderful they were and how they would soon be forever memorialized in story, I thought.

The air grew thick and the fire more smoky and gray and our minds wandered into each other and out of touch with reality. It was in fact too strong, as the old man had predicted. So it was an insecure high for all of us, a wakeup call if you will. See—in our altered states of consciousness we always attach ourselves to those whom we are most comfortable—and if not a person—those thoughts most comforting. Aden and I talked and joked while Faith and Kara did the same. We were all together but had only met weeks before and it showed.

Aden went to bed paranoid that Kara and Faith were judging him.

So I stared at the fire alone and listened to Faith's sultry music about heartbreak and lost love, letting her and Kara giggle to themselves with Aden already in the tent. I stared at the fire for hours actually, transfixed inside my own thoughts—no different than any other time. I thought about Andrea mostly and missed her ripe—I missed her like a fresh eulogy sitting in the pews of Yosemite. If I stared long enough into the fire, she would come back I thought, from across the land and away from this heat—into my arms like a cure for common sadness. No matter how deep our blood ran, Aden would never fill this hole. I was surrounded by those who cared about me, but no one who loved me enough to feel uncomfortable while saying it out loud as Andrea did.

See—Andrea rarely told me she loved me—knowing the word wasn't enough, as if the word cheapened the feeling. And I, in fact, *never* told her that I loved her because I was an adolescent and therefore immaturely stubborn—and stupid. But now I was able to listen to my heart and remember its name and analyze its purpose in ways I wasn't able to prior. I had previously locked it in a cage within my mind and told myself that my wife would be a good-enough-girl present at the right moment when it was most convenient to have children. I thought of love like a frozen left over to be taken seriously only if nothing else was available. But after some time my heart picked the lock of my psyche and started screaming loudly as if at war with my inflexible reason. So battle after battle, I warred with myself and my yearnings and shoved my desires down into the ground, all until they finally grew wings and flew higher than I was able to reach. So there I sat, a smoldering war zone of emotions, sore from the fight and a little bruised from the neck up, left with only one giant heartbeat, violently pounding out of my chest as if it was trying to pull me towards Andrea.

I leaned back in my chair and extended my right hand, palm up towards the empty seat next to me, and imagined Andrea holding on tight, the two of us white haired and wrinkled there together, giving our firewood to a youngster next door and asking him if he knew what 100 Kush was.

Chapter 11

SAN FRANCISCO ROLLS AWAY from the rest of California, even rolling away from itself like a scared armadillo with its rusty shell all curled for the weather. Its hills wave in all directions and its boulevards crisscross on plateaus just large enough for a few cars to settle on top of, just before jutting farther up or farther down, and there is the uneven earth too and flags spitting out of narrow houses. The San Francisco Valley tilts the houses ever so slightly down hill, as if everyone is constantly falling down, clinging to their pasts if only to feel stable. It looks as it should from postcards, more red than anything else, with the unsettled bay in the foreground.

We arrived for the attractions right off: Fisherman's Wharf, Berkeley Square, the Golden Gate Bridge, and Castro District. We took the appropriate pictures with the appropriate smiles and were happy to check each of them off our mental lists of things to see but didn't notice their significance more than their names implied. Maybe we were burnt out or maybe the timing wasn't right? After coming straight from the natural wonders, from thousands of years of river architecture and the real ground of Yosemite, nothing an architect could throw together after a few summer work sessions was going to compare. I appreciated San Francisco then for its people more than for its signature.

The locals there walked more slowly than they did in Los Angeles and certainly their eyes shined brighter towards the curiosities of the day, but each person felt that hopeful sincerity more on purpose than I'd expected. It was as if they *had* to care about the world's problems because no one else would; they were so used to shouting down the establishment and the powers that be, were so astute at the grassroots version of life, and were so painfully aware of their limitations to change anything, that they walked around as if acting by muscle memory. I sensed that their faded murals and poems of the generations past were just that, faded murals and faded poems. The urgency to which the youth bucked the system back then, in the 60's for example, all that is now mutated against towering billboards for new coffee flavors and New York skyscrapers and beeping taxi cabs. The once fertile fog from the once lively bay is now confused with the smog of a burning city, as if the history of the past century finally brought it back to its rightful place of honor, a place far out west where stories can be exaggerated and retold, convincing the do-gooders of our great country to move there, and then become jaded working at a Walmart plopped in downtown.

Though I needn't be so harsh — there were a few remnants of the "old ways" still left near Haight Ashbury — like the torn together runaways sleeping on the corner nestled into their brown baggy clothing together, with only the warmth of their solidarity to settle their minds. I took solace in their freedom and so bought them a few cans of food from the local store. We were cut from the same cloth, them and I, except mine had been freshly washed in comparison — and of course I had a car and a plastic card in my wallet. What a difference eh? Even an old man straight from a Grateful Dead reunion asked me about my shirt and said he liked it. I wore the aforementioned tie die shirt I had previously bought to feel alive, and thought it was fitting for San Francisco, in its official color being the rainbow.

"Are you guys alright?" he asked us a little jittery.

"Yeah we are good thanks man."

"Well that shirt man…I mean, dude…are you *sure* you are alright?"

"Yeah we're just passing through trying to check out the sites."

"Oh yeah, yeah right man. That's great man. I dig that. You guys aren't squares I can tell. But I mean, seriously, are you alright?" — he repeated this for the third time but this time now while pointing to his head and then he swirled his finger towards the sky. Just then I realized what he was actually asking.

He asked again more explicitly — "I have some LSD and since you guys seem legit I can get you some. Want any?"

I thought him sad just then—not that I had any negative opinions about LSD or the people who choose to use it, but rather because I could tell he'd asked that same question a million times before. He too, was stuck. He was stuck no less than those stuck in cubicles working for multinational corporations, typing away the same numbers for thirty years and then off to the grave. He too was the same as he was thirty years prior, except with less money in his bank account, and a fried brain. And in the end all he had to show for it were a series of stories he'd tell from his youth. He had lived a different sort of monotony on that street corner, talking to the tourists high on acid. And surely the view was better for him, with all the colors speaking to him and all the smells able to be heard and with all the amalgamations of picturesque thoughts trickling down into his opened consciousness—but after a while even tie-dye seems a little drab.

He complimented Ann Arbor like it was the great shining light of the Midwest and told interesting stories of Dead hideaways stuck in the woods next to the university hospital. We laughed and joked with him, staying there for quite some time watching his filthy beard and its crumbs crawling to the floor, if just to get away from his smell. Though he was nice I must admit. He was actually very nice. After a while he even offered us free LSD because he had too much he said, and therefore didn't really need the money by now since he owned his house up the street. I didn't care if he was lying or telling the truth because he was like a funny cartoon character in real life, except for adults, and very high. He was very entertaining.

We declined the LSD and moved onto chocolate crepes and souvenir shops instead.

Then we ate dinner with Aden's uncle, smoking pot with him at his house. He's a professor at one of the universities there, a professor who is obsessed with good wine and weed—like most professors. We then spent the night drinking too much in Berkeley and so later found ourselves sleeping late into the afternoon all over the floor of Aden's cousin's house.

Aden's cousin and his wife had moved there from Israel to work in the school and do research and raise their child in an environment devoid of bombs. I thought them wonderful and hospitable, like a family who knew what that word meant. But again — they were too normal and too predictable in the way they woke up each morning excited only for what they would cook for dinner and tired for their crying newborn. I had told myself I wanted children one day if only to watch them dance ballet or throw a baseball like my country tells me to. But the anchors associated with feedings and car seats and white picket fences and being careful all the time sound and feel like something I would only appreciate in hindsight, after they were all grown up in the best ways. But then I thought myself selfish and judgmental and they were opening their house to me after all and they were getting by because that is what we do — we get by the best way we know how, in small apartments sometimes — under the same blanket as someone who loves you dearly for all your faults and your wild ambitions — and so I should appreciate them I thought. So I appreciated them. And I thought of San Francisco and her past.

So I went to bed saying sorry to San Francisco for my unfair expectations and for my buying into first impressions. She forgave me in my dreams, I think.

On our way to Mount Temple Pious we stopped to see the great Redwood Forrest in northern California. The trees stuck themselves plainly in the ground, sprawling every which way, taking up more space than they probably needed to — reaching and stretching themselves like a contortionist only slightly too tall. I hugged one of them and walked through another and took the tour and they were amazing feats of godly resolve, in how they were so still, so alive, and yet so comfortable in their own skin, as if they were bored with their own grandeur. But I couldn't help but think of Aden more than the plants so wished I had more mental space to accurately appreciate the diversity of foliage surrounding me. I thought of him being alive right now, and being dead soon enough — dead long before these great trees would ever fall or burn. So Aden was more of an obvious point of contention — he was more delicate and therefore I thought of him instead of the trees.

That morning he had told me the story of Mount Temple Pious — the story of his spiritual mother of long ago. When she was still very young, before Aden, she had moved to Japan on a whim, after knowing Aden's father for only a few weeks and married him there almost as if on accident. But she visited the then great San Francisco and her brother who was also young back then, the now pot smoking professor who we had dinner with just the night before. And as the legend goes — upon climbing the Mount she heard a voice that whispered to her, "Go back. Go back and conceive me."

She tells this story out loud as if there weren't anything to doubt or question, like a statement of unquestionable fact. So she convinced Aden through tellings and retellings that it was in fact *he* who spoke to her that fateful day, there on a protruding rock near the summit. So the whole day, naturally, was to be just a dress rehearsal for that moment to come, where he would face his own birth like a Bodhisattva in the flesh, culminating in a series of meditations and realizations to match. Or so he hoped…

When we arrived near the top the view was spectacular as would be expected — the breeze subtle and sultry, it tickled our eyelashes just enough to see them perk up. The sun hid behind a few blanket white clouds but still warmed us lovingly. Even the children playing on the rocks grew mature and silent if only for a few moments so that Aden would have his peace. We trudged up the path and could see all of San Francisco before us: the bay, the ships, the bridges, Berkeley, and the cars swarming together in the mist. Each of us went our separate ways in location, but all of us only thought of Aden and his moment — his moment with himself of old, just his ghostly version and him speaking through incantations of the mind. I didn't believe any of it and Aden didn't either but the story felt so comforting, like the warmth of an expected heaven, that he couldn't help but entertain the idea.

"Did you hear yourself?" I asked him on the way down. I said this quite seriously but in my sarcasm being more subtle than most, he interpreted me funny and responded in kind.

"No. Unfortunately I didn't," he reported, "but really I was hoping for a talk with someone other than myself, maybe my future wife or something or another?"

And that didn't surprise me much. As much as he talks about himself and finding himself, it will always be about finding someone else with Aden — that person who will figure him out so he won't have to do it himself.

We cursed down the long lines of California that next morning, sober, but tired still. It was as if we needed a day of calm to escape from all the hurry we'd forced ourselves into. Even the beaches and the relaxations felt more anxious than they should have. There was always the next place to go, or someone else to meet, or one last thing to see. So the car felt like home again and the road regenerated our hopes pleasantly and for just the cost of a tank of gas. California became part of our rearview shortly after we left, more in our minds than in reality, but we pushed the petal down to the floor anyways, as if racing towards new memories, sick of California and its edges, sick of its expectations.

See — California is a disastrous irony in that way — with its expectations. It's the new New World. So everyone already raised there is helpless to their own ambitions.

"Well — I'll just move to California," we say when everything goes to shit or gets too boring. But what happens if you are already there? What happens if you already live in heaven? What if the Garden of Eden feels lonely? Where to next?

...At least it explains all the drugs.

But we drove without drugs, just our minds pounding, arriving in Las Vegas well after dinner stopping only for bathroom breaks and the occasional outlook. Once the thermometer read 115 degrees so we stopped on the side of the road and got out just to feel the natural temperature for a moment without air conditioning. It was hot like a sticky film of fire, like a stretch suit of hot coals, so its novelty wore off about as quickly as it took for us to step out of the car. We only stayed there in the desert of California just long enough to appreciate its contribution to California's geographic diversity. No other state claims intimidating skylines and sunny sea-sides the same as world class skiing and untouched streams and unholy cities and stifling deserts. California has it all! California is its own country in a lot of ways.

So while leaving I said goodbye firmly, as if returning would be impossible.

+

AFTER HOURS OF DRIVING the sun rested behind our heads and fell away in the distance, leaving only the sparkling machine of Las Vegas to guide us in the wrong directions.

The desert is sweet in its temperament. It's patient and minds its own business, generally speaking. It knows itself well so doesn't allow more than the simplest of pleasures to infiltrate its parameters — like an alchemist who really believes in the power of his rocks. The falling dollar bills and the cashed in dreams of Las Vegas shout into the quiet of the desert like a too loud neighbor. The cops are all bought off in that their salary depends upon it — so the sands and the red cliffs and the scorpions buzzing along their days have no real case against the powerful lights. They vibrate luminescent like a stabbing into the night. And the darkness bleeds out silicone and makeup.

See — we went to Vegas more because we *had to* — because it calls to us like a magnet of pleasure and excess. It tells us it's OK to let loose for a while and forget about our problems, so we thank it with our money and little chunks of our spirit.

"Oh look, there it is!" Faith shouted.

Even though I was only meekly excited Vegas did show itself like a stunning red head — unexpected and therefore more noticeable. The old mafia hotels had long been overrun by their flashier and more technologically advanced versions closer to the strip. So as we passed through the final valley with the near dead mafia casinos of old lining the highway, and I thought of them like sad hobos with their thumbs outstretched still, not realizing that we didn't do that anymore — we were over it. The novelty had worn off decades ago and so the lonely mafia bosses now only sat there in their big suits holding their still stuffed bellies and they drank one last whisky to the old days, back when everything made sense in the desert. I felt bad for them, even, because at least they were honest about corruption and stabbed you with eyes wide open right in your stomach instead of shooting you in the back while running away. At least they were honest about how hard they wanted to fuck you over?

We arrived with the city buzzing because that city is always buzzing. There are no clocks in Vegas after all and rather than time standing still, our morals do instead, like a time capsule for regret. But I eventually put my hasty assumptions aside and pulled myself into the hotel. We had to pay for it which hurt, but we wanted to walk everywhere and sadly the residential areas of Vegas weren't appropriate for children or high schools and therefore developed as far away as possible from The Strip. We immediately went out because there isn't anything else to do. We hadn't the money to spend on the world class entertainment which is by far the only legitimate reason for going — so instead we called a promoter-friend we had and got ourselves on the VIP list at some club.

I slicked my hair a bit and drank more than a bit, wore a more reasonable outfit than normal that included a blazer and a button down, and generally expected to make a fool of myself hitting on girls far better looking than me. And mostly all my predictions came true immediately upon arrival. The girls, Aden, and I all met in the center of the club, which looked like a movie set for a Roman orgy. There were white leather couches lining the outer edges of the dance floor with red carpet and roped boundaries so that everyone knew who was important and who wasn't. Each of these VIP pods included a bottle of Grey Goose Vodka, a personal bouncer in a pitch black suit, and a group of blondes in skirts without underwear. Usually all this was accompanied by old men without their wedding rings for the night. Aden and I saw the first couch that wasn't occupied by any of these old men and began conversing with the Barbie dolls sitting there upright, breasts out. After a few polite sentences I drunkenly asked for a drink from their stash because I didn't want to spend any more money than I had to.

"What are you poor or something?" the girl asked me. She said this almost as if fighting her own puffed lips. They were so pumped with Botox and chemically pealed back and wrapped with gauze and then shoved out into the world as if constantly screaming, that I rather stared at her mouth more than listened to its sounds.

"What? Can I have a drink?" I repeated.

She turned to her friend ignoring me and shooed Aden away who was actually doing well with his Barbie. Soon after we left, I saw one of those old mafia men with a hairy chest and gold chains with smelly sweat dripping from his back, walk right up to those Barbies and kiss them both on the mouth. I felt bad for them and bad for him too, that their vodka was more valuable than their pride.

We sunk ourselves into the outside dance floor which rested next to a pool with laser lights and golden statues of David, but bigger than the original, because everything is bigger in America, and even bigger still in Las Vegas. There were a few honest girls who were there visiting from Kansas, so we danced with them most of the night and kissed a few of them and fantasized about the models dancing in bird cages above our heads. They swung back and forth like hypnotists who knew their audience well. We drank so much for such an exorbitant cost that we decided that we had paid our way into the realm of lost inhibitions — so danced with more and more women and pointed at them like we were back in Iowa City for the first time.

At some point I found myself being asked on more than one occasion if I wanted to go back to said girl's hotel room, and although I wanted to believe deep down within my heart of hearts that this was because I was so strikingly handsome or so incredibly smooth that each girl hadn't the capability to resist, I knew better. Las Vegas is the land for legalized prostitution, and although I was presented well and firm, I wasn't *that* attractive and knew it. So I kindly rejected them, one by one, not wanting to pay for love, and then I watched them immediately throw themselves against the next nearest male. I felt sad for those girls right then, and wanted to ask them to dinner, out on a proper date even, if only to know their story and write it down for them. One day they would be doctors or lawyers and would be done with this part of their life and look back upon it not with pride of course, but with an understanding that they made it past the dirty condoms and were finished with hotel rooms devoid of life. And they would be proud of themselves.

Maybe?

I found Faith for a while and danced with her alone in the corner of one of the many corners of the club. She was almost fall-over drunk and I was giddy drunk as usual — watching her smile at me and bend her neck back sensually without knowing it. She gazed towards me and eventually felt my lips on hers. It was almost as if we tripped into each other and both startled, kept it up for only a few seconds unsure why. Kara had just arrived at that very moment to see all of this, like in the stories typically, but she just shrugged at us as if to say, *"You are both stupid."* But she didn't mind, not really. I ran away towards Aden and didn't see Faith till the next morning which was actually the next afternoon, not because I thought it would be awkward but because I didn't want to be tempted again and cross a line neither of us wanted to cross.

Ironically, after all my thoughts about prostitution, Aden and I had a limousine pick us up and take us to the local strip club. I don't know why, except that it was included in the VIP package. We got seats real close to the stage and didn't have to pay anything to enter. We went in being exclusively led by our libidos while intellectually questioning the actual fun we'd have there. The girls were about as beautiful as a group of girls can be — and that's the thing — they were definitely girls. The women, like the old hotels, were relegated to the outskirts of Vegas, off The Strip, near the dust and the shining buffets. This left only the most stunning specimens of human creation gyrating before our eyes. For all the moral fiber I attempted to muster, I finally admitted to myself that it was OK and that even if it *was* terrible, I couldn't help but enjoy the view. Right? Rationality told me that this was the most famous strip club in the entire United States and so charged exorbitant amounts for minimum tips and lap dances and even higher prices for other less spoken of activities. All the strippers were probably making thousands of dollars a night and so made conscious decisions about their lives. And there I was a patron, and I didn't necessarily feel good about it, but after some convincing I decided I didn't feel all that bad about it either.

I bought Aden a lap dance from a sultry Colombian girl who spoke to him in Spanish. He spoke back in Spanish and she smiled almost genuinely. Though it was hard to tell with them. Every girl who passed would touch the inner of my thigh and lean in real close to my ear, pressing her breasts firm on my chest, and they would say, "can I sit on your lap?" real-sexy-like and I felt bad saying no over and over but I did anyways. I was waiting for one that I could see, actually see, and not see through like the rest. While Aden sat there smiling the Colombian ran her hands up and down his neck and swirled her ass high up towards his face and he gave me the thumbs up and the girl didn't seem to mind any of this but she was an actress by trade so I didn't think much of any of it.

Just then a cute, not hot, but "cute" brunette sat across from me with her legs crossed. Her body was tight and groomed accordingly but in a way that looked more like the result of a gym membership than a trip to the doctor. Her face was healthy and full but long the way I like. She parted her hair down the middle as a hippie would, long and straight, reaching towards the floor. She wore a skirt and a white bathing suit top to show her flat yet soft stomach. I was impressed by her lack of makeup and generally calm demeanor.

"May I sit on your lap?" she asked like all the rest and I was disappointed in her just then, and it showed. I subtly rolled my eyes and suggested that we talk instead, her sitting across from me. She crossed her legs tighter and pulled her arms inward as if closing a coat around her that wasn't there. It was as if I had made a stripper self-conscious, and not that this is a difficult achievement, but I did it without touching her, and that *is*, I think.

I asked her about her life and why she was there, stripping. I told her I would pay her for her time as if she had actually given me a lap dance because I knew I was costing her money by chatting. There were hundreds of wealthy men from all around the world there who were all ready to throw fifties into her mouth if only for a fantasy of youth. But she didn't seem anxious to leave and told me of her boyfriend back home and about the schools she was applying to. She asked me what I was doing here and why I was at a strip club if I didn't care for lap dances and I didn't have a real answer and I told her so. I felt bad then, like I was there just to point out the sins of others and illuminate the impoverished ethics of the whole town. It was arrogant at best and callous at worst. But I told her all this and she said she understood and that I wasn't alone. She had met many such men, she said, who wanted what they wanted but felt bad about it. She said I shouldn't worry about her and that this was a choice and that she made good money.

"I wouldn't come out to Vegas each weekend from San Diego if it wasn't worth it economically," she said. "This job is a choice. And sometimes it sucks but I'm not a prostitute like some of these girls. Prostitution is legal here you know? ...So I keep my pride intact."

I wasn't sure about that but didn't press her further. We talked like this for the better part of a half hour and seemingly enjoyed the company, both of us, like a coffee break with a good friend at work. I apologized for taking up her time and gave her what money was left in my wallet. She told me this was deserving of a lap dance and began to take off her top for me. I told her that she was the most beautiful girl I had seen in Vegas, and that I knew this even without seeing her naked. She smiled and gave me back some of my money while kissing me on the cheek whispering, "thank you," like she meant it, and moved on to the next guy still fully clothed.

I thought of her that whole night and wished I could have taken her away from the hustle and bustle of Las Vegas and into the quiet of the desert. We would talk there and maybe set a fire and hallucinate under the stars together—but it would be real and genuine and I wouldn't touch her because a girl like that needn't be touched to be loved. Men looked at her like an object to be bought because she sold herself as if on layaway. Each man would give her a dollar and she would give them more and more of her soul until it was battered and beaten down, until it was relegated to the off ramps of her dreams, far away from the city.

We spent another day in Las Vegas almost laboring ourselves into the idea that something new would happen to excite our fancies, but of course, we were only left to stuffed bellies and another exaggeratedly beautiful club. So Las Vegas was sad, but only in its predictability. We knew what we were getting ourselves into and it delivered on every promise it uttered, so I felt bad leaving so trite, but sinning is only fun when it's unique after all.

After seeing all the emptiness, we left never soon enough. We'd be at the Grand Canyon by dusk and shortly after would say farewell to Kara and Faith. We all knew it was coming — the goodbye.

+

THE NIGHT I BROKE up with Andrea, Aden and I sat on our favorite barstools, drinking our favorite beer. I had called him to have a "guy talk" and ask for his advice. The lights were too bright. The place was too loud. But nothing could have made me comfortable to be honest — my whole life was spiraling out of control.

"You want to talk about the road trip?" he asked. "I'm so excited. July can't come soon enough."

"Yeah man — I'm excited. But I don't want to talk about the road trip right now, or, well, I guess I do but..."

"What's up man?"

"Andrea."

"How you guys doing? You still thinking about breaking up with her?"

"I think I'm going to do it today."

"Fuck."

"Yeah I know."

"You sure that's the right decision?"

"No."

"Talk man. Talk to me."

"Well you know I'm taking care of my dad now, and I'm working all the time and what not, and school is pretty hard right now — I think I signed up for too many classes. I just have so much shit going on..."

"Do you need money?"

"Who doesn't?"

"You know what I mean."

"No I'm OK for money — it's more that I just don't feel like I have any space for anything. There is so much going through my head and so many people that I need to be good to right now ya know? Like I want to hang out with you and the guys, but I have to work all the time, and then I barely make my classes...and I just wish I didn't have to deal with my dad being here — I just...I don't' know man. It's just all really hard right now."

"Listen man if things are tough right now, as they obviously are, we don't need to go out all the time ya know...we have this whole summer to hang out and...I'm just saying — don't worry about me and the guys and what not. It's all good."

"Yeah yeah I know I know...but it's just...it's all too much. I can't turn my back on my dad. He's my family. He'll always be my dad."

"Is he in the shelter still?"

"Yeah — and — well — I just need some weight off my back. I need some weight off my back man. I can't quit school. I can't stop working. I can't stop helping my dad. My friends are never going to go away. And Andrea is going to Belarus in September so we probably won't last anyways right?"

"I don't know? You could probably make it if you really tried."

"That's what everyone says. But then they leave each other for a year and it's hard to stay committed for that long...even if you do love them."

"True."

"She just seems like the only variable in my life that I can cleanly get rid of. I'm not saying I 'want to' get rid of her necessarily — but like I said we'll probably break up anyways while she's in Belarus — and I just — I just need to not have to take care of her anymore."

"You take care of her?"

"No — but being in a relationship is work. It's something that I have to take into consideration. And — I just can't anymore."

"I get it."

"So what should I do?"

"You aren't going to get that answer out of me. I'll support whatever you do man."

"I know."

"You want to back out of the road trip? Take it easy this summer?"

"A part of me is considering that — but no — not really — I need this road trip."

"Yeah me too."

"I just want to get away from all of this."

"Me too."

"I think I love her although I've never said so to her, but I'm young ya know? How does anyone know what love is anyways — especially in college? We're all so young."

"If you love her you should stay with her. You think you'll just find someone else or what? That's a risky proposition my friend. Very risky."

"I'll probably regret it later."

"I hope you don't."

We talked like this for the better part of a few hours until finally I had to go. I called Andrea soon thereafter.

"Hey!" she answered.

"Hey."

"You coming over soon?" We didn't live together but we might as well have—we stayed together every night.

"Yeah."

"You OK?"

"Ehhhh...I don't know."

"What's going on?"

I paused for a very long time. I didn't know what to say.

"Kristopher—what's going on? Are you OK?"

I gulped silently, took a deep breath and calmly said—"We need to talk."

+

THE SPECTER MULES AND their broken backs collapsed alongside the tarnished hobos and disheveled natives of northern Arizona—the empty highways shown lines of holy women with their crafts held in their leathery hands. They folded their hopes inside of themselves and buried any ambitions for their own futures deep past the greatness of their ancestors. It was all just a sordid complex of Mexican looking shacks and hand painted signs the likes of which would be envious of South Dakota. The whole ground lingered and seeped upwards into their shoes and the creases in between their elbows and forefingers. Their faces drooped and dribbled almost as if upside down, like melancholy pears, elongated and wretched. I was scared of them while entering the gates of the Grand Canyon. The entrance fee was but ten dollars and a blackened memory seared forever into my subconscious.

I didn't know if those women on the side of the road were Native Americans or simply ghosts with their sad donkeys parched and only partly standing, as if they leaned upon their owners for nothing but mere survival, like anything more and they would shatter like sandstone. I thought we all had noticed their sadness on either side of the road, like time had stopped for those ancient civilizations. Their lands were now tourist attractions no more worthy than a baseball game, and certainly less frequented. But we did the only thing we could and passed by on to better views and cooler vibes, forgetting still the women of the Grand Canyon selling their trinkets like ghouls caught in between the living and the dead, somewhere between yesterday and tomorrow.

"So that was a little creepy right?" I asked everyone hoping they had noticed too.

Faith kept singing and Aden was reading a book, and Kara was nodding, but I wasn't sure about what. I was the only one in actual observation, I thought — and wondered if any of this meant anything to anyone but me. Was it simply *I* who cared deeply — who wanted to remember and learn — and if so, what is going through their minds there in the car? I wanted to feel anything but the cold plastic of the wheel in front of me, and after driving for so long, wasn't sure if I was right in the head.

"I think we are here," I said grounding myself and stopping the car.

We exited together and set up our one tent stuffing it with lights and crumbs, the occasional bed bug, and a few sleeping bags still rolled up. Aden and I played football as well as you can with only two participants and then fell back into our childhood and threw rocks against trees, or tried to throw rocks against trees, most of them zipping past our targets and we'd laugh and high five each other, remembering what it felt like not to care about anything.

At this point Kara and Faith were reading and setting up the fire. We came back proud of them for no particular reason; they were absolutely as capable as Aden or I would have been at starting a fire, but our masculine tendencies and traditional beliefs caught us off guard, and so left us proud.

The fire roared that night in a way more liken to a celebration than a form of destruction. It crackled and we ate food we had bought from the only store at the national park. All the food was overpriced and catered to families who would be eating mostly over a fire — but there was a section labeled "camper" that still had frozen pizzas and baked goods that intuited the existence of an oven. The campers, those big gaudy examples of American excess and opulence would come stomping into the parks of our country's great historical parks like a brand name next to hand made. And for the life of me while sleeping on the ground, the bitter ground, I felt jealous. I wanted a damn camper. I wanted a bed. Really I just wanted something soft. Like Andrea. Maybe Later?

That night before shuffling off, we had a great debate about the beauty of outside and how much wood to put on the fire, and whether mosquitoes contributed anything substantive to the balance of things.

"Maybe its nature's way or god's way if you are into that sort of thing, of showing us that we aren't that powerful us humans — that this little flying gnat of a creature can still annoy us. In a way they are a reminder of our mortality — that we are no better or worse than any other creature," I said almost quoting Aden from an earlier conversation we had had in Yellowstone.

"No," Faith argued, "they are shit devil flies and that is that."

She won the argument flat out and I put my arm around her to tell her such. I held her close to me and then Kara on the other arm, and then Aden past her and we had the fire in front of us blazing too wildly as Kara had predicted but we didn't care — all of us looked up at our last full moon together and said little after that. There had been so much already said and so much already done that nothing was necessary anymore except to feel our arms on our shoulders and our foreheads on our brows and the moon twinkling above us like a spotlight, as if the sky was our audience and all the stars shined brighter with applause for such a beautiful moment. This was to be our final act together, after a glorious two week long play where everyone in attendance left having learned how to speak to strangers.

And if ever the moon spoke in song, it was that night, that faithful July night in Arizona. She, the moon, knew the next day would be the Canyon's so like an understudy's only opportunity, she bellowed out such a note of peace and rest that I closed my eyes and still heard her voice immaculate in the night. I felt her momentous joy for having been finally recognized on equal footing with the sun—that I had cared enough to notice her hanging there all alone in the sky. So I stood with outstretched hands up towards her and ran from the fire. I could still see every inch of the ground before me, illuminating from her glow.

She is the protector of my nights, my unholy and disastrous nights of substance and substances both, I thought, and she let me look at her straight in the eye the way the sun never would, and I thanked her for that with my hands cupping her face softly, wanting to smooth her rough edges so that she could shine this bright, always.

I slept cold and alone under the tent of the moon. The glimmering bed bugs and I made a truce in knowing this was neither the time nor the place. Aden slept next to me with his feet peeled and bruised. Kara and Faith snuggled wearily in the car holding each other's hands without actually touching. All the while the Grand Canyon was whispering to me about tomorrow, slightly jealous for my attention, but I would converse with her later, after the quiet.

And so the morning hurried past without us really noticing. By the time we came to see the canyon plain, now up close and personal, our minds were open and ready for what it had to say. I went in not expecting much, like it was an overly hyped movie that I doubted would live up to its trailer. I had seen so many pictures and heard descriptions of grandeur told with wild enthusiasm from otherwise shy individuals. People come alive after they leave the Grand Canyon, so like having heard the song already, I anticipated a more predictable live show.

Though I was wrong as I usually am. It came up at me big, in the way the word should be used. It's a simple word—"big"—one that most writers run away from—the way they run away from "very" or "awesome." But it was in fact very big, and awesome. It's slated on its sides with alternating reds and tans and browns all the way down to the bottom. But the ironic part is that what we care about, the vast endless space, the haunting openness that makes us feel oh so small, is actually nothing. We aren't bothered by the sheer drops or the walls because we can see those in Ireland or Canada, in California even. It's the space that confronts us, falling out in front of us. It's the other side in fact. It's the gap.

If the Grand Canyon was not in fact a canyon, and only held one drop straight down leading even twice as deep — no one would care. But we can see the other side — on our same line of vision — calling to us in the distance. It's carnal even — bringing us back to the days of hunting and gathering and trekking between climates and yes, around canyons.

So we began without much talk or care for anything except for our own budding thoughts. I ran down the trail while everyone else patiently walked. They would catch up with me later — a few miles later deep into the canyon. I had sat there for quite some time throwing rocks over the edge and watching them slowly fall one by one. They would balloon out into the empty air and curve back towards the Earth like dirty falling stars. And I thought of Israel again stroking my forearm, feeling it for its flaws and its defects, its perfections and its tones, its tensed muscle sinews and all of its stress being released. Throw a rock. Pick up a rock. Throw a rock. Pick up a rock. Swirl finger around in the red clay and clean my hands with its purifications. I didn't need anything but the rocks.

Faith and Kara were already in pure contemplative mode in knowing they only had a few more days left. They hadn't actually understood the ways in which they had been changed, nor did they want to know right off, but they were nearly done experiencing by this point. See — when you pack a lifetime of spontaneity into a few crazy weeks — you become hopeful for the rest home provides. They didn't want to stay anywhere in particular, but they wanted to recharge before the next adventure.

"I think we are going to go back up," Kara said to Aden and me, now sitting together on my ledge, throwing rocks and talking.

"OK we'll meet you back up at the top in what — an hour or so? Hour and a half?" I asked.

"Whatever. It's whatever. We'll see you there."

They put their arms around each other as they walked up the trail. It was narrow and slippery in spots, dangerous in others, but we hadn't thought to see them through it. At this point—everything was a given. We were survivors. They would thrive up that trail, together, and every trail thereafter.

"They are awesome," I said to Aden after they were out of earshot.

"I agree man. I agree. They are the first girls that I have ever been completely comfortable with. I feel like they hear what I'm trying to say more than what I am actually saying."

"What do you mean by that?" I asked already having an idea of what he meant.

"Well I feel like a lot of times I'm hit or miss with people and even the times when I hit it right perfectly, eventually I do something to screw it up."

"That's because you are too forward and selfish," I said to him outright. I was completely over tiptoeing.

"What does that mean? I..."—He right off got defensive but I wouldn't let him get angry.

"You have this belief that you should live to be happy. I share this belief and so do many people. It's fundamental. But you associate that with getting your way, rather than enjoying whatever comes."

"That's not true," he said honestly. "I enjoy a lot of things, and not just those that I wanted to do beforehand."

"Sure that's fine, but the truth is that you are a 'leader' in an annoying way. The way you communicate with people doesn't allow for discussion. You say things like 'I want pizza. Let's get pizza' and then are surprised when people aren't jumping at your every command?"

"I don't understand what is wrong with that kind of statement? I want pizza so I say I want pizza. And then I lead the group towards what I want. That's not only making me happy but it is also making me a leader. I like that. Why would I not like that? You do the same thing."

"No—I don't. Firstly it's a matter of asking. If I wanted pizza I would ask the whole group what they wanted first, then with everyone's opinions in mind I would explain to each person, from their perspective, why getting pizza is the best idea for the group. For example if someone wanted Chinese and another person wanted a sandwich and another person wanted pasta I would say, 'well it probably just makes sense to go to some Italian eatery that has pizza, some Italian sandwiches, and pasta— and we can then get Chinese for dinner?' and everyone would probably agree. Now we have two scenarios that both end up with the whole group going to the pizza place except in my scenario people don't think I'm demanding."

"Fuck"

"Fuck is right."

And we continued that line of conversation for the better part of an hour. He asked me a million questions and put me in hypothetical situations and asked me how I would socially wiggle my way out of them and make sure everyone was still happy. I made a lot of my answers up on the spot and have no real knowledge of social dynamics or psychology and surely I am not a therapist but I know that Aden, big heart and all, has an incredibly difficult time communicating with people past a smile or an exclamation of joy. He's wonderful—but unsubtle to a fault.

"That was the best conversation we ever had," he told me while stretching his legs. We had been talking on that ledge with the Grand Canyon in front of us, throwing rocks into the abyss, for longer than we intended. It was getting late and we had to go back.

"It was definitely good," I said hugging him. But halfway back up the trail I got that intense desire to run again—so left Aden behind.

"Do what you have to do," he yelled to me already running up the trail.

I ran up and up and my legs burned. I wanted to stop and walk but imaginary voices pushed me onward. Don't stop. Don't stop. Up and up the Grand Canyon walls until I reached the top and saw Aden still snaking his way up the trail hundreds of feet below.

Kara and Faith were sitting there waiting for me, not annoyed that I was an hour late.

"How was the journey?" Faith asked me smiling.

"Long," I said.

Chapter 12

I MET MY GRANDMA north of Phoenix. I don't particularly know what she does all day except clean the same few spots over and over again. She has a nice little car and drives around playing bingo and the slot machines at the local casinos.

But it makes sense, somehow — because she's all alone.

My grandpa is dead.

His death wasn't all that big of a deal to me at the time. He had been slowly wasting away for a few years. Then one summer he asked for the whole family to come see him (presumably before he died). See — upon retirement and inconveniently, upon my birth, he and my grandma moved to Arizona to get away from the Michigan winters and mine for gold. They would have been better suited for the nineteenth century I do believe. They would send me pieces of gold for my birthday from a thousand miles away with a card or something, as if their photographs were better than their hugs. I only saw them a few times a year, so maybe a dozen or so times in my entire life.

So when my grandpa was dying we all flew down to Arizona to see him. We were the last ones in the family as all my cousins and other uncles and such had already visited that same year. My dad cooked my grandpa's favorite meal that night, scallops and some potatoes. Grandpa couldn't really eat all that well with his crusty mouth and swollen tongue and he was still yelling about politics and the goddamn government and the goddamn women all ruining everything, but we all just smiled at him almost nostalgic for his anger. He died that night. My mom told me at the time that he chose to die, that he had been waiting until he could see all his family and eat one last great meal. But I remember hearing him a room away that night and he was not choosing to die. He was fighting for his life in him being an atheist and therefore not wanting to fall heavy into an atheist's blackness.

He called out for his wife and she told him it would be OK but it wouldn't be OK and my dad stood over him and I heard the whole thing really although I pretended to be asleep when my mom woke me up and told me to come into the living room. I don't remember how old I was, but I do remember writing a poem about the death, about death in general, and I wanted to read it at his funeral but I was too young and therefore didn't have anything to say that anyone else wanted to hear.

My grandma has been alone since then.

We tell her to move near us but she enjoys the weather and the deserts of Arizona more than her family, or so I tell myself when I'm lonely. I do love her though, in a real way and not just because I should. She's had a hard life and did everything she could do to provide for her family and just survive the way her generation did so eloquently—as if their dreams were manifest so long as food was on the dinner table.

She lives in a retirement community where everyone has to be over sixty or something. It's off this empty highway with an abandoned railroad next to it. It's mostly widows by now she told me. They have breakfast with each other real early in the morning and spruce up their mobile homes and RVs for fun. They all can afford better but don't need better. The bigger the house the more empty space, and the emptier the space, the more they realize how alone they all are.

I jumped out the car to give her a great big hug and was surprised at how small she was. I had to bend down quite a ways for her arms to stretch up towards my shoulders. She smiled a really wonderful and full smile upon seeing me the way grandmas do sometimes. It's an older version of a smile, I think. Smiles have evolved with technology and new worries—like what kind of cell phone we have—but the old kind of smile isn't distracted by all that modern thought. For grandmas there is just a table with food and a grandchild and a great big hug.

Kara and Aden and Faith left after a feast because they knew I needed some alone time with my grandma. They went to Phoenix and couchsurfed with a local and drank and partied because that's what they do, all while I stayed with my grandma. I played bingo with her and went to the casino with a few dollars because that's what she likes to do and we drove around Arizona together getting lost but not really caring because that just left more time for conversation. I asked her about our family and about our history and about what my dad was like when he was young and I asked her why she moved to Arizona and what grandpa was like and where we all come from and all that.

"You come from Kentucky hillbillies," she said with a sly smile.

"See how far we've come?" she meant.

So my grandma and I talked for the first time just then. Sure we've conversed and danced, smiled and held hands — but we've never really talked. Not like adults. And so as the stories rolled from her tongue, she felt like those sages past, captivating my every thought.

And so she went on, Mark Twain-ing tales of dirt floors, coal mines, fire roasted game, train jumping, rugged clothes, torn shoes, red hair, blue eyes, sweated brows, and the plural of love.

She told me I come from the civil war and hand-me-downs. That graduating high school wasn't quite possible for her. She told me that the men went to war and the women loved them.

"Everyone has a vice," she said.

"Comedians today are crude."

"When you get old you know who you are, and you know what you like."

"It's nice to hear your voice."

"It's nice to see you."

"You should visit more often."

"I'm sad to see you go."

I realize now that I prosper only because I can. I hope wildly because I am allowed to. I dream big because I sleep well at night. I believe because I am comfortable in my own skin. I live because she struggled before me. And so true are her words, even calling them wise would insult.

I was still sitting with my grandma when I heard Aden spinning into the complex. The speed limit around the neighborhood said 10 mph. It actually said that—10 mph. It was illegal to jog briskly. But Aden didn't care about any of that mess—he wanted to rescue me from the old people as if I needed busting out of jail. He gave my grandma a great big hug and Kara and Faith followed suit.

"Oh why, I mean I don't know..." my grandma stuttered at their outstretched arms—"I guess if...well oh Jesus...just come here." She wasn't a physically affectionate woman, and wasn't sure if they were safe or crazy. They were neither, but she hugged them anyway.

We then stopped off at a Middle Eastern restaurant because we had decided to start this crazy journey in one just like it. We were suckers for nostalgia. They eagerly told me about their nights out in Phoenix and the people they had met while away. We didn't talk about anything that had happened prior, nor made any claims about the future. We didn't reminisce or cry or even laugh really. It was a quiet contemplative conversation describing their experiences, almost scientifically—just the facts and logistics.

We drove them to the airport without much emotion.

"Well..." I began to say.

"I understand. I know," Kara said slowly, not wanting to speak of goodbye.

"We'll see you soon," Faith said.

And that was that. After a few weeks that felt more like years of friendship and an honest realization that we were all going to be changed forever, and therefore remember this moment forever, we said goodbye as if we'd see them for breakfast the next morning.

We said goodbye without even saying it. We couldn't.

+

Everything is shattered in west Texas. It doesn't look like it because its residence have an incredibly resilient culture, that or they wear a thick skin so as not to be cut too deep, but it is shattered nonetheless.

And needless to say — Todd didn't fit in.

Todd was wearing a collared shirt but it wasn't button down, and he certainly didn't have a tie. That was a little unexpected considering the company he worked for controlled a considerable share of the world's oil supply, and therefore the world's money too. The billionaire Texans aren't worried about all that fuss about them fancy brands n' all — not like those too-good Manhattan bankers are. So they don't wear ties.

"We actually make stuff happen," Todd had once said about his company. That's probably true — but they do it while wearing 2 dollar shirts.

Todd's about 5'10" with something colored eyes, always wearing glasses and smells like too much cologne. He wears his jeans tighter than normal for his age, especially around the ankles, but not because he's a hipster or stylish or any of that mess — he just wears them because he wears them. He walks briskly even if he's not sure where he's going, leaning forward usually, as if he were in a perpetual state of falling, but saves himself each time by stepping forward at the last possible minute. Some days he wears a green collared polo shirt and some other days he wears a blue collared polo shirt and sometimes he even wears a black polo shirt. Tennis shoes, straight jeans, polo shirt, glasses, and a sort of beady nose which only seems natural in size due to his glasses. He generally looks upstanding but won't ever be considered "handsome." He looks like an engineer basically. That's it — he looks like a twenty-three-year-old engineer.

"How are you doing?" I asked him upon arrival.

"Shitty," he said honestly.

"Ahh that's the Todd I know and love."

"So—I mean it's great that you are here, but, well, I mean—what are you doing?"

"Good question," I said. "We're just traveling around not really sure what to do with our lives. I got an interview tomorrow morning for a marketing position for this company in Nicaragua. I need to use your computer."

"Typical," he grunted under his breath, "but Nicaragua? I mean—won't you get raped or killed or something or both?"

"Probably. Probably both."

"Well at least you know. So…cool. But I mean—well—I wish I could go travel everywhere too. I'm pretty jealous actually. You should see these absolute douche bags that I work with. I mean these guys are absolutely fucking retarded. No one knows what they are doing…well that's not true they are all pretty smart but they are boring as hell. I'm learning a lot of technical shit but…"—he gestured to the empty land to his right—"…I live *here*."

I had in fact noticed the deplorable state of the city while entering. We found his house via GPS so I didn't have to do much looking around, but that was probably for the better. What I did see were a series of empty farms, lacking even cattle, spotted with barracks looking subdivisions that were probably built by the oil companies to house their employees. They built this imaginary city in the middle of western Texas using faded yellow and blue paint, and a series of bland housing structures which distinguished themselves only by name.

"So what do you do?" I asked him.

"Well right now I'm still learning how to analyze the cost…"

"Right. I don't really care about the oil engineering stuff…what do you do-do? Like what do you do on the weekends when you aren't working?"

"I do nothing, that's what I do. There is this one bar that some people go to but I'm pretty busy with work and the bar sucks anyways. It's full of middle aged men who have a lot more money than me and it's just depressing. It's seriously depressing."

"Because you don't want to be them in ten years?"

He eyed me very seriously — "I won't be them in ten years."

I looked around the apartment for a while. He had a beautiful table and chair set, a leather couch, a fancy plasma TV, a nice grill, and a full fridge.

"Nice place you got here," Aden finally said. He was friends with Todd in college but only because I was. They never really connected. Todd is hard to handle if you don't understand him. He would give you the skin off his back if you needed it, but he would complain about it the whole time.

"Thanks man. I do my best. Ya know the funny thing about this job? And I don't mean to say this to sound arrogant or whatever because god knows I don't make enough money for what I do — but I do pretty well."

"Oh yeah I heard that you are making like…"

"No no no," he stopped me, "that's rude."

"True."

"My point is that I bought that TV with my first check and then that leather couch with my second one, then the grill, then the bed…a new computer and a few knick knacks or whatever. I basically have all the 'stuff' I could want." He said this emphasizing "stuff" as if it were a nasty word. He knew I didn't care about "stuff." So he continued honestly in asking, "…and now what?"

"And now you go party," Aden suggested.

"Well yeah, but whatever — again that's not the point. The point is that I can't have two plasma TVs and I can't fit two couches into the living room because it's not big enough. I could get a bigger place but then I'd just fill that up with more shit. And then I'd be sitting in my living room with four leather couches, which would just be depressing because that would remind me of how many people are not visiting me. I don't need more space—if I have more space I'll just fill it up with more stuff—and the more stuff I have then the more space I'll need, and on and on and the stuff, my point is, the stuff is fucking terrible. I absolutely don't want another couch and I don't want another TV. I already have a car and all that shit so what now? What do I do?"

"I still stand by my original statement," Aden laughed, "now you go party."

Todd rolled his eyes at me but sort of chuckled as well. "Yeah," he said, "maybe you are right."

He didn't like his job but he accepted it. For this I both envied and pitied him. He had found himself a job that paid well in America and would soon find a girl to love him and make babies with him and it would all turn rosy in the end—so I envied his acceptance. I envied the fact that he held himself in such high esteem, if only for his new social class. He was never a confident fellow in college—angry and temperamental, caring and socially capable, but certainly not confident.

But if I had had his job I would have been even *more* self-conscious actually, not wanting to admit to having been caught up in "the system" so easily. I viewed the working middle class no different than the working upper middle class, or the rich white collar class for that matter. Only the poor did I accept at face value, because if they were stuck in a job that would eventually kill their spirit, at least it was more acceptable—at least they didn't have a choice.

So I listened to Todd talk down to the rest of our country, the less educated or the less ambitious, but didn't see his justification. See—he believed in his superiority deeply, as if he had earned it, and was therefore content. But I knew that he had so much more than western Texas. He had so much more than Midland or big steaks and a room full of nice stuff. He had long journeys and intelligent women and new languages and political influence and hope and all those beautiful things that don't seem to exist in west Texas.

"Did you hear about Craig?" he asked. Craig was a friend we both knew from high school. He was a famous running back from our town—the prototypical jock—the locally famous.

"He's working at a Walmart or something. What a shame..." he finished.

"Well is he happy?" I asked challenging Todd's assessment of Craig's life and his own at the same time.

"I don't know. I guess? I think he's married or something? But I don't know. He just always seemed like he was smarter than that. Or maybe he wasn't?"

"As long as he's happy," I said superiorly like I wasn't even more judgmental than he was.

"That's what happened to our high school though," Todd defended himself, "there were a lot of smart kids...well not a lot but whatever. My point is that I feel like a lot of the cool kids or whatever from high school are all still there. No one has moved out."

I immediately thought to say, "Well Ohio is better than this shithole," but I thought that would sound harsher than I meant it. But—actually, that's exactly what I meant. So I digress, it was just that I didn't want to be impolite.

"Someone has to pump the gas, right?" is what I ended up actually saying out loud.

"And someone has to drive around the country doing whatever he wants," Aden smiled.

"You guys are ridiculous. But it's cool I guess," Todd told us while covering his last piece of steak with some more gravy. "I wish I had the time to do all of that but I'm stuck here in this job."

"You think you'll stay with it?" I asked sincerely.

He kept his head down chewing for a quite some time. I knew he had asked himself this very same question before and he probably hadn't come to an answer. I put him on the spot. Sometimes in order to make a decision we just have to be forced into one.

His glasses twinkled in the light, but slowly, like the reflection was taking its time for effect. The whole scene ran in slow motion. "I don't know," he said sadly, "I really don't know. I hope not. Or at least I hope I get to go abroad. My company has offices all around the world."

His eye flickered and his voice jumped just a little when he said that last part. He looked like someone who believed he could make the jump, but also knew deep down that he didn't have the guts to try. He was a contradiction in this way. He knew himself capable of anything, of everything, but for whatever reason wouldn't risk anything. It was as if he was comfortable so long as he was not uncomfortable. What a sad baseline.

"You are right about high school, but I mean everyone can't be engineers like Aden said. Some of the coolest people we've met on this trip have been random waitresses or some guy sitting on the other side of a truck stop, or a farmer on the side of a hill, the little fat girl eating ice cream, and all of that. I know I sound silly but it's true man—after seeing many parts of this country that I hadn't ever seen before, I'm starting to realize that I am a seriously judgmental person who, just like you, makes fun of people who haven't 'made it' or haven't been educated and what not. But at the same time my mom isn't educated and she's my mom. And she's awesome. Basically, I think, America's is just a country of cool moms."

"Some are shitty," Todd was sure to add. He spoke from experience.

"Yeah for sure some are shitty. But a lot aren't. And listen man I'm talking to myself here too. All this judgment about whose life is better and who's isn't—I don't know man—we're all just trying to do what we can to be happy. You have this awesome job and this awesome experience living out here alone and becoming an adult on your own and you can save a ton of money and you're going to get to go abroad and it'll be awesome, and then we're out here just traveling around for a while…"

Aden's phone rang. He excused himself because he had heard all this before. I didn't mind because I was hoping it would be Andrea. I hadn't talked to her since Yellowstone.

"...and who knows what will actually happen but it'll be pretty fun along the way. I think some of the kids working in a factory or whatever, they are doing more than I am right now."

"Well listen I get your point," he said trying to defend me, "but I mean getting out of that place, no matter if you got a job or whatever, doesn't really matter. And I heard you were writing. I've been reading your blog you are going to write a book or something right?"

"Who knows man? I've tried to write many books and never got past a hundred pages or so. I'm not predicting anything."

Aden butted in. "We have to talk," he said.

"What's up?" — I was worried that something serious had happened.

He picked up his dish and headed towards the sink. "Dinner was seriously awesome Todd. I really appreciate you cooking for us like that," he said leaving me still in anticipation.

"Not a problem."

"Alright brother," he said seriously, "how do you feel about DC?"

"You mean Washington DC?" I asked stupidly.

"Yeah."

"I'm going to take a shower and start getting ready for bed," Todd said after washing his dish, leaving Aden and I to our dreams.

"Alright see you in the morning," I said to Todd.

I looked at Aden and plopped down on the couch — "I mean — what's up? DC is fine. Do you want to go there? I thought we were going to San Antonio next, then Austin, and then the Deep South and what not? Right?"

"Well yeah that was the plan but you know how we are with plans. That was Billy on the phone. He's leaving for Japan in a few days and wants us to meet him in our great nation's capital before he leaves. He knows about the road trip because he's been reading the blog and says we should just drive across country. What do you think?"

This is a really silly idea, I thought. If we went to DC our plans for Miami and New Orleans and basically the whole geography of the next few weeks would be turned on its head. Washington DC is more than a thousand miles away from western Texas. We already skipped New Mexico to have access to a computer and for all my complaining about Texas I figured it had a lot more to offer me. I was anxious to see all its long highways, and great steak restaurants, and I wanted to go to a Rodeo with real cowboys. Plus I wanted to actually give Midland a chance and take Todd out on the town and hit on the country girls with him and make fools of ourselves together. Maybe we could find locals and really do some cow tipping? I thought Todd deserved more than just one dinner and polite conversation. He's all alone out here. I hadn't seen Billy in a while but he should have given us more notice than one day, especially considering he would be in Japan for at least a year. If we went to DC we would have to skip Austin which was one of the cities I was the most excited about.

None of this made any sense. We couldn't *actually* go. I really thought that this was an incredibly moronic idea. There is being spontaneous and then there is wasting gas money. It just doesn't make sense. There is no way we could go on such short notice—not all the way across the country at least...

"Well it's fairly obvious that we have to go," I said to Aden.

"Let's pack now," he agreed.

So we went.

We left in the dead of night across the plains of Texas, up through Arkansas and its hills, past Tennessee, stupidly not stopping for the live music of Nashville or the BBQ of Memphis, and then into Virginia, and then we took a sharp left north towards the great non-state city-capital of our country — the enigma of the U.S. In total the trip was more than twenty-four hours of straight driving. It wasn't a scenic, beautiful drive as it should have been because we were both so tired. We were so worn from the road that its metaphors fell short at our knees. We drove sanely, but in a dreamlike stupor, arriving if only by accident, not remembering what we had just done or where we had just been.

"So we're in Washington DC?" Aden asked when we first arrived, "I can't remember — why exactly?"

My eyes were puffy and hands swollen. And my butt felt like Jello past its expiration date, so I drooled out my words angrily. "Honestly," I said, "honestly Aden — I don't know."

+

We had no good reason for being there, the same way I had no good reason for not being with Andrea. But sometimes spontaneity and snap judgments rule our lives so brutally, so aggressively, that we can't help but fall empty to their consequences.

Similarly, I had chaotically decided to break up with Andrea. My dad was still homeless. I still had to work 50+ hours a week. I still had to finish school. I still had to deal with her insistently moving to Belarus within the next year because of her schooling. And most importantly — I still had to deal with my own doubt — doubt for love — doubt for compassion — and my doubt for us. So I decided to break up with Andrea before it all became too overwhelming. I had such a cacophony of unrelenting decisions to make about my future, about my family, and about *her* in particular, that I had to make a snap decision — and sadly (oh so sadly), she lost the contest. I interpreted our relationship as fleeting, as "one of many to come," and so chose to let her go.

And in knowing that she would hold true to her convictions for the ubiquitous "us," I made every attempt for her to hate me. *"If she hates me — she'll move on,"* I thought. *"She deserves to move on."*

"I don't have emotional room for you," I had told her.

"I'll wait for things to calm down in your life," she had said. "I understand it's difficult with your father and all…"

So in not wanting her to wait around for me, and then, in not knowing that I would almost immediately regret my decision to separate from her, I found a pretty girl — (pretty girls always came so easily to me) — and I kissed her as quickly as possible. And to add fire to Andrea's already smoldering flame, I kissed a girl who she knew intimately — a mutual friend — just to prove to her that "you can't trust me."

I *wanted* her to hate me. It would be easier that way. I would move on. She would move on. Everything would be clean and simple. Like death.

"Did you really kiss her last night?" Andrea asked me crying one night. Her eyes were gaunt. She looked empty. Everything had been taken from her.

"I did."

"Why?" she cried. "Did you like her while we were together?"

"You have to move on. I want you to move on," I said.

"I can't move on," she sobbed. "I'll take you back. Just come back to me."

"Andrea." I was very resolute. Very still. Very confident. "I didn't like her while we dated," I said, "and I don't like her now still. But it happened — so you have to move on."

"Do you still like me?"

"Of course. You can't just turn it off like a faucet. I just can't…See — you're going to Belarus and my dad…ya know? I have to take care of my dad. I just don't have the emotional space for anything right now. You have to move on."

"Kristopher — please — just — stay with me."

"I can't," I said. "I'm sorry."

Chapter 13

Her apartment building looked and smelled like an old insane asylum, like something left behind from an old Negro district. All the districts in DC are old Negro districts. Squealing revolving doors greeted us upon entry. I saw a few potted plants but otherwise the grand entry room was unnervingly empty. And worse, it led straight up old marble stairs towards a hallway lined with wallpaper. The colors were all too on purpose: hushed yellows, faded greens, and floral pinks. It was a color scheme your grandma would pick out for your bathroom.

After we realized that turning left down a long mirrored corridor was our only option, things became even more worrisome. A desperate old man swayed back and forth with his industrial vacuum partway down the corridor, giving us a humble nod while vibrating to and fro. He carried himself like a man who defined himself as colored rather than black. The whole place felt like this man, completely lost in time. I looked to my left at the mirrors and saw myself there in the dim light. I walked slowly, even more slowly than I normally do, and wondered if my reflection thought much of me.

One step. I noted my lanky arms flowing down towards the ground, like my grandpa's. Two steps. I was noticeably brown, "like a caramel," my mother would tell me. Three steps. Deep brown eyes almost too dark to notice, like a hollow sea. Four steps. Rusted jeans and a meaningless t-shirt, dirty white shoes, and a full backpack. Five steps. I looked like I was on a leisurely journey up a mountain, like climbing Everest by starting on the beach. Six steps. My curved hands and my gilded smirk. Seven steps. Nod, almost bow to the colored man out of respect. Eight steps. Back to the mirror. Nine steps. My hair is too long already. Ten steps. I couldn't help but skip just a moment to see my backpack shake, to feel its weight more intensely as it fell with gravity. Eleven steps. Aden is many paces ahead of me because he always is. Twelve steps. Relapse.

The lady at the counter asked us a few questions. She was a security guard, but looked more like she was dressing up as one for Halloween. All security guards do. What's a badge if it's attached to an XL shirt and 50 lbs of love handles? I could crawl backwards and still make a clean get away. We signed in as Emma's guests and scurried upstairs, taking the elevator too high because we always take the elevator too high.

I called Emma to tease her before making our entrance. While walking down her hallway she answered, "Hello?"

"Hey we are at 59th and Stevenson and can't find anything. Where is your apartment again?"

"59th and...where?"

"We're right next to a government building," I said.

"That doesn't help." She was not amused.

I laughed and bellowed out, "We're at Smith and Weston," while laughing even harder.

"Kristopher," she asked me quite sternly with a pause between each word, "where...are...you?"

I tapped on her door just then. She smiled and said not meaning it, "you're such an idiot," while walking to let us in.

Aden and I almost knocked each other down trying to get in the first hug. We both loved Emma dearly. I was not only interested in how she could affect *my* happiness; I was interested in hers as well. And this is big for me.

We met each other while in college, all of us, through many meetings and fights with bureaucracy and through sleepless nights on each other's couches and hell if we weren't the best damn student organization in the country, all of us together—we'd change the world soon enough, we had thought. She had been our rock through college—but still so soft. We loved her and so needed big bear hugs even though she wasn't very affectionate.

When you first meet Emma you right away notice she doesn't believe in God. She comes from the aristocracy of Philadelphia so was born with the wisdom of gray hair, even though she wears it a crimson brown. She slouched most of the time like a middle aged divorcee, and for some reason I always envisioned her skin tasting peculiarly of salt. Her nose was soft and edged the way one would expect from someone of her eastern rank, but her breath only came from her mouth in short anxious spurts as if she never learned how to inhale through her nostrils. She's perpetually anxious, knows it, and therefore lives with an ever increasing bout of insecurity. Her mind isn't able to keep up with her face, even though they are both beautiful in their own ways.

And she *was* actually beautiful and smart and what a damn wonderful women although most guys wouldn't think so at first glance. I always hated being only a good friend to her, and I hated how she wore herself asexually, as if feminism's kryptonite was a pretty dress. She didn't give herself enough credit or enough makeup, so no one else did either. And isn't that the way it always goes anyway?

She was wearing something, but it didn't matter because she wears a flowing skirt from the sixties even when she doesn't wear a flowing skirt from the sixties. She belonged there in the past, I think, with her fall-away hair, with its wraps and her deep-set eyes—she was simply born too late. Everything is too tight in the twenty first century. Back then she would have worn everything loosely, and sure she would have surrounded herself more often with the productive hippies who secretly had too much money, but she would have been happier back then, and certainly would have had more sex.

She's too big for our generation. She lives for causes that no longer exist.

"How are you?" she asked now genuinely smiling.

"Oh we're swell," Aden answered not sarcastically though he sounded so.

"I really like your place. It's very well put together, as I would expect," I complimented.

"Oh thank you. I got a lot of this at random stores around town and that from the internet over there," she said while pointing towards a sheet overhanging on a bookshelf.

She said it was a wall divider. That's fine. I don't really care about decorating, or clothes, or anything with cloth really (maybe the American flag?). But you could tell *she* did, so I continued to gesture towards pillows and at her bed sheets and, "oh look at the table cloth over there how wonderful," I would say. I made gestures at all the cloths and said things like—"oh and that's really nice as well."

Aden rhythmically nodded in agreement. And I don't want to imply that I was faking interest for the sake of faking interest because I wasn't. I was faking interest because Emma is wonderful and she deserves my dishonesty. I highly doubted many people had been in her apartment. She is much more of an "I'll meet you there" type of girl. She wishes she wasn't because her pillows match too perfectly for her to not show them off. But alas—that is that.

"Are you hungry?" she wondered. "I don't really have much but I assume you are famished from all that travel. How long was the drive and what are you doing exactly?"

"We just ate at this wonderful taco place in Virginia so thanks but no thanks about the food," Aden said.

I made a mental note that we rarely ate so when we did we gorged. Once a day we'd pack ourselves into some local joint, whichever looked most "out the way" and least visited, and stuff our faces, usually ordering appetizers to share and desserts of all sorts and shoveled piles of extra side dishes near our chins and then we would stop to say something about the interesting bird flying outside the window and then we'd make a toast usually with water and it would splash out onto our plates but we didn't care because it was just water and the accented waitress would clean it up soon enough and "yes I will have both" and "well which would you prefer if you could choose?" and "I'll take whatever the chef wants to make at this very moment" because how fun, and then we'd slouch down and crawl out the front door, bell ringing and belly's full, and would leave exorbitant tips just in case the diner wouldn't have remembered us otherwise.

I tried to answer all her questions in one clean sentence — "The drive has been very long and we're not really doing anything."

"That makes sense," she said.

She's often sarcastic.

"What are you doing here lately?" I asked her. "You still working for that women's thing?"

She must have hated the way I said "women's thing" as if all the specific problems facing women could be generically categorized with a pronoun. But then again she was into "women's studies" which isn't that much better.

Feminists confuse me.

"I was working for the NCWO," she corrected me, "but now I'm working for URAC."

"English?" I said confused. "Washington DC is the land of acronyms, it seems. How and the hell do you keep it all straight?"

This city is just a bunch of grown up fraternities, I thought, and they've all kept their letters and handshakes and secrets — especially their secrets.

"Are you going to remember if I tell you?"

"Of course not."

"So why did you ask me?"

"I'm trying to ask…well…what are you doing in Washington now? And more importantly, are you happy?"

At this point Aden was taking a shower. He is always bored with small talk. Although small talk with Emma is always more genuine and certainly more sincere so I didn't quite mind. She obviously didn't either.

She was short sure, but she's always short. She was smiling from ear to ear.

She answered me while wiping down her counter and taking out a bottle of tequila from the refrigerator — "We are a healthcare lobby basically. But it's a nonprofit so I am in charge of fundraising. I should get paid way more considering everyone's salaries depend upon me."

"You could have told me you were in Obama's cabinet and I would have insisted that you deserve a raise. So I'm with you there. I'm always on your side."

This was true. She was the only reason Aden and I had any success in college. We were entertainers without an agent before we met her. She's like a clock, reliable to the very last tick.

"Well are you happy?" I asked again predictably.

She put her head down slowly and handed me a glass. She looked to her left and up and we all know what that means — she was about to lie.

"Yeah?" she said more asking than stating.

"So no?"

"I haven't had sex in a while Kristopher..."

I smiled a great big smile right then and there. See — I've never been one to believe in exclusively platonic friendships but she said this with such trust, with such a forceful exhale, with such relief, that I couldn't help but sink in deeper to our friendship. She thought of me so openly, so beautifully, that she could admit such a wonderful truth without hesitation. She's blunt — but not *that* blunt. This was a secret that only a few were privy to.

"I won't tell Aden," I chuckled at her.

"Oh god. Thank you. I wouldn't expect you would anyways."

"I feel like you've had this problem since college," I whispered so as not to be overheard.

"I know!" she said emphatically and annoyed equally.

"Well you know I think you are absolutely beautiful and you're so smart and well, sadly, this must be your fault," I said honestly and sharply. "There is no reason that you shouldn't have willing and ready suitors knocking down your door. And in the least, you should have some sleazy Georgetown guys trying to buy you drinks. Just pick a cute one and end the drought. There is no shame in that. Just wear a condom and enjoy yourself."

"At this point I just might. But not a lot of people approach me to be honest."

"You're scaring them all off then."

"I'm not!"

"You have to be."

"I don't know…"

"No this is true," I said, "…you are intimidating. You look at everyone like they are in an interview. Wear a dress and a pushup bra and take a girlfriend out to a happy hour and get hit on and be responsive in a nice way. The guy won't be perfect but it'll at least get you practice being nice to guys."

"Yeah I *am* pretty judgmental."

"That is the understatement of the century Emma. You know how some people read body language really well? Well no one needs to be an expert to read yours. You have your own, very loud, version of body language and it is usually saying 'why are you talking to me?'"

"Oh god that's bad. I know that's bad." — She said this laughing. My tone hadn't been to berate her or to make her feel embarrassed. I was concerned and she felt it.

"We'll try tonight."

"That won't work," she said.

"Why? I hope you know that you are going out with us tonight?"

"Yeah yeah I know but I'll be with you guys the whole time and you are staying here so I can't take a guy back *tonight*. And besides, no guy will talk to me if I'm surrounded by you and Aden."

"Oh no...this will be even better. I'll hit on you and kiss you all night and the other guys will see how much attention you are getting and then I'll go talk to someone else and they'll move in for the kill."

"This all sounds terrible."

"It *is* terrible," I mused, "but we're trying to get you laid. So everything is on the table at this point."

"OK I'm down," she said smiling bigger even than before.

Aden conveniently walked in right at that moment. "So what's the plan for the night?" he belted out wearing only a towel.

Emma turned in her chair and dangled the bottle of tequila in front of him.

"Perfect," he said.

I took a shower and when I came out this sorority-looking girl was sitting at the table in a bright turquoise dress — one of Emma's friends I presumed.

"Who are you?" I shouted hastily.

She looked at me standing their dripping wet in my towel. She pointed to herself and then looked at Emma confused as if to say, "*Who is this strange man in your house?*"

"I'm Kimberly," she said while sticking out her hand.

"I don't shake hands," I said while hugging her. This confused her and frightened her equally.

"Kristopher, stop scaring her!"

Emma came to my defense saying — "This is possibly my best friend and he and Aden, who you already met, are traveling to — where are you going? It doesn't really matter. The point is that they are traveling and they went to Michigan with me and they're staying here for tonight, or maybe a few days? I don't know anything because they don't ever plan anything. They are fine."

I don't know why I had such a hostility towards this girl and so immediately nonetheless, but she was very small, very fit, very pretty, and in an overly put together way that screamed Ivy League. She was everything and everyone who made it impossible for Emma to have sex in a city like this. She was hit on by guys at her work and was asked out on dates by men in the street and had many drinks bought for her at the bars and probably had a boyfriend who exclusively wore Ralph Lauren so I just didn't like her. I'm not sure exactly how to describe this girl any further. What's the opposite of a people person? She represented everything that Emma hated, but Emma needed friends and girls to hang out with and most of them thought they were prettier than her but god dammit they weren't. I wouldn't stand for it.

Tonight will be Emma's night, I thought.

"Do you remember a time when you didn't care about your haircut?" I asked Kimberly while putting on my pants in front of everyone.

"What?" she asked angrily.

Emma gave me a mother's look that I deserved.

"I was just thinking about that today. I remember a time in my life when I didn't care about my appearance. I wish it were still like that."

I stuttered backwards with one pant leg in. I was hopping all over the apartment trying not to trip, finally falling on the bed.

"You care what you look like?" Aden asked to lighten the mood.

"Well true," I came back, "but what I'm saying is that I'm conscious of how I look. Surely I don't care very much compared to other people. For example there are some girls who take hours before they go out picking out the right dress and methodically put on their makeup not realizing that they are just making themselves uglier. Now, I don't care compared to a superficial girl like that of course. Actually I care a lot less—but I'm still consciously aware of what I'm wearing and my style, even if it *is* thrown together. So I ask you—do you remember a time when our moms wanted us to go to school in terrible outfits and too-perfect haircuts and we couldn't care less except for what was for lunch that day?"

This girl didn't deserve any of this but I was on a roll so I continued— "There is a picture in my second grade yearbook of me standing next to a drinking fountain. I was wearing what looked like my father's sweatshirt, which was tucked into my skintight acid wash jeans that only reached a few inches past my knees. And on top of this I had velcro sneakers and highwater socks pulled up as high as they could go. My hair was faded sort of the way it is now, except parted with gel and very much on purpose. I looked like a hipster with terrible style—which is saying a lot. And you know what was the best part?"

I had been acting out this entire bit, sticking my jeans tight to my thighs and tucked in my shirt real deep and walked around like a nerd for Halloween. They all laughed as I contorted my body and made fun of myself. Kimberly laughed most of all so I felt only slightly forgiven for being so mean to her only moments before.

"What?" Emma laughed while pouring a tequila shot.

"The best part is that I didn't even know that I looked stupid. None of us knew anything. I was most concerned with recess and not getting a note sent home and gym class. I exclusively cared about gym class. I miss that," I said genuinely.

"I do too," they all said.

Kimberly shifted in her skin tight dress and excused herself to the bathroom. I bet she thought about wiping off some makeup just then. That would have been nice. Although I'm sure she didn't.

Five shots of tequila later Aden and I stumbled out of Emma's apartment hoping she would take care of us. She would. And I don't know why we drink so much anyways? Mostly alcohol is a tool. We use it because we're all lost and think it will navigate us towards something, anything really — fun, sex, love, a release? I don't know. Those are all the same thing anyway. We drink because if we didn't, no one would dance, and only the sluts would have sex, and only the extroverts would have any fun. We drink because we're too afraid not to.

Or maybe it just tastes good?

+

THE WEEK BEFORE CHICAGO, Aden and I went out to the bars to get a good taste of Ann Arbor before leaving. We drank and smoked and danced and climbed our way into our memories to take a good look around, making sure we wouldn't miss anything. That week we wanted Ann Arbor, college, and all the beauties of having a home. I wanted to stumble back into my apartment and kiss Andrea. God I wanted to kiss Andrea.

Michigan, in being a university and all, it has to show off its wealth of knowledge and wealth of architecture and it's wealth of artistry in order to show off its wealth, of course — so it built a new wing for the modern art museum in between the gothic law quad and the ivy drenched union building. To its left was the literature and philosophy building with its Greek pillars and just beyond that was a great depression-era, salmon-colored, bricked building for studying politics. The modern art museum would stick out as much as a shell on a beach, with its flat walls and its unnecessary clumps of glass. I don't know why modern architects think building museums that look like warehouses is a novel idea? It's not. It's not cheeky or ironic or modern. It's boring.

The museum had its grand opening on a Friday night and so would stay open 24 hours for the students. The organizers of the event advertised all over campus that they were going to hire DJs to play different styles of music in different rooms to commemorate the reopening. They would have free food and extended tours and nothing would be off limits even at four in the morning — my favorite time of the day. They figured that in order to get students interested they had to promise them a party and snacks—and they were very right.

Aden and I had it all planned. That night after having drank at our favorite watering hole we shouted out orders for Mexicans working at La Cantina, which served food as Mexican as their American customers would allow them to. The menu read like a dietician's list of foods to avoid. After a night of drinking fishbowls of alcohol, college students don't care what they eat so long as it is big. Bacon laced beans, fried rice and cumin, cilantro, fried chicken and fried pork, melted cheese, guacamole, sour cream, hot sauce and salsa, extra sour cream, and I had it all wrapped in a machine pressed burrito much bigger than my head. Aden had his as well, so we were armed and dangerous, packing two tinfoil wrapped burritos without napkins into our holstered coat pockets.

There were many students there but they weren't alive yet, we noticed. They all were politely mingling with their hors d'ouvres and their whispered personalities. Right off I recognized the DJ as a friend of a friend who occasionally played at a local club on Thursday nights. I was still wearing my coat because I didn't know where to put it and I wouldn't have cared if I had, because I just danced and danced and then gestured to everyone looking at me that "yes it is OK to dance," and so slowly a few others joined in. Aden had called a few girls he knew but at this point I was already anticipating, or hoping to get back with Andrea permanently so ignored them. I could tell Aden wasn't as drunk as I was and wished I had been more of an honest wingman but I had a terrible habit of sleeping with girls I didn't care about and was trying to quit cold turkey.

The music pulsated inside of me. I jumped rapturously while taking chomping bites of my burrito, half finding my mouth, half spilling out its contents onto the uber clean floor. A bar bouncer would shrug at such a site, a drunken idiot spitting out rice and sour cream on the floor while spinning around in circles—but here at the museum there weren't any bouncers. There were only old women and men with glasses, all wearing straight black pants and straight black collars and straight black jaw lines and straight black individualities. I was a splash of color to them, and they hadn't the courage to stop me, questioning if only for a moment whether I was part of the show or not, like a mobile art exhibit titled "what I learned in college."

So they let me go. They let me dance. It was 3 am and I was encouraging others to dance with me. And the organizers wanted to be able to say, "Yeah it was a great success the kids had a lot of fun dancing," to their colleagues the next day. They hated me but they needed me and they knew it. So they let me go.

After there were dozens of girls and guys still drunk from the bars already dancing, I left to go run around the museum by myself. I stared at each piece: a blue phone this time and a lobster, a twenty foot mural of a straight line, a robot sitting on an old rocking chair, a video of someone screaming on mute, a chess set glued to the ceiling, but only for a few seconds each time. And in between each painting or each exhibit I ran. I ran to the next one spilling out more and more chicken, and accidentally smearing more cheese and more guacamole. Eventually a young boy about my age dressed up as a police officer told me I had to calm down or leave but I told him I didn't speak English, in English, and ran off to the next piece of art. The ceilings were high the way I like and empty so echoed while I staggered into my loud sentences.

"What do you think this means?" I asked a nice couple holding hands next to a pile of bright pink bricks in the middle of the floor.

"I think…"

I took another gnaw on my burrito and ran away to the green pile of bricks in the other corner of the room before they could finish. "Yeah but what do you think *this* pile of bricks mean?" I would cackle while running away again not listening to anything, not even myself.

Aden later found me with two girls on his arm and I think I was supposed to have sex with one of them or distract her from her friend or at least be nice to her or something, but I wanted to move more quickly so I pulled everyone onto the dance floor which was really just the entranceway to the museum and thrashed my head up and down to the beat beat beat, boom boom boom, and the laser lights pointed at me and then careened away just as quickly—red, blue, green, bite of the burrito, red, blue, green, and I lost my coat somewhere too.

"Where is my coat?" I wondered to Aden.

"You must have put it down somewhere. Let's look around."

"No—let's go home," I finished. "I'm done with Ann Arbor."

+

WE FOLLOWED EMMA AND Kimberly into a modern bar—the type where all the lights come up from the ground, and are generally neon and awkwardly red. It looked like a gutted hospital room, and smelled only slightly better. I prefer bars where male bartenders wear t-shirts and tell you to "fuck off" if you complain about anything. But here I asked for a beer from a fake blonde, her tits spilling out almost touching the top of my bottle. I sighed thinking *"let's make the best of this."*

I turned to Emma and gave her a big wet kiss on the cheek because I wanted to and because there was a friendly looking group of guys standing behind us.

I left her saying, "I'm going to go meet some girls," very loudly so that no one could question whether we were together or not. I don't know if she appreciated that, but I had good intentions regardless.

I ended up sitting on the floor next to a group of girls and guys, and made more than polite conversation with one of the girls specifically. Emma quickly noticed and ushered me towards her.

"You met my friends?" she asked knowing the answer already.

I turned back and pointed at the group sitting behind me—"Those ones? Those are your friends?"

"Yes. I know basically everyone here. I toooold you. This is a party for my friend's birthday," she said hitting me on the shoulder.

"I absolutely did not get that part at all. I was wondering why we were at such a stuffy bar."

"I know right?" she agreed.

"But yeah your friends are nice."

"So Melanie," she said like she was about to tell me something important. She paused and grabbed my shirt collar and pulled my eyes down towards hers—"Melanie is dating Rob right next to her so I would back off a little bit. He can get jealous."

"Melanie and Rob are the people I was talking to?"

She nodded in the affirmative.

"Rob? First—Rob is gay. And second, I'm just being nice. I'm here for *you*. All these people can drop off the face of the Earth and it could just be you and me and I'd be perfectly happy. I was just hoping you would talk to some of these guys. I was trying to give you some room to breathe," I said truthfully.

She grabbed my collar even stronger this time so I had to lean over closer. She whispered, "I think Rob is gay too," in a way that denoted she was relieved to finally have found someone with such common sense.

"Well what do you want me to do then?" I asked confused. "Do you want me to hang out here and we'll just rock out or do you want me to go talk to your friends and leave you time to get hit on?"

I paused while she thought to herself.

"You look hot by the way," I said to distract her.

She smiled briefly.

"Thank you," she sighed. "Uhhh…let's just go over there together so they all know we know each other and you can be introduced instead of just being crazy like you always are."

"This makes sense," I responded but I didn't mean it.

She looked sexy in her dress and she really had done her hair that day and I could tell she wasn't going to start talking politics at a moment's notice like she normally does. She was relaxed because we were there. She knew she had allies. This was the perfect time for her to go out and feel pretty on her own. But she didn't. She wanted our comfort instead. She treated herself like a scab desperately needing to be picked, so I was naturally annoyed though appreciative.

Aden was hitting on a girl closer to the entrance to the bar because he's always hitting on a girl. He was also trying to find out where Billy was. We were supposed to meet up with him near Georgetown.

After saying goodbye to all of Emma's friends, gay and straight and confused alike, we headed in a cab up the street towards Billy. We had literally and figuratively traveled thousands of miles to meet him here on the peak of our journey. After him we would slowly descend upon the south, jumping and skipping along the way, but only as an affirmation of what we had already achieved. Billy was our summit, the farthest north we'd go, and the closest to home we'd ever feel while still afar.

The bar looked like a bar and that's all I can remember because I met Billy there. He takes up a lot of mental space for me, physical too when he gets drunk and starts dancing. See — he does everything big. His personality expands outward past his skin and touches everyone around him like a topical cream prescribed for depression. You can't help but smile when you are around him — the way he acts out stories with his whole body and turns himself into characters with specific voices, the way he only compliments people when he means it, and the way he compliments people all the time.

He speaks like an exploding firework, gesturing in every direction. He is noticeable from every angle. Watching him is like watching television in color for the very first time. He reminds me of a thoughtful Jim Carey though even more talented, and funnier, because unlike a movie star, Billy is in real life.

I think he always wanted to be a movie star actually — and probably dreams of having a recognizable name and looking taller on television than he does in person. But don't we all?

Though if ever there existed a person who was made to be famous, it was him. But sadly no one is made for fame; they just sort of deal with it the way that we all deal with it — each of us from our own side of life's two-way mirror.

"How the hell are ya doin my brother?" I said while giving him a big bear hug. From the outside we held the hug much too long, but for us it was too short. It's always too short.

"I'm good man," he said into my ear patting my back strongly with his hand, "I'm doin' really good."

Emma and Aden knew him but not the way I knew him. I knew about his ninja turtle bedspread in grade school and his first kiss in junior high and his first love in high school and roared around in his first car and we saw movies together and went to our first teen clubs together and talked on the phone in college when we needed a trusted comrade on the other end. Our mutually close friends always teased us that we would one day finally declare our undeniable love for each other.

"I do love him," I would say in response.

"I do love him," he would say in response.

And that was the way with us. We were past the filters of masculinity and certainly past the limits of apprehensive communication. We were brothers in arms, reuniting after our long journeys while apart. He had been sailing around the world near Australia and had stopped off in Fiji to find his wife and saw New Zealand too, just to try the food. He had swam on the South Asian beaches and tasted the culture of China, and had backpacked through Europe with me only a year before all of that. And I had traveled to Central America and around the great American Plains and fiddled my way through a million different accents and cultures and had backpacked through Europe with him only a year before all of that too. So our reunion was a reunion for two souls that although separate, had an internal magnetism. We were metaphysically required to come together at least once a year for a proper refueling.

Friendship is the same as love in this way. A true friend brings himself unapologetically open and empty to the other. A true friend acknowledges himself similar to a spouse. There is an understanding that in order to definitively separate it would take a betrayal of such magnitude, that the thought of such a scenario is neither tolerated nor spoken of. In this way, a best friend is superior even to a spouse.

Friendships have much higher success rates than marriages though, and without all the paperwork.

So Billy and I mostly hung onto each other's shoulders and bought rounds for the whole gang. There were other people at the bar I presume, but I didn't see any of them. We built a tent around our own depravity and pushed down hard on the fast forward button. Everything spun around into our mouths, splashing and swirling around, and we'd squint with the tequila and pucker at the lime, hiding our expressions for the rum, and so all the dirty fluids of American bars saturated us. And we loved it. We yelped and danced and jumped in our tent, just happy to be home once again with each other.

After that nothing particularly exciting happened because nothing particularly exciting ever happens when we drink. We become so comfortable with the speed that we don't mind missing everything in the blur. Drunk is the new tipsy. And tipsy is the new happy.

Emma got us home without much difficulty although I could tell she was a little more than "happy" herself. She had experienced the curse of all women that night. She wanted to fully let loose but couldn't, because she had to make sure her boys wouldn't kill themselves along the way, like a mother at her son's wedding. But she didn't mind much I don't think.

When we got home I slipped into nothing, stripping all my clothes off, throwing them down on the kitchen floor, and grabbed a bottle of water. Aden did something similar and plopped down on the couch. I sat down at the kitchen table, which was in the same space as the living room and Aden sleeping, which was in the same room as Emma's bedroom and bed, which was in the same room as her library and entranceway to the bathroom. It was all one big room. City flats are incredibly private, unless you have someone over and then you can't ever get away. She did her best to partition off sections of the area with her pretty cloths and shelves, but there is something about a real wall that just can't be replicated.

I put my head on the kitchen table trying to melt into the wood, with the bottle of water still mostly full because I couldn't muster up the ambition to lift it up to my mouth. It was as if my whole body was swimming in a thick pudding of bad breath and malnutrition, and I couldn't move except for what gravity helped me with.

"Kristopher you have no pants on," Emma said to me from the other side of the room, toothbrush still in her mouth.

"Emma I don't have a shirt on," I grumbled not looking up and she laughed.

The black world underneath my eyelids was spiraling out of control. It was how a blind man must feel like after spinning in circles. I pried one eye open with my index finger and thumb, holding it open like you would a cadaver's. I was close to being one anyway. And through this forced open and inebriated eye, I noticed Emma there in her nightgown walking back towards the bathroom sink. I only got a glimpse, just a secret, a flowing hint of an upper thigh and a sheer bottom. And so I noticed her there just then as an object of my affection, a truthful attraction, for the very first time. It was partly because I was drunk and partly because I hadn't been with a girl in a few weeks, but mostly because she really did turn me on.

There is something about a nightgown and glasses that really gets to me — the juxtaposition of intelligence and sensuality, and the warm feelings after a conversation about a recently read book. There is nothing hotter than a girl reading a book in glasses except for a girl reading a book in glasses while wearing a nightgown. I don't know why I hadn't noticed before, but she had always been that girl. I only needed to see that nightgown to put me over the edge.

I wish I could have thought myself away from those urges, but I couldn't. See — everything is emotion. Emotion is the drug and its withdrawal and its recovery and its relapse all in one. It's the whole damn process. Logic only grovels at the feet of emotion and hopes to be heard. But it never is.

We curled in bed next to each other not awkwardly, but only because she never could have imagined what was crossing my mind. It had never been like that with us. If it had, then I certainly would have already tried. We had 4 years of college to figure this out, and yet, still, after all this time, I wanted to reach across that line. I wanted to so anxiously that I worried she would be able to feel my heart as if it were pounding inside of her own chest.

So my hand rested there, frozen only a few inches from the dimples of her back. But for all my self-proclaimed grandeur I couldn't mount the courage to reach any farther across the bed; there was a great chasm of proclaimed friendship already deeply entrenched in those inches. I told myself it was all Aden's fault for snoring loudly on the couch and thus ruining the mood. Only then did I relax enough to fall asleep, having given myself an ample excuse. And it's a good thing I didn't try anything too — it would have been too meaningless for her. She wouldn't have obliged me because she's not one who generally obliges, but even if she had, even if only out of sheer boredom or curiosity, it would have been too quiet and too clumsy.

And she deserves better than my randomness. She deserves better than what I was willing to give her — as all girls do.

Chapter 14

WE WOKE UP SOMETIME after Emma. She had already been to the market and was planning a trip to an apple orchard. She would later cook a beautiful apple pie, but we wouldn't be there to eat it. It seems — sometimes we're too late even when we show up early.

She woke us up, ushering us to a Jewish deli owned by Koreans in an old arts district. I ate a bagel and lox, and then promptly threw it up in a back alley next to a dumpster. Then I ate another bagel with cream cheese, and too promptly threw that one up in a marble, black speckled urinal next to a balding man and a clean mirror at the Hilton across the street. I spread my remnants from the top to the bottom, from the fat cats to the alley cats, from the high rises all the way down into the abandoned subway lines. We all throw up, I thought. The only difference is what comes out. I prefer moonshine because it feels like you are giving something back to nature. But that's just me.

I stumbled back into the deli and an old Korean woman at the counter made fun of me. "Do you want to try a third bagel?" she asked while chuckling.

"No," I said sickly.

"I've never seen you like this," Emma said accurately. "In college you rarely if ever got sick from partying."

"I know," I said sickly.

Aden piped in, thoroughly enjoying his egg sandwich — "Did you throw up two times?"

"Yes," I said sickly.

"Well…" Emma paused not sure what to say considering my mood—"What next?"

"I don't know," I said sickly.

No. I know. Yes. I don't know.

The story of my life.

I felt like time had snuck up behind me and bopped me in the head real quick saying, *"you're not young anymore you know? You gotta grow up."* She might as well have killed me. All I had was my youth, I thought. It was my excuse for everything—my excuse for breaking Andrea's heart, for treating other women so badly, for drinking too desperately, for caring so little, for caring so much and so randomly, for beating down my body just enough to peal it off the cement and force it to run marathons, for belittling my generation so exquisitely and for berating my elders with such sardonic zeal, for throwing up bagels just for the hell of it, and most of all, it was my excuse for still being hopeful after all of that.

Without youth we have nothing. This is true even when we're old.

They eventually convinced me to pick my head up off the table, and only twenty minutes after that, did they convince me to leave the deli. Emma had made her decision to leave us for the day. She had to meet one of her friends downtown for a lunch date, but assured us that she would find us for dinner—though she wouldn't.

We drove around downtown not saying much, a few blocks here or there, and Emma pointed around to every building, explaining their histories to us. I was slowly feeling better, with every step I could feel it, my body having fully gotten over its hangover. Wouldn't it be nice if breakups were just as quick? If we could just vomit it all out and go about our day as if nothing ever happened?

"Drop me off over there," she said.

"No," Aden insisted, "we can take you to wherever you need to go."

"You are stupid," she insisted back. "I have to walk only a few blocks east, which is left, and you can't go left up here because of the one way. Just drop me off over there and I'll walk a few blocks — it's not an issue. That way you guys can go west on State Street and that will take you right up towards Ben's Chili Bowl. That's where you are meeting Billy right?"

"Yeah," I said.

"OK I guess that makes sense," Aden finally agreed.

She had to go; she needed time on her own. See — Emma clinches tightly to herself. We all do, but her especially so. So although she rather enjoyed us, and in fact needed us like a gasping breath after being under water for too long, she also rejoiced in and was therefore proud of her unadulterated independence. She was a woman through and through. So she left us then rather womanly looking, asking us if we knew where we were going and demanded that we reassure her that everything would be alright, that we wouldn't kill ourselves.

"We know exactly what we are doing," I said as she scurried out of the car, shutting the door.

She smiled and waved.

We smiled and waved.

"I promise we'll be fine," Aden insisted knowing she didn't believe us for a second. He then proceeded to turn left down the ass end of a one way street. He slammed on his breaks and beeped his horn to the traffic behind him insisting that they "move it or lose it," annoyed, as if it were their faults he had to back up into oncoming traffic.

Though he eventually wiggled his way into a successful right turn and we were off, Emma all the while standing on the sidewalk staring at us like we were zoo animals making funny noises. She smiled and waved again, this time rolling her eyes. We smiled and waved again, this time shrugging our shoulders as if to say, "We'll...probably...be fine?"

After turning the wrong way a few more times, we eventually made it to Ben's Chili Bowl. It was famous, or so we were told, for DC residents. It had grown legendary in the middle of a horridly depressed part of DC, or a beautifully romantic part of it—depending upon which story you believed. The area was once a burgeoning center for jazz clubs and poetry, a place where all the educated and working class of the black community could dance and smile together. *"If you're white, you can go in through the back,"* I imagined their bouncers saying. Though they probably didn't.

But as is the story, eventually the roaring 20's fell into the coffin of war and a great depression, one that didn't reverse discriminate. But then like the rolling tides of our ever changing economy, U Street and the Lincoln Theater became alive again just before Martin Luther King's assassination. It was nicknamed "Washington's Broadway" and teemed with life and fashion.

Then there were riots, and the roller coaster continued, with those harrowed inhabitants only enjoying one smell of consistency—the smell of spicy chili and juicy sausage emanating from a few blocks away. Like a lone soldier carrying his wounded, Ben's Chili Bowl brought hope and laughter, celebrity even, to an otherwise stale and broken part of the country.

Upon arrival we found Billy kissing a statue of a polar bear which nestled itself on the sidewalk adjacent to our car.

"What is he doing?" Aden asked.

"Being Billy," I answered.

I walked speedily towards him and his cousin, who was also equipped with a friend. I had met the two non-Billy participants in our adventure the night before, but didn't really notice them and still don't remember what they look like without reminding myself forcefully by way of a photograph. They sort of blended into the scenery for most of the afternoon. No matter—I kept towards Billy and gave him a very similar hug to the one I had shared with him only a day earlier.

"There's my brother," I said sternly, wrapping my hands around him, "How are you doing my man?" This hug was crisper, harder, and more sober. We needed more sober.

"I'm doing really good," he said again. "I'm doing really good."

We all analyzed the statue some more. It was no taller than any of us, but certainly was human sized, and was painted very mismatched like, as if a rainbow had tried her hand at corporate art. Later we found out from Emma that children in fact were the producers of these bears. Each school had been commissioned to paint one, and subsequently they were bolted down at odd locations all around the city, to show its care for children and the arts in one fell swoop. The rainbow now made sense. Children are all rainbows. It was painted with geometric shapes and almost exclusively with primary colors — spirals and triangles taking up most of its space.

Billy wondered while analyzing it more closely — "How do you know it's a Polar Bear?"

"Because his undergarments are white," I answered.

"Undergarments? I'll ignore that," he continued, "and how do you know it is a he?"

"Because it's a bear. All bears are males."

"This biologically cannot be true," Aden said, adding some reason to our silly argument.

"Well..." I paused, "that doesn't matter. Bears are too vicious and too mean and too big and hairy not to be men. The same way all cats are female because they are too dainty to be anything but."

"I just kissed it," Billy shouted curtly, "so it can't be a guy."

"I'm telling you, that statue, that one right there, with all its color and cuteness, is still a ferocious and dominating..."

"Wait," Billy yelled with his hands flinging up towards my face, "Ferocious and dominating you say? That is sexy...definitely a girl."

We all laughed and took inappropriate pictures with the statue because, well, because we are stupid.

As we entered the restaurant we realized it was completely full from the inside although we hadn't noticed any activity while outside of its doors. Right away a tall black man yelled at us—"Wait there for a second will you? We'll get to you real soon now don't you worry. You ever been here before? Well...have at it then. We're famous. Look at the walls why don't you? Eh? Well what are you waiting for I tell ya, order right here and we'll get everything sizzlin' right quick eh?"

I leaned into Billy asking him, "Which question should I answer?"

Aden took charge exactly as he always does, walking deep into the restaurant and interrupting a server. I could see his arms gesturing towards us and towards the ceiling, not sure why, and then towards a back table that seemed to be open. He smiled and then became stern, and then smiled again and touched the waitress on the shoulder. She eventually turned around to refill a drink for someone, giving him a nod. He then held up two forceful thumbs and ushered us towards the back room.

"He's good at charades," Billy joked.

"He's good at flirting," I corrected him.

No sooner than that were we sitting down in the back room. It was covered with tarp paper and red cups, plastic bins for cleaning, televisions all strangely turned to c-span, and was covered with signed pictures of celebrities the likes of which Hollywood would envy.

"You know President Obama ate here once?" one of the waiters bragged to us while walking by, like a proud parent.

The place was loud and boisterous but polite all the same. I imagined I could hale down a passing busboy with a whistle and no one would mind, so long as I appreciated his hospitality with a smile and didn't take too much advantage. We ordered chili and hotdogs and sausage and all of it came with cheese and French fries and a scattering of Freetos. We all ordered different meals but it all came out the same really, having been all cooked in the same half-century old frying pit and all seared with the same iconic sweat.

"These hands are my daddy's hands and before that my grandaddy's hands," one of the cooks would say, *"and she over there is my cousin and her too my sister, and you see that fine young lad he'll be off to Princeton next Fall we're so proud of him, yes we are, but he's my brother too and yes sir we've been splitting open this pork and frying it up real good since before your parents were even thought of yes sir and yes ma'am."*

You could tell they were Virginian blacks. At least they spoke like it. And they cooked like it too. All the flavors lingered slowly in our mouths, and all the cheeses melted and dripped back onto our trays. We sipped up frothing shakes and covered it all with the freshest damn water since Yosemite, watching television and pointing at all the history.

It was beautiful.

But then came the bill.

I hate bills.

In fact I hate eating with strangers if only because it's too intimate. At the end of the meal you always find out if the person you are eating with is a good person or not. It's like knowing their childhood and their values and their historical and spiritual worth after only half an hour. I feel like a voyeur, like I'm peering into their souls without their permission. What I'm talking about, of course, is how someone tips. There are only two types of people in this world, good people and bad people, and there is only one way to accurately find out who is who — look at how they tip.

A friend of mine who was only a friend of mine for a few dinners in college once told me — "It's not my responsibility to pay for them. A tip is a tip, and therefore is not required."

"Well it is not their responsibility to work for you without you paying them either, is it?"

"They should get paid more from the restaurant," he countered.

"No they shouldn't, because that is our custom. Tipping is a part of our culture. If we didn't do it this way then we would have indifferent servers like in Europe who don't give a shit how many times you've asked for a refill because they're not going to make any more money if it takes them twenty minutes."

"Well I just don't like it. And I'm a poor college student."

"So are they…and at least they have the decency to work and not go out to eat with their daddy's allowance and then have the gall not to tip. It's absolutely pathetic."

"I'm not pathetic!"

"You are pathetic. If you don't want to tip them then you should go get your own damn side of sauce and go refill your own drink, and pick up your own damn food from the cook and bring in your own extra napkins as well. McDonalds exists for a reason. You ask them to serve you and then you don't pay them for their services? It's like stealing. It's pathetic," I told him very angrily.

"Well it looks like I shouldn't go out to eat with you anymore," he said dejected.

"You should never go out to eat at all. You're not worthy of it," I finished.

Billy has a history of saving his money, but when he goes out to eat he's always a good tipper. He was a waiter so he knows. Aden also has a history of saving his money, but when he met me and I gave him my behind-the-scenes perspective he immediately changed his tipping habits. Our friendship would have seriously suffered had he not. This trip probably would have never happened. Tipping is *that* important.

So I sat there waiting to find out if Billy's cousin and his sidekick were in fact good people. They weren't. Unfortunately they were worse than bad people. They were crooks.

"You owe more than eight dollars," I said to Billy's cousin.

"My fish sandwich was eight dollars," he said to dismiss me.

"*Fish sandwich? Hungry? Me. Pay. Look. Eight dollars. Good. Me. Happy,*" is what I heard.

"And you had a coke and you ate half the appetizer and there is tax and you have to tip because you had a waiter. Do you want me to do the math for you or do you think you can handle it yourself?" I said to him.

Billy gave me a look like "*whoa man this is my cousin,*" but also knew not to say anything. He'd been there before with me. He knew not to push this button.

I have a very warm heart normally, but there is a fiery rough part of it that only shows itself when confronted with bad tippers. I can talk about the Holocaust academically with a Nazi sympathizer, discuss the problems and nuances of gay rights in Wyoming, and calmly articulate my feelings about abortion with a Baptist minister from Georgia — but if someone doesn't tip well, then hell hath no fury.

Though I got over it soon enough, and so we made a collective decision to "go see something cool" close to the monuments. We started at the northern end near the National Museum of Art, but skipped it in lieu of seeing the grassy mall instead. We walked up to it and just sort of hung out for a while.

"Is this supposed to be important?" Billy said pointing to the capitol building.

And of course he joked, he teased — he joked a great ironic joke.

The Capitol Building? Important?

...It looked like one enormous carving, like the great Titans, still ruling over Zeus and his brothers, forced those gods to chisel away through the centuries until they finally cracked the Earth so carefully, so perfectly, that it gave birth to that grand building before us.

We had no words or discussions — all standing in complete awe, feeling like peasants at the foot of our kingdom's great castle. It laid there in a wild musicality, balancing its sharp intimidating edges and its serene white carvings with such an exquisite stability that it hardly boasted though it could have. There it stood, surrounded by the greatest particularities of antiquity and other daunting architectures, next to all the warm museums and their intellectual innards, peaceful in its regality. The Capitol Building, busy with its powerful men and powerful women all scurrying about signing laws for moneys and futures so frequently, can and should accurately be described as the most important building that has ever existed on this great Earth. Of all the countries and of all the capitols and all the lands and all the churches and all the histories and all the dominatingly contented governments, there exists no serious competition for the power of this great building. In no other space does there exist such supremacy. In no other location, should there be an edifice with such an equivalent authority. In no prior scene had their ever occupied such a sturdy leviathan. So there we stood, on the bottom step of the world, and fell silent.

Feeling a combination of fear, pride, and sadness, I ushered Billy and Aden away from it to start the long journey down the mall.

We walked around quite slowly, which was in no part due to our attempts. We rushed along straining our muscles every which way trying to zip past each monument, only wanting to take the picture, skip the significance, and on to the next. But still, we walked quite slowly. Washington DC is completely underwater in this way, with the calamity of tourists and picture flashes and indistinguishable children; everything is under water. We bound onwards in our minds, tearing at the air and violently we clench our muscles, but each statue or bell, each plop of melting ice cream or carved word, each momentary flap of the flag or each marbled stair, they all fight back at us like a thick water. No matter our indifferent tempo, Washington DC demands our attention, and so slows us, requiring a reaction each and every time.

So we sauntered like a French film in fast forward, maintaining only a daft awareness of what was going on around us. We ignored the museums and kept on towards the monuments in the distance. Sure we were just a few feet away from the entrances for a few of the greatest museums in the world, but I didn't care. I had my friends, and they were better than anything I could have seen in a box.

We continued walking diligently, now on the actual grass.

"Is this sacred grass?" Billy asked. "Are we allowed to walk on it?"

"I don't think so. No — I mean, I think we *are* allowed to walk on it. I don't think it's sacred. I don't…think?" Aden said.

I wasn't sure if Billy was serious but had a similar question myself so treated it sincerely. "Well we are a secular country right?" I said, "…I think that means nothing is sacred."

"Yeah, we own this shit anyways," Aden said.

"Tax dollars at work," Billy agreed.

"Let's go throw the football over there," I suggested, running outwardly not waiting for a response. Billy launched it but by the time I caught it I was butted up against the mouth of the Washington monument, it jutting up pointedly into the sky.

At first glance, Washington's monument is unapologetically phallic. This makes sense considering the way he indulged in his slaves. But neither should I be so bold as to only give Washington credit for his monument's nerve. Most of the buildings in Washington DC are also purposefully audacious. Americans are like Romans in this way, except cockier. We build giant statues but not for any particularly good reason. We just do.

Billy rushed up towards it and gave it a great wide hug.

"Thank you Mr. Washington," he said sarcastically, "Thank you Mr. Washington so much for giving us freedom and thank you so much for not allowing women to vote and for giving us slaves to build the White House with and this great city also. Thank you so much for everything. You're such a great example for us all."

I then lied down at the base of the monument staring upwards.

There I was, with my insignificant speck of this world, me in my tiny little spot, with my devilishly selfish perspective on everything, carrying only an acutely tunneled version of reality, all of it forcing my eyes upwards into the ever shimmering above. All I could see was what I could see: blue and blue and blue and a white cloud mirrored by two twin flagpoles and their huddled banners waving near their peaks, more blue and still even more blue after that. I could hear the laughs of children playing next to me and smelled the sweet smell of newly created bubbles, and heard even the faint pitter patter of a rushing helicopter in the distance. The breeze and its inhabitants swirled into my nose and filtered through my lungs and in and out, and there was more blue above me still, another laugh, and the snap-snap of photographs all around. I was intimate with the whole thing, intimate with each part of that moment.

Though just as quickly as I had settled there, wanting to forget where I was and pay closer attention to the falling away sky, Billy's face came full force into my line of sight, completely engulfing my peripheral, framing the edges of my world on one side with his chin and the other side with his draping hair.

"Get up, get up, get up, it's time to save the world," he said mouth wide open.

"Makes sense," I said only mildly discomforted while pushing him away from me.

He jumped back just then and began skipping with his hands flailing high into the air, legs thrashing to and fro. "Perfect," he chirped, "and now we're off to see the wizard."

He always wore the same thing, Billy did — flip flops, jeans, booted, a desperately plain t-shirt, and a hat. Some days he would wear a white t-shirt and others a light blue, but on this day he wore a faded yellow one. I think he dressed so averagely because otherwise he would be unbearably audacious. Very often the shyest people are those who wear the most peculiar and therefore most noticeable outfits. They do this because they are so inwardly panicked, that the only way they know how to express themselves is through outward fluttering. Billy fits perfectly within this thesis, except that he would fit on the opposite end of the spectrum, as an outlier of such ferocious volume who therefore must, if only for survival, carefully suppress his visible appearance.

So we kept on in that way, skipping and hooting, separating if only to come right back towards each other. Though all of that only lasted a few short meters.

Soon came the calm of a memorial for a great world war, which naturally shone dim and was therefore demanding of our attention. There was a quiet pool, in which rested an even quieter fountain, dripping and dripping with the memories and the snapshots of a far away and just war — quite possibly the only just war. Around this glass of water stood cemented and therefore striking, a circle of carved states. Each state was represented in the war, and therefore each state had its own engraved plaque of sorts.

You could predict which states were where if only by the people huddled around their sections...

The longhaired veterans and their families, many-many families, all crouched together over California. I saw an old man with gray socks pulled up tight around his veiny legs, wearing a bald eagle sweatshirt, standing purposefully next to West Virginia. And there over by Oklahoma was a heavy set man, wide legged, sprawling tall, taking up as much space as possible. A large crowd gathered around next to another of the states, many of them as black as night, but regal looking, and proud. I imagined there near carved was the word Mississippi. And so on this went as I stood there, taking a look at Michigan quickly, giving Ohio even less time, and moved on to whichever state I saw next. I felt like they were all mine. I had a personal connection with them all, and if I hadn't yet, I would soon enough, I thought.

Just when I was about to round up my own troops, not knowing where Billy or Aden were, I felt a tap on my shoulder.

"Come," Aden encouraged me.

He was very resolute and very clear, already walking away from me. I had already been to where he was headed to, so paused for a moment, interpreting his enthusiasm as being an Aden version of the word, and therefore not necessarily reasonable. Though I ultimately posited that this time might be worth it, but only after he had turned around once again and emphatically waved me towards him.

When I arrived, fully expecting him to point out a pretty girl, I was surprised to see that although he *was* pointing out a pretty girl, she had only been alive for what could not have been more than two years.

She waddled unknowingly in a polka dotted red dress. Her miniscule arms were no longer than the long end of my forearm. What hair she did have was pulled up carefully into a red bow. She looked like a Christmas present, no bigger, yet incomparably more valuable. The top of her head would only reach to my knee, but I couldn't help but picture her all grown up, one day standing at the very same spot she was just then, though older.

And what was most significant about this scene, more than her simple cuteness, was that there seemed not to be a parent in sight. Of course, actually there were dozens of parent-looking adults all standing beyond her peripheral, all watching her the same as Aden and I. I assumed one of those watching pairs of eyes were her father's, and another owned by her mother, but even so, they let her roam as she pleased, as did everyone else there.

Each of her steps felt controlled, very heavy, and incredibly labored. She looked as though she was thinking quite earnestly to herself—"now left, now right, now left, now right"—still learning how to manage her own body. And each step, each careful advance, brought her closer to the edge of that pool. And carved there, was a word, a very simple word, etched and fortified in the stone. She walked towards it, as if drawn by some innate desire, some inalienable craving, finally pressing her hand gently upon the indentation of the first letter.

She looked up at the word, not knowing what it read, and neither understood its meaning, but still paused. Then she looked back at what now was a large crowd of adults, half crying, half taking photographs, and touched the second letter now.

This tiny little American with her red bow and her even redder dress, there at the epicenter of a monument, at the epicenter of a mall, at the epicenter of a city, at the epicenter of a country, there she touched the word "freedom" for the very first time.

+

FREEDOM IS A TRICKY thing. Most often, just when we finally understand its definition, almost immediately thereafter, we come face to face with its consequences. So too with Andrea, after a month of being separated from her, Aden and I went to Canada without her for a party.

I was free. I had made my decision. I accepted it — and was therefore finally ready to show myself to the world. I was ready to try and find someone new. I was — free (of her).

We drove in a limousine because we had too much money to spend, and thought we should therefore arrive in style — like good Americans. We passed the entrance without paying because someone we knew, knew someone who knew someone who knew the owner. Or something like that? The point is that we drank and danced and drank and danced. I saw blue lights and black girls and white dresses and gray suits and yellow shoes even — but only one blue dress.

As I twirled to my left, adjacent to one of the woofing speakers, a simple drop of sweat catapulted from the top of my bangs. It soured peacefully and my eyes followed it out and out, past a few teenagers, past a few leather shoes, past everyone, landing calmly near the toes of a girl in a bright blue dress.

Andrea.

It had been a month since I had last seen her in the flesh, and it was immediately obvious that my daydreams and memories about her were completely inadequate. "She's even more perfect than I remembered," I thought. I only saw the whisper of her profile that second though. She was spinning away from me, swiveling her hips, head held upwards, arms raised to the rafters — her eternal stance. Her dress shimmered in the blackness — I kept spinning — she kept reaching and I gulped. She swayed ass-up, hair-back, with high heels, dripping of sweat, with the music blasting — until the music stopped of course, and that's when our eyes met.

The last time we had spoken she had told me that she hated me — that every ounce of me was a sad evil to her. Everything about me repulsed her. I had betrayed her. Though still, everything about her melted me.

So I melted, but to my astonishment — she stayed with me. Not for very long of course, but if only for a few seconds, she lowered her hands, put them gently at her side, slowed her sway to a stop, locked her gaze with mine — and stayed.

She bit her lip shyly. I shrugged as if to say *"hello."* She gestured towards her then-boyfriend dancing beside her as if to say *"I'm with him now."* I shrugged again — not knowing what to do. She bit her lip again, this time to hold back tears, and turned around. Then she raised her hands again, lifted her head, and swayed her hips. I stared at her for quite a while, dancing robotically, until finally receding deeper into the dance floor. Maybe I would see her later that night, I thought? Maybe later?

+

EVENTUALLY WE CAUGHT BACK up with Billy and walked along the reflecting pool, every few feet crouching down to touch its waters. I thought for a moment about all its history and clenched my eyes tightly in daydream...

When I opened them, the whole world went away. All the people and the tourists, all the birds and the cars, all the sounds and the commotions, they all vanished like we were standing in a post-apocalyptic world, a peaceful one. We roamed around like cows in India thinking to ourselves "we own this shit" because technically, we did.

We took out our signs and stood in the middle of the million man march, listening to the great echoes of Martin Luther King reverberating into us. We changed our clothes and grew out our hair and heard Abbie Hoffman whispering to our left. Even the pool itself vanished if only for a moment, and I saw F.D.R. walking hopefully along the grassed prairie.

Then I heard a faint whisper from a far, as if the clouds were chanting to me. The sound grew stronger and stronger, louder and louder, clearer and clearer. I couldn't make out what it was so I ran up the steps of the Lincoln Memorial wondering if that great president himself had a message for me. I yearned to know so desperately what those words were. Clearer and clearer they came in, until I heard them directly and perfectly...

"That girl is eye-fucking you," Aden said.

Billy laughed a great big laugh and ushered me over for another picture next to still another monument. "I don't think she is," Billy said to Aden, "or if she is, we should talk to her parents because she looks about sixteen."

He shooed Billy and I farther to the left saying, "No I bet she's eighteen and she for sure wants one of you..."

"...I can tell," he said while snapping the picture.

"Well then we better put our best face forward," Billy said, always ready to find humor in any situation..

"Oh God," I countered, not knowing what that meant, but knew that it would be embarrassing.

It was. He widened his stance and stuck out his chest like a girl wanting a free drink, placed one fist at his waist, and with the other he reached towards the ceiling—like superman. He was posing like superman.

"Come on come on, let's be superheroes like Lincoln now," Billy insisted. "It'll impress the high-schooler I promise."

"Oh God," I said doing my best impression.

"Very sexy," Aden judged.

It was impossible to be serious with Billy, even with police officers around, or while being flanked by etched speeches about slavery and war, and with a view to end all views, with children, and echoes and tours and classes and passions and all sorts of serious endeavors — even in the face of absolute emotional reflection, Billy was a bottle of laughter, spilling himself all over the floors of whichever setting he found himself in.

"Now let's go talk to this girl and her babysitter," Billy laughed to make fun of Aden. "We must be off to ruin her life…"

"Oh God," I said.

Next we stopped by the Vietnam memorial and touched it and walked past it but that was about it. None of us had any grandparents or uncles or whomevers to stop us from being indifferent, so we stayed indifferent and ran over towards the White House.

We eventually found ourselves within view of it. There lived Obama, newly anointed and very much already a historical figure for our generation. We found ourselves there next to a few old women protesting something about gay people, or something about the Bible and how it wasn't being taken seriously enough, or maybe it was abortion? I don't know. But either way it looked pathetic and sad. Even though I found their politics disagreeable I felt as though they were a great example for the decline of my generation's activism. Had there been a glorious crowd of angry and organized protesters, youthful and vibrant, at least I would have felt more alive. Here we were at the foreground of the president's house, a man who had more influence on this world's goings-ons than any human being on Earth, and only a handful of hallowed women, sore from the weather, taking breaks in lawn chairs, had the decency to protest outside his door.

It was a sad time.

A war was raging somewhere in a desert but you'd never know it. Antiwar movements were distant and forced. Their organizers begged not for real participation because they knew they'd never get it — they simply hoped that anyone, someone, would feel anything above apathy. Rallies were blotchy now and even those in attendance more showed up for shame than passion — friends of friends all guilting one another saying "we should probably care about something eh?" as if they were deciding which movie to see that night.

We were a society of teenagers that cared for the shine of our cars more than the quality of our engines. And the politicians knew it, so they used our guilt and our bumper stickers and our empty slogans for their own gain. We used 9/11 like an "I heart New York" t-shirt, proud just for having been there when it all went down. But the shirt is dirty and stained now, and no one wants to scrub that hard. It will all settle in though, with time, and clean itself up, or blend in enough that we'll forget what it originally looked like — after the caskets come back, with the half dead soldiers in airplanes with their limbs in cargo boxes below them, sometime long after they're done holding cardboard signs on off ramps asking for help, sometime long after we pass them by in our minivans without giving any, after we're all dead except for our black and white leftovers, smudged all over the history books — yes — then we'll remember. We'll be given a nickname like The Great Generation. Ours will be something bold and unwarranted like theirs is. It'll be a holiday or something.

I repeat — it was a sad time. But even so it was also a time of hunger, and dinner no less, so we cozily walked back up the mall, this time on the street's edge, talking about girls and girls and sex and girls and girls, until we had reached our respective cars, picked out a place to go, and drove there together.

Though somehow we found ourselves at an outdoor art market instead because we wanted to see what warriors looked like up close and personal. We wanted to meet those who roughed up all the smooth edges, those who held their lives tight by the ends of their dreams and smashed down hard upon the city, bursting it with color and bending it into shapes and designs, inventing new forms of expression, desperately wanting to speak on behalf of something, someone, anything, anyone — bigger than themselves. The warriors of color — the artists.

"Good day'eh to ya young chaps, houw'r yas all dooin dis fine afternoon?" a gentlemen shouted to us as we walked by. I couldn't make out his particular brand of accent, but that made him all the more alive.

"I'm quite perfect," Aden answered boastfully.

"Wells der ain't nuddin more perfect den perfect ars there muh bruddah?"

"No there's not," Aden smiled back. "What'cha got here?"

The man was dark and regal like a Nigerian but certainly wasn't Nigerian. He had a Caribbean flair to him which most artists do, wearing a paint spattered Hawaiian shirt, old and baggy. In front of him were long rectangular paintings and long tubular sculptures of jet-black figures, almost alien shaped, playing trumpets or saxophones or bass guitars. You could almost hear their jazz in three dimensions.

"Do you like Jazz?" I asked him plainly.

"Oh's I like some Jazz now'n again," he said.

"Are these characters in your paintings playing jazz?" I pressed him more purposefully.

"Some of dem are's sure I bet'cha they ars. The ones that like Jazz…dems playing great Jazz. Each one play their own music whatever they like ya know? Like us."

We wished him well and moved on towards the next booth.

"Don't yas want anytin?" he asked us as we walked away.

"We're poor artists just like you," I said. "I'm sorry. We can't."

And I was — sorry. So much of my life was bound up in adventure and packed tightly in a backpack that I couldn't help but see the greener grass on the other side. Someday I would buy a great big statue of a great big black man playing his great big black tuba and maybe the music would be a soulful hip hop or a fast rock'n'roll but either way I would buy the damn thing and put it in my house and collect tiny monuments for all the artists — in solidarity — to say, "I'm with you muh brudda. I'm with you."

But I couldn't. I had no place to put any art. I had no wavering money in need of meaning. I had no one to show off to except for Aden and he would have much rather bought a handle of vodka than street art. No no no — we were with him and we felt his call — but we were miles away after just one glance.

"Do you think you'll ever build up the courage to go this far with your writing?" Aden asked me bluntly.

"What do you mean?"

"To call yourself a writer out loud and what not? ...To make a living at it. To really try-try?"

"I already do."

"No you don't. Not like these guys. I mean look at this girl...hello there ma'am." He tipped his hat to her, shuffled around her homemade cards and continued in saying, "she is pushing against what her parents told her and what her education taught her and she's at this market with her little stand and she's ready to make a living with these little cards because these little cards are what she wants to do. You know what I mean?"

I got real defensive and asked rhetorically — "Well I don't see you with any holy grail?"

"I know. I don't have it. But you do. And I would kill for one. You are always writing or talking about writing or reading or whatever and you *do* have your holy grail. You have the light at the end of your own tunnel but you don't have the balls to walk towards it."

"Well walking towards the light is ill advised in most cases."

"Come on now."

"I know man. I know." I really did know.

I continued — "But what's a writer anyways? That doesn't even mean anything? What do I do? I write something and hope to god someone wants to read it? And let's say someone wants to read it? …then what? I hope to god that someone wants to pay me for it?"

"Well," Aden asked me, "What's the difference between a writer and everyone else?"

"Nothing," I said confidently.

"Well there is your problem."

"What problem?"

"You're scared."

"Of course I'm scared! There is no starting point with writing. There is no blueprint. Fuck the finish line…that could be in Tibet for all I know? The finish line…whatever…I don't' care about the finish line…my problem is that I don't even know where the starting line is."

We then walked to the next booth to meet the next warrior. This time it was an old women standing in front of a bunch of paintings of Washington skylines. I wondered if she cared much for the skyline of Washington or if she just knew that tourists would buy that type of painting?

"Is this always what you wanted to paint?" I asked her stubbornly.

"I always wanted to paint," she responded, "and for now — this is good enough."

I'm not sure whether I was bothered more by the "for now" or the "good enough" but either way I felt worse after her response than I had before. But she still was a warrior. I could tell. I could see it in her eyes. She was there in the thick of it. She was out in the trenches battling each and every day…putting in her time…waiting for some recognition. Most people go through their days like ants, walking along the same scent lines all day until they find their way back home. But no, she was living out on the edges of her own expectations and although she had "sold out," slightly, and altered her art for the sake of profit, she was still an artist. And oh how I admire artists!

Artists are the heroes of their own lives—only they have the courage to face their own limitations head on.

The next booth was made of glass. I was in a trance. All the light from the day's happiness was reflecting in every which direction, falling into my eyes like a gentle calm. There were glass blues and glass pinks and even some glass yellows all dangling from tubular sockets.

"So what do we have here?" Billy asked the old women sitting behind the spectacle.

"Wind chimes."

This was odd because there was certainly wind and nothing was chiming.

"Right," Billy said fondling one of the larger ones.

"I like this one," I said looking at a specifically colorful one dangling above my head.

"So…are they meant to chime?" Billy asked her.

"Well they are more…art pieces…than musical pieces."

"Makes sense," I said.

We moved on quickly because it didn't actually make sense.

"Wind chimes without chiming?" Billy whispered to me.

"They were pretty," I said defending her, because I thought her art interesting. And after all, I'm often most interested in those things most breakable.

"So are you excited about Japan?" I asked Billy as we walked along in between more booths, passing most of them, waiting for something to catch our eye.

"I wish you were coming," he said.

See — I have always been one to make grand declarations. I've always lived on the peripherals of my own possibilities. I've always said yes to everything. I've always been one to oblige those around me in a way that dilutes my own sense of belonging. I've always committed to things I hardly had the ambition for, nor the ability to pull off. And so this was also true with Japan.

A very long time before this Washington DC visit, Billy and I had talked about moving to a faraway land together with all the romance and fun ingrained in such a trip. We had planned haphazardly to teach English to foreign students and have sex with foreign girls and learn funny sounds in funny new languages and fumble around the other side of the world together because fumbling is funny. We had plans for saving money except not really because we probably would spend it all on trips to New Zealand and Thailand because we would hear there was something to see there. It had all been planned in the "sure man" sort of ways that we live by. Except this time Billy went on and did it. He made the plans. He met a girl and made the plans and got the job and paid the rent and bought the plane ticket and actually did it.

He called me one day saying, "So everything is set for Japan. I'm just waiting on you to get your act together."

"You may be waiting a long time my friend," I said.

"…"

I broke the news to him softly — "Listen man…I'm in no position to fly out to Japan for a year and I don't have the credentials to teach like you do and you have a degree already and I don't know man. I need more time and you're rocking out this Japan thing and you're going to have a blast but it's going to be more of a 'me visiting you' thing than a 'me being there for the year' sort of thing. Ya know?"

"Fuck man," is all he said.

That was as nice as he could have put it. I didn't so much as spoil his fun as I tuned the music off. He could still dance but he'd have to find a new DJ.

I paused for a moment, looking ashamed, bending my head upwards if only for pride. I swirled my thumb around the inside of an empty mug. It was hand molded and therefore unique. Each subtlety was its own. Each flake was its own. Each eccentricity was its own to share. But unique is often lonely. And so we shared that haunting emotion — surrounded by those who most understood us, those most alike us, and yet were so desperately unique that neither consolidation nor touch could bring us back.

"*I wish you were coming,*" he said. My heart sunk.

"*I wish you were coming,*" he said. What am I doing?

"*I wish you were coming,*" he said. I let him down.

In seeing that I had no proper response he pulled out three cigars from his pocket and asked, "Anyone have a light?"

Billy was kind in this way. He had a Christian sensibility about him that allowed him to dance and make funny voices and smoke cigars and have sex before marriage, sure, sounds good — but it also taught him to forgive at a moment's notice — and for that, I would always be eternally grateful.

So we smoked the bright smoke into our lungs and forgave each other for all of our transgressions and talked about writing and painting and about our dreams too. We stuck our noses up at the art but only because we wanted to smell each artist more thoroughly. We were fully ingratiated in the whole lot of it. We envied their serenity and everything was amazing and everything was awesome and we couldn't believe how she had done that or how he managed to pull that off and we kept taking puffs of smoke because at some point your nervous system just takes over and says "ahh that's the stuff."

We looked at the art but we didn't really know if it was good or not. No one does. Sure people go to art shows, yeah, but all they ever do is make small talk with big words. No one knows anything about art—not really—because there is nothing to "know." Art is faith. And so that's about all we had just then—faith in each other. Faith that one day it would all be better.

+

THE WAITRESS WAS QUITE stunning at dinner. And at this point it may seem that I meet many stunning women, too many in fact, and this is absolutely true. I humbly accept this critique but it changes not my impressions. To assume there are not enough beautiful women in this world to fill the pages of a book is to assume a world that does not truly exist. We live in America after all, the land where thousands of years of other nations' communal incest finally has the opportunity to blend itself out. The sharpness of an Eastern European nose is softened ever so slightly by a Japanese's more buttoned version. The red freckles of an Irishman are illuminated brown by mixing with the skin of a Kenyan. The caramel softness of a Columbian is elongated by the height of a Norwegian. And so on. America blends and mishmashes its bloods, its colors, its ideologies, its religions, its tones, and its faults too, until what comes out is often a most invigorating and surprising composition. So the waitress was stunning, like many others are in my great America, and that is that.

She stood averagely, but had a regal tallness about her. Her eyes would have been envied by even Faith. She had pitch black skin, held her hair back softly with a pink hair clip, and although her uniform was an unflattering polo, I couldn't help but notice her modelesque figure.

She looked at the table with her small nose and started very simply. "What can I get you guys?" she asked.

You could tell she was mildly annoyed with having to deal with a group of guys who were firstly, guys, and secondly, were all friends, and therefore would uncontrollably flirt with her the entire evening. Though, in the same way, she could tell we were also some version of men, and therefore would tip well.

…And so continues the double-edged sword of life.

"I'll have a dark beer…a Guiness, I guess?" Billy said.

"A coke please."

"Also a coke, thanks."

When Aden is faced with a pretty girl he always becomes very "on purpose." He stiffens his lip, becomes incredibly efficient with his communication, polite, and shares wicked eye contact.

"I will have a glass of water please, and I would also love for you to place a few lemon wedges in the glass. I very much appreciate you doing this for me. Thank you very much," he said. Little did he know the unspoken code of all waitresses—"*hate those who ask for lemon.*" He was already at a disadvantage despite his politeness.

I was looking at Aden thinking about what he said.

"And for you sir?"

I wondered why he communicated so differently with girls than he did with us? I always thought that he would be better off just being himself.

"Excuse me sir. What would you like to drink?" the waitress asked me again.

I looked at him, wondering about his past, and if his mother had anything to do with it. I always grew up with women around me: my sister, my cousins, my mother, and so for some reason I felt comfortable with them. I don't know why, but I just do.

"Are you having anything today?"

As I thought these thoughts, Aden gazed back at me with a peculiar look of emphasis. He shook my shoulder as we stared at each other, and pointed up to the waitress.

"Are you going to answer her?" he asked me.

I had forgotten about her—zoned out if you will. I turned back to face her, looked up, and calmly said, "Oh I'm sorry...I'll have a brownie sundae."

I ordered a brownie sundae right off because it's a goddamn brownie sundae. If you need a reason to order a brownie sundae then I feel sorry for you. Chocolate is the only useful antidepressant, I think. If I were a psychiatrist I would prescribe brownie sundaes for suicidal thoughts, Oreos for PTSD, and double fudge ice cream for anxiety disorders. I wouldn't keep my patients for very long, sure, but at least I'd be groundbreaking. And that's always important.

The whole gang got a kick out of this.

"You are the dumbest smart person I know," Billy said hitting the table with his hand.

Aden wasn't laughing as much as he was confused. He asked me, "What are you talking about? A brownie sundae?"

I didn't understand all the fuss really, so I looked up at the waitress and asked, "I don't get it, do you not have brownie sundaes or something?"

"No no no," Billy said to me and looked up at the waitress.

"Don't worry, I'll handle this," he said to her. She was laughing too, and now getting attention from her coworkers for doing so. She shrugged her shoulders and let Billy lay into me.

"First, Kristopher...she asked you what you wanted to drink...as you should assume because you have extensive experience in this business, and you'll also notice that we don't have drinks yet and that she only just came over to introduce herself...and second...if in fact she was taking our order...a brownie sundae?" He turned his head sideways, which is the universal signal for *"you're an idiot,"* and then continued in saying—"And it's dinnertime on top of it. This kind waitress comes over and all you say is 'brownie sundae?' You're absolutely an idiot."

So I realized why everyone thought this was so funny.

"OK," I said to her, "I apologize. Though I still would like a brownie sundae. But you can get me a water to start. I'm sorry...I wasn't really paying attention obviously."

She composed herself, wrote down my order, and walked back to the servers station snickering.

"You are really an idiot," Billy said again, still laughing.

"She's pretty hot," I said.

"Yeah and you fucked up any chances you have with her," someone else said.

"No I didn't."

"Yeah she *was* pretty hot," Billy agreed.

Aden has a special place in his heart for black girls, especially ones with accents, which this waitress had, and so emphasized this point even further—"Hot? Oh my god she's a goddess."

"I bet she's Ethiopian," I said.

"You know what," Billy said turning to his friend Chuck who was black, "and I mean no disrespect by this..."

Chuck was a friend of Billy's from college. He was black-black, but not African-black. Although he carried his color like a badge more than a shield. And that was relieving. I had met him a few times before—good guy, upstanding, well educated, liberal, and polite. The only problem I had with him was that he always wore very preppy outfits, like he was constantly going out to a horse show in Nantucket, if they have horse shows in Nantucket? I've never been there so I wouldn't know. And I've never been to a horse show either but hell, what are stereotypes for if we can't use them without warrant? But the picture is set no less—he wears perfectly framed glasses, usually a pink button down, and nice shoes— *always* nice shoes. And none of this really bothered me as much as it made me feel dressed down. I always thought, "*You're making me look bad man,*" but of course never said it out loud.

Billy paused to look at Chuck more seriously before he continued, making sure he wasn't being racist which was silly since they were friends already. But white people in our generation have to be careful after slavery and the shit their parents did and all that. Even with a black president we're all still a little on edge, careful not to go in reverse.

"For some reason," Billy said slowly, "I don't know...but I'm not really attracted to very many black girls."

"Halle Berry?" I said interrupting him.

"Right I mean, I know there are beautiful black women out there..."

"Beyonce?" Aden chimed in.

"...look all I'm saying is that..."

"Lauren Hill." Chuck started in as well.

"...I know...I know...listen I'm not trying to say..." — Billy was starting to become flustered.

"Rihanna."

"You know how some guys really like Asian girls? Like Kristopher...you really like Asian girls. You are always talking about how they are so small and..."

"Jada Pinket Smith."

"...like some guys like Asian girls because they are very thin and their hair and all that...we all have our tastes right? It's just that I haven't really been that attracted to a lot of black girls so far..."

"Naomi Cambell"

"Kristopher...come on man help me out here..."

"Oprah."

"Oprah? I'll ignore that. Oprah? ...Well I guess you have a point," he said now laughing. "Listen guys I know there are..."

"Tyra Banks"

"...I think the waitress is..."

"Diana Ross"

"You guys are annoying," he finished realizing he wasn't going to win with us.

"Annoying?" I said, "At least we're not racists. Chuck I can't believe you are friends with Billy he is such a racist."

"Alright brownie sundae..." Billy butted in.

"Yeah. Sure. Brownie Sundae? I see your 'brownie sundae' and I raise you 'I'm telling the waitress you think she's ugly because she's black.' How about that?"

"Fuck you," he said putting his head down.

The waitress just then came back to our table with our drinks and said, "I didn't put in your Brownie Sundae yet because I assumed you'd want it with their meal. Is that OK?"

"Well I asked for it first didn't I?"

"Oh I'm so..."

"No I'm teasing," I quickly added, realizing she thought I was serious. "Let me tell you something about myself please. If I may? See—yesterday I drank a lot so I'm fairly apathetic about everything right now. When the brownie sundae comes the brownie sundae comes. That is my philosophy for today."

"OK that works for me," she said shyly, almost blushing.

Everyone ordered their meals and as the waitress left we all leaned in closer to the middle of the table as if we were about to create a secret "no girls allowed" club in our backyard.

"Oh my god Billy you're a moron she's stunning," Aden said quickly.

"I know," Billy whispered, "did you see her hands? They are so petite and..."

"I don't even like black girls and she is definitely perfect for me," Chuck added.

"You don't like black girls?"

"No," he said plainly.

"But you're black?"

"I know I am."

"And you don't like black girls?"

"His girlfriend is white," Billy let us know.

"You're a racist," I said.

"I can't be a racist. I'm black."

"Really, no black girls?" I asked again.

"Well for this waitress...I could make an exception."

"Oh my god I know...I swear to god..."

Billy sat back in his seat very quickly and gestured for all of us to sit back in our chairs as well because a girl was in the vicinity.

"How are you guys all doing?" the waitress asked.

"What's your name?" Aden asked back.

She looked startled and calmly replied, "Veronica."

"Awesome," Aden said to her.

She left again.

We huddled again.

"Awesome?"

"What?"

"I mean Kristopher's 'brownie sundae' fiasco was bad but you may have just topped it with 'awesome,'" Billy joked.

"Yeah man. 'Awesome?' Really?" Chuck said as well.

"What?"

"You just ruined your chances man."

"What? I don't understand. What's wrong with 'Awesome?'"

"You never say 'awesome.' Awesome is the great highway to masturbation land."

"Nooooo…"

"Oh yeah man" — I was loving all of this — "You don't know that? You were doing really well and then you said 'awesome' and now it's all over. Sadly it's now just between Chuck, Billy, and me."

"You mean Chuck and me?" Billy laughed. "You've been out of the running since 'brownie sundae.'"

"Well now that I know that you are both racists…"

"Hey now!" Chuck snickered.

"I know you are black Chuck but that is no excuse for blatant racism against black people. The jury has spoken — and you have a girlfriend anyway. Do…not…think," I said slowly, "that I will not tell her that you have a girlfriend and ruin you!"

"Fuck," he said putting his head down.

"...and I am NOT a racist," Billy said.

"You are definitely a racist," Aden countered. "But guys...I mean just because..."

"Yes," Billy finished for Aden. "Yes Aden, just because you said 'awesome' you are finished. I'm sorry but it's over for you."

At this point we were all laughing great big laughs, still huddled together and having the best of times. Just as the waitress was walking towards us I said, "This is now a one man race," and sat back in my chair smiling.

"Does anyone need a refill?" Veronica asked us.

We all looked around the table and realized that no one had taken even a sip of their drink. We were too busy making fun of one another. We all widened our eyes to one another thinking, *"why is she asking us this?"* because it was so obvious that none of us needed a refill.

"Well...actually," she started timidly, "can I ask you a question?"

I was looking at Billy. He gestured his eyes towards the waitress to tell me that she was talking to me.

"Oh...yeah...what?"

She laughed and Billy now said out loud this time — "I'm sorry he *really* is an idiot."

She covered her mouth knowing I was joking and continued, "...well...my friend, well she's another waitress. I mean...I guess she saw you at the table and we were talking in the back and...well...we were wondering what you were?"

"I don't understand the question," I said to her completely understanding the question.

The whole table fell silent. Everyone's eyes were on me and the waitress. They all knew I was very comfortable, and therefore silly, in these sorts of situations — so watched me on the edge of their seats.

"I mean..." she continued even more bashfully and slower this time. She looked at her friend who was standing within my sight line maybe ten yards away. I waved to her and she too blushed so hard that I could feel it across the room. "...I think you are Arab and my friend thinks you are Indian. But we both think you are mixed regardless. Which is it?"

"Neither," I said, "but I *am* mixed."

"Oh..." she said surprised. "Dammit. I thought I was right."

I didn't say anything — neither did anyone else at the table. Normally I would have just told her that my mother was Mexican, but I wanted to milk this as much as I could. So she stood there waiting for a response that would never come. The seconds melted past awkwardly, me just looking at her smiling. Finally she turned her head to the side, but this time not in the *"you're an idiot"* way. She turned her head to the left and then to the right, looking at me very closely, analyzing my features and my skin — trying to figure me out.

"I don't know," she finally said flustered. "What are you? Aren't ya' gonna tell me?"

"Well how about if I guess what you are, then you have to guess what I am? Fair?"

"Deal," she said quickly, feeling very confident.

"Ethiopian," I said just as quickly.

"Oh my god," she cried out and ran away to her friend completely forgetting all semblance of professionalism.

I looked at Billy without saying a word. He could hear my silent film, even directed it as he wanted sometimes. So often we didn't need words, him and I. We were at a level of sub-communication that only best friends can ever achieve. No one said anything though I up kept at Billy with my eyes.

He looked back at me, then gestured towards his mouth so that everyone would listen to what he had to say, and then very methodically, very emphatically, and yet very calmly, said — "Fuck...You."

At that exact moment the waitress came back and asked me, "How did you know that?"

"Eyes and nose," I said.

"That doesn't make sense," she responded. "What about my eyes and my nose?"

"Everything," I said again.

And I wasn't being seductive, or sensual. I just answered very matter-of-factly while taking a sip of my lemonade.

She ran away again.

"No seriously," Billy said for the second time, "Fuck...you."

Chapter 15

AS YOU WALK THROUGH the lit corridors of America, especially those in Washington, you become terribly aware of everything you are missing. Behind each gate and in each apartment, through every window, there are stories of bustle and movement and hurried papers and shredders and secrets. As a consequence, rarely are there very many people on the streets—even the cabs feel strangely foreign. Everything belongs indoors in Washington D.C., or so it seems. So much action, so many decisions, so much power and control, all just a few feet away from us on the other side of some random brick wall—though all the while we walked the streets as if alone.

I had friends who came to Washington to change the world. I had thought of doing the same myself actually. It's a city with a youthful buzz that is for sure—but everyone is a worker bee while the queens just sit in their offices and point to what they want and smoke cigars and not much else.

…Saving the world in Washington is an illusion. It's a hologram invented by old men who are too lazy to get their own coffee. But it works, somehow. And so members of my generation keep buzzing along, making copies of unimportant documents because one day they might be able to help pass a piece of legislation that might, someday, possibly, if it works, hopefully, help someone, somewhere—maybe? And that's good enough.

Though at least it's not New York thank God.

As we walked in the night, I noticed something about Billy just then that I hadn't noticed before. This was the first time I had walked with him in a dangerous city. We had always ridden our bikes around the suburbs and after that strolled around college towns which are just practice suburbs.

But this was different. This time he only nodded at us with his hands in his pockets not so much for warmth as for cover. They were shaking, nervous, his hands, and he didn't want us to see. This was obvious. Though we did notice.

After each sentence, after each nod of his head, he would look behind his shoulder. He would check to his right with his eyes, never quite making eye contact—there with us, but not actually there *with us*—he was worried about something.

To our right were a series of benches smelling like dirty laundry baskets, hollow trees, with the homeless hiding behind them. Rusting blankets and elegantly assorted boxes and well-used bicycles and layers upon layers of clothes—there were remnants of better lives carefully folded into the fault lines of this park. A man with a somber look and a crusty beard gazed through us, passed us and into the insides of DC, waiting for someone to govern his life for him. Another man with a somber look and an even crustier beard looked at Billy, making eye contact for only a moment before Billy scurried his eyes towards the sky. Another man with a somber look and the crustiest beard of all sat at an adjacent bench, chin resting on his chest, absolutely still, like a depressed monk. The whole park was full of them—the gypsies of America—the jaded drug addicts of its most powerful city—the anxious souls just passing the time, struggling along a road called Death.

And it doesn't have to be this way, the homeless men all lining the streets. But patriotism is lost now. It's just a color anymore. It has a heartbeat once every fourth November and then hibernates until the next slogan wakes it up again. All the while there are homeless men and women sleeping on benches, under the penetrating light of our nation's wealth, and even their dreams are frozen solid.

And why?—because Washington needs them. So many of us take pity on those of us without a roof and so many of us become angry at the thought of poverty in the richest nation. I know I do. But it's hard to if you see their eyes. It's hard to if you take a moment to ponder the why as much as the what. It's about choice. Sure we've all been born into different starting points and we've all been lead into precarious situations, and yes some of us have been given the shortest end of the stick possible—but there is always choice. There is always a limit, and then there is pushing past that limit. So Washington needs this park. It needs the bottom in order to work as hard as it does. It needs something to fight for. It needs a baseline. It needs a reference point. We all do I think. And sure it's sad that inhumane and inhuman are so different—but this is the world we live in.

The trick, then, is not to give homes to the homeless. The solution is not to give them all thousands of dollars. What we must do is treat them as equals. Set up a system whereby they can slowly, ever so slowly even, pull themselves up from their park benches if they want. We must never look over our shoulders and assume the worst. We must hold firm to our eye contact and hold firm to our convictions, and hold on tight when the world tells us to be scared of the shadows in the forest. Because it's all superstition anyway.

"Why are you afraid of them?" I asked Billy.

"What?"

"Why are you afraid of the homeless people?"

"I'm not."

"You're shaking and looking over your shoulder every three seconds."

"Well I just don't want to get jumped or something."

"Have you ever been jumped?"

"No. But that's not…"

"Has anyone ever stolen anything from you ever in your whole life?"

"Probably not. But that's because I always…"

"All I'm saying is…there are 5 of us on a lit sidewalk on a main street in a huge city…Relax."

"Whatever. One day someone is going to steal all of your shit and I'll say 'I told you so,'" Billy said to me.

"Cool," I said.

"Cool?"

"As long as I don't have to look over my shoulder my entire life. I'll take that trade."

"Whatever."

We eventually found ourselves back at Emma's apartment, showering again, making sure to wash off all the stench of the car before heading out for the night. Aden had a friend who worked for the Clinton campaign that we were going to meet for a few drinks. After that, who knows?

We drank top shelf liquors in fancy glasses on the roof of a newly renovated apartment building. There were well kept benches of black leather, a smoldering fire in iron grating, and a view of Washington lit from its head down. It's safe to say that we were far from Texas by now. Instead of chugging we sipped. Instead of dancing we talked — and about politics instead of sex.

"So what are you going to do with your life?"

"So what's this road trip all about?"

"What are you going to do after this?"

"Do you have a plan?"

These were the sorts of questions this crowd wanted answers to. Billy had half an answer with his plans for Japan but Aden and I were consistently left dumbfounded. Neither of us had even considered answering seriously. As if being assisted by destiny's eternally cheeky lawyer, we answered only with "yes," or, "no."

"So what are you going to do with your life?"

"Yes."

"Yes...yes what? Come again?"

"No."

And on and on we went, mastering the art of changing the subject. The real answer was something entirely more complicated than any soup question would appreciate. These questions aren't asked out of interest, but rather are used as a barometer. But how do you tell someone that you are living under an entirely different scale—that money and the future aren't as important as happiness and spontaneity? It takes a long argument—one that sounds both pathetic and life changing equally.

I stared off into the distance, high above everything, feeling both Maryland and Virginia, The North and The South, and worried for the very first time in months. They say that success breeds success—but so too does success breed competition, and competition breeds expectation, and worry, and trouble, and stress. So I asked the requisite questions to myself this time, and in struggling to find any legitimate answer, I let my cosmic lawyer speak for me.

"Yes." "Yes." "Yes." "Yes."

Over and over and over again—my eternal answer is yes.

Now if I only could remember the question.

+

EMMA ROUNDED UP EVERYONE so we headed out to meet Chuck and his girlfriend at a bar. She could tell that none of us were all too excited about sipping anymore. We needed to feel the liquids a little faster in our throats. Her too.

The entranceways to all the dusty bars were alive with shimmering electricity, all of us glimmering into the otherwise ragged streets. We brought our A game and gulped until we couldn't distinguish walking in a straight line from spinning in a circle. We were lucky to even have been let into *any* bar we were so drunk already. We weren't going to buy anything, and if we did, we would do more spilling than drinking. But Emma flirted and Billy pushed past a crowd and so we found ourselves upstairs again, at a beach themed bar. The whole place was crawling with bored twentysomethings, on the verge of collapse after a week of filling up coffee mugs and making cold calls to offended citizens. This was the buzz in full flight. The girls were better financed than those of Vegas, so dressed similarly, except spent more money on their accessories. The guys mostly wore suits, or college t-shirts (if they went to a good school). It smelled like hair dye and sounded of CSPAN—a very strange combination indeed.

Aden was talking to a few girls because Aden is always talking to a few girls. Though I was more focused on the group in general, making sure there were no stragglers who weren't having a good time. I hated loneliness and could smell it from a mile away. So while Aden and Billy teased a few girls, I instead sat down with Chuck and his girlfriend at an open table—trying to sober up and change their mood from "why am I here?" to "this isn't so bad."

Somewhere between gulps of whisky and coke, somewhere between the banal "how are you - I'm fine" conversations of the bar, somewhere under her dress, and somewhere near the edges of his smirk, I noticed their hands clenched lovingly below the table. I don't know why it hit me so hard, but I remember an insatiable gulping feeling, as if my attempts at swallowing my throat were all but futile. She came back to me like a rushing storm over Missouri—I saw her coming past the horizon, but it was still shocking how quickly she arrived. She always came to me in furious waves, never a subtle trickle or a silent afterglow—no—she poured all over me, heavy, leaving me sopping wet, happy, and gray.

Every beautiful crack of Chuck's strong hand resembled my own. Every curve of his girlfriend's white knuckles smelled of her. The crackling opposition of their colors, black and white, fervently cusped, reminded me of our bodies intertwined. Andrea. Oh God Andrea. I wanted to be touched by someone who knew how to touch me. I wanted that familiar muscle memory orgasm, the one that comes as if by mistake, the kind that surprises you if only for its casual intensity. God I missed her skin.

The waters of evolutionary trial and error had washed over her, smoothing all of her pits, leaving only a silky cascading ivory, so peaceful, so nonchalant, that even *she* didn't know what to do with it. Her skin is like an enormous diamond in the sand — it is generally made of the same parts as everything or (everyone) else — but she shines so much brighter still. And no one knows why. She just does. Like the sun.

"You OK?" Chuck asked me.

"Yeah," I said looking through him.

"You sure?"

"Yeah — it's just..."

I paused for a moment not sure whether articulating my predicament would have any positive effect or not. See — I had always ruled my emotions with an iron fist. I am a dictator to my feelings. They do as I say, and not the other way around. But somewhere underground, in the dark corners and the back alleys of my heart, in the wilting buildings, under the dripping pipes, armed with nothing but fists and fury, my emotions were organizing. They were planning a munity to tear down the high walls of oppression that had stifled them for so long. Sure they were acknowledged every so often with a little nourishment and they were entertained with the occasional conversation, but their existence was more one of survival than enjoyment.

So I paused, ready to change the conversation and suppress the uprising once more, but this time I felt something different. I don't know where it came from, or why I allowed it, but a small gathering of words tip-toed their way onto the end of my tongue.

"...it's just...there is this..."

An historic moment was in the making. I could feel the weight of those words pressing down hard on the edge of my mouth, filling it until I couldn't breathe, until I was suffocated, and had to let it out —

"...there is this girl."

But I bit down hard. That was enough. That was all the mercy I had room for.

"Oh," Chuck said grievingly, giving me the space I needed.

But the uprising pushed back even harder this time, and I collapsed.

"You two remind me of me and my ex-girlfriend. It hasn't been a while since I've been with a girl…but it's been a while since I've held anyone's hand ya know? At least not like this."

I pointed to their mutual fist now resting peacefully on the counter. I half expected him to give me a break from all the reminders but he didn't. He only squeezed tighter and looked lovingly at his girlfriend.

"You were in love with her?" she asked.

This question initiated an attack on me the likes of which I had never before experienced. It had been so long since I was able to speak out loud about her. Even with Aden or Billy I played her off as another chess piece to be moved around only if absolutely necessary. She was a last resort. My queen. Sure I cared about her but I was fine I would say. *"No…really,"* I said, *"I rarely think about her."* Which was true only in the same way that we rarely think about sex. We don't, normally, except for all the time. It's so obvious and so standard, that we lose sight of its existence — like a ringing in your ear that never goes away. Eventually it blends in as background noise.

"I love her," I said.

The war had been decided. I had raised the white flag. A new leader would have to take over. Sound the alarm. The dictator is dead.

"Excuse me," I said while rushing to the bathroom.

What happened in that tiny bathroom was neither a transformation nor a peaceful exchange of power. The last remnants of my former, harder self, exhaled profusely all over the sink. My eyes had been cut, so bled and bled, until all of their superficial expectations for love were dried red. I looked at the mirror, unsure if there was a proper next step? One part of me wanted to call her then and there, another part of me wanted to run to the next airport and fly into her arms, but the new humble version of myself hadn't the courage for any of that. It simply looked into the mirror and said a few times, out loud, "I love her," until it felt normal. Until it felt right.

"You OK?"

"Oh yeah," I said embarrassed upon returning to the table.

"Let's just say that is the first time I've ever said that out loud," I explained.

"Well you can't say tonight was boring?" Chuck said to his girlfriend. And I smiled knowing that that was all I had ever wanted.

Just then Aden came back to lighten up the mood. The bar was too dark for anyone to notice my bloodshot eyes. So I was able to continue covertly, without having to make a big scene about the whole incident. Chuck gave me a little nod when everyone arrived back at the table as if to say, "*we won't say anything if you don't.*" I appreciated that. I'd talk about it with Aden, but later, after Emma and Billy had left.

Then we went dancing in places where no one else was dancing — hoping to start a more insatiable party than swirling rocks glasses would allow. So we danced our goodbyes then and there, under the dark night, and hugged one another to the sound of the beat.

Though underneath all this commotion, or somewhere behind it, I felt an idea creep up my neck so I spit out its words like a cough, involuntarily and suddenly — "Let's go see a sunrise."

"What?"

"Let's go see a sunrise."

"That'll have to wait till morning," Billy said tilting his glass towards me.

"No I'm serious."

I emotionally left Billy just then. Emma too. I needed a distraction from my own distracted head. If I was to ever get over Andrea, if I was to ever exist, anywhere, without her there breathing down my neck, I would need something more spectacular than a seedy bar to absorb me.

"Let's go see a fucking sunrise," I said with emphasis.

"When?"

And so it was only Aden and I just then. Everyone else washed away. We were back to scheming, and when we scheme, the world falls apart at our shoulders.

"Now."

"Wait a second," Emma mothered, "you guys have had more than a few drinks so that's not exactly smart and besides, don't we deserve a proper goodbye?"

"Do you want to go see a sunrise?" I asked Aden. "You know, one off the coast of America…the Atlantic…with the sun coming over our country? I've never seen a sunrise over the ocean. Have you?"

"No."

"Want to go?"

"Fuck man, I mean sure but…"

"Let's go."

We said our goodbyes for a few hours and even got some food. I hugged everyone properly and walked Emma back to her apartment but I had to go, and although Aden was more along for the ride at this point, he had his hands up the whole time — ready to leap off of Washington's cliff with me.

"It was really nice to see you," Emma said honestly.

"I love you," I told her.

"I love you," Aden told her.

We had never said that before, at least not to her. We wouldn't think about her much after we left and I had already forgotten about the small of her back, but she was loved ferociously nonetheless, right then and there, so it was worth saying. I don't know if she said it back or not but it wasn't about reciprocation anyway. The trip, in fact, wasn't about reciprocation. We wanted to spread as wide as we could to reach every corner of our country, even down in the cracks — and the only way to do that is to love unconditionally.

I kissed the crease between her neck and cheek, an intimate spot, seriously but gently, and held her opposite shoulder with my hand. She held me comfortably too, but softly, unsure how tightly she could squeeze. This made me laugh. How much more intimate can you be with someone than to sleep in their bed and tell them you love them? I guess sex would have helped.

So we left after holding hands too long, first letting go of one hand, then palm to palm, fingertip to knuckle, and then just a whisper as we walked away.

"Goodbye."

Chapter 16

TRAVEL IS A DRUG.

We feel its vibrations and it calms us. We live for those fucking vibrations of the car and the night, and it'll probably kill us one day but none of that matters when you're going that fast. None of that matters when you're chasing the sun.

That very brand of monotony lulled me into a sort of cathartic drowsiness, like a depressing comedown. No matter the strength of the hit, no matter the scale of the vibration, eventually the road melts your eyes like gravity pulling in both directions. Highways are so predictable, so devoid of anything interesting at night, that lines become sheep, and you count them, and you count them, and you count them, and you count them until you're almost dead. My eyelids began to squeeze together so although the intelligent decision would have been to pull over and take a nap, I couldn't — I had a deadline — there were no extensions for the sunrise. It would come and go with such a lackadaisical indifference to whether or not I saw it that I had to push through. Even if it killed me I would keep driving south. Even if it killed me I would run away from whatever I was running from, and get to a new place, wherever that would be, and everything would be better. Makes sense, I think?

Though just as I careened over the yellow line mostly asleep at 70mph, I saw the faintest hint of something not black to my left. There was no sound. Aden wasn't snoring. There was no smell. The car had been cleaned. There was no touch. The road felt smooth. There was no taste. My mouth was dry. There was only sight, and me, now wide-awake. For the sun had said hello.

So there in the dark I realized that black doesn't actually exist. Even without fire there are stars. Even without stars there is the moon. Even without a candle there are the illuminations behind our eyes. No matter how pitch the black, there is always light. No matter how vigorously we emphasize the dark, no matter how sternly we attempt to blend in with it, no matter how energetically we lock ourselves into our own voided rooms, the light will find us still. It'll seep in through the window, and if we patch the window it will come in through the cracks under the door, and if we stuff those cracks, it will simply come sweltering from within.

This is why we worship the light as God — and why the sun has historically meant so much.

So from there on the car floated the entire way there. It simply hovered above the pavement, only touching down for brief moments like a weightless astronaut bouncing on the moon.

I screamed at Aden to get up.

"Get up!" I shouted frantically while taking the key out of the ignition. "We're about to miss the sunrise!"

I shook him hard and repeated the same few lines. Though he wouldn't respond sternly and only grumbled something about, "It's OK." But it wasn't OK. I didn't have time for him to wake from his dream. I had my own to finish.

So after sprinting onto the boardwalk, jumping over a possibly locked gate, falling down and scraping the bottom of my knee, crawling back towards the Atlantic, hobbling all the way to the water's edge, I wet my feet only to my ankles, sunk down deep into my spot, and watched the light turn on over America.

And all of the eyes of the beach were upon me, staring at me from tip to top — which is to say that no one was looking at me because I was the only one on the beach that morning. So I envisioned myself the only one on that whole road of sand reaching downwards towards Miami and all the way up towards Maine and yes the whole right cliff of the eastern shore was bare, only me and the sand, like an obtuse and ancient cross, my hair for the sky, my feet for the floor, empty forever to the right, and empty always to the left.

I dug my feet into the sand, sitting idly, waiting, knowing I had made it in time. And just then I noticed the moon still saving face, still showing until the very last moment. And I love when the sun and the moon are visible at the same time, when they come to a truce like soldiers on Christmas day. See — they need each other, both sides, good and evil, night and day, the sun and the moon, Kristopher and Andrea, ying and yang, left and right, truth and falsity, up and down, happy and sad. And if only it were true, that old adage, "opposites attract." If only opposites were in fact like magnets? Instead they are usually in opposition, and rarely, very rarely, do they ever coexist. But when they do in the early morning on the beaches of North Carolina, when the sun and the moon are both glimmering ever so faintly in the sky — there is nothing more beautiful.

So it came, the sun, ever so slowly still. And it wasn't so garish that morning, but rather shown itself humbly and evenly. See — there is no particular moment during a sunrise that is superior to any other. It's a gradual beauty, a wandering and lingering happiness that shakes all the fickle thoughts from our minds. A sunrise demands our attention. It's the only thing — the light. Though I wonder — when does it stop grabbing our attention? When is the exact moment when it stops being a sunrise, stops being beautiful, and transforms into an average sunny day — the type of day we are so used to and therefore treat so irreverently? Honestly? I'm not really sure. But either way, it came, and I sat, vowing just then to see the sunrise always, and in all places.

Though the tiny little writer in me peeked through the cracks of my insecurities and said, *"The sun is a hologram you can feel."* I laughed at myself for trying to describe, in that very moment, what I was witnessing. I didn't and still don't have the decency to let a moment pass as it passes without trying to bottle it up in words like a doggy bag for lost memories. I yearned so deeply for words, and so desperately wanted to call myself a poet, a narrator, a storyteller, an actor, a writer, anything, out loud, so badly, that I couldn't help but tell my own story back to myself over and over again. I was determined to become the most infamous monologist of my head. So I sat there thinking of yellow, orange, beautiful, spark, light, shadow, happy, Aden, blue, cloud, Andrea, analogy, sand, thick, soft, thin, car, road, sex, write, sun, rise, fall, moon, home, travel, dance, and ordered those words into different combinations until they combined with one another and formed sentences. I didn't take a mental picture of the view; I took mental footnotes of words to describe the view.

I was either destined to be a writer or to live in a mental hospital. And I'm still not sure which will happen first.

By this time Aden had climbed out of the car and was sitting high above me in the lifeguard's chair. He looked like a king as I swiveled around to notice him more obviously. He smiled but not at me and gestured with his chest but not at me. He was in "full expression" as he so eloquently coined. He was dancing with the sunrise, some more sensual version of The Tango, a silent and still version — a tantric intimacy.

I walked towards him and hailed him like the best cab ride I would ever take, and he smiled again but this time at me. He belonged up there on the top of the world, I thought, above me with the sunrise and his hair blowing in the morning breeze. He belonged on the beaches of everywhere because beaches are for the bare-chested of us who aren't afraid of their own faults. I noticed his broad shoulders and red forearms, his blue shorts and his leather sandals, his ruff stubble and his brazen eyes. I noticed all of him there, loud, and glowing. Even his shadow was bright.

"Not too bad eh?"

"Not too bad."

He had his faults as did I. He had his idiosyncrasies as did I. He had his difficulties as did I. And although the world hears me shouting more boisterously than he and therefore misinterprets our relationship as one of leader and follower — we knew our truce. We knew the atomic equality of our relationship. Sometimes I'll sit down real low, close to the water, and sometimes he'll sit way up high above me, and sometimes I'll tell the story and he will listen, but no matter the details, we understood our places. We were intuitively aware of our roles. One of us was the main character and the other was the main character as well. And we'd have it no other way.

+

LATER IN CHAPEL HILL, a beautiful soul named Jason let us stay at his house. He opened his door as a stranger and we left still thinking him a stranger, but this had little to do with him and everything to do with his gender and the subsequent gender of his friends. He was quite an interesting character, lanky and clean, gay though he didn't admit to it, smiley and very southern. We gave him hugs upon arrival because we always give hugs upon arrival and instead of reacting unsure he wrapped himself tightly around our chests and gestured towards his couch.

"My home is your home," he said.

"I appreciate you having us here," Aden said. "We were in DC last night and somehow found ourselves in North Carolina today, homeless. You really rescued us from a night in the car."

We had sent out a few emails to couchsurfers in Chapel Hill because it was a college town and thought someone, anyone, might be crazy enough to let us stay with them with four hours' notice. Jason, in fact, wasn't a couchsurfer himself, but his friends were. They weren't in Chapel Hill that night but vowed to find us a place to stay anyways. Jason was the answer.

So I thanked God. Because what is God, if not exactly what we need exactly when we need it?

In the morning we helped him move a couch, ate some breakfast at a local café, and toured the campus of the University of North Carolina. Jason was a tour guide so we pretended we were incoming freshman and walked around with an enormous group of giddy yet terrified 18 year olds. Most of them looked older than me so I got away scot-free. Aden looked older than them but I think that made him seem cooler. He was.

There was quite a history there, beautiful red bricks aligned in rows, housing books and books and books and people who read them and people who study them and people who talk about them. That's all a university is—just a town full of books and people who love them. All the trees breathed old but the grass smelled new, matching the professor student relationship.

Jason made a note to talk about UNC being a public school. And I do have respect for public schools. They are at a categorical disadvantage by the sheer fact that they are public and not private. Private implies prestige, separate and intentionally not equal, and therefore for a public school to garner any respect it has to be even better than good. It has to prove itself even better than average, otherwise it's acceptance to the club will be questioned, like a minority after affirmative action. It's not fair. But it's true.

While leading the tour he gestured randomly and talked about meal plans and the best places to eat and old folklore about where they would meet their future spouses and "look at that gargoyle." Stuff like that. I felt a tinge of jealousy being amongst real live freshman. They were like zebras on the great plains of Africa. I watched them. They did nothing exciting. They just grazed around the campus and whispered to their parents. But I watched them. They had the whole world ahead of them — all the drinking and self-discovery and sexual adventures and wasted tuition and late night pizza they could handle. They had worlds of adolescent revelry right behind the doors of their soon inhabited dorm rooms. I wanted to be them. In fact, I was them. But they had an excuse. I wanted an excuse to do nothing except read books and have fun. Though as it stood I was homeless with a bank account. Not exactly admirable.

We hurried back to eat and made plans to meet the mystery couchsurfers because they were girls. Enough said.

Ester came in, and she was named Ester, so that was strange. I wasn't sure what to think except to judge her appearance — something I had much practice with. Her hair was fire yellow and curled from the tips upwards — each strand clung to the next as if she carried giant ringlets of adolescent tresses, clumping together, spiraling in perfectly eccentric circles. If she had the patience to straighten it I imagine it would reach down near her ankles. She wore it how it naturally laid, but for some reason I couldn't help but envision her wearing pigtails. She probably never did, actually, but she wore them no matter, the same way that Emma always wore a flowered skirt.

...She looked like Goldilocks except with bigger teeth.

She was so cute and so small, like she was a teenager who stumbled into college by accident, looked around, and decided to stay. Every part of her face was small, as if her nose, her mouth, each of her eyes, her tiny cheekbones, all of it—as if each part were constructed by delicate children in the clouds of heaven. She was so dainty, so innocent, and so pale; she looked at me like a middle-schooler with an ever intensifying crush.

Sara was a darling too. She had wide laughing eyes that fluttered and turned with each of her breaths. She wore a skimpy t-shirt though she was too heavy for it. Dark brown hair like my mother's probably once was draped down covering her ears. Her soft cheeks were red but not from makeup. She seemed happy. So happy. Happy into her bones. Though I worried that she had some deeper insecurities that she distracted herself from by athletically smiling. Like she trained for it.

Sara was the ringleader of the two. I imagine this is because no one named Ester could ever be a ringleader. She was relegated, at birth, to a life of missed eye contact. No one can be confident with a name like that, and although she probably received more male attention than Sara because she was prettier, Sara was certainly the one calling the shots.

"So what are you guys doing?"

"Traveling around," I said.

I still hadn't come up with a good answer to this question. Everywhere we went someone would ask us this. Aden usually answered with some version of "whatever we want" and that was beautiful to him and beautiful to me most of the time as well, but I couldn't help but feel a little helpless. So often when we are driving squarely in one direction, dead set on a destination screaming to us in the distance, we look through the rear view mirror and wonder "what if?" There were so many paths leading out from so many starting points that even though we were the bosses of our own destinies, the cosmic hugeness of each subtle decision left me feeling small. Every place and every decision, every determination, every "I want to" declaration seemed cheapened by the randomness to which we made them. Did we want to be in North Carolina? Did we? Really?

"We're doing whatever we want," Aden answered Sara more thoroughly.

"That's awesome."

"Like you're just going wherever you want? Traveling? That's incredible!" added Ester.

I could see it in their eyes. They envied us. They desired our freedom. They were attracted to the mystery. Our mystery. They were attracted to us even. And although I would have rather they liked us than not, it seemed disingenuous. Would they have liked us if we stayed forever? If we weren't the roaming cowboys of their Friday night, would they still have noticed us? So often I convince myself that people are meant for my stories, when in fact, I am meant for theirs.

We packed up our stuff and headed to their house for a party. I made tortillas for fajitas and thought of my mother. She never taught me explicitly how to make Mexican food because my father thought "that kind of stuff is for women." But my mom's a sneaky teacher. She taught me math by playing store with me. And I never played a game of monopoly without being the banker. And let's just say she never paid with exact change. And so also she would inject techniques for making tortillas into casual conversation.

"Thank you for dinner mom," I would say.

"Well you know I think the tortillas are especially good today," she would compliment.

"Yes I agree."

"...because I made sure to get the pan really hot before I cooked them."

...Moms are sneaky.

"These are the best fucking tortillas I've ever had," Sara said slightly tipsy after having had a few margaritas.

I noticed that I had been drinking what seemed like every day since we had left. Wherever we went our hosts thought of us as a break from their normal humdrum lives. So they would buy spirits and celebrate strangers coming to their houses. They would always throw a party. I felt like how a rock star must feel. Every city deserved my best show because, for them, this could be one of the highlights of their year. But for me it was just another show in just another city.

Needless to say I didn't know how to feel. So I took a shot of tequila despite my better judgment, to catch up. And after cleaning up the kitchen, feeling a little loose, I joined the group in the living room, most of them still eating and refusing to quiet down about the tortillas.

"I mean really...these are..."

"Yeah I know," I finally said. "It's like eating Wonder Bread your whole life and then going into an Italian bakery. Taco Bell, sadly, is not where Americans should learn about tortillas."

"I'll say."

"That's the quickest way to a women's heart," Ester said, "through her stomach."

"Makes sense."

"Though," she continued, "the best cook I know is just a friend of mine so maybe not?"

"Oh you shouldn't have said that," Aden quipped. He was right. I am obsessive about convincing people that guys and girls cannot be friends.

"What?" Sara asked.

I told her from across the room — "I don't think guys and girls can be just friends."

"But I just told you that my chef friend and I are just friends," Ester argued.

"No you aren't."

"Yes we are!"

"I have plenty of guy friends," Sara commented.

"They probably would have sex with you."

"That's not true," she said though enjoyed the compliment.

"It is for sure true. And if not, then you probably would have sex with them."

"That's not true."

"You really don't think girls and guys can be friends?" Ester asked perplexed.

"No."

"Really?"

"Really. It's simple actually. I think people are more than friends if one is attracted to one or the other….if one of the parties wants more…then you aren't 'just' friends. Since you are already friends you like each other emotionally. You enjoy each other's company. You care about them. You find their personality attractive right?"

"Right."

"…then the only thing left is for you to be attracted to them physically. Now what are the odds that one or the other will not be attracted to the other physically?"

"Pretty high."

"Zero. The odds are zero."

"That's not true."

"One will always be more attractive physically than the other and the lesser attractive one will be attracted to the more attractive one. This is just biology."

"What if they are both ugly?"

"Then they have lower standards in general. Ugly people know they are ugly so they are attracted to other ugly people, not because they aren't attracted to pretty people, but because they know what they can get and what they can't. So if two ugly people are friends it's even more likely that they'll hook up."

"I have plenty of friends who are guys. I don't care about your reasoning."

"How many guy friends does your mom have?"

"huh?"

"How many guys does your mom just go out to the movies with — as friends?"

"I don't know."

"Are your parents still married?"

"Yes."

"Does your dad have any girl friends that he hangs out with without your mom?"

"I don't know."

"Come on…answer the question."

"Probably not."

"Why do you think that is?"

"I don't know."

"You think he never had 'girl friends' when he was younger? Of course he did. Your mom was probably one of them. But when you get married you aren't allowed to be friends with people of the opposite sex because it's inappropriate. And why is it inappropriate? ...Because guys and girls can't be friends."

"Fuck" Sara said.

"It's not a bad thing. It doesn't mean that every one of your guy friends is fantasizing about you every moment. It's not weird. We're all adults and we all have filters and we all can make decisions about how to proceed or how not to proceed, but to say that guys and girls are doing anything other than going through the motions with each other until they are married would be a lie."

"You are depressing," Ester said.

"It's not depressing. It's not even weird. It's natural."

"I still don't believe it."

"Does that mean we aren't friends?" Sara asked thinking she had cornered me.

"Friends? Sure. But only because the English language doesn't have a better word for it. We're friends but we're not friends-friends. There will always be some tension. We just met right? When I met you I judged you physically and still I am currently judging your personality. And I don't mean 'judging' in a bad way I just mean 'making a mental decision about you.' 'Do I like her or do I not?' You did the same to me. You thought in your head 'oh he's cute' or 'oh he looks homeless' or 'oh he's ugly.' Of course you did. It's not bad. You just did. This always happens when two straight people meet each other. They size each other up and decide whether or not they are interested in being 'just friends' as you call it or 'more than friends.' So are we friends? Sure. But I think the jury is still out since we just met each other."

Aden has heard this argument close to a thousand times. He was silent just watching the conversation unfold before him, drinking a vodka and coke, munching on a burrito. Just then there was a very long pause in the conversation. I wasn't sure whether or not they thought I was reasonable or a creep. Maybe a reasonable creep?

"I think we can be friends," Ester finally said.

I ended the conversation with—"We aren't going to be friends. It's just that simple."

I spent the rest of the night proving this to her, once in the pool, and twice in her bed. Though, to be honest, I'm sure there is *something* to be said for guys and girls being true friends. Probably only one thing—but surely—*something*? I don't know what it is. I've never heard it.

And then everything sped up. Jason came over with another friend and Sara's ex roommate showed up with more alcohol. Eventually the room became more familiar, looking like all the others I had been to that summer, because everything appears the same when you're spinning. I felt home there in that spot, that spot somewhere between four and ten shots of liquor.

"I'm going to kiss you. Is that OK with you?" I asked Ester a few hours later in her neighbor's apartment.

"Please do," she said. So I did.

"Do you have a condom?" she asked me while unbuckling my belt in the kitchen with people all around.

I whispered into her ear, "yes in the car but I think we'd better not do it right here in the middle of the party."

"Yeah—that's a good idea."

So we snuck out and found condoms and then snuck back into her apartment, away from all the commotion of downstairs, and I noticed Aden and Sara on the balcony. I knew we had all night for horseplay, and didn't want to leave Aden by himself all night, so we went outside and stood with them before making our way to the bedroom. They had cigars and red cups like college kids do and they were talking about philosophy and politics like college kids do. Sara was a little too close to Aden for his comfort I could tell, so I stood in between them and looked up at the stars. We were on the third floor of a four story apartment building. Below us was another balcony overflowing with even more red cups, some of them blue, listening to the guttural shouts from boys trying to be men. Across the way were two more apartment buildings, both identical to the one we were in. And in the middle of all this was a lawn, an outdoor pool, a gate, and a bonfire.

So I looked down upon this glassless shimmering pool in the sparkling twilight and saw a group of almost naked students sitting just outside the still closed gate. Some didn't have any clothes on and others only their underwear. They sat around smelling each other like a meditative fraternity. They were sprawled there all exposed, glistening wet, shot-gunning beers and quoting Hegel.

"Sara wants to have sex with you," I whispered to Aden only feet away from her. "I can tell."

"I know," he said even louder than I had.

I shrugged my shoulders as if to ask, "*Are you going to go for it?*" though I knew his answer already. It's not that I don't have standards. I do. But compared to Aden I'm a bottom feeder. He is determined to sleep exclusively with super models. I keep telling him that for one night, sex is sex, but he has a pride about the girls he sleeps with that baffles me. It also doesn't get him much practice.

"*No*," he shook his head.

"Right, well I'm going to sleep with Ester tonight," I told him.

"I figured."

I assume Sara and Ester were having the exact same conversation as we were except a girl version, which is more assertive though simultaneously more insecure.

I indulged in her soon after. The sex was fine. She was very specific about pleasing me more than she cared about being pleased herself which was also fine, but the quickness to which all this happened made me wonder if she would go further. So I asked — "Do you want to have sex in the pool?"

I wouldn't have cared if she had said no.

"Yes," she said quickly.

"Alright let's go."

And as we walked outside I saw Sara kneeling next to Aden trying to sleep on the couch.

"You can sleep in my bed," she told him.

"I'm fine on the couch. I don't want to impose," he said.

"No really Aden — you can definitely sleep in my bed it is no skin off my back."

I looked at Ester and we chuckled silently to ourselves, me in boxers, and her only in my white t-shirt. *Only* my white t-shirt. Sara was drunk so kept asking him and Aden kept telling her no.

"I apologize but I am not going to sleep in your bed. That is final," Aden finally said sternly.

Sara was hurt but wouldn't be broken. When Ester and I left she was still next to him on the couch insisting that she "wouldn't mind." Desperate. But cute.

The water was cold, especially without any clothes on, and especially in the dead of night. We saw many people standing on their balconies, lights on, conversations being had only a hundred feet from us or so. But no matter — the rush of public indecency washed over us the same as the pool. It was technically illegal and that was exciting. Freedom is a right that is rarely fully taken advantage of in this way. Rules are bullshit. Fences are annoying. At least sometimes. You know?

Though, it was also lazy and we were shivering. It was a little awkward and we really only had one position to work with, one that required us to kiss a lot, which wasn't so bad except for it demanded an intimacy that I would regret the next morning. I liked it. I did. We invented strange new languages of the flesh. But besides the audience, I preferred a bed like a good Catholic. My mom would have been proud.

+

THE MORNING TWISTED INTO us. Aden was awake, cooking breakfast, and although we all knew that a goodbye was in order, none of us acknowledged it. We had pushed so hard into each other, at moments quite literally, that we all needed some time to slow down. So there wasn't much talking. There wasn't much reflection. There was only recovery.

Aden must have felt a little awkward after having so blatantly refused the advances of Sara though you wouldn't have known. He smiled and jeered and talked about staying for another day even. Though I knew he actually didn't want to stay. We had had our fun. We saw the movie and it was good and we'd recommend it to friends but we wouldn't go back to see it again. Maybe if the DVD was cheap we'd pick it up but that was the extent of it.

Sara additionally kept up quite a front of normalcy. Though maybe it wasn't a front? Maybe they were so adult, so understanding, so calm and gentle, that even such a divisive conversation as "no, I will not have sex with you," didn't affect them? Or maybe they were too drunk to remember?

Either way we all decided that getting to know one another was appropriate.

"So...what's your major?" Aden asked Ester.

"We all know that Ester and I spent the night together correct?" I asked.

The girls giggled and Aden appeased me by saying, "of course."

I continued, "Isn't it funny that we don't know anything about each other?"

"Funny?" Sara asked, "I would say awesome."

I wasn't expecting her to say this. I would have expected some version of "terrible" or "slutty."

"I study the environment," Ester answered.

One time Aden and I ventured out in Ann Arbor. Aden wore a kimono. I don't know why Aden wore a kimono but he wore a kimono. I distinctly remember the kimono because it was a kimono. So we entered a bar and left a bar to head to another bar and stumbled across a pretty short haired girl with very large breasts standing outside the local salsa joint. Aden convinced her to leave her friends and come with us. I ended up sleeping with her, too drunk to remember much of anything. In the morning I asked her "What's your name?" and she responded, "Does it matter?"

I thought for a second that "I study the environment" was Ester's version of "Does it matter?" But I looked at her eyes just then and I saw in them a gentleness, a longing that couldn't go unnoticed. She knew I would leave and I knew she would stay, and we both knew how fickle the previous night had been, but somewhere, deeper, somewhere within her pupils, there was a part of her that wondered "maybe?"

...And she got to me just then. Her soft skin. Her kind ears. Her frantic hair. Her thin waist. There was something about her, sitting there sipping on her coffee, an environmental girl from North Carolina, that got to me.

And so often that's how it is with sex. It doesn't necessarily have to mean anything, and it certainly doesn't necessarily have to be "good." It's not even about the sex. Masturbation is better half the time.

We collide into each other because we don't have a good reason not to. My generation values sex like we value the change in our pockets. We don't really *need* it—so we give it away sometimes.

And even if I did like her, even slightly, it wouldn't have mattered. Every ounce of my love was held in a cataclysmic vault. Every second of my life was held hostage to some other girl's combination. So although I yearned, worked for, and begged for the freedom to love someone else—I couldn't.

I couldn't imagine my life in North Carolina. I couldn't imagine myself with "good enough." I couldn't counter the everlasting pull of Andrea. Every time I met a new girl I compared her to Andrea. Every time I yearned I broke. For every positive gesture there was an equal and opposite retraction.

"You should visit me again," she would say.

"I will try," I would offer.

And it wasn't that I didn't want-to-want-to, it was just that I didn't want to. I wouldn't even if no one else better came along. And I would not have even fancied the idea of sleeping with her in the first place had Andrea not blindly given herself permission to do the same before the summer even began.

"What's your dream in life?" I asked her.

"So what is your favorite color?" is what I should have asked her. The answer would have meant the same to me—nothing.

And dear God it wasn't her in the real way. It was me in every way. It was me in the cosmic, depressive way. She offered everything I should have, could have wanted, at that very moment, and in every moment to come: a soft stomach and a happy bed, a charismatic lifestyle and an unforgettable smile, an ageless body and an enticing mind. It really, desperately, wasn't her. It was the comparison of her. It was the end of my ability to think logically. It was my intrinsic desire to leave. It was my heartfelt capacity for nothing meaningful. It was Andrea and exclusively Ester not being her. It was pathetic in the most beautiful way I could have ever hoped for.

"I'm not sure," she said solemnly.

She asked me where we would go to next, if we would go anywhere next or not? I didn't have an answer so I mumbled. I kept on mumbling. All I had done all summer was mumble.

But the choice had to be made. So we did the only self-respecting thing we could think of—pick out a map and point randomly. We were effectively dysfunctional.

This must have frustrated the girls—seeing how carelessly we used the map—how carelessly we used them. Though the choice, if you can call it that, was between Florida and Alabama. Florida had the better weather and beaches and more partying and a more obvious sun. But we'd have no more of the sun. It's too bright anyways. So we left just then, on a moment's notice—on to the capitalized South—on towards the Alabama of our songs.

I think we said goodbye though I forget.

Chapter 17

DRIVING INTO THE SOUTH is just as exciting as flying into Jerusalem, or Rome, or Mecca, or some blank wall in Tibet, or whatever Buddhists think is important—because it's a pocket of the world that is ludicrously and unapologetically religious. It wears its bumper stickers on its guitars and speaks a strange language of drawled bible verses.

I woke up from a thud. Aden had careened off the road, crashing into a parking spot in the early morning.

"Why'd you stop so fast? Where are we?"

He said this very slowly, very methodically, as if each letter was its own word to be worshiped—"Talladega Speedway."

"NASCAR?"

"Yes—NASCAR."

Now, I had never watched a single moment of NASCAR on television nor had I cared to for the entirety of my life, but we were in Alabama to hear accents and meet a few racists and eat some fried chicken and glorify all the stereotypes in person. We wanted to sink our teeth into every ounce of this new strange land, and what a better way to start than to go to the NASCAR Hall of Fame at Talladega Speedway? We should have paid but we found a back door that was open so we just let ourselves in. Many famous cars, or cars that were famous to someone, and many framed pictures of famous drivers, or drivers that were famous to someone, lined the walls. We sped through not really understanding all the jargon except enough to say things like *"oh wow it says here that this car was the one that Dale so and so drove when he won his 200th race"* and *"this car broke the land speed record for a turn."* We took pictures and touched things we shouldn't have touched because *"there isn't a sign saying we can't."*

Typical.

Soon after the museum we got it in our heads that we would be able to drive on the track. Of course this was impossible but we planned that if we got caught we would say *"but there isn't a sign saying we can't."* So we raced towards the arches, towards the track, but were soon met by a Dunkin'-Donuts-style police officer — red bearded with an enormous belt and all that. He stood in front of us at the entrance way ominously. It was obvious that he was the only thing standing between us and the freedom of an empty race track.

"Want to gun it right past him?" I asked Aden.

"Yes," Aden said quickly though we were all talk. We were scared.

...We let him tap on the window.

My heart was pounding. We were probably past the "restricted area" already and we had snuck into the museum just a few hundred feet away and he had probably saw us or someone did, and they had told him and he had already called his buddies from the station to *"come lock up these Yankees."* I didn't want to go to prison and if I did ever go to prison, I hoped it wouldn't be in Alabama. We were ready to bolt. We were ready to leave Alabama forever after only a few miles into the border — ready to leave this officer and his overstuffed belly, his hand on his hip, his walkie-talkie and all its history of oppression. He would use a hose on us. I knew it. The Mexican and the Jew — locked up forever in the hell of Alabama.

"Well how'r ya'll two boys doing this fine morning? Is there something I can help you with?" he asked in a sincere, joyful, almost too-nice sort of way.

"Well," Aden kind of stuttered. He usually is very suave in these sorts of situations. He is always the one who talks to authorities for the two of us. In college I, on more than one occasion, told Aden with my hands on his shoulders — *"You have to talk to the cops. I can't handle this."* But Aden could. And he did. But this time you could tell that Aden felt out of his element. Sure there were accents in North Carolina and sure some of them snuck around with the Confederate Flag but Alabama is like a foreign country comparatively. So Aden stuttered.

"Well...officer...we were hoping to see the track more up close and personal?"

The officer took a step back from the window and put his hands on his hips. He paused. It was a very dramatic pause. A police officer's pause is never subtle. Then he pointed back from where we had come.

"Over there is where we'll take you off to jail for sneaking into the museum ya damn Yankees," he was about to say.

"Well you know boys if yous hurry quick I bet ya'll can make the next tour. Go talk to Rose in the gift shop and she'll set yous up real nice and easy. Have yous boys ever been on a NASCAR track?"

"No sir."

"Oh you'll love it and it's pretty reasonable you know. "

Was this really happening? Was he really this gentle? Was he really this nice?

"Uhhh..." Aden felt a boost of confidence so asked a real question—"Do you think we could take a picture of the entranceway before going on the tour?"

"Oh of course, it's a real pretty view eh? ...Do you want to get out and I'll take it for you so you two can be together?" he asked.

Surreal. Completely surreal. It shouldn't have been. But it was.

"Here's to southern hospitality," I cheered on our way to the tour.

"Agreed."

As we entered the bus with a few obvious natives, Alabamians from Mobile or something, armed with NASCAR shirts, I noticed that Aden was wearing a new shirt as well.

"What is that?"

"Oh I bought a shirt while you were in the bathroom."

"Who is that?"

"Jeff Gordon."

"Really?"

"We're in Alabama man."

I love Aden. What's not to love about someone who so unequivocally and so insatiably throws himself into whatever fire is in front of him without a moment of hesitation? He wasn't making fun. He wasn't teasing. He was full-on accepting, deeply, everything NASCAR had to offer — so wearing a shirt made sense to him. It made sense to me too, though I never had the guts to be as obvious about it as he was.

As our tour guide entered the bus, with only us, a family from The North, and the Mobile tourists, he struck me as normal. He looked old in all the typical ways. He leaned over while he walked to keep his balance. He held firmly to railings. He had liver spots and a funny red hat that he didn't know was funny. He had wrinkles but not too many — just the "old people have wrinkles" sort of wrinkles — like they had always been there. The man sent to explain the fastest part of America was as slow and innocent as Alabama itself. He was a great irony, a kind gentle irony.

But then he said hello. And everything changed.

Aden and I looked at each other immediately. The man continued with the introductions though we hid our heads behind the seat back in front of us like kids at the back of the school bus who were hiding from the bus driver. We giggled like little girls and cupped our mouths into our hands.

"You are kidding? Right?"

"Do you think that is real?"

"There is no way that he really talks like that. There is no way. It's an act."

"I'm not sure. It might be real?"

+

A FEW YEARS EARLIER Aden and I had gone to Columbia together. On a bus ride packed to its max capacity, which in Columbia means people standing for a six hour adventure, swaying back and forth on some of the world's worst kept roads, Aden and I broke into the thickest, most obviously American-Spanish accents we could muster.

"Maaaay Goooos - Tay - reeeeeah ahhhh eeer aaayl Bon-yo," we said, which translates to "I would like to go the bathroom." We kept at this the entire time just for our own amusement — wanting the locals to tell the story to their friends about the crazy Americans with the most *"ridiculous American accents ever."*

This is how this man sounded — but more extreme because he was actually speaking English. It must have been fake, I thought. There was no such thing as an accent this thick. It was as if he was picked out of a Disney cartoon and plopped down in front of us. It was so outrageously exaggerated that no stereotype, no faked accent that I had ever heard, even remotely compared. I can't even begin to describe the accent phonetically because I didn't understand half the words he was using — if they were even words?

"Are you getting any of this?"

"Not really. Isn't it great?"

"It's beyond great. I'm so glad you stopped."

"This guy is too fun."

"This is perfect."

And it was. He was Alabama in all its glory, sitting right on the border, their tour guide on high, as if Alabama conspired to hire as its host the most sincere and simultaneously most insane man they could find. They lined up all the crazy old NASCAR fans and asked them all to tell a story in their thickest accents about "the good old days." And this man had won the contest with an audition to end all auditions—a fiery yet calm monologue about hospitality and the kindness of strangers. He was everything I could have ever hoped for. The track didn't even matter. The winner's circle, the Harley Davidson test-track, the pit, the enormous embankments because "otherwise the cars would fly off the track," all of the pictures, and all the statistics about near death experiences—none of them mattered compared to the man telling the story. He was everything I ever needed to know about Talladega Speedway.

He wasn't talking about NASCAR. He was NASCAR.

After, we stopped at a local diner right off the highway where we met some real southern comforts.

"I'll have a Sweet Tea," I told the waitress.

"I'll have a lemonade," Aden said.

"Now," she paused very purposefully, chomping on her gum, hand in pocket, other hand swirling a pen in her hair, "Have ya'll eva had sweeayt tea befo?"

I chuckled asking—"Is it that obvious?"

It was.

"Alright honey it's no problem. I'll bring y'all out some sweet tea and if ya'll don't like it I'll just run quick and get you sumthin' else. How does that sound honey?"

"Perfect."

So we really were somewhere new. Sure the highways were strange sometimes. Sure the mountains were different and the great national parks were isolated and sure some of the big cities were busier than we had expected—but never had I felt so foreign in my own country. Even Wyoming, though scary, ate the same food as everyone else. But here we ordered country fried steak, grits, black-eyed peas (which are really just beans), cornbread, and sweet potatoes. And everything was covered in gravy. Even the pecan pie. Well not really the pie. But almost.

"Home sweet home," Aden said while finishing his pie.

"What?"

"Home sweet home," he repeated.

"This feels like home to you?"

"Everywhere is home in Alabama."

I liked that. And no sooner than had I really started to believe it did we arrive in Birmingham. We picked out Birmingham because it was close to North Carolina respectively and a couchsurfer had, again, on a few hours' notice, agreed to let us stay in her house. Plus there was Martin Luther King and a famous church and all that to see. We were ready. Or so I thought.

We never in our wildest dreams could have expected to meet such a fire cracker as we did on that lonely street in northern Birmingham.

"I think we are here," I said to Kalyn on the phone.

"OK then I'll come out and let you in," she answered me. She speaks with the accent of a howler monkey.

So just as we picked out our backpacks from the trunk we saw her bounding, vibrating towards us in the summer light. Kalyn was constantly vibrating. She threw up her hands in the air and shouted to us, "hello," as enthusiastically as she could. Her wistful dress flowed in the gentle breeze but it seemed out of place. She was louder than such a feminine dress. She was jumping and swaying and crawling and smiling and wondering all at once. She ran towards us, hands still up in the air, like a dirty hipster with a manicure.

But then I saw her face. Oh how I saw her face! Uncountable are the troubled men who have seen her smile. Unknowable are the sorrows told by those who have so witnessed her lips. She was devilishly small, compacting herself so exquisitely, and so proportionally into the minimum available space allotted to her by her creator, that her heavenly grin shown even the brighter in comparison. She must have been so bored with claims of instantaneous love, so fervently and unrelentingly aware of the spell she naturally would cast upon those poor men who dared bend into her presence, that no bounding show of affection would ever leave her impressed. No—she had been hardened to love and those men who played it like a hand of poker, winning her as a reward and then running off with their new chips before she had even the chance to play another hand. It was so typical, and so normal to her, and in that it had let her down so many times before, all she could do was smile over and over, hopeful that the next time would be different. That's all she had left, it seemed—a hopeful smile.

See—she was not slowly digestible. She demanded to be swallowed all at once, and didn't quite care if you didn't enjoy the flavor, nor would she allow you the time to acquire her tastes more acceptable. You either liked her or you didn't, and she would go on bounding and smiling regardless of your decision.

Sound familiar? Had we met our match?

+

IN CANADA I DANCED mildly, constantly checking over my shoulder amidst the lights and techno music, searching for Andrea. *Had she hidden away after that first encounter? Did she really hate me that much?* No matter—I grabbed Aden by the shoulders and told him that Andrea was here. I had to find her.

"I saw her earlier man—but I didn't want to say anything about it...she's with her new boyfriend."

"I don't care."

"Do you want to see her? I thought you were over her?"

"I am."

"No you aren't."

"I know."

"Well then let's find her."

We elbowed people and stepped over others, turning ourselves into bloodhounds in search of our fallen prey. I could no longer hear the music. I could no longer see anything — just the color blue — where is that blue dress?

I found her swaying drunkenly next to the bar. But with her back to me, head bobbing, I saw her differently just then. She wasn't proud and happy and full of hope with her new boyfriend like I had thought she was. See — ever since the breakup I had spent all my time consciously trying to forget her, attempting to quell the annoying sound of regret that was constantly beating into my scull. All the while, which is usually the case with loneliness, I thought she was perfectly content. I thought she had met a new guy happily, and therefore had "moved on" easily as I had predicted. — But something was different. Her posture had changed. Instead of giddily swaying with the music, she was stumbling back and forth, awkwardly and numbly. I stared at her — sad for her — sad for me — sad for us.

"Turn around," I wanted to yell.

"Come back to me," I wanted to scream.

Then she turned around, and to my utter shock — that's exactly what she did. She turned around as if on auto pilot, locked her gaze with mine, and ran towards me. She fell onto me actually, arms resting around my neck, lips resting against my ear.

"Hello," she whispered, her breath smelling of heaven and vodka.

I didn't know what to do. This was all so unexpected — it was all so — perfect.

"Hello," she whispered again — "we are both here."

"Yes we are," I said while looking at her new boyfriend who was now standing right next to us, probably wondering who I was since we had never met. I made a face as if to say *"who is this drunken girl hugging me?"*

and he simply shrugged (little did he know). He must have been used to her falling down. Since the breakup I would learn—she was rarely sober.

"I miss you," she whispered into my ear, "but I'm not allowed to say that...because...you know...my boyfriend is here...and well...I still hate you."

"I miss you too."

"Why are you doing this to me?" she said sadly.

"Doing what?"

Just then her boyfriend pulled her away from me. I wouldn't see her for another few weeks.

+

IT WAS IMMEDIATELY APPARENT that our leading role in the story was over. We were crazy adventurers who had decided to come to her only the day before, and Kalyn was interested to an extent, sure, sounds good—but really she was probably wholly unimpressed by us. She had seen this game before. We weren't anything special.

So we asked her questions more than she asked us questions—"Why Birmingham?"

"I'm going to school here now because I ran out of money while I was traveling. My family is from sort of allover because my dad is a military dude and met my mom in the Korean War or something and yeah—but we're from Alabama."

"Makes sense."

"How did you run out of money? You were traveling? Where?"

"Yeah I lived in China and Japan and Australia and visited South America and lived in Nicaragua and Guatemala for a few years and ya know, just traveled until I ran out money and then I applied to nursing school and that's what I'm doing next week at UAB."

We then understood why a little jaunt around the US wasn't a big deal to her.

"I got hit by a car," she said.

"Oh god! Where did that happen? Were you OK? I think..."

"Oh shush. It was the best thing that ever happened to me."

"Yeah?"

"That's how I got all that money to travel! ...I rehabbed for a few months and then left until I don't know how long."

"You know I may live in Nicaragua soon?" I told her. "I actually should find out today if I get a job down there."

"Oh yeah? Nicaragua is awesome. What is the job?"

"Something with marketing but it sounds cool. Have any advice?"

"Don't do cocaine."

"Right."

"No I'm serious. Drugs aren't just drugs down there. It's a lot easier to get involved with and stuff, you know what I mean?"

I didn't.

"I do."

"Promise me you won't do the crazy Cocaine?"

"I promise."

"Do you guys like Kimchi?"

"My roommate in college was Korean."

"Do you guys like Kimchi?" she repeated bitingly.

I was falling in love. I love when girls challenge my stupidity.

"Yes I think we do. Aden?"

"Yes we do."

"Alright well I'm glad you guys are here so we're going to have a Korean meal, Korean style, on the floor and what not. Are you guys cool with that?"

"Authentic Korean meal on the floor in Alabama? I'm all about that."

She was faster than us I realized — she kept talking at a pace that I had never experienced before. Her brother was going to come over and another friend might stop by and she just got back to Birmingham yesterday and…

"Wait…you just got back yesterday?"

"…Yeah I just moved in. You guys are the first two to see my place. I don't even really have any friends here yet. Well I did. So I guess I do. But I haven't called them since I arrived so I need to do that. I should do that. I'll do it later. Do you guys care if I grill the meat or would you rather have it baked?"

"uhhhh…?"

And she kept up like that, and would, for the entire visit. Even at dinner on the floor…

"Could you pass the hot sauce? So do you guys like traveling around? You guys seem cool. I think some people would be scared to have two big guys come into their house right away but I did so much surfing around the world I have to give back ya know? It's only fair. And you guys are cool big guys. Right?"

Aden passed her the hot sauce and answered one of her questions, kind of — "We like traveling around, yes."

"This is really good food. Thank you."

"…and even better with chopsticks," Aden added. "You think we are big?"

"Oh you know what I mean. You're big compared to me." She said this while flexing her muscles, looking like a stick figure in 3D. "Want to go out tonight?" she asked.

"Of course."

"Obviously."

So we went. And we didn't know where to go or how to get there or who we would meet, but we knew that it would be unforgettable. Nothing with Kalyn was going to be forgettable.

"I don't think this is a 'one night' type of place," Aden suggested to me.

"I completely agree."

"Kalyn?" Aden then asked her, "Do you mind if we stay for more than one night? We've decided that we like you and want to see more of Birmingham than just one day's worth. Is that cool?"

"Of course. You can keep me safe at night. It's my first couple nights in my apartment so I'd actually rather you guys be here," the tiny girl said to the two strange men who she had just met.

This exact sentiment precisely summarized her entire life philosophy. She was moving back home but it looked different and felt different than what she remembered, so she was a little on edge.

See — after we travel our homes rarely change, but *we* do, and so we view every part of our past through new, wider eyes, as if we never stopped traveling — and now we have a once familiar city to relearn all over again. But so too is she small and so too is a city sometimes a little too quiet at night. So she invited strangers into her house right off, good ones, to fend off those other strangers, the ones who actually lived in one place — the scary ones. We were more relatable to her than her own city because we understood her. We understood the road. We weren't necessarily heading in the same direction — but at least we were both moving.

"So there is this independent bookstore that's really cool and I think there is a show there tonight. Is it cool if we just go there?"

"Oh Kristopher is a writer so yeah let's do that," Aden insisted.

"I'm not a writer."

"He's a writer."

"You're a writer? What did you write?"

"I'm not a writer."

"He's a writer."

I wasn't annoyed by Aden's persistence. I needed his persistence. I didn't often have the audacity to root for myself. I needed his confidence.

I needed him.

But then Kalyn quipped something to deflate my ego. Something like — "Oh just shut up. If you're a writer you're a writer. Stop being so stupid."

"I'm not I'm just…"

"Oh shut up."

So I did.

"So listen. Listen to me," she continued, "So I heard from one of my friends that there is a band from Boston playing upstairs or something at this bookstore right? It's a really cool place and I think they are running out of money so that sucks but maybe if they get this grant they'll be able to stay in business and they do shows like this for extra money and I don't know if anyone will really be there but I think it might be cool anyways. Even if its just us there it could be fun — it for sure might be cool or we could go into the city instead and I'm not really sure but I think we should go there since you're a writer and all that…"

"OK," I said.

So we went.

To get there we passed a series of abandoned factories that we would later learn were in fact haunted. The air felt thick and cold even though the temperature was sizzling. Only desolate street lights guided us farther.

"Are you sure this is where it is? No wonder this place is going out of business."

"Yeah trust me. I used to go here all the time."

See—Kalyn lived exclusively in back alleys…from one to the next…she slipped past all the lit safe areas of Birmingham, scurrying into the seediest parts of her city like she was in a maze, doing everything in her power to stay lost. And the closer we got the darker and more desolate the city became. But the more we reached into its empty bag, the more at home I began to feel. I knew something big was coming. I knew something magical was headed my way. And sure enough, as we pulled down that last empty street, I could hear the bookstore from a few blocks away. I heard it loud and clear—like someone—or something—was shouting. And this made sense in a way—because a book is the only shout that's ever really heard.

The place smelled like old books because it was full of old books. There weren't many mystery novels or romance whatevers. It was a homage to real live literature—this bookstore's curators were like bouncers who only let the prettiest words in.

"This place," I said happily to Kalyn, "is full of…literature. They really take their time with this place, it seems."

"It is pretty dusty and crappy looking to me."

"I'm not talking about the decorating," I said. "I don't care about the decorating."

"It is pretty dusty and crappy looking to me."

…I kept falling in love with her.

"No. Listen. I'm talking about the books."

"What's the difference between literature and a book?" she asked me.

"30 years…a college reading list…or suicide?"

"No really?"

"I don't know. Really. — If it says something timeless?"

"I don't like time."

"Neither do I."

"That's good."

"That is good."

We didn't say anything for a bit until…

"Want to go upstairs and see the show?"

"Not yet."

"Aden do you want to go upstairs and see the show?"

"Yes."

"Kristopher…come on now…"

"I'll meet you guys up there. I want some more time with the books," I said.

"Don't you mean the 'literature,'" Kalyn said to me faking a British accent, sticking her nose up really high into the air.

"Rock out," said Aden.

"Yeah," Kalyn quipped, "'rock out.'" She smirked and walked upstairs with Aden.

Melville. London. Austen. Shakespeare. Dickens. Thoreau. Burroughs. Dickenson. Wolfe. Whitman. Frost. Twain. Kerouac. Salinger. Tolstoy. I had all my friends there with me and we needed a few moments alone together. I did a little spring cleaning and wiped away the smudges on the edges of their pages. I loosened up their jackets and gave them a little shake to get rid of all the cobwebs. I raised my finger along the edges of their collective brilliance and hoped to feel some inspiration, to hear a story in my own head, anything, as if I would learn something from them through osmosis. How I loved their soft touch — their weathered faces in faded photographs — and all that black and white, all the patience, sentences of all shapes and sizes, just waiting to be read.

...And with all this beauty available for fifty cents a pop, my generation has now learned how to read a book without having to actually touch one, I thought.

We're fucked.

But then I thought of the fine book-store-slash-attic-music-venue that I was standing in and it comforted me. -There wasn't a line out front. There wasn't a cover. There wasn't anyone for that matter, except for two bearded fellows sitting on a couch near the door. They said they were working, or some version of it. There wasn't much difference between working and hanging out since no one there got paid. It was as if a group of friends stumbled upon a great empty warehouse and decided to pool their book collections and start a store. Everything was handmade — even the shelves were nailed together with such blissful ignorance that I couldn't help but be reminded of 7th grade shop class. Worse even.

"So we need some wood," the one said to the manager at the lumber yard.

"We need wood and nails and a hammer," another one said.

"Well what kind? What size? How much?" the manager asked importantly.

"I don't know — just give us some wood."

And so they made shelves and they threw books on them and made up prices based upon how much they liked each one.

"The better the book — the cheaper we'll sell it for. That way people can read only good books."

It was a very benevolent crowd. Whether money is a useful tool, whether it is necessary for the organization of a civil society, is still up for debate there.

"Want a book? No money? How about a hug?" And that's all they ever needed.

I walked up the creaky stairs and immediately heard music drowning me in all the perfect ways. It started near my toes as they began to tap. Then my ankles shook. After, my hips swayed and it was a little chilly, this beat, with the drums banging at my sides. Then my arms and my head nodded and climbed higher and higher up the stairs, up towards Aden and Kalyn and a band of Boston rockers who had come all the way to Birmingham to give us a private show.

There wasn't a bar. There weren't chairs. There were just angled beams and splintering boards — just an attic — an empty attic. All the lights were turned off except for those just above the band at the opposite end of the room. Aden and Kalyn sat there next to each other Indian style beside one of the bookstore "workers," one of Kalyn's friends who met us there, a guitar player who "opened" for the band, the girlfriend of the lead singer, and the girlfriend of the drummer. They all sat as if in a drum circle. There was endless space on the ground for anyone to fit anywhere they wanted, but everyone sat knee-to-knee, almost palm-to-palm, all edging their necks towards the band. Sure no one really had shown up for the show but that made it better as Kalyn had predicted. It made it intimate.

And as I sat down next to Kalyn, Aden just on the other side of her, I waved to everyone sitting as if to say *"I come in peace."* They all smiled as if to say *"you are welcome here."* There was something spiritual about the emptiness of that attic. There was something metaphysical grounded in it — live music for a few strangers. And Kalyn too, had a big smile — though it was a vague smile. You were never sure if you were the reason for her happiness or if she was just being polite. And she wanted it that way. She lived for that exact brand of confusion.

"How's everyone doing tonight?" the singer asked us.

We all cheered as loud as we could. We yelled to the heavens.

"Anything you want to hear tonight?"

"Something we've never heard before. Your favorite song!" Aden shouted.

So we danced. Because, of course, it's always important to dance.

They played songs of rock n'roll and I don't remember if they were any good or not. I imagine they were. But it didn't matter. We danced, just the five or six of us and the music pulsated just feet from our bones, sometimes so close that we could feel the atomic composition of each note pressing up against our temples. We were frantic in the dull light, and happy. Everyone completely forgot how to frown. We were savants of dance. We always had been. We all are, in fact. See — learning how to dance doesn't make any sense actually. Learning how to dance is like learning how to smile.

For the first time it was as if I was living backwards, living so ferociously and so exquisitely that time had turned on its head and so I grew younger, physically even, falling for the first time not closer to death, but farther away from it, like a car careening down hill while still in reverse.

"This is the best concert I've ever been to," I yelped.

"Me too," Aden said.

"Me three," Kalyn squeaked.

But it ended as all things do. It ended like the end of a road after a sharp corner — we didn't see it coming. The night crept into us like a silkworm under water.

"Keep playing," we yelled.

"No please stop. We've got to go home," a few of the workers said. "We have 'real jobs' to wake up for tomorrow."

Real jobs. Real jobs? I had forgotten what life felt like.

"How about this," the lead singer suggested, "since we don't have any money to get back to Boston except for what you guys bought in t-shirts, let's go get a drink at a bar. We'll take the party there. Just give us a second to pack up the equipment. Though you have to buy us a beer." He said this into the microphone even though I was standing arm's length from him. I liked that. I would definitely buy him a beer.

So we left the attic forever, never to return except for in our memories. That attic is probably dead by now, or forgotten. But that barren attic was once alive, at least for one night, and that's all that mattered.

I kissed my fingers and placed them on the floor while walking down the stairs to say goodbye peacefully.

But we lingered around the books for a time before finally leaving, thumbing through pages and reading passages out loud to each other.

"Oh oh listen to this…" Kalyn would shout from one end of the shop to the other.

"Oh you'll never believe this line…" Aden would say.

But beyond all of that, or somewhere underneath it, I stood silently next to the cash register and picked up a card board journal. It had obviously been handmade— only consisting of a few blank pieces of construction paper folded into a piece of thick cardboard, a few staples in the middle, oh, ya know, and the entire world.

…That's all.

"How much for this?" I asked a girl. "And did you make it?"

"Oh yeah we had a bunch of random boxes so we just made a few of them. They are really simple as you can tell."

"How much?" I asked again.

She curled her lip as if I had insulted her. But she paused. She calmed — and asked me the most important question I had ever heard — "Well are you going to write anything important inside?"

"I would like to," I shuddered.

"You promise you'll try?"

"Yeah. I promise I'll try."

"Then just take it..."

Then she handed it to me, I thanked her, and I was born just then.

It was a wordless poem. It was a blank sheet of paper, an empty journal, or a plain white document—nothing and yet everything all at once. It was beautiful not because it already was, but because it one day could be.

"What do you have there?" Aden came up next to me, looking at the piece of cardboard in my hand.

"A journal," I said.

"*The rest of my life,*" is what I meant.

"Well now it's obvious my man. You *have to* write this story man. It's a sign. You have to write *this* story." He said this casually while patting me on the back and walked away, but nothing about what he said was casual—not to me.

So I looked down at the journal, held it tightly with both hands, and I prayed. I don't know to whom or to what or why. I don't even know what I prayed about. I didn't ask for anything. I didn't even think. There were no words—just a feeling of gratitude washing all over me. As if the whole universe had conspired on my behalf. As if it had always wanted me to be here in this bookstore in Birmingham. It had always wanted me to go to school in Ann Arbor and meet Aden. It had always wanted me to break Andrea's heart and leave her at her most vulnerable moment. It had always wanted me to search for myself through America. It had always wanted me to see the sunrise in North Carolina, and accidentally pick Alabama and it always wanted everything to look like chance. The universe wanted my life to seem like a series of unrelated fantasies thrown together if only by the sheer randomness of my scattered mind. But no—it was all clear now. The whole damn thing—all of it—my whole life—was for this journal. It was for this story. It was for this moment.

Aden walked away.

"It *is* a sign," I whispered to him though he didn't hear me. "It *is* a sign."

Chapter 18

"LET'S GO GET DRUNK!" the drummer screamed while running down the stairs from the attic.

"Yes let's do," Kalyn agreed.

And so we did. We found the tiniest, strangest, most random bar we could have ever possibly found and decided that it would do just fine.

"This place is awesome. There won't be anyone here. But it's awesome," Kalyn told us. We trusted every ounce of her at this point—all 12 of them.

There was a sign out front reading "Bar" in pink neon. It dripped with gunk and putrid water and saliva and cum. It sat next to the most wretched brick wall I'd ever seen. It was red and dark red and brown and black and also was made of gravel and was covered in graffiti from top to bottom. For a second I thought the same people who built the bookstore had built this bar. This excited me.

Another sign showed an arrow pointing down. Even farther down. Farther and farther down. It was a basement bar, somewhere in Birmingham, somewhere on a street, somewhere in America—just the way we like. Though we walked down the stairs too politely I realized. This was an unholy bar for lushes and patriots and nuns and dancers. It had no room for silence. It had no room for civil conversations or high heeled shoes or collars either. It had no room for date nights. It was the proud gum on Birmingham's shoe.

Everyone in the joint had a face or neck tattoo except for Kalyn who was wearing a bright yellow sundress. It fit somehow. Though she did have two paintings tattooed on both of her arms. She said she liked them. This made sense. There were scribbles everywhere on the walls. Everything from "love everyone" to "for a good time call" to "Fuck Bush" to "I hate niggers." It all fit somehow.

The only thing we could do was fill the jukebox with as much money as we could afford. Which was a lot. And we danced, of course, to no one's surprise. We danced. And we danced — the only ones dancing, sure, sounds good — but that's how it always has been with us. And Kalyn, by this time, was one of us. In half a day she had evolved from a stranger to a lifelong friend, like bunkmates at boot camp — except dancing is much more fun than killing people.

The jukebox and Kalyn were the only things glowing. Everyone else and everything else was black and torn. So like watching a light show at a rave, hopped up on her acid — I tripped. I had all sorts of visions and strange thoughts and awkward mood changes and I was too cold and too hot all at once. I saw her like a hologram I could touch. She was quickly becoming the Estella to my Pip.

We said farewell to the poor rock band from New England and saluted their expressions.

"One day you'll be famous," I told them.

"Probably not."

"One day you'll be famous," Kalyn repeated.

"Well thanks."

"Hey," Aden added, "Someday you'll be famous!"

And with a tip of their hats and a roar of the engine, they were off. We left each other but knew we had solidarity with them. We would never see them again, but the road is the road. We'd feel them everywhere.

Aden passed out right away on the couch upon arrival at Kalyn's house.

"Do you mind if I play some music?" she asked him snoring.

"I don't think he cares," I said.

"I think you're right."

"Do you want to talk?" she asked me.

"Sure."

"Let me run into my room and get into something more comfortable."

I did the same. She came back. We talked.

We sat there in a nook, and I can only call it a nook because no other variation of such a space would be appropriate. We were framed on three sides by walls, only one of which was an actual wall, the other two, the back of a couch and a desk respectively. Her apartment was desperately small. All the lights had been darkened and Aden was miles away on the other side of the couch, far from our sightline. We sat there crouched Indian style, a candle flickering somewhere in the distance, so saw each other's shadows more than our colors. It felt youthful, like we were two toddlers up way past our bedtime, chatting and drawing things in the carpet together.

She was wearing a very short nightgown, the type you would receive as a gift on Valentine's Day. It was soft pink, cotton, and nearly sheer. She sat in this gown cross legged and so showed me very openly, and surprisingly very comfortably, her white underpants. They were spotted with red flowers, and very organized. And in it being so late and therefore so close to bed, neither did she wear a bra. And so too each time she leaned into a gesture closer to me, the strings of her nightgown fell lazily around her shoulders, exposing not only the tops of her small breasts. She must have noticed, but carried on with such an absolute indifference that I couldn't help but ignore her flesh. I would not have been shunned for interpreting her dress, the time of night, the moment, and its literal nakedness as her coming onto me—but I accurately didn't. This was just another example of how she lived. I easily imagined her prancing around near her family with a similar carelessness. She wasn't trying to show me anything, she simply did, and hadn't bothered to address it. She liked her nightgown, and she felt comfortable sitting that way, so that was that. She wouldn't change for anyone, even if it meant they saw her more privately.

We talked like we were in a basement in Denver. At first she spoke her usual way, fast, and flowing. She talked about Birmingham and told me all about her adventures in Nicaragua. She was a scuba dive instructor at one point.

"But you're so small?"

"So?"

"Good point."

She loved her mom and couldn't really relate to her brothers as much as she liked them. She isn't happy being back in the US but she wasn't happy traveling either. There was a boy and boys suck.

She kept up like this for some time, staying firmly on the surface of possible conversation. She went only so far down before coming back up for air. Understand—Kalyn spoke in free verse and she knew it. Like a river that controlled its own dam, she was careful not to open up too long for fear of divulging too much.

She was someone who would love E.E. Cummings if she hadn't thought poetry so trivial. "Don't talk about it," she would say, "just live it." And don't ask her to define "it." She'd just say "doesn't matter" and continue along dancing. Which I guess is true—it's always important to dance.

But the dam broke eventually. The flicker of a candle. The pink warmth of her cheek. My chin resting on a leaning palm. A song in the background...

"My father is dying," she said.

There is nothing appropriate to say when confronted with such a secret. There is never a right answer with death. There is no magic one-liner that quenches the thirst of such a ferocious fire. It's better to stay silent, stay calm, ration your sympathy into careful little piles, and weather the storm together.

"Is that why you came back to Alabama?"

"That's why I came back to Alabama."

She cried. She didn't sob. She wasn't loud. She was careful not to wake up Aden—such a good heart. I could barely see the details of her face by this time, with all the lights dimmed and the candle on its last breath. Everything relaxed. Everything rested peacefully. Everything gave her the space she needed.

So I didn't say much after that. I just looked fully into her over and over again. I let her words pour out of her without trying to catch them. They deserved to splash and scatter all over the floor beneath her. She deserved that mess. She needed it. And when she was done she quietly, calmly, asked me if I would sleep in her room with her.

"Of course," I said and placed a simple blanket on the floor.

I wasn't sure if she wanted me to hold her or listen to her more or touch her more instinctively? I didn't care either way. I simply laid my blanket down on the floor, turned off the light, and said, "Let me know if you need anything. I am right here."

So eventually talk turned into tears and tears turned into worry and worry turned into thought and thought turned into a dream and a dream turned into a very peaceful rest. She used me like a nightlight for a very dark sleep—and I was happy to oblige.

"Thank you," she said in the morning.

"No—thank *you*," I said in the morning.

And that's all we needed to say.

+

I ANSWERED A CALL congratulating me on getting the job in Nicaragua. I was excited but only mildly. This meant I would have to leave soon. In only a week's time they wanted me in Nicaragua. In only a week's time they wanted me packed, moved, and ready to start work. It wouldn't be work-work. My office would have a garden and my boss was my age and everyone had a sort of youthful "let's go change the world" attitude that didn't allow for any sort of corporate humdrum—but I didn't want to go. I wanted to stay with Aden for weeks, months longer and check out Austin and Miami and then ride the coast up towards New Hampshire to see Andrea's home and eat some syrup. I needed more time to devolve, I thought. I needed more time for I didn't know what. But I wasn't ready to go anywhere with a plan just yet, I knew at least that. The impending doom of a schedule frightened me.

"I got the job," I said.

"Ha!" Aden shouted while opening his arms for a hug, "I knew you'd get it my brother! I knew it! Kalyn we have to go celebrate Kristopher got the job in Nicaragua. I knew you'd get it man I knew it you've always had a knack for…Kalyn! Kalyn get out of the shower you have a lifetime to shower. We have to go celebrate! I knew you'd get it man. I'm so happy for you. Are you happy? I'm so happy for you."

And he was. He was happy for the two of us.

Though he quickly changed his tone—"when do you start?"

I shook my head in disbelief. "Not good man," I said. "It's not good."

"Fuck. You have to go soon?"

"I have to be there in a week. So I'll have to fly back to Michigan soon and get my things settled."

"Fuck."

It only took a moment though. All the thoughts that could have possibly swarmed around in his mind did, were decided upon, and left all in one big flash. He made an instantaneous decision to be happy regardless of any outside variable—including me.

"Well then we have a few more days. Let's make the best of them."

I shook my head.

"I'm happy for you man. This is what you wanted."

"I know but it's so fast."

Just then Kalyn bubbled into the room yelling and smiling and hugging and talking a mile a minute. I had to go here and there and talk to this man and this woman and couldn't miss out on this place and must visit that one place over there. I forgot all of it before she even finished.

"You promise me you'll go everywhere I recommend?"

"I promise.

"Let's have a drink," Aden said.

"What time is it?"

"I don't know. Let's have a drink anyway."

"Why?"

"Because somewhere the sun is setting."

"This makes sense."

So we drank at a bar that had been picked as one of the best bars in America by some fancy magazine.

"So what makes this bar so special?"

"It was in a magazine."

"Well yeah but why was it in the magazine?"

"Because it's sooooo special," she said sarcastically. I was still falling deeper and deeper in love.

Today she would try hard. She would take us to all her favorite places and let the sun shine down on our day with purpose. We were actually *trying* to get the tan this time. Usually it just falls into us.

So next was a BBQ rib joint that smelled like heaven.

"Oh my god my ribs are so tender," I said, "the meat is falling off the bone due to gravity. I'm in love."

"With whom might I ask?" Kalyn piped in.

"With you," I said only half-joking.

"Shut up."

"Yeah he's definitely in love with you," Aden agreed.

"You two boys are just too silly."

The sauce, the air, the conversation, the gravy, everything about this restaurant was thick. Thick accents, thick hips, thick knives, thick — everything. Except for Kalyn. She was still small.

"Any girls in your lives'?" she asked us more seriously this time.

"Nope," Aden spouted.

"Yeah but I fucked it up. Typical bullshit story…" I admitted.

"What did you do?"

"Broke up with her."

"That's all? She'll take you back."

"I slept with someone the same day I broke up with her."

"Idiot."

"I know."

"She'll take you back nonetheless."

"Well she did but…"

"But what?"

"Well she did but then she didn't."

"You left?"

"I left."

"Idiot."

"Yeah but now I have you."

"Not the same."

"I know."

"Whatever. She'll take you back."

"I hope so."

"She'll take you back," Aden said. "She loves you."

"I hope so."

"New conversation," I insisted. And we left.

The closer Michigan came in my mind the more Andrea came back to me. I had done so well for so long. I hadn't bothered her the whole summer as I wanted to. But I would see her soon. I knew I would see her. I would see her. Not maybe later—but actually later—in real life.

After that we bought bubbles and rolled down hills. When did bubbles lose their charm? When did we stop rolling down hills? We are stupid for not continuing this tradition into our maturity. There should be hill rolling clubs and bubble clubs in major cities. It would catch on. It would.

We lost all semblance of adulthood and skipped openly and threw grass and rolled and rolled and rolled and rolled up to the sky, the ground, the sky, the ground, the sky, the parking lot, the sky, the ground, a statue, a hint of Kalyn, the sky, faster, the sky again, the ground, laugh, the sky, parking lot, Aden, a shirt, laugh, the sky, sky, sky, sky…thud. Up—and again and again—until our sides ached.

"Best day ever," Aden said.

We laid at the bottom of the hill head to feet breathing heavily—a tiny triangle of friendship.

"Best day ever." Cue background music. Overhead shot. Spinning.

"Best day ever." Quick close up. Big smile.

"I'm seeing a friend tonight who I haven't seen in a very long time," Kalyn said randomly still lying on the grass.

"That's badass," said Aden.

"Friends are good," I said.

"Friends are definitely good," Kalyn said.

"To friendship."

"To friendship."

"To friendship."

Our fists reached towards the sky naturally. And we knew the symbolism. We knew that a similar fist, for a much greater cause than friendship, once pointed sharply to the sky above Birmingham. The tension of the day's humor and its celebration compared to its setting was something we all felt most earnestly just then. Needless to say, a few hours later as we stood outside of the 16th Street Baptist Church and thought about those four little girls, our fists fell limp. They extended and turned up, palms towards the sky.

"I'm so sorry God," I said. "I'm so sorry."

I had done nothing of substance. I had jumped on the memories of the martyred ghosts of Birmingham. I looked past the oppression and the segregation, past the poverty and the thick black smoke, and focused only on my most hedonistic desires. I saw The South as a playground more than a memorial, and no sooner was that glaringly apparent than in front of that faithful church.

"I'm so sorry," I said to myself and to anyone who would listen. "I'm so sorry."

Back then, well before I was born, my grandmother was going to be put into a lower grade because she couldn't speak English.

"Give her a math test!" my great grandmother had shouted.

So too, her entire generation shouted. All of Alabama shouted so loud that it ripped itself apart. It had to. It was the only way to put itself back together again.

My mother told me of the race riots in Saginaw and her black friends telling her — "you probably should go home now."

So there was real solidarity running through my veins. Or there should have been? My skin was caramel, sometimes even more so than my African brothers and sisters. I was "The Mexican" if I tripped. I was just another white kid if I shined. So I felt it sometimes too — injustice. Not often but sometimes — and that should have been enough. I had felt that toxic indifference for justice, that putrid disrespect for the righteous, that very insensitive and bigoted mindset, it was exactly what had led to packed buses and sit ins and peaceful marches and water cannons and now…to this…

A statue. A silly little statue. And guilt. A whole church full of guilt.

So I cried. For Alabama. For everything. For all of it. Outside. Inside.

And that was that.

+

A FEW DAYS AFTER the Canada foolishness, I passed Andrea at an intersection on my way to class.

"Andrea?" I said after a double take.

"Oh…hi," she said shyly this time. There would be no hug. There would be no "I miss you."

"How have you been?"

"Fine—actually really good." She was lying. "...and you?"

"Alright."

"How is your dad?"

"Same."

"I'm sorry to hear that."

"Yeah well you know…"

"Hey Kristopher—I actually should get going I have to…" She didn't want to see me. Sure, in her drunken stupor a few weeks before she had been honest—but not now. Now she had to be stubborn. She had to be strong and distant.

"Well…I actually wanted to talk to you."

She rolled her eyes irritated.

"Can I walk with you?"

Class? What class? I had my Juliet to walk with.

She didn't answer but I took that as a yes.

"Do you remember what happened in Canada?"

"Canada?"

"You know—in Windsor?"

"Oh yeah—we saw each other right?"

"You told me you missed me."

"I was drunk."

"I know but…"

"Kristopher—I was drunk," she said sternly.

"I miss you too," I said. "I regret everything."

She smiled. And then she smiled again.

"Can I take you out to ice cream again?"

"I have a boyfriend Kristopher. You told me to move on remember?"

"I know…just as friends," I said.

"Just as friends?" she said sarcastically.

"I know."

"Kristopher—I can't."

"Well—how about…well…" I would try anything. "…Have you heard about Aden and I's party? We are having a DJ from Denver come for it. It's a black light party—starts at 8:00 on Friday. We're expecting about 300 people there. You should come. You'll like the music. You can bring your boyfriend. It'll be fun."

"Well…"

"Come on Andrea—it'll be the best party of the weekend for sure. We're spending over $1,000 on it. It's in one of the abandoned sorority houses. It's going to be absolutely incredible. I know we aren't on good terms but I want to be. Whether you want to admit to it right now or not—you miss me. You told me you do. And I miss you too. And I know it's complicated but fuck—let's just go to the same party—dance a little—and maybe…I don't know…maybe we can talk or something?"

"Just as friends?"

"Just as friends. I promise."

"And I can bring my boyfriend?"

"You can bring your boyfriend. Bring the whole gang—your sister and everyone. It'll be fun."

"Friday at 8:00?"

"Friday at 8:00."

"And I can bring anyone?"

"You can bring anyone."

"Alright Kristopher — I have to go."

"So are you coming?"

"Probably," she said and walked away.

I smiled then. I smiled a great big smile and fist pumped the air. I jumped up and down in the middle of the sidewalk as she walked away. I was so damn happy. — But not as happy as I would be that Friday when she finally let her guard down and told me to kiss her. That — was ecstasy.

Though — of course, I had to go on this fucking road trip right after that kiss — so instead of kissing her for the rest of the summer, I went to a bar in Alabama, trying to forget about her all over again, trying to find Kalyn...

+

"WHERE IS KALYN?"

"I really don't know man she was talking to her friend, what's her name?"

"Katherine." Aden is excellent with names.

"...She was talking to Katherine and then she just fell off the face of the planet."

"They have really funny pictures in the bathroom. You should check it out."

"I'm not going to check out pictures in the bathroom."

"Why not?"

"Good point. I will in a bit."

"So what do you think?"

"Of Kalyn?"

"Of Kalyn, this place, the trip, leaving, what do you think?"

"Oh fuck man I never know. I'll change my mind tomorrow."

"That doesn't sound like you."

"I know. —I'm happy right now. I've got my best friend here…" we paused and clinked our glasses together—Aden's favorite—Long Island.

I continued—"…Kalyn is a rock star. It was nice seeing Emma and Billy. We've got New Orleans coming up and that's a 'bright light at the end of the tunnel' sort of city. I'm happy."

"Excited about Nicaragua?"

"With all my heart yes and with all my heart no…I don't want to leave any of this."

"Do you think we could live like this forever?"

"We could win the lottery maybe?"

"Well you could write? I could make money online with social media marketing? I think we've got big things ahead of us. The lottery isn't our only option."

"I can't think that far ahead. I'm just a little flustered right now."

"Feeling good?"

"Drunk?"

"Yeah."

"For sure. I was drunk a few drinks ago."

The bar was very brown. The music was loud enough that we could still tap our feet and the band was in full crescendo by this point — sun drenched accented hipsters lined rows of chairs next to us — Kalyn was still lost — everything was jumbled — but a drink resting on a brown bar, no matter where, is calming.

"How about you?" I asked after a long pause (the two of us listening to the music in camaraderie). "…Where are you headed to? What's your next move?"

"Well after New Orleans I'll probably go to Austen and couchsurf and after that maybe Kentucky? Miami? I'm not sure though it won't be the same without you."

"That's not what I mean."

"Well I'm even less sure of that. LA? Boulder? I liked a lot of places."

"I'm with you wherever you decide. Let the fates take you ya know?"

"Definitely."

Just then Kalyn sat down next to me. She didn't run towards me. She didn't bounce onto the stool. She didn't hop or skip. She didn't rush. She slowly, depressingly, sat down — like she was "*too old for this.*"

"What's wrong?" I asked her patiently.

She gestured her left palm towards me — "*stop*" it said. It wasn't an angry stop like from a police officer or a cross walk guard. Her pencil fingers drooped down somewhere between a fist and a point — as if she was giving the air an inverted handshake. Her head sagged with gravity. She was hanging by a noose of air — of sadness.

I looked at Aden in disbelief. I had seen her cry the night before but it fit then. There was the cancer and the candle and the nightgown and the scary newness of a too-clean apartment. But here she was home. She was in her element — a rusty bar full of carvings and dyed hair and a crushing drummer, old friends and well water.

"Why is she crying?" I shrugged towards Aden.

"I dunno," he said with his eyes.

"Are you ready to go?"

"Oh no no, let's stay," she said still staring at the bar.

"Are you sure?" I hate that question. I don't know why I asked that question.

"I'm sure."

For some reason I had had her pegged as stronger than that. She confused me. I didn't know the full back story. Maybe she saw an ex that had hurt her? Maybe her friend was a little awkward and she realized that friends change too? Maybe she wasn't feeling well because she was drunk? She weighs 12 oz. after all. But either way—I wanted her to pick herself up. We had all been there—wherever that may be—somewhere—in a place of unreasonable sadness—a place of unwarranted desire. We all had judged ourselves too harshly and fed the flame of our own self-doubt with too much enthusiasm. But we pushed through. We didn't outwardly wallow. We didn't publically engage such negative emotions. We travelers, we fighters, we humans—we fight until the happiness is pealed back from each frown. We dedicate time and energy into practicing positivity until the flat line of optimism becomes our standard. And she was one of us. So where was this coming from?

"You have no reason to be sad," I wanted to yell at her. *"This is so random!"*

Instead I ignored her.

"Let us know if you want to leave," Aden said.

She nodded.

So the awkwardness of the moment came rolling into us with the same, ever increasing momentum of an avalanche. She just moped there, sitting with her drink next to us in silence. Something violent was happening in her mind, and neither I nor Aden were privy to such secret information.

We "weren't old enough to understand" she might have said in a cheekier mood. And isn't that the devil in all of us? — That full bodied distrust of ourselves to deal with life as it stands currently. So quickly we choose the path of most resistance and swing swords of silence and isolation when there is an army of support waiting for us just over the ridge if we only had the courage to acknowledge it. Sure we didn't have anything meaningful to say but we carried mean smiles and intimidating optimism and resolute empathy. We were there, just a bar stool away, waiting for our cue though it never came. The music played and the music played, and that's all that comes through in those sorts of moments — just the ever-presentness of music cluttering everything.

"We'll follow you anywhere," we said in posture. And I don't think we made much of a difference except for what a tissue could have done. But that didn't matter. We waited anyways. For the first time since we had left Ann Arbor, and probably since much before even then, we hadn't waited for anyone but each other. But she had touched us in a way no one else had. She left us speechless. So we waited.

But just then, in a flash of delirium, something equally random occurred, or clicked, or fell, or changed — something bipolar happened — something immediate — her loneliness committed suicide. Sure she cried a bit before pulling the trigger. But it was worth it. She was pulled by some force so foreign to her and yet so buried inside of her all along, that she fluttered the rest of the evening like a butterfly moments after its birth.

"Let's go outside," she hopped.

So we did. She didn't follow us for a second but not because she wasn't with us, but rather because she was with everyone by that point. The whole lot of the bar — the ex, the friend, the band, the bouncer, the bartender, the randoms, the stools, and the toilet seats: she was in harmony with all of it. So she pulled herself from one goodbye to the next, hugging her way towards the door, until finally, after far too short of a time, she reunited with us standing outside of the entranceway. We were all shivering in the Alabama heat, pretending to be cold.

But as we walked back to the car Aden had an old idea, like a benevolent parasite finding its new host — "you should come with us to New Orleans."

"OK," she said.

And that was that. Aden didn't convince her. He didn't persuade her. He didn't decide for her. He just laid it out on the table before her and she picked it up like finding a match while playing "go fish," as if she had always been waiting for the invitation...like she knew all along. So it was settled. She'd come with us as Faith had, as Kara had, but with her own flavor and story.

I cut out pieces of her energy and swallowed them. They were big pills in dark bottles. One was called "jump on the car" and another was called "climb up a billboard" — the last was called "dance way up high."

Though just as soon as Kalyn had decided to journey with us she ran back into the bar. So we sat on top of the billboard, twenty feet up, a mile high, in outer space, and looked down upon all the hippies and darkened strangers of Birmingham, telling their stories to ourselves as they spilled out into the grassy parking lot. All the parking lots of Alabama are just grassy fields, I thought. Or so I assume.

There were literal spotlights shining up into our eyes, highlighting each one of us — Aden, myself, and Kalyn's long-lost-friend Katherine. We sat high like saints, like de-petrified mummies, with all the wisdom of time between us.

"What are you guys doing up there?" Kalyn yelled still wearing her tiny yellow t-shirt.

"Does it matter?"

"How did you get up there?"

I pointed to the car parked directly beneath the billboard.

"That's too high. I'm staying down here."

She spun in circles like Kara in Iowa City. Except it was later and drunker and more alone—it was different. But eventually she fell to the ground heaving her chest towards the sky and then quickly back towards her stomach—ground, sky, ground, sky, ground, sky, Alabama, not-Alabama, Alabama, not-Alabama, inside the bar, outside, inside the bar, outside, happy, sad, happy, sad, happiest, saddest. She is an unsatisfied coin, always flipping back and forth from one side to the other. The problem, if there ever is a problem, is that neither side is right—neither side is better—it's all just luck. We dart in and out of our lives as if any of it means anything, as if choosing was any different than falling. We're not in control of damn near anything. "Heads or tails?" Sure. Whatever. They are both the same thing anyway.

So her heart pounded fiercely. She stayed on the ground and then climbed up, or we swung her up, and then she climbed back down, and then lay down again. She was strong. Her heart was strong. And although the heart is the strongest muscle, it's also the softest. So she fit. She fit everywhere. Like us.

After all that it took us a very long time to find home. We needed a very long time to sit on that billboard. We needed even longer to get down. Even longer still to find food. And only after the night collided with the day, after we began to realize that "tonight" and "this morning" were interchangeable, did we find our way back into our spots. This time, though, I passed out abruptly on the couch and left Aden and Kalyn to their nook. Aden said it was as romantic for him as it was for me the next morning. And although I do believe him, and although I fully believed that Kalyn enjoyed Aden's softness more than my hard edges, I couldn't help but wonder if that had more to do with Aden or more to do with me or more to do with Kalyn? Was she just a romantic?

Either way I woke up with hot sauce on my lips because "Aden wanted to show me how deeply you sleep." He proved his point and so they laughed heartily in the morning.

"Why are my lips sticky and spicy?"

"Maybe you had some left over hot sauce from last night?"

"I didn't have any hot sauce last night. I think I just had French fries."

"I think you were drunk."

"I was definitely drunk. This is absolutely true. But it is also absolutely true that I didn't have hot sauce."

They couldn't contain themselves and therefore admitted to their prank.

"Romantic my ass!" I said joking.

Aden put his arm around Kalyn saying, "Very romantic."

"Yes," she agreed, "very romantic."

I smiled. I liked them together in the night, romantically putting hot sauce on my lips. I did.

+

"WAKE UP WAKE UP wake up!" — Kalyn shook me asleep in the back seat.

"I'm sleeping."

"Wake up wake up wake up!"

"What's going on?" I noticed we were pulled over to the shoulder.

Aden was driving. He turned his head back to me, holding the brake steady, and pointed towards the rearview mirror. My eyes were hazy and my dreams were still poking their feet into my reality, so while still in a strange delirium, I twisted my neck backwards to witness the cause of all this commotion.

Kalyn pressed her head onto my shoulder and hugged my arm as if hiding — "I hope he doesn't kill us."

Hitchhiker. It was a hitchhiker. They hadn't stopped at first, I would later understand. Much more on purpose-like, they had seen him walking brazenly down the expressway leading towards Montgomery, passed him, had a conversation about "the sad hitchhiker-walker man," turned around, then turned around again, and stopped about a hundred feet in front of him. Aden flashed his lights to signal that we were peaceful.

Kalyn had jumped into the backseat because — "I don't want to be next to him."

So I stared out the window still spinning, still half asleep. I could only make out the faintest glow of a black figure in the distance. Cars were whizzing by and Aden was asking if this was a good idea. Kalyn still clung to my arm. I looked harder — like I was studying a difficult question on the SAT. The more I stared, the more frustrated I became.

He came at us wildly. He ran, or rather, sprinted towards the car. We were a friendly watering hole in a desert of anxious strangers. At first he looked normal, like a man, like a man who had been walking — but the closer he came and the more I stared the worse the situation became. Each step he took was like a trigger punching bullets into my abdomen. So my stomach retreated up into my throat for warmth and shelter. He came closer like a monster we were inviting to stay under our bed. His disheveled everything, his smelly everything, his torn everything, his hand me down everything — everything about him screamed "crazy homeless man." I had read many glorifications of his type — his soft soul and his daring glare, all the world resting on his shoulders and the beauty of the freedom of the hope of the sundrenched whatever of the homeless. Blah blah blah. I bought into it even. I had read the books. I knew what was up. But it was immediately apparent to me just then that I preferred my serial killer look-a-likes in books much more than in my car.

"Hey guys thanks for picking me up I really appreciate it," he said plopping down in the front seat.

Aden gave me a look that simultaneously said both, *"We probably shouldn't have done this,"* and *"Fuck it we're already committed."*

We were facing our deaths right there on the side of the road. Though what does "facing death" mean anyway? No one faces death. There is nothing noble in death. It's like giving yourself credit for being born. Death is the most average of all acts. Actually it's not even an act. Death is passive. It's like a pebble that we trip over. So we tripped over our fears and picked up a suicidal veteran — or they did — and I went along for the ride.

Whatever.

I noticed his hands right off. They were crusted and torn, newly cut, and putridly dirty — like he had just been dumpster diving at a nuclear waste facility. He also only had three fingers on each hand. Now, I do pride myself on being open to even the most random of deformities but hell — the guy was missing a bunch of fingers. I couldn't help but stare a little. And couple that with how he was walking down the road and all, and the creepy duffle bag which wasn't actually creepy but was creepy by default, and his unfinished long hair, and his yellowish rotting teeth — yeah — I judged the fingers. I did. I'm not proud of it. But I did.

"So where you heading to?" Aden asked.

"Montgomery."

"What's in Montgomery?"

I didn't say anything. I never say anything in these types of situations. Put me in the middle of an ideological debate or in front of a group of beautiful cheerleaders or in front of a new set of parents to impress, and I'm golden. But when our lives are on the line, Aden is in charge. He's more forceful. I would be just as likely to say "well yes sir you may kill me if you would like" as I would be to argue in favor of my life. I have a hard time disappointing people, even if it causes me harm.

"I need to go to the VA."

Oh god.

"Where are you coming from?"

"Birmingham."

"Oh yeah we just came from there."

Kalyn was smart enough not to tell him that she lived there.

"They don't have a VA in Birmingham?"

I looked at Kalyn and she squeezed my arm tighter. The worst was over. The anxiety was fading. Now she squeezed out of excitement. *"We picked up a hitchhiker!"* she wanted to scream. I did too. This was the first time any of us had done so. We were losing our virginity together — and it was a little rougher entrance than we had hoped for, but things were starting to loosen up — we were starting to actually enjoy it.

"Oh those damn ya know they just don't know because we fought for this country and the VA ya know they aren't those people over there they well the place isn't open and I need to see a doctor to fix me right up ya know?"

"Well what's wrong?"

He spit every time he said anything which made sense in a way. He didn't have but more than a few teeth.

"I'm suicidal and I ran out of my medication."

"Right."

It was official. We had picked up the worst possible hitchhiker in the history of hitchhikers. This was the hitchhiker from the movies. If it walks like a duck and talks like a duck and all of that. My mother always warned me but I had always kept an optimistic perspective on the whole situation and therefore assumed that one day I would pick someone up off the side of the road and we'd have a glorious conversation together and I'd tell the story later and maybe even meet up with him later down the line after both our lives had smoothed over. We'd become great friends. That's what I *thought*. Wonderful. — But my mom was right. This wasn't as magical as it was scary.

And what got to me, above all else, was the fact that he didn't attempt to hide his psychosis. He plopped down in the car, waved a few fingers in the air, kept his hand right next to the zipper of an ominous black bag, and said outright — *"I'm a crazy person."*

He was homeless, or at least acted like it. So he was insecure about his ability to function socially, causing him to stutter at every syllable. He was understandably frightened by a world that didn't think on his level. I get it now. But I didn't then. Then, I was just frightened. I didn't want to die. I think this makes sense.

"So you need a doctor for your medication?"

"Yeah them doctors at the VA they real nice but ya knows they aren't open and dem peoples before they took my medication and I just can't take any of this anymore."

"What happened?"

Aden meant — *"What happened that you are unhappy right now?"* or *"What happened that you don't have a car?"* but he got an answer to *"What is the crux of every problem of your life?"*

"Panama happened and all muh' men died around me and ya know the US and the VA they aren't taking care of us though the VA people dem nice sometimes and I need to get to Montgomery. Can you take me there?"

"Kalyn, are we heading to Montgomery?"

"We'll pass it," she said softly.

"OK then," I added, "then we'll take you to the VA hospital in Montgomery. You know how to get there?"

Stupid question.

"...you know those Panamanians and they didn't want us there and all muh' men just sitting ducks in the sky and all those bullets and ya know the VA..."

"Do you have a family?" Aden asked.

Stupid question.

"My daughter oh she's the world but we don't get along much and the VA and my medication ya know is good most of the time but sometimes I get depressed when she's not around and the hospital will help but I don't have no money and the VA was closed back in Birmingham and my daughter I love her very much…"

"Do you get to see her often?"

"Oh well Jesus ya know Jesus is the savior and he saved me when I was low almost in the ground ya know I just couldn't take it a few days ago and that medication but I don't have none ya see? Do you believe in Jesus as your personal lord and savior?"

"We'll get you your medication."

"Those last people they just sped off with my medicine they need Jesus I think with all the VA hospitals and I pray you know? I pray. I pray and prayers are answered because I was about to end it all yesterday and my daughter didn't want to see me so much anymore…haven't seen her in quite some time ya know but they just took my medicine. All them boys we were just boys ya know and ya know they just dropped us off — first damn day at war and we jumped out of planes ya know?"

"Oh were you a skydiver?"

"…Well but we had guns and they just shot at us while we was floating down ya know? And the men, my boys and we were all friends ya know and the bullets just came flying from the jungle and that's how this happened," he said while holding up his tattered hand. "…They just wasn't ready for any of that and they hit my hand but I was lucky ya know with Jesus there and I need my medication but they stole it."

"So you were in the Army?"

"Second battalion Roger 3rd Company and Colonel Maddison and we just floated down but most of them were dead by the time they landed us just floating down and we couldn't even shoot back with our packs and the jungle is dark and cold and lonely and I was shot ya know. But I got the bronze star and they have shows for us sometimes and yes they do treat us well at the VA ya know sometimes they do."

In an instant everything changed. He wasn't going to hurt us, I thought—or maybe he was but it wouldn't be his fault even he did. I was no doctor but he screamed PTSD, and all the Oreos in the world weren't going to help with his issues. In fact, he would probably never escape his cocoon. He was shot while still incubating. As much as I wanted to see his butterfly—I never would. The war had sucked him out of himself. He had survived—but only physically.

We called the hospital and were informed that the VA wasn't open, though we could drop him off at the emergency room and they would take care of him they said. So we did just that.

And as we drove past the University of Alabama, with all its beautiful fraternities and sweaters and old white money, we noticed a preseason football crowd blocking most of the roads. Everyone was clean-shaven and drove suburban cars and saw their daughters off with hugs and kisses and they had all their fingers intact and had never held their best friend in their arms while he died. They never spent two weeks eating bugs in the Panamanian jungle. No—this was the shiny part of Alabama. So we carried our darker, angrier, sadder version of America, a forgotten soldier, towards a hospital full of bumper stickers reading "support our troops."

"Thank you," he said genuinely while exiting the car. "I don't know if I would be here if it wasn't for you guys." And I don't know what he meant by "here" but I know he didn't only mean the emergency room.

Kalyn got out of the car to see him into the hospital. She took a drag of his cigarette before entering. I hadn't noticed that about her. I didn't think she smoked. I think her face distracted me. Or maybe Alabama distracted me? —All of it in all of its Alabama glory. I left knowing I didn't see enough. We all left having had experienced so much more than had expected though not enough all at once.

So Alabama said goodbye politely, at night, on the dark highway towards Louisiana. But it left us with something—a parting gift—a bottle of whisky and a cigar bought at gas station. So we toasted to hitchhikers and smoked in the breeze racing through our windows.

Overall, Alabama seemed melancholy to me, but I don't mean depressed. I mean melancholy the way I used to define the word in my head as a child. When I was younger and still learning my own language, I had always thought that melancholy was a terrible sound to mean sad. "Meeleenkaaauuully" I would say out loud. Someone had mixed up the translation, I thought. This used to be a word meaning love or hope and then it got changed, or maybe some poet had used it ironically and it stuck? To me it always sounded like it should mean cheerful, or be the name of a ripe fruit, or be an adjective to describe how someone might feel while skipping down a hill. Suffice to say I don't appreciate how such a kind sounding word has such a wretched meaning. So Alabama was melancholy, but my own version, the more attractive one. And that's that.

+

WE ARRIVED SOMETIME AFTER midnight. The skyline looked like a Tetris board of fallen stars, and I wasn't sure if the ocean reflected the sky, or if it was the other way around, because they blended into each other with such symmetry that all the while I thought the whole city was floating on a giant black cloud.

See — New Orleans was watching me that day. We raced across its bridges as if they were conveyer belts. We stayed in one place. The city came to us. And that's the way it is with new skylines — with New Orleans and the final chapter. You slow down and take one last look, one last mischievous picture, without anyone or anything noticing — just you and a few Pilars in the distance.

"It's too bad about Katrina eh?" Aden said.

Kalyn was sleeping in the back.

"It is."

"I blame Bush."

"I blame the weather."

"You know what I mean."

"I do—but I actually blame the journalists."

"Hey man Anderson Cooper was up to his neck saving people."

"I bet he could have saved more people without a microphone."

I had no sympathy for the public, the country, the journalists, or for myself. No one did anything. Everyone watched their televisions like they did on 9/11 thinking "how terrible" except Katrina lasted years instead of moments. We weren't helpless. So it's not the same. Though I really blame the writers and the journalists for not having had the courage to stand up to the big bad wolf that is the schizophrenic American public and demand a reaction. We needed to fear and loathe something, someone, anyone.

Poets are not creative enough to write novels, I thought. Sure. And novelists aren't creative enough to write poetry. Makes sense. But journalists aren't creative enough to write anything, or certainly not anything useful—at least not when it's critical.

"You want to check out the wreckage?"

"Not really."

"Neither do I."

We had noble reasons for ignoring all the pain. We didn't want to drive by slowly as if on safari, waving and taking pictures of all the abandoned poor people. We didn't want to embarrass anyone. We were doing everyone a favor by skipping that neighborhood, I thought—the neighborhood whose coat of arms was a spoon, a lighter, and a half full syringe—the color of abandonment. We had no room for such disaster. Though the truth is, we didn't want to feel guilty. It's the journalist's fault, I thought again. They are the reason I don't care enough to do anything to help! At least that's my story.

"Kalyn," Aden asked shaking her awake, "Can you call your friend? Where does she live?"

I was driving.

"What time is it?" she grumbled.

"Early — or late — yeah — very-very early," I said. The sun was way on the other side.

"OK give me a second," she stretched.

We plugged in the address to our GPS. It took us to a tattoo parlor.

"What was the address again?"

She told me.

"That's what I put in. It says that this is it. Can you call her back and ask her for the address again? Maybe there was a mix-up?"

She did but got the same address.

"Well," Kalyn told her friend, "we're right in front of a tattoo parlor so that can't be right."

We all listened, tired.

"Oh — so we're in the right spot? Wait…where are you?"

Just then the door of the tattoo parlor swung open and Kalyn's friend ran down the stairs. She was wide awake at a tattoo parlor. Strange. Strange though karmically perfect.

"This is a sign," Aden said.

"This *is* a sign," I agreed.

Way back somewhere in my past, somewhere in Iowa, before all of this meant anything to either of us, we had met Jake and promised ourselves to get tattoos. We had promised to get tattoos "when the universe told us to." And if this wasn't the universe screaming in our ears that, "*the time is now,*" then I don't know what is.

Kalyn's friend was a painting of herself. She framed herself with a skin tight tank top and boy shorts. Her hair was highlighted with radical whites and heavy blacks, like a fashionable skunk. There were a few piercings here and there but none of that mattered — it was all a warm up for the enormous wings tattooed across the fullness of her chest. It started at her neck, stretched up to her shoulders, and finished somewhere lower than I was privy to. She looked like a high school cheerleader: fit, tight, young, big teethed, smiling, and yet the tattoo loomed so large over her that nothing but *it* said anything of substance.

"Here I am," it said, "*now deal with it.*" -Kind of like Kalyn.

Her boyfriend, the owner of the tattoo parlor, was even showier though his demeanor was even more subdued than hers. He was figurative more than literal. There were skulls and pirates and baby girls and words and neck markings and both arms and both legs and pretty much everywhere, something, yeah, even under the dreadlocks I thought for a moment — tattoos were everywhere. But no matter the brightness of their bodies, immediately I felt their warmth.

We felt an honest camaraderie. It fell strong and immediate. We understood one another, in all of us having been subjected to the plight of America's spoiled youth.

"Have a seat guys," he said.

So we did, outside on a deck.

"This is a nice place you got here," Aden said.

"Thanks man."

"So are we staying with you or...?" I asked.

"You guys tired?"

"A little tired, yeah."

"Well we were thinking about going out tonight."

"Tonight?"

"Yeah."

"This morning?"

"Well tonight, this morning, ya know…what's the difference? Welcome to New Orleans."

His deck winded around and down to a back alley. The whole place was a back alley actually. Though, inside, the parlor was clean like a surgical station. Even the posters were covered in plastic. A back alleyway hospital.

"Tattoos are serious man," he told me later. "I take them very seriously."

A Harley Davidson looking gentlemen with a soft voice was getting an enormous queen of hearts tattooed on his back.

"She's my queen," he said rubbing his wife's shoulder. She was tattooed almost as much as he was.

Everyone is beautiful. Everyone is too damn beautiful, I thought.

"Want to head out after I'm finished with this tattoo?"

"Sure," we all said.

"We'll stop over at my house, it's only a few blocks down the road and we'll drop your stuff off."

So we went out and drank more than we had all summer which, for having had been in the company of Kara and Faith for that long—that is saying a lot. We drank shot after shot and the music was rough—like the sounds of angry sex. Everyone was sweating. Everyone wore black except for us. I wore bright blue. The dance floor was in a basement although it was actually on the second floor—it just seemed like it was in a basement. Kalyn and her friend caught up and then danced separately. We drank more and more, until the wreckage of ourselves spilled out onto Bourbon Street.

It could have been ecstatic or heavenly. It could have been the last radical night out with Aden, and in a way it was, but emotionally I was far away.

I was in bed with Andrea. I already had dreams of sweeping her off her feet a few days before she left for Belarus. I would leave in little more than 24 hours and she would be waiting for me at the airport, having had smelled me coming up from The South. So I danced and drank and the red hue of Louisiana buzzed around me. It was all on fire. Though the fire of New Orleans was too close to us, actually. It was at risk of being burned.

We stumbled down the street squawking as loudly as possible, pressing our arms from one end of one sidewalk to the other, from one shoulder to the next, making a giant line with the tattoo artist on one end, then me, then Aden, then Kalyn, and then Kalyn's friend on the other end — all of us stomping and spitting, in love with the undercurrent that was holding us together.

And then everything sped up. We got food and listened to street performers and drank on the streets because it's the only place in the country where you are legally allowed to.

"Where is a police officer?" I asked. "I want to go talk to him while drunk and drinking. He won't be able to do anything!"

This probably wasn't true but it was my dream. And all we have are dreams in our twenties so why squash them with reality?

We ended on the big red trolleys of the French something or other — everyone's hair blue or purple — and immediately fell asleep. There was no in between. We entered the trolley and instantaneously we were sleeping on a foreign couch. That's how it is in New Orleans. New Orleans is faster than jazz — like a pupil that grew up to be even greater than her teacher.

+

"WE HAVE TO GO to a Casino," Aden said excitedly.

"Why?"

"Because it's the Sabbath."

"It is?" I perplexed.

"Oh…I don't know," he answered.

"Right. I guess that makes sense." And we were off.

The casino wasn't as fun as Las Vegas. It wasn't as big. It wasn't as glamorous. I sat at the penny slots actually playing penny slots, spending $4 on five whisky and cokes. I didn't even have the balls to try and win a significant prize.

"At that rate, even if you win the jackpot to end all jackpots, you'll barely have enough for the plane ticket back to Michigan."

"I just want free drinks."

"What if you win though?"

"What if I lose though?"

"Have to risk it all to win it all…"

Little did he know, I was already planning my biggest risk yet. Though I wasn't risking money—I was risking my heart. I purposefully left myself a few extra days in Michigan that I didn't want in order to see Andrea before she left for Belarus. She had a boyfriend. Sure. Whatever. He was her summer captor and I was the prince and I'd ride in on a shiny white plane and rescue her. She'd love me back and we'd commit for real this time. I'd visit and she'd visit and it would all be perfect. It was an "if I win the lottery" scenario and I knew it—but I believed deep down in every crevice of my heart that it would work.

"I know this all too well," I said. "I'm all about the risk."

"Then what are you…?" he stopped himself mid-sentence. He knew. He knew all along.

"Well I want to win some *money*," he finally said.

"Someday," I said.

Aden had spent hundreds of dollars in Las Vegas and hundreds of dollars in the last few hours trying his hand at blackjack.

"It's about skill," he said.

"Sure—but you're no expert."

"I'm smart though."

"Of course you are smart. But odds are smarter."

He lost his plane ticket back to Michigan. But that didn't matter. I was already there. The whole day we explored the French quarter and ate shrimp and Cajun everything. We skipped down the streets and met the cocaine-friendly friends of our tattoo artist. We laughed and smoked and drank and yeah yeah yeah—I wanted to go to Michigan. And that's always the way I am with travel. It doesn't matter how amazing the trip was, the last few days aren't magical—they are depressive and anxiety ridden. It's not that I won't miss wherever I was, it's that I don't have time to think about it. I want the airport now. Now. Now. Now. —Like a good American.

"So I heard you were thinking about getting a tattoo," the tattoo artist said to me.

"Yeah I think I might."

"When?"

"Well I guess it will have to wait. I'm leaving early in the morning. It's already past midnight ya know. But I'm sure I'm going to get one. I met a guy in Iowa and…" —I told him the whole story, finishing with—"…So when I pulled up to your tattoo parlor I was in shock. I figure that is all the fate I can ask for right?"

"…You have to get one right now," he said.

"Where?"

"I'll do it."

"Oh man you don't have to do that. I figured I would ask one of your guys or something. You're already letting us stay at your place and you've been so nice showing us around the city and..."

"This is my passion," he said very seriously. "Remember? This is my art."

"I get that but I don't even know what to get and it would be a rushed decision and ya know the plane is just so close and I have to...ya know? Aden, and well..." —I sounded like a hitchhiker.

"Tattoos have nothing to do with the picture, or the symbol, or whatever you actually put on your body—it's not about the physical thing—it's about the time. Like this one," he said pointing to his right hand, "...this one isn't all that meaningful, just a kind of cool design. But I got this when I was in Hawaii—the first time I had ever left the continental US— my first real traveling experience, kind of like you ya know with all your travel—it's important right?"

"Yeah."

"So I don't care about whatever this symbol is. It's a representation of some part of my life. It's a photograph. It's a memory that I'll never forget because I fortified it with a tattoo."

"I know but it's really late and..."

"Irrelevant! Just get the fucking tattoo," Aden yelled from across the way. He and Kalyn were helping each other balance on a fountain outside the casino. "I'll get one too."

If he hadn't said that I probably would have never done it. For all the beautiful speeches about memories and travel, for all the non-coincidences of staying with an artist who happened to do tattoos, I wouldn't have done it without Aden. In fact, I wouldn't have done any of it without him. All along, for all the monologues and all the lectures and all the critique, the whole time he was the one leading the way. He was the backbone that I had used for walking forward. He was the catalyst for everything I ever had the courage to do. He was everything. And I was leaving tomorrow.

"Alright," I said.

"Let's do it?" he said giddy.

"Let's do it."

"Oh—you all can have your fun I'm going to go to bed," Kalyn said. "Though you have to take me to the bus station at six in the morning. You'll pick me up?"

"Of course."

So—early, fucking early, a little drunk, and all the way hopeful—he opened up his shop and we entered. I picked out a tattoo after much deliberation.

"Let's be hypothetical for a moment," Aden said, "and for argument's sake let's pretend that you cared about anyone other than yourself…"

I had to laugh at this. So true.

"OK?"

"What message would you want to say to the world? Let's say this tattoo isn't about you but is about everyone who will see it on you after you are famous and a world leader and all of that. What do you want this to symbolize?"

I ended up picking a tattoo because I picked a tattoo. It meant something to my family. It was nice. World leader? Really?

I looked at my tattoo artist and thought about the complete randomness of this moment. Here I was with a complete stranger. I slept on his couch because another complete stranger knows his girlfriend. And I met that complete stranger by pointing blindly on a map. And now he was giving me a free tattoo at the crack of dawn because he "felt like" I was "a good person." All the while Aden was penciling away, drawing his own tattoo. And I was about to leave after two months of complete randomness to try and execute the most on-purpose romantic gesture I could possibly think of. Fuck.

New Orleans is like a Walmart for original sin, it seems. It's open 24 hours and if you want it, they have it.

"Does this look good?" he asked placing the stencil on my arm. He looked like a carved oak tree, spotted—both regal and ugly.

"Aden?"

Aden looked up from his drawing for only a moment, though he didn't really look.

"I love it," he said.

"I love it?" I shrugged.

"So you ready?"

"I'm ready."

The first pinch wasn't so bad, and neither was the second.

"This is going to take about an hour so just try and get used to the pressure. Imagine that this is how your arm always feels. Imagine it'll have to feel like this for the rest of your life. It'll go by quicker that way."

"OK."

"So you're leaving yeah?"

"Tomorrow, yeah."

His tone changed just then. He wasn't at a casino anymore. He wasn't at dinner or smoking outside. He was a professional now. The muscle memory kicked in—so he started rifling off conversation starters to keep me distracted from the needle poking my skin a hundred times a minute.

"Excited?"

"Yeah."

"Kalyn said you guys had been traveling around the country for a while?"

"Yeah."

"How'd you like it?"

The needles were starting to hurt now — lifetime my ass.

"It was a blast. Best experience of my life so far."

"So far?"

"Well yeah. I hope this isn't *it* for me."

"He's going to write about it," Aden yelled from across the room.

"Oh you're a writer?"

"No."

"But you want to be?"

"Yeah."

Then everything went numb. I couldn't feel a thing. He hit the sweet spot.

"So you want to write a book?"

"I do."

"What do you want it to be about?" he asked me.

"Something I'm passionate about," I said.

"Yeah and what's that?"

"Well that's the problem," I said, "I'm passionate about everything."

"Everything?" he said surprised. "That's not possible."

"I know."

He laughed and asked — "What'll it be called?"

"Something people like."

"That's a strange title."

"You're telling me."

"So when do you write?"

"Late at night."

This is true, I thought. The best writing is done right before you go to bed, and not on paper but in your head — though, then, of course, it's lost forever as you doze off. See — the totality of literature is actually just the sloppy remnants of what some poor soul forgot while he was still asleep.

"What's your favorite book?"

"I have many."

"Well what's one you like?"

"I like literature more than books ya know? I like things that are well written."

God even the shyest authors have big mouths.

So I continued on a rant — "There hasn't been anything written but reality television novels since about 1970 — too many vampires and star trek and bad horror and what the hell is a romance novel anyway? At least D.H. Lawrence could actually write…"

"It sounds like you are jealous," he pressed me.

"Of course I'm jealous. I'm very jealous. I mean nothing is literature until at least 40 years after it's written anyway. That's all writing is — a bunch of insecure intellectuals trying to outdo one another."

"Are you calling yourself an intellectual?"

"No. I'm even worse — I'm a critic."

"Why don't you just be a journalist? Isn't' that easier?"

"What's your favorite article?"

"Article? What do you mean? About what?"

"Exactly."

"Ahh I get it. But isn't there something to be said for changing the world?"

"Be careful what you say."

"What do you mean?"

"You might change the world."

"Are you being sarcastic?"

"I don't know if we really *can* change the world. And what does that mean anyway?"

"I change the world," he said sternly. "I change people's lives. I make their bodies into art."

"When did you decide to be a tattoo artist?"

"Since I can remember I always loved drawing and something about tattoos always spoke to me. And then I got one and they are addicting."

"You think I'll get another?"

"How many people do you know that only have one tattoo?"

"I don't know."

"Exactly. It's an addiction."

"That's how I feel about traveling."

"Is that how you feel about writing?"

"I think they are the same thing."

"How so?"

"I can't travel without writing about it and I can't write about anything I haven't already done. So they are symbiotic."

"That's how I feel about mechanics."

"Yeah I noticed all your tools in your garage. You have quite a collection."

"This gun," he said holding up the tattoo gun in his hand to show me, "...I made it."

This calmed me for some reason. He now had a Zen and the Art of Tattoo Maintenance vibe to him. All the better.

"So do you love what you do?"

"I wouldn't do anything except for what I love to do."

"Love is very important," I said, thinking about Andrea.

"It is."

Just then Aden came over and showed me a tattoo that he had drawn. I couldn't move so he placed the paper in front of my eyes as if I were in a full body cast.

"Do you like it?"

It was simply the word — "love."

I chuckled. "I love it," I said.

I cannibalized his feelings and so shot, somehow, tactically, spiritually, all of Aden into my tattoo just then. I would remember him forever. All his pictures and all his love — no matter what happened and no matter the journey ending — I would always remember...

"What time is it?" I asked my tattoo artist.

I hadn't known the time in two months. I didn't carry a watch nor did I have a phone. I just trotted around like in the olden days — with the sun.

But now the deadlines of planes and buses loomed over me, like a very heavy rain after a long drought.

"4 in the morning," Aden answered.

People have always gone to bed around 10 pm in America because they have always had to wake up at 6am. The reason they have always had to wake up at 6 am is because they have to be to work at 8 am. Needless to say I don't go to bed at 10 pm. And neither does New Orleans — the immortal city. It reminds me of death in this way, because death is the only thing you can't ignore. It's a 360 degree sadness. No matter where you turn, there it is, ready for you all along. And so the opposite of death is not life — the opposite of death is 4am — that subtle crack in each day, that unwarranted smirk for having had the courage to sit merrily on the fence of time, defying both the day and the night. Which is why New Orleans opens at 4 am — it's not for the money or the exploration — it's instinct — it's survival. 4 am is New Orleans' fountain of youth and every day its citizens drink buckets from it.

So I drank my tattoo like it was a mirage come to life. I drank in the whole moment. And when that didn't satisfy me, I condensed it, life, into a vibrating needle and shoved it into my skin. Over and over and over and over — only a subtle pain compared to its value. All of the sadness. All of the loneliness. All of the lost adventure. All of the love. All of my country. Every inch of it. All of this crazy 4am New Orleans American bliss — tearing my skin open with each hit. Hit hit hit, ink ink ink, life, hit-hit hit-hit, more, one more hit, just one more hit…

Exhale.

"…we're almost done," my tattoo artist said.

"Yes we are," I said.

Chapter 19

KALYN SAT THERE ON the curb, was cool to the touch, yet completely on fire. She had just vomited and was crying, but didn't seem embarrassed. Her glazed eyes looked up wearily and sadly, though we weren't sure why exactly? It could have been her father, or her brother, the shock of being home, or the expectations of America and all its weight, or maybe it was because she had to leave her good friend, or because she had to leave us? Or maybe because she hated the bus? Either way I didn't know what to do. I rarely know what to do when faced with sadness. It's awkward.

Aden helped her up and we walked with her towards the bus station. Aden knew her better than I did, their connection felt deeper, and I was jealous a little, but then I felt happy for them just as quickly. He deserved that connection. She deserved it too.

"I had a dream about you and it was nice," Aden said to Kalyn.

"Oh really? When?"

"I don't know. Sometime."

"What happened?"

"A lot of good things."

She smiled.

"A lot of good things?" she smirked.

"Goodbye?" I said with my hands extended.

She hugged us both and was off.

"Hurry up," Aden said lastly, "but not so fast that you'll fall."

I'd miss her forever.

"Airport?" I suggested.

"Fuck," Aden said.

"So what do you think?" he asked.

"About what?"

"Everything."

"I think this was the greatest experience of my life."

"What about it?"

"Everything?"

"What did you learn?"

"Everything?"

"Really?"

"I didn't know anything before and yeah I don't know anything now either but I'm that much further along now so that must be worth something right? So you're going to Austin?"

"Austin my brother."

It was a strange conversation. It wasn't awkward because we don't' know how to do awkward with each other. It wasn't too-quick because we don't know how to do too-anything. It was just — lazy. After all that — all we had was small talk.

"Where you going to next?"

"So you going out tonight?"

It felt like a random Thursday in Ann Arbor. Though maybe that was for the best? –We didn't need any drama. All we needed was a solid hug and a serious "I love you brother" and that was it. We knew we'd see each other again. There was no goodbye. There was only "till next time." And that was relieving.

As I entered the plane I took one last inhale of the trip. I let it soak into me. I let all of Aden and Kara and Faith and Jake and Kalyn and Emma and Billy flow through me. Big inhale, and then a forward step — back to Michigan to make my dreams come true.

We had lived a truthful exaggeration that summer, having not accepted the paradox. We had ventured into the corners of our minds and the corners of our country equally, sure, makes sense — but there was more still — back in Ann Arbor. Everything had always been in Ann Arbor all along.

And the circle goes round and round.

It was as if I had just woken from a long dream. I leaned against the glass, armed wrapped, unshaven, without sleep, and visibly hung over from two months of nonstop action.

"Did he really get a fresh tattoo just moments before boarding a plane?" my fellow passengers would ask themselves.

"Is he homeless?"

"Yes and yes," I would whisper.

"But why?"

"...Well that's a long story."

I must have died, I thought. I must have died and been placed into an incubator for lucid dreams. This was all unreal. It was too nice. It was too easy. My life was one giant dream.

And so on the plane there was a list of places. Favorite place. Nebraska. Best drive. Idaho. Best city. Chicago. Best view. Yosemite. Best meal. Alabama. Best stranger. Everyone. And all at once the dream became real. My eyes resting. Sleep.

When I awoke I would be in Michigan.

+

I ARRIVED AND VISITED my family—I think? But that didn't matter. What mattered was finding Andrea without a phone number. I used all forms of Internet communication possible to try and communicate with her. Though she ignored all forms of Internet communication possible. So for two agonizingly long days I searched all through Ann Arbor, emailed friends, visited funeral parlors, waited around her favorite restaurants, all in the hopes that somehow, someway, I would be able to see her before she left.

"Hey man I got your number from a mutual friend. I heard Andrea is at your place can I talk to her?"

"Who is this?"

I was conversing with the enemy—her new prince.

"One of Andrea's old friends."

"She's sleeping," he said ruggedly, angrily. Why was a guy calling his girlfriend?

"Listen man she won't mind if you wake her up I promise. Can you just get her on the phone for me? She's leaving for Belarus tomorrow as I'm sure you know. Please?"

"She's sleeping."

"OK that's alright no problem man, but let her know that Kristopher called and tell her that I'm in Ann Arbor."

"Whatever."

"I'm serious man—she's going to be angry with you if you don't tell her. This is bigger than you."

"This is bigger than you." —He must have chuckled inside. Bigger than him? It was bigger than me. It was bigger than her. Love is bigger than Belarus, bigger than road trips and distances— God I had to see her.

So I waited and waited. Each tick of the clock was a lifetime, and each one of those lifetimes slowly grew darker and sadder and smaller, as if I had been banished to an eternal regression of worsening reincarnations. So I took matters into my own hands and called every single one of her friends, again, demanding to know where she was staying.

Please not with him, I thought. Please not at his house, I hoped.

And to my delight, she wasn't. She was staying with a mutual friend of ours who, if there were sides, was on mine. She met me for a late coffee to debrief about Andrea…

"Her stuff is at my place. She'll have to come back and pick it up before leaving."

"Can I come over and surprise her?"

"I think that would be wonderful." She was even more on my side than I had originally thought.

So we rushed over to her apartment building. It was old with red brick, maybe four stories tall, with an enormous parking lot behind it. And as we pulled into a parking space and got out of the car — there in the distance, opening the far door — I saw a figure. It was just a figure at first, then a girl…a girl, then a short girl…a short girl, then a brown haired girl…Andrea!

At the exact moment that I was arriving, she was leaving. Fitting.

I saw her there walking under the dull light of an empty parking lot — a sunrise in primetime. I had found her. The lost generation you say? Hell no. We are the found generation. We are the generation of princesses and romance and rose petals and ruby red slippers, magic pumpkins and sleeping beauties.

See — the darkest shadows are always the most pronounced on the blackest of nights. And oh God her shadow stretched farther than I could see, beyond the horizon even of the trees. She towered so high, so beyond me, so vibrantly, standing there in the dead of night, spotlighted as if on stage. I saw the stars behind the stars just then. The whole moment was perfect—because she was.

So I ran over to her, or rather sprinted over to her, and kissed her right off. No words—no hello—no hug—just a kiss. See—mouths should only be used for kissing, eating, and talking, and always in that order. And although she kissed me back, held my back even with her hand, I could feel her tension on the tips of her fingers.

"Why are you here? I mean…how are you here?" she asked me smiling.

"I came back to see you."

"I'm leaving in the morning."

"I came back to see you."

"My boyfriend is here!" she whispered to me tilting her head.

"Whatever…come with me."

I pulled her over to the side of the building and continued to kiss her. She held my hand and touched my thigh—she lost herself in me for moments at a time—but kept opening her eyes, peering off to the side. She was, of course, technically, cheating, again. But it had all happened so quickly, and with such fidelity, with such intimacy, with such intuition, that she hadn't had time to decide whether or not to continue. She just did. It just happened.

She was one of the mad ones. God I love her.

A screeching car pulled up beside us. It was her boyfriend. He looked like a boy, I noticed. He looked like a boy, not necessarily sad for having just seen his girlfriend immediately kiss her ex in front of him hours before leaving, but angry. He was an angry type of person I could tell. He wasn't about love or connection—he was about screeching tires and angry looks.

"Call me when you are done," he yelled at her and sped off.

She melted.

"I am such a bitch," she said to me with her head in my chest.

"No you aren't."

"Why are you here? This was supposed to be our last night together. You ruined it."

I kissed her again.

She looked like a lost and abandoned room in a weathered mansion — with all its candlesticks and the light glimmering horizontally, with its painted shadows and its romantic chill, with its old oak desk and beautiful fireplace — except, sadly, she had her cobwebs and her dust as well. It was obvious. No one or no thing can go that long without love. Neglect makes ugly even the most beautiful of God's creations. So although she had been touched, I could tell she had also been neglected. So I would touch her more gently than I had anything that summer.

"It's good to see you," I said. "I missed you."

"God I missed you too," she said. "But…"

"Let's go inside."

"I can't stay with you."

"Yes you can."

"No Kristopher," she yelled at me, "I cannot!"

"Let's go inside."

I held her hand the whole way. I could tell she was angry with me. She resented me being there. I just swooped in, unannounced, unexpected, and had ruined her last evening with her boyfriend. She wanted me, a big part of her wanted me, which is why she kissed me over and over again — but an equally ardent, let's call it moral, part of her was upset. I was an old song to her that brought back memories — too many memories. See — for her, even the most beautiful music is bothersome if played too loudly.

"Why did you leave?" she asked me, both of us sitting on the floor in an empty room.

Our mutual friend was moving out and with Andrea's stuff already packed up for Belarus—all we had were the walls and the floor.

"I didn't want to but I had to."

"No you didn't."

"We would still be together if you hadn't left. I kissed you at your party. I thought that was a new beginning," she said.

"Andrea I told you that I would be with you unconditionally. I told you. I asked you, 'do you want to be with me monogamously while I travel?' and I told you, 'I will commit to you right now—just say the word.' —but you didn't say it. You wouldn't say it. You didn't want it."

"I was so hurt Kristopher. I still am hurt. You killed me. You killed every inch of me. You were supposed to fight for me!"

"You killed every inch of me too."

"So that's why you left? Revenge?"

"No. Listen. I had already made those plans. I thought you hated…"

"Hated you? I did hate you. I hated every fiber of you. I still hate you. But you should have stayed…"

"Don't say that."

"…And then you came waltzing back into my life like nothing happened…just like now. Fuck you! You always do this."

I kissed her. She kissed me back.

"Fuck me? Andrea I just cut the trip of my life short and embarrassed myself to everyone I once knew in Ann Arbor searching for you. I just flew across the country for you. Fuck me? Fuck *you*! I can't believe you are mad at me?"

"I'm not mad at you…"

Another kiss. Still holding hands.

"…You just kill me. I don't know how to act with you," she said.

"Stay with me tonight."

"I can't." Her lip stiffened.

"Yes you can."

"Why did you leave?"

"I don't know. I didn't trust you to love me back? I was stupid? I'm always stupid. You know that. I would have given you my star if you wanted it. Fuck Andrea — what do you want? What do you want me to do? I'll do anything. I love you."

"Don't say that! You never say that! …God…I don't know. God you just fucking kill me Kristopher. You really do."

"Please just stop thinking."

"Stop thinking?"

I kissed her softly — so softly. I wiped the tears from her eyes with my thumbs and kissed her gently like she was the only girl in the world because she was.

"I'm such a Bitch."

"I love you," I said.

"Oh come on — be honest," she said. "Don't give me that shit."

Honest? What feels honest? Can you feel honesty while burning alive?

"I do love you," I repeated.

"What am I supposed to say to that? I'm leaving in the morning."

"You don't have to say anything. Just stay with me. We'll talk. We'll talk and make plans and I'll come visit you in Belarus and you can come visit me in Nicaragua. We can do this."

"I have a boyfriend."

"Sure," I said and kissed her.

"God dammit!"

She pounded her head against the wall though I put my hand behind her head and rubbed it gently. She then put her hand on my knee. She felt numb and yet better for it. Her previous state was that of wallowing and hatred—so she felt proud of numb. Numb was better. But it's important to remember that numb is not comfortable—it's just numb—it's nothing to be proud of—it's like being proud of being able to die.

"I regret so much. But I'm here. I'm here now. I'm finally ready," I said.

Though I didn't really believe in regret because living without regrets is impossible. A life without regrets is a life lived in absolute selflessness, which no one can do, nor should anyone attempt to do, not really. So regret is actually a good thing sometimes, I think. Regret is a signpost for a life spent taking risks.

God I'm the king of regret.

"It doesn't matter if you're ready Kristopher—my boyfriend is going to be here soon and I'm leaving in the morning."

"I'll take you to the airport. You can stay with me."

"I can't. That is so mean."

"You are already being so mean."

"I know! Fuck. What are we doing? God what are we doing?"

"…the only thing we know."

"I really am glad you are here though. I missed you," she said.

"I'm sorry."

"I know you are…I have to go."

She wanted to unlearn me.

"You don't have to go."

"He'll want to fight you if he sees us here."

"I don't fight."

"…yeah… 'Monkeys fight. People talk.' I know I know. But I'm telling you that he won't care about your pacifist psychobabble philosophy bullshit."

"So you're dating a monkey?"

"Don't start."

"Come on Andrea—you know that I'm a lover not a fighter," I said picking her up in the air while swirling her around.

"You're so cheesy."

"I know."

Though she kissed me, smiling, her fingers running through my hair.

But just then I heard the lonely screeching of an angry car. The door slammed shut. He was done waiting.

"Andrea!" he yelled from below into our window.

"Oh God." Her whole body clenched. "Put me down."

"Take a deep breath. This is OK. Nothing is going to happen."

"God I'm such a bitch. Fuck!"

"Andrea…."

"Why are you here?" she screamed at me, though not too loudly.

"Andrea…"

"Fuck!" She wouldn't let me talk.

Though I finally got through—"Andrea. Listen. Stay with me yeah? Please? I came all the way across the country to be with you. Let's have one night before we both go to opposite ends of the world eh? Just one night. It's obvious that we still have something here. You wouldn't just cheat on this guy at a moment's notice if we weren't something important. It has nothing to do with him and everything to do with us."

"Fuck. I know. I want to stay with you. I do. I've always wanted to stay with you. I've always wanted you. All I ever wanted was you—you're all I've ever wanted—but you left. So I moved on. You told me to move on."

"Stay with me."

"You messed it up. You messed everything up. It's broken now."

"Some things have to be broken before they can be put back together properly…"

"God shut up Kristopher with your psychobabble. This is real life. I mean I care about you. I never stop thinking about you…I love you…"

"Same for me."

"…But you ruined everything."

I got down on my knees, her standing stiffly, legs together. I hugged her knees, my head buried in the crease between her upper thighs. It wasn't sexual. It just fit. I was reminded of a similar situation from just six months earlier, except the roles were reversed now.

"Andrea—please—just—stay with me."

"I can't," she said. "I'm sorry."

"*You have to move on,*" is what she meant. Though I couldn't. I needed her—everything.

I looked up at her as I felt her legs stiffen. I kissed them. I didn't know what to do. How do I convince her? What did she want? I settled for something — anything — "Well then let's have breakfast in the morning? I'll see you off in the morning. How does that sound? I'll take you to the airport. You're staying with your aunt right?"

I didn't know but I assumed.

"Yes."

"So just call me in the morning and we'll meet at a breakfast place. She can come too. We'll have one last talk. I don't even want to sleep with you anyways…"

"Oh shut up," she said. I patted her on the butt. "You're ridiculous…"

"So we have a deal? The morning? You'll call me when you wake up? Let's do it at like six or something so we have a lot of time together before your flight. Hey — it'll be great because I'm anxious to hear about Belarus anyways."

"Oh Belarus…God. What's your number?" she asked. "I only have my Belarusen phone now so I'll have to call from my aunt's and I don't have your number memorized anymore."

I tried to kiss her but she recoiled. All this time, I didn't realize, she had already left. All this time I thought I was the one running away from her when actually she was running away from me. She was already long gone. I tried to kiss her again, softly, touching her shoulder with care. Though she pushed me away still.

"This is too hard," she said. "I can't do this anymore."

"What is too hard? What can't you do?"

"I don't know. God I'm going to go in the car with him and he's going to want to kiss me and what do I say? What do I do? This is all…gross. I just…just give me a second."

I tried to kiss her again but she recoiled again.

"Kiss me!" I yelled at her. "Goddammit what are you so fucking scared of?"

"I'm not scared," she said sternly, grabbing my collar and shoving me against the wall forcefully.

Just then she kissed me passionately, intensely, sexually, but not so lovingly. It was as if she was trying to prove something to me. And I don't know what it was, but she proved it nonetheless. I was aroused, and she was so pressed up against me that I knew she noticed.

Just then the door knocked. The monkey.

"Hide."

"Hide?"

"He's going to want to fight you."

"Like a monkey?"

"Whatever."

"Just go around the corner."

"I'm not going to fight him."

"He won't care."

"…Like a monkey?"

"Andrea!" a strong voice shouted from the other side of the door. He was pounding furiously by this point.

"Kristopher — Please?"

"I'll see you tomorrow morning?"

"Yeah I'll see you tomorrow morning I promise."

And then she tip-toed up to me for one last kiss.

"*Goodbye*," she mouthed as I rounded the corner into the kitchen.

Then I heard the door shut.

Chapter 20

6:00 am PASSED WITHOUT A CALL. 7:00 am passed without a call.

I sat there shocked and worse still — the moment's water slowly boiled hotter and hotter, so like a soon cooked toad, I made no attempt to save my own skin. I felt something particularly repugnant about her not calling me, but hadn't the intelligence to understand that which was so obviously happening all around. She had no real intention of contacting me, and so would continue lighting my pot, boiling me still, stoking the fire beneath me hotter and hotter, until I would be found later that day after having been cooked alive, never having had the courage to save myself.

The refrigerator was nearly empty, I noticed. I took out an egg and fried it. I turned on the television. I toasted bread. I turned on some music but didn't dance. I sat next to the Piano and thought of Aden. I burnt the egg. I fried another one. I opened the refrigerator again. I turned off the TV. I turned off the music. I turned off the lights. I put the fried egg in between the toast. I grabbed a fork. I didn't need the fork. I put the fork away. I sat down. I took a bite of my sandwich. I was all alone. In the dark.

Just then the phone rang.

"Kristopher?" Andrea said out of breath.

"Yes," I answered politely.

"Kristopher I'm so sorry I overslept and my aunt had to rush me to the airport and I just got up — I just barely got here in time and I might still miss my flight you know I don't have a cell phone anymore because my Belarusen one doesn't work in the U.S. I'm so sorry." I could tell she wasn't breathing.

I listened to her silently, sitting down on the couch, almost relieved that she had at least called. But I knew still that I was angrier than I gave myself credit for, and therefore it was better to stay silent.

"Kristopher?" she asked knowing I was still there. "I'm so-so sorry I know this is terrible but I was really shocked when you came yesterday and I didn't know what to do so I couldn't sleep all last night so I stayed up and then I fell asleep at four and my stupid Aunt didn't wake me up at five like she was supposed to and my alarm didn't go off...Kristopher?"

"You absolutely don't care..." I said sadly. I had to catch from choking. I couldn't continue without crying.

"Kristopher..."

She kept saying my name. I didn't like that she kept saying my name. She had only recently remembered the sound of it, I thought.

"Kristopher I'm so sorry and look I'm going to think about this the whole flight and I'm so pissed I really wanted to see you and it's wonderful that you came and saw me and it's so wonderful and yes it's so wonderful but I don't know what to say Kristopher. Kristopher?"

"You don't care about me Andrea," I said now actually blubbering. "Your alarm didn't go off? Fuck you! You absolutely don't care about me."

"Kristopher I do! I thought about you all summer and you hurt me so badly but then you just came and I fell asleep and I'm so sorry I don't want to leave like this and I'll come home and you can visit me in Belarus yeah? Kristopher? Kristopher? You can come visit yeah?"

She was now crying a bit too.

"Don't cry!" I yelled at her now raging. "You don't care about us at all! I come to see you across the whole fucking country and you don't have the decency to set an alarm? You fell asleep? You were tired? Fuck your sleep. I didn't sleep either but only because I was so excited to see you this morning. God this is uncontrollably cruel, this is..."

I had absolutely no filter because even that was all wasted away. I had nothing left.

"You are..." —I was sobbing at this point—"...you are..." —and I couldn't stop sobbing—"viciously...cruel. You are vicious."

The phone fell silent.

"I have to go," she said, in much the same way I had told her only a few months earlier.

"I'm," she said, "I really am so sorry because I know you don't deserve this and you don't deserve this and you don't deserve this but I don't deserve this either," she said finally being honest with herself.

"...I'm sorry but we'll talk later right? We'll talk when I get to Belarus you and I? Kristopher? I'm sorry."

She was very much crying too.

"This is so stupid," she said to me very slowly, finally wiping her tears away in between each word, "we...are...so...stupid."

"Goodbye," I said.

"I'm sorry," she said, and hung up.

When she hung up I continued to cry. No. Actually I wailed. It was one of those flat on your back sobs that should be embarrassing but never is in reality, because no matter who sees you in such a state, no matter how robotic that person is, they can't help but shower you with empathy. Yes—it was one of those absolutely desperate, soul and heart and body and elbow and cell and cheek bone and third to the left mole on my right shin—deep aching, and wretchedly torturous feelings of uncontrollable despair. I writhed on the ground streaming pools of unrelenting tears onto the carpet beneath me for what seemed like hours. This is what heartbreak feels like, I thought.

I could feel nothing and everything all at once.

Though then it hit me. Wasn't that what I wanted all along?

So I proudly tightened up my eyes and blew my nose, walked outside to get some fresh air and looked up towards the sky. I stood silently in that chilly morning, with the sun only barely visible to my left. I then walked into the middle of the driveway and noticed how familiar it looked — I knew each of its cracks. It felt comfortable and familiar, normal even. Sure I still owned only a backpack and a few journals, but it felt like some version of home, and that was nice.

I looked up and I swear I could see Andrea, floating there in her plane. And I wondered if I'd ever see her again? Maybe later? See — it's always "maybe later" with her.

I paused for only a moment, took in a great deep breath, and quickly went back inside to pack my bag.

Nothing more happened.

I had to go.

Available from

Curious Apes Publishing:

by Steven Parton

Hello, World

by Donovan James

Saudade

curious apes
publishing

Jonathon Kendall is a novelist, a journalist, a poet, a wanderer, and a semi-professional Couchsurfer. He hails from Vancouver, WA though he is most often found traveling. He also likes to dance.

This is his first novel. His second will be released in 2014 — titled *On Being Human*.

ISBN 978-0-9910088-0-3